REBEL ROSE RISING

Rebel Rose Trilogy

Book One

K.T. MARTIN

REBEL ROSE RISING

For information contact:
ktmartinauthor@gmail.com

eBook ISBN: 978-1-949913-46-0
Paperback ISBN: 978-1-949913-47-7
First Edition
Editing: Tami Stark

CHAPTER ONE
Reyna

"Easy, Ember. Not yet." I tightened my grip on the reins, steadying my mare as she pawed the ground beneath us. The battlefield stretched before me in a vast expanse of mist and shadow, the distant army waiting like a storm on the horizon. My pulse thrummed with anticipation, but I forced myself to remain still.

Waiting.

Calculating.

To my left, Jaila, my second-in-command, sat atop her chestnut mare, her dark eyes sharp with readiness. To my right, my half-sister, Cassia, stood beside me, her armor too clean, too new. Unblemished by battle. The excitement in her bright blue eyes made my stomach clench. I had fought for years to keep her safe, but now there was no avoiding it. She would fight. And she would bleed.

I reached out, tucking a loose tendril of golden hair behind her ear. "You stay close to Jaila. Do you understand?"

"I can do this. You don't have to worry about me." Cassia lifted her chin as if fear didn't course through her like it did every Iron Swordmaiden before her first battle. I would have believed her, but her grip on her sword was too tight, her knuckles white.

I swallowed the urge to tell her no, she can't do this. To order her back to the barracks where she belonged. Where she would be safe. But she was seventeen, and in our world, that was old enough to die. All I could hope for now is that the training I'd given her meant she was faster, stronger, and smarter than her opponents. That she would survive.

Different mothers had gifted us different features—her golden hair and blue eyes a striking contrast to my dark locks and emerald gaze—but we had endured the same horrors. Though we shared only a father, the harsh realities of our childhood had forged a bond between us that ran deeper than mere blood. Our shared struggles had turned half-siblings into two halves of a whole.

Cassia stood at my side, blade in hand—too young, too beautiful, and far too valuable to be here. I had fought to keep her from becoming a breeder, the position her rare beauty should have demanded, leveraging my battlefield successes to secure her place in my army instead.

For three years, she had been safe at my side. But safety was an illusion in our world. And now, as the battle loomed, I wondered if I'd only saved her from one death to deliver her to another.

Still, I'd take that over the alternative. A warrior's death is swift. A breeder's is slow and soul-shattering. I'd seen what became of women forced into that gilded cage. My mother. So many others.

Cassia was mine to protect. And in this world, women had only two choices: bleed or breed. I would see Cassia bleed beside me on the battlefield a thousand times over before I let them turn her into a docile broodmare forced to bear sons for a man she did not choose.

"This is your first battle. Just remember what I've taught you. Don't try to be a hero."

Jaila cast me a look, her expression conveying that she would keep my sister safe. If anyone could, it was her.

Jaila had been my shadow since we were both thrown into the Iron Swordmaidens. We'd bled together since childhood, two frightened girls turned warriors. We had trained side by side, our bond forged in the sweat and blood of countless battles. She was my second, my right hand, the one person I trusted beyond question. If I fell, Jaila would step in without hesitation. If Cassia stumbled, Jaila would be there to keep her standing. And I knew, without having to ask, that she would die before she let Cassia fall.

I turned my gaze to the enemy. The Steel Storm's warriors were formidable, but they had made a mistake. "We pull them into the center. The ground is soft—too soft. When they get bogged down, we flank. They'll have no choice but to surrender."

Jaila nodded. "It's a solid plan. *If* they fall for it. The Steel Storm is known for her battle strategy."

"They will." Though I'd never faced her, I knew of her reputation for winning, but The Steel Storm, as they called the leader of the Stormspire kingdom's army, wasn't in the position of power this time. This was my turf they marched on, and I knew it well. I'd defended it many times in my reign as the Iron Rose. I knew the ground here flooded during rains, like the ones we'd had all week past. But to an outsider, they would never know the hidden condition of the ground, and no doubt she would lead them straight at us, confident in their greater numbers.

A sound cut through the morning quiet. Hoofbeats.

I didn't need to turn to know who it was.

A silent snarl tipped my lip.

Sir Asher.

The king's dog.

I kept my posture straight as he rode up toward me, his dappled grey horse restless beneath him, two guards on bay steeds flanking his sides. The silver details on his black armor glinted in the misty light, emphasizing the wide set of his shoulders and the broad planes of his chest. His chiseled face held no emotion as he approached, his jawline, strong enough to cut steel, clenched tight. His piercing blue eyes locked with mine, and though I'd seen them hundreds of times, they never ceased to stun me with their intensity. Ice-pale and just as cold, they created a stark contrast against his ebony hair and warm, tanned skin. Those eyes, though inarguably beautiful and as striking as the man himself, held the detachment of someone who had long since bid goodbye to emotion.

"Iron Rose." His voice was deep, steady. "The king orders a full-frontal charge."

I stiffened, barely restraining my rage. "That's suicide. The terrain will slow us. We'll be sitting ducks. The past few days of rain have made the ground between us saturated. Stormspire's army doesn't know that, so my plan is to lure them into it, and while they are struggling to move forward through the muck, we can easily surround them. End this with minimal losses."

Sir Asher's face remained impassive. "His orders are final."

I clenched my teeth so hard it hurt. "And what do you think? Or does the king do all your thinking for you?"

A flicker of something—annoyance, maybe—crossed his face. "I think the King wants to show the strength of our army. He wants a full-frontal attack to send a message to the other kingdoms that we fear nothing and no one. You have your orders."

Bastard. He was one of them. A man with power, free to live as he pleased while we fought and died at their command. Men's lives were too valuable to risk in open battle, but the women of the seven kingdoms were considered expendable to die for their whims. I wanted to spit at his feet. To tell him to run back to his king with my message that I wouldn't send my women to die needlessly. That we would run my plan, spare countless lives and still come out the victors.

But I wasn't a fool. I had disobeyed the king once, and he had executed five of my warriors for my defiance. Hung them in the streets to the cheers of the men to teach me a lesson I wouldn't forget. I would not let him take more. Though defying him would likely save far more lives than he would take as punishment, my swordsisters would rather die in battle than in humiliation.

I fixed Asher with a glare sharp enough to cut straight through his armor. "Go tell your king I'll carve his message into the bodies of the fallen," I said, my voice like iron, "but their blood is on his hands, not mine."

Asher didn't flinch. His expression was unreadable, his eyes as impassive as ever—but that only infuriated me more. How could someone so perfectly sculpted, so effortlessly commanding, be utterly devoid of a will of his own? It disgusted me. And yet, for one maddening moment, my gaze lingered on his perfect face, drifting to his lips, which parted as if he might speak before thinking better of it. A flicker of something twisted inside me, sharp and unwelcome. I shoved it down, burying it beneath the weight of my loathing. He was a blade sworn to a master, wielded by the king without hesitation. And I despised him for it.

I exhaled through gritted teeth, pushing away the bitter fury curling in my gut. We had no choice but to obey. But that didn't mean I had to like it. It was just one more reminder of the life I was born into where the only choice I'd ever made of my own free will was to ensure I would die on a battlefield and not in a bed.

I touched the scar on my cheek, a deliberate mar to my beauty. When I was fourteen and my mother's striking features had begun to show through, I'd decided it was better to be scarred and fight than to be beautiful and bred. The penalty for such an act was death, but they couldn't prove my own hand had made the deep slice across my cheek. My skill, even at fourteen, had been too valuable to waste with my death, and I'd been assigned to our army, the Iron Swordmaidens. An army I had risen to lead in the past seven years since joining, and one I would fight to my dying breath to protect my swordsisters, and my real sister, from the threat looming across from us. But I wouldn't relish cutting down those warriors, because it wasn't them who wanted our blood, it was their king and the men who ruled their kingdom and controlled their lives.

They were just like me.

Fighters.

Survivors.

Slaves to a system that saw us as nothing more than flesh to be sacrificed.

But as much as I hated knowing that bloodshed awaited us below, my loyalty lay with the women I commanded who stood behind me, ready to fight and die at my command. The women I would fight with every ounce of my strength to protect.

I turned to my army, my swordsisters, the only people in this wretched world who mattered. "We fight not for our king, but for each other! For the sisters at our side, for those who came before, and those who will come after! We fight because we must, and we survive because we are strong. Iron in our blood!"

"Iron in our bones!" The response thundered across the battlefield, a promise, a battle cry, a prayer.

I gripped the reins tighter, turning back to the women waiting across the field, waiting to die for a king who would never remember their names. The Steel Storm and her warriors were not our enemies—not truly. They were pawns, just as we were, just as expendable, just as doomed. But that did not mean I wouldn't slaughter them if it meant saving my own. I had no choice.

None of us did.

I raised my sword, and my army surged forward, iron against steel, blood against blood, knowing we would pay the price men never had to.

Ember surged forward beneath me, her powerful muscles straining as she galloped into the treacherous, mud-choked battlefield. She moved as though she knew my thoughts before I did, ducking her head when arrows rained down and shifting her weight to keep me balanced as I swung my sword. We had been through too many battles together for me to doubt her instincts. She was not just my mount—she was my partner, my lifeline.

A spear came for us from the left. I barely had time to pull the reins, but Ember twisted sharply, her hooves kicking up wet earth as she spun us free. I let my blade do the rest, slicing through the soldier who had dared to threaten us. Blood sprayed the ground, mixing with the rain-slicked mud, but there was no time to process it. No time to breathe.

Cassia held her ground. I saw her out of the corner of my eye, cutting through enemies with practiced precision. A swell of pride warred with my terror. She was good—but good wasn't always enough.

Jaila fought beside her, a wall of iron and fury.

Ember reared back as a soldier lunged at her, her hooves colliding with armor, sending the woman sprawling into the muck. I leaped off, landing with a guttural roar on top of the stunned soldier. I didn't hesitate. One clean stroke, and she was gone. Not because I wanted her dead, but because she would have done the same to me. Survival left no room for mercy.

I pulled out my second sword, the two weapons singing as I fought opponent after opponent, my well-honed skills slicing through them as my muscles screamed for rest. But I ignored the pain. Ignored the guilt as each one fell. And finally, when my armor and blades were soaked in blood and sweat, The Steel Storm called the retreat. Just like that, it was over.

I stood on blood-soaked ground, my shoulders heaving with my breaths as I watched them flee. I surveyed the carnage around me. My warriors were alive. Not all of them, but enough.

Ember trotted over, my loyal steed always nearby, as if she knew to be ready to offer me an assist or an escape. I pressed my forehead to hers for the briefest moment. "Good girl," I murmured, running my fingers through her damp mane. She had saved my life more times than I could count, and today, she had done it again.

My gaze searched the wounded women stirring around the battlefield, panic rising in my chest as I tried to find her. Finally, I exhaled a sharp breath of relief when I saw Cassia and Jaila walking toward me, unharmed.

"Well fought," Jaila said, brushing dirt from the sleeve of her armor. Her tall, lithe frame, hardened by years of battle, moved with the effortless grace of a seasoned warrior. The braids in her dark hair clinked softly against her steel armor with the movement, each one threaded with small metal rings—a testament to every battle she had survived.

Cassia's hands trembled as she sheathed her blade, and without thinking, I pulled her into my arms, gripping her tightly against me. I felt the rapid rise and fall of her breath, the tension in her muscles.

"Are you hurt?" My hands ran over her arms, her sides, checking for any wounds she hadn't noticed in the heat of battle.

"I'm fine," she assured me, though her voice wavered. Training for battle and being in one were two very different things. Nothing could prepare you for the horrors of taking your first lives, and I ached for the pain I knew tore apart my sweet sister's insides.

"Just a few bruises. Nothing worse than what you've given me in training."

I exhaled, pressing my forehead against hers for the briefest moment before pulling back.

"Your arm," Cassia said, her fingers tracing the deep wound on my arm. "That looks bad."

I glanced at it, paying little attention to the deep wound I knew would heal rapidly.

Jaila scoffed beside me. "Of course it's already healing. I swear, you heal faster than any of us. It's unnatural."

Cassia frowned, brushing a finger near the wound but not touching it. "You've always been like that. Since we were kids. I remember when you broke your wrist—only took a few days before you were using it again like nothing happened."

I shrugged, unwilling to dwell on it. "Luck, I guess."

Jaila gave me a look that said she didn't believe in luck.

Before she could press me more, the king arrived.

He walked the battlefield as if he owned it, stepping over the bodies of my fallen sisters without so much as a glance. Behind him, Sir Asher rode in with the rest of the Kingsguard, his sharp blue eyes sweeping over the carnage, pausing just long enough to find me.

I met his gaze, rage rising in my chest like a tide. He had known. He had known this was a mistake, that this battle was unnecessary, that my strategy could have ended it with fewer dead. But he had followed orders like the good little dog he was.

I tore my gaze away from him and back to the king as he stepped around Lorna without so much as a glance. Her body lay twisted in the filth, her golden hair streaked with blood, her hands still clutching the sword she had refused to let go of, even in death. Lorna had been one of my best—fierce, relentless, loyal. She had fought beside me in dozens of battles, and now she was gone. A life stolen for nothing more than a king's posturing.

I clenched my fists, nails biting into my palms as the king spoke.

"That will send a message," he said. "Let the other kingdoms know Ironhold is not to be challenged."

He didn't see the blood on my hands, the way my fingers still curled around my blades, aching to run him through. He didn't care that these were women, not pawns. To him, we were all disposable.

I glanced back at Sir Asher. His face was carefully blank, his posture rigid, his grip on the reins firm. There was no pity, no regret—just cold detachment, the mark of a man who carried out orders without question. Without care. Without consequence.

I hated him for it.

The king turned to leave, mounting his horse on the stepping stool Sir Asher provided.

As the King rode away, Sir Roland, the Warden of the Warhold, our jailer for all intents and purposes, swaggered up, his piggish eyes gleaming with barely contained delight. Sir Asher followed behind, his expression unreadable, his movements precise and controlled, like a blade always at the ready.

Roland smirked, stepping closer, and I had to resist the urge to put my blade through his throat. "I see the illustrious Iron Rose survived to fight another day. It seems we won't have to replace you yet."

I didn't respond. The venom on my tongue was too sharp, too eager to strike—and I wouldn't give him that satisfaction. He'd love to see me fall in battle, wouldn't he? The iron thorn in his side finally gone. Then he could crown a new Iron Rose, someone softer, someone who would turn the other cheek to his cruelty.

He hooked his thumbs on his belt, the one straining to contain his belly, and rocked back on the heels of his finely polished boots. "I've just received word the king has a special honor for you."

My blood turned cold at the way his eyes gleamed with the simple sentence.

"King Ruthio of Shadestone arrives soon," Roland continued, his tone thick with amusement. "And he has requested entertainment fit for one of his status. What better way to honor him than with a grand spectacle? A showcase of strength, a clash of warriors."

Jaila stiffened beside me.

Roland's grin widened, his yellowed teeth bared like a predator savoring its kill. "Ten of our finest against Shadestone's warriors.

To the death. And you, Iron Rose, will lead the charge. And I've decided what a grand display it would be if I pair you fighting beside your sister."

My breath stilled.

The words were deliberate. Calculated. He let them hang in the air as his smirk lifted, savoring the moment, knowing exactly what he was doing. He had seen the way I fought for her, the way I defied the king to keep her from the breeding beds. This wasn't just a selection. This was punishment. It was personal.

Roland had been searching for a reason to put me in my place ever since I stopped him from taking liberties with one of my younger soldiers in the Warhold where we lived. He ruled over our barracks like a fattened hog, abusing his position, picking and choosing his victims under the guise of authority. Just a month ago, I'd had enough, stepping between him and a terrified girl barely past her sixteenth year. I had nearly broken his hand, twisting it back until I heard the snap and saw his face turn red with rage.

It should have been a death sentence for me. Any defiance against a man was. But breeding with the Iron Swordmaidens was forbidden—we were meant to fight, not to carry heirs—and if I had exposed him, it would have forced an uncomfortable reckoning with our King. So, he had said nothing. Had let it fester. And ever since, he had been waiting for a chance to make me pay. He hadn't forgotten. And now, he was making sure I wouldn't either.

Jaila's hand found my arm, a subtle pressure, an unspoken warning not to react. She could feel the rage vibrating through me, the storm coiling tight inside my chest.

I barely heard the rest over the roar in my ears. The Shadestone Sentinels weren't just warriors; they were executioners. In all the seven Kingdoms of The Southlands, they were the most feared. Ghosts of battle, clad in Nocturnium—the one metal no other could match. It was found only in the cliffs of their kingdom, and they guarded it with unmatched ferocity. They would carve through my women like beasts set loose in a pen, slaughtering them while the kings watched and cheered.

And Cassia would be one of them.

I forced my face into an expression of cold indifference, knowing Roland wanted to see my reaction. See me unravel. I wouldn't give him the satisfaction. Stone cold and steady, I answered, "We will fight with honor."

Roland's smirk deepened. "Good. The king will be watching closely. Don't disappoint him."

Roland turned on his heel and left, but Sir Asher lingered, his gaze flickering over the battlefield before settling on me.

He opened his mouth. Then closed it. Whatever he was about to say, he swallowed it down and followed the warden without another word.

Coward.

I looked at Cassia.

Although pale, she held her chin high.

I exhaled slowly. I had fought to keep her safe. I had bled to keep her safe.

And now, I would kill to keep her safe.

Shadestone would not take my sister.

Not while I still drew breath.

That night, after we returned to the Warhold—our barracks and our cage—I sparred with Cassia until my muscles screamed. Until she could barely lift her sword. Until the wounds that had already begun to knit themselves back together screamed in protest.

Wood thudded against wood as we circled each other, our wooden blades the only weapons we were allowed behind Warhold walls. Real steel was forbidden. They feared we'd turn it on them—rise up in the dark, storm the castle, end the reign of kings and men alike with blood and fire.

They were right.

Instead, we were forced to accept our fate locked inside the Warhold, a high-walled and heavily guarded prison inside Ironhold's capital city of Ironheart. Revolutions had been attempted in the past, but each one had been snuffed out before it started, and the swift and severe punishment to all the women in the kingdom kept us from repeating the attempt.

But even with only wooden swords, I would use every second I had to make sure Cassia survived. To make sure she was faster, stronger, and deadlier than she had ever been.

I adjusted her stance, knocking her arm into position. "Again. You're too slow on the recovery. If you miss your mark, you have to be ready to defend."

She sighed, shoulders slumping. "I'm exhausted, Reyna. Can we pick this up tomorrow?"

Even though I knew she ached from her first battle, her mind and body weary like my own, I tightened my jaw, setting my eyes on her with determination.

"The Shadestone Sentinels are unlike anything you've ever faced. You're a better fighter than most already. But it's not enough. Even if you're stronger, faster, and more skilled, their Nocturnium weapons will slice through your armor like butter. Your weapons will bounce off them like hitting stone. The only way to beat them is to be twice as good a fighter so you can survive long enough to take advantage of whatever tiny advantage you get. We will train until I know you will survive. Now, I said, again."

Cassia gritted her teeth, nodding, sweat dripping down her temple. "I won't lose."

With my rage against our circumstances, against the threat to my sister driving me on, I raised my sword. "Then prove it."

She lunged.

I wouldn't lose her.

I couldn't.

This world had given me nothing. Had taken everything. My mother. My freedom. My choices. But the one thing I wouldn't let them take was Cassia. They could have my blood, my bones, my body—but they would never have her. And I would kill anyone who tried.

CHAPTER TWO
Reyna

The roar of the crowd echoed in the long, shadowy tunnel leading to the arena floor. It wasn't fear pushing my heart to racing, but a potent mixture of rage and anticipation. I gripped the hilts of my twin iron swords, feeling their familiar weight and balance, my muscles twitching at the ready.

Beside me, Cassia bounced softly on the balls of her feet, a bundle of nervous energy. Her golden hair, pulled back in a braid like mine, swung with the movement, and her blue eyes focused with fierce determination at the entrance to our battleground. I stared at my sister, my resolve to protect her hardening as we prepared to step into the blinding sunlight and chaos of the coliseum.

"Ready?" I asked, my voice low and steady—calm despite the anxiety ripping apart my insides. Could Cassia survive a battle with the fiercest warriors in all of the kingdoms of the Southlands? Had I made a mistake saving her from a fate as a breeder only for her to be sacrificed for sport in a different way?

But instead of meeting me with worry in her delicate features, Cassia flashed a fierce grin. "Born ready, sister."

My anxiety softened as I saw that my beautiful sister was indeed a fierce warrior, one I had honed myself and molded like hot iron on the blacksmith's anvil. She could survive this. She *would* survive this. I would make sure of that.

We clasped forearms, pressing our heads together for a brief moment.

"Iron in our blood," I began.

"Iron in our bones," Cassia finished.

A single sharp blast of a horn signaled our entrance. We gave each other one last look then slid on our matching iron helmets. Squaring my shoulders and straightening my spine, I strode forward, Cassia at my side. We stepped out onto the sandy arena floor, thunderous cheers and jeers from the packed stands of men filling the world around us. Even in the open air of the colosseum, I smelled the metallic tang of blood and the acrid stench of sweat and fear.

My gaze swept over the arena, my eyes widening for a moment at the carnage from the earlier matches. Dark, bloody stains marred the sandy floor. Broken weapons and discarded pieces of armor littered the ground. My jaw clenched and the rage inside me rose as I watched them drag away the crumpled bodies of fallen warriors. How many women had died for their entertainment today?

As much as I wanted to scream or cry at the senseless loss of life, I pushed the thoughts aside. There would be time for mourning later. Now was the time for survival.

Across the arena stood our opponents — two of King Ruthio's feared Shadestone Sentinels. They were clad in midnight-black armor that seemed to swallow the light. Their faces were obscured by gleaming Nocturnium helms carved into snarling beast visages.

A sharp laugh caught my attention, and my lips curled in disgust when my eyes found the sound came from King Ruthio, lounging in the royal box. He was young for a king, barely thirty, having inherited the throne of the most powerful kingdom in the Southlands only two years ago when his father died. Though undeniably handsome with his dark hair and chiseled features, all I could focus on were his cold, calculating eyes. He reclined on a gilded throne, his Nocturnium crown perched on his head while sipping wine from a jeweled goblet as he surveyed the bloodsport he'd commanded in his honor.

Beside him sat my own king, Lothaire. The stark contrast between the two rulers was jarring. Where Ruthio exuded youthful arrogance, Lothaire appeared aged beyond his years. His shoulders were slumped, his rheumy eyes unfocused. If the two were to battle one on one instead of using their armies, the fight would be over before anyone could exhale a single breath. But that would never happen because it had been centuries since a single king had marched into battle, and instead, we fought and died in their place.

A gong sounded, reverberating through the arena and snapping my attention back to the looming battle. My muscles tightened like coiled springs as I settled into a fighting stance, swords at the ready. Beside me, Cassia mirrored my pose.

"Remember your training," I said, my voice low and firm. "We fight as one and we watch each other's backs. Always be three steps ahead."

Cassia gave a sharp nod, and our eyes locked onto our approaching foes.

The Sentinels moved with surprising grace for their size, spreading out to flank us. Their black armor made them appear as living shadows slipping effortlessly across the sand. The one facing me carried a massive axe, while the other wielded a wickedly curved scimitar and round shield, both forged from the Nocturnium I knew could slice through our skin like a knife through butter on a warm day.

For a long breath, all was still. Then, as if by some unspoken signal, we exploded into battle.

I darted forward, my twin swords flashing in the sunlight as I unleashed a flurry of strikes at the larger Sentinel. She parried with surprising speed for her size, the clash of iron on Nocturnium ringing out. Sparks flew as our blades met again and again in a deadly dance, and we seemed evenly matched in skill and speed.

From the corner of my eye, I caught sight of Cassia engaging in her own furious duel. Her enviable agility was on full display as she ducked and dodged around her opponent's attacks, striking like a viper whenever an opening presented itself.

I allowed myself a brief smile. We had trained for this, honed our skills until fighting together was as natural as breathing. Though young, Cassia showed skills that matched and outperformed her well-trained opponent.

The battle raged on, neither side able to gain a clear advantage—their armor too strong for our superior fighting skills. It didn't matter how many times we made contact, our iron swords bounced right off their Nocturnium armor. My arms burned from the effort of deflecting the crushing blows of my opponent's axe and crashing against her protective armor. A thin line of pain erupted across my arm as her blade slipped across my skin, drawing first blood. I hissed in pain and anger but pressed my attack with renewed force.

A sharp cry from Cassia sent a wave of icy fear through my veins. I risked a glance toward her in time to see my sister stumble, her leg giving way beneath her, the bright red blood on her calf catching my widening eyes. The Sentinel shadowed over her, scimitar raised high and ready to descend in a killing blow.

"No!" The scream tore from my chest as I launched away from my own fight, diving toward my fallen sister.

Time seemed to slow. The curved blade began its descent. My gaze connected for only a split second with Cassia's wide, terrified eyes. My legs burned as I pushed myself faster... faster.

At the last possible instant, I caught the scimitar with my crossed iron blades, halting its deadly arc before it could exterminate my sister. The brutal impact reverberated up my arms, but I held firm, muscles straining against the attack.

"Get up!" I shouted at Cassia.

She scrambled to her feet, battle-ready in an instant, but favoring her injured leg. I pushed off the ground, landing on my feet and pressing my back to hers. As one, we spun slowly to face our opponents, who circled us with measured, deliberate steps, advancing cautiously.

What followed was a whirlwind of raw determination and fury. My fierce, protective instincts took over, my body moving of its own accord. Block, parry, thrust. Duck, weave, strike. Cassia and I moved around each other with lethal choreography, slowly but steadily pushing our opponents back. But for every strike we landed, it deflected off the impenetrable Nocturnium that rendered our opponents and their army elite.

My muscles screamed for relief, begging me to quit, but I pressed on, hunting, searching, for an opening. Finally, it appeared, and I seized it. When the larger sentinel raised her axe to strike at me with another powerful blow, my left blade found a gap in the armor at her armpit. With a powerful scream, I drove my sword into the small opening, feeling no resistance of her impenetrable armor as her flesh gave way to my iron blade. Her hot blood gushed over my hand and down my arm as I wrenched my blade free.

The Sentinel stood unmoving for a moment, then fell to her knees, her axe clattering to the ground. We locked eyes for a moment, and from behind her black helm, I saw the fear of her death reflecting in her brown eyes, and also, the forgiveness of my hand in it. My stomach clenched as I saw the life flitting out of her, a needless waste of a worthy opponent who deserved a better fate than choking on blood to the roar of the crowd.

A loud grunt and roar from my sister ripped me from my moment with the fallen warrior, and I whirled to aid her, but it wasn't necessary. Instead of turning to see her wounded and battling for her life, I found Cassia executing a lightning-fast series of strikes that left her opponent reeling. A final devastating blow dislodged the warrior's helmet, and it dropped into the sand, rolling to a stop. The red-haired woman's eyes flashed wide as Cassia's sword swiped once more, this time opening the woman's throat in a spray of crimson.

Silence fell over the arena as the last Sentinel collapsed into a lifeless heap. For a moment, I heard nothing but my own ragged breathing and the whooshing of blood in my ears. I looked to Cassia. She gave me a soft nod, then the crowd erupted in deafening cheers.

While they screamed and cheered for our victory, Cassia and I stumbled toward each other. We fell into a hug, then pulled back and I clasped her shoulder, both to steady her and myself. We had survived. Against all odds, we had emerged victorious. Together.

"Well fought," I managed out on heavy breaths, my voice hoarse.

Cassia beamed up at me, her face blood-splattered but radiant in her triumph. "We did it," she breathed. "We actually did it."

Though my sister had survived the fight, I still had one last battle ahead of me. The legendary Shadow Raven. The leader of Shadestone's powerful army. Though my body ached and I knew the battle ahead would be one of the hardest of my life, even if I fell, I knew my sister would live on, and that was all that mattered to me. Her life hadn't been sacrificed for sport to the cheers of weak, bloodthirsty men.

A horn blasted, cutting through the crowd's roar and quieting the masses to a whisper.

"A magnificent display!" the master of ceremonies bellowed, his voice amplified to reach every corner of the arena. "Truly, the Iron Rose and her Iron Swordmaidens are a credit to Ironhold and its king!"

More cheers. My eyes narrowed as I glanced at King Ruthio looking so disinterested as they dragged away his warriors we'd slain for his entertainment.

"And up next," the announcer continued, "for our final match of the day—a battle between legends! The Iron Rose herself, Reyna of Ironhold, will face the Shadow Raven, Alana of Shadestone!"

The crowd's excitement reached fever pitch. My pulse quickened. I had heard tales of the Shadow Raven's prowess on the battlefield, not to mention her sheer size. Shadestone kingdom was known for breeding large women for their armies, and Alana's size was whispered about across the entire Southlands. Said to be larger than most men and as strong as an ox, the Shadow Raven's name echoed through the kingdoms with awe. This would be a true test of my skills, perhaps the greatest fight of my life. And it *would* be for my life, because one slip, one mistake, and her legendary Nocturnium greatsword could end me with a single blow.

"But first," the announcer said, "let us see the faces of our brave warriors! Swordmaidens, remove your helmets!"

I grumbled under my breath but complied, tugging off my helm. My long dark braid tumbled free, matted with sweat and grime. Beside me, Cassia did the same, shaking out her golden hair, her face still beautiful despite the blood speckled across it.

As she stood in front of the crowd on full display, a hush fell over the arena. A chill ran down my spine like ice skating across my skin. My heightened instincts for danger flickered inside me, and I searched for the threat nearby.

And then I saw it. But it wasn't a warrior coming toward me or an army ready for battle. The danger causing me to feel the depths of true and real fear was something far more treacherous. Something I couldn't battle away with my swords.

The danger sending me into high alert was the hungry gleam that entered King Ruthio's eyes as his gaze locked onto Cassia.

The Shadowstone king leaned over, whispering something to King Lothaire. I strained to hear, but their words were lost in the restless murmur of the crowd, all regaling in the beauty of my perfect sister. An unexpected sight as swordmaidens weren't known for their beauty. My stomach twisted when I saw King Lothaire nod, a look of interest etched on his craggy features.

"You there, girl," King Ruthio called out, his sophisticated voice dripping with arrogance. "Step forward."

Cassia hesitated, looking to me for guidance. I wanted nothing more than to grab her and run, to flee this cursed arena and never look back. But I knew that was impossible. To defy a king's direct order was death, and there was no way we could escape with our lives. Still, my fingers twitched at the hilt of my sword.

We shared a look, an understanding between sisters. She warned me to stay quiet with her gaze, and though my stomach clenched with worry for what may transpire, I gave Cassia a small nod I would comply, trying to project a calmness I didn't feel. She squared her shoulders and strode forward, chin held high.

Ruthio moved to the railing, his elbows leaning on it as he gazed down on her, his predatory gaze raking her over and lingering on her delicate features and lithe form. His lips curled in a smile that sent ice through my veins.

"How is it," he asked, his voice smooth like silk, "that such a rare beauty came to be wasted on the battlefield? That one, though beautiful, has a scar, so I can see why you'd forgo her." He pointed to me, and my lip twitched in a slight snarl. "But this one is flawless. I can't say I've ever seen her equal, and I have some of the most beautiful wives in the Southlands. Surely there are... better uses for one so fair, King Lothaire?"

King Lothaire tipped his head. "I have never seen this warrior before. How did she end up in my army?"

"My sister," I said loudly, stepping forward. "She is my sister and having her assigned to my army was my gift for winning the Battle of Belgrand."

He barely acknowledged my words, instead jutting his bearded chin at his Kingsguard. "Bring her to me."

Bile rose in my throat. I knew where this was heading, had feared it since the day Cassia came of age. My hands clenched into fists, nails biting into my palms. Two guards moved to flank Cassia, gripping her arms. My sister's eyes were wide with fear now as understanding dawned.

"No..." The word escaped my lips in a strangled whisper, hoping, praying, against all odds that they would return her back to me after regaling in her obvious beauty.

I watched in mute horror as the guards led Cassia up the steps, stopping her before the two kings. King Lothaire rose from his seat, circling my sister like a wolf eyeing its prey. He gripped Cassia's chin, tilting her face this way and that, like appraising a horse before purchase.

"I would never let such a face or a body fight in my army," King Ruthio said, appraising her with the same hungry eyes. "Perhaps if you won't take her as a wife, you'll give her to me. I am always looking for more beautiful women to add to my chamber." His eyes sparkled as they searched Lothaire's, awaiting his decision.

My stomach clenched, and I felt the sands shift beneath my feet as the world around me seemed to wobble. Though only a king for a few years, Ruthio's cruelty was already a thing of legends. The women he took as wives endured unthinkable horrors to satiate his depraved needs.

"Yes," Lothaire said, "yes, I think you're right, King Ruthio. It's a shame to waste such a beauty on the battlefield." His eyes lit with lust and greed. "Perhaps it's time she was... reassigned. But I'll keep her. She will give me strong *and* beautiful children."

"No!" The scream tore from my throat as the last shreds of my composure snapped. I launched myself forward toward the Kingsguard holding my sister, no thoughts to the consequences. All I knew was that I had to reach Cassia, free her. I had to save her from the nightmare awaiting her in a king's bed chamber.

I made it three steps before a Kingsguard launched in front of me. Without thought, without care, my sword swung through the air, slicing across his throat and sending him to the ground, choking on blood as he clasped the fatal wound gushing blood from his neck.

The men in the crowd shouted, gasping in horror as I charged forward toward my sister, rage and fury blinding me to anything but her freedom. Two more guards moved to stop me, but with blazing speed from the years of honing my skills, they met the same fate as their friend.

"Stop her!" King Lothaire boomed, and he grabbed Cassia, shoving her into the waiting arms of his guards. "And get her out of here!"

"Reyna! Don't! Please! Don't fight them! They'll kill you!" Cassia shouted as they dragged her away.

"Cassia!" I roared back, prepared to slaughter every man in this kingdom who dared stand between me and my baby sister.

I lunged, my mind a single, violent command: Kill. Take her back.

But before I could reach Cassia, an iron grip wrenched me backward, slamming me into a wall of muscle. A hard arm locked around my throat, and another crushed my arms to my sides, immobilizing me. I thrashed, a snarl ripping from my throat, but the hold only tightened.

"Let me go!" I screamed, kicking back blindly. I connected with something solid—flesh, bone—heard a grunt of pain. But my captor didn't loosen his grip.

"Stop fighting," he ordered, his voice steady, unshaken. Like restraining me was no different than saddling his horse.

I recognized his voice instantly. Sir Asher.

A red haze descended over my vision, rage and sorrow and fury. With a primal scream, I redoubled my efforts to break free. I drove my heel into Sir Asher's instep, slammed my head back into his face. I heard the painted grunt, but still he held on.

Rage boiled over. "You bastard!" I twisted violently, but he was stronger, his grip unrelenting.

Ahead, Cassia's wide, terrified eyes met mine. "Reyna! Don't fight them! Please!"

Her voice pierced through me like a blade.

I struggled harder, my body wild with desperation. "Cassia!" My scream ripped through the arena, raw, frantic.

But the guards shoved her through the gate.

The heavy doors slammed shut.

And then...

She was gone.

And I was too late.

Something inside me shattered.

I went limp, the fight bleeding out of me faster than any wound ever had.

Two guards appeared on either side of me. Sir Asher's arms fell away as they hauled me to my feet. Only then did he release me. Not gently. He shoved me away from him, like he was done dealing with an inconvenience.

I stumbled but the guards caught me, and I turned to face him, wild, hate-filled eyes locking with his. The man who'd stopped me from saving my sister. He didn't look sorry. Didn't look regretful.

He just looked... cold. Distant. As if my pain meant nothing.

And I hated him for it.

"You—" I snarled, my breath ragged, uneven. My hands clenched into fists. I wanted to tear him apart.

But he only adjusted his gauntlets, shaking out his hands like I had been a mere training exercise. Then, finally, he spoke.

"Take her to the dungeon."

The words were simple. Unfeeling. As if my entire heart hadn't just been ripped from my chest.

I shouldn't have been surprised. He was a man. A cold, calculating loyal lapdog to the King. The man who'd stopped me from saving her.

Cassia. My baby sister. Gone.

The world around me faded away until all I was aware of was the sand beneath my feet, the hands restraining me tight, and the gaping void in my chest where my heart used to be. Where my sister used to be.

I felt the last of the fight had been ripped out of me knowing they took my sister away to a fate that had been the death of my mother. Humped and ravaged by her abusive husband until she finally snapped when she saw him strike me, killing our father and losing her own life dangling by her neck before the cheering crowds.

I'd watched firsthand the cruelty men bestowed on their breeders, and bile rose in my throat knowing my beautiful, strong, sister would eventually break.

As they led me away, I spotted an unmistakable figure across the arena. I knew instantly who she was. Alana, the Shadow Raven, stood impossibly tall and silent where she had been waiting for our match to begin. From beneath her black helm, I caught a glimpse of her sympathetic gaze. Our eyes locked, and we shared a look, an understanding, between two powerful, dangerous women relegated to simple playthings for men.

In that moment, in that look between us, a spark of something dangerous ignited in my chest. Anguish and fury consumed me like fire burning through a dried log.

My gaze locked with Sir Asher's, and I let my fury burn brighter, all my hatred and anger narrowing into a singular, deadly point aimed straight at him. Without his iron grip, surely I could have slaughtered every man in this kingdom who stood between us and stole her away to a life far from all the cruelty bestowed upon us by our birth as the wrong sex.

I would survive and free my sister. Somehow. Some way.

I would kill every last one of them that stood in my way.

My eyes narrowed at Sir Asher as they dragged me away, his cold blue ones unwavering as he watched.

And I would start with him.

CHAPTER THREE
Reyna

The chains around my wrists dug into my skin, each heavy link a reminder of my failure. My failure to save Cassia. My failure to fight through the sea of guards. My failure to slit King Lothaire's throat before he stole my sister away.

I paced in my cell as far as my chains would allow, the iron bars casting long shadows in the dim torchlight. The damp air of the dungeon clung to my skin, thick with the stench of mildew and rot. My body still vibrated with unspent rage. I wanted to rip the bars from their hinges. I wanted to scream, to tear through flesh and bone until there was nothing left but blood and ruin.

Instead, I clenched my fists, my knuckles whitening as I forced myself to breathe. Cassia was gone. That single, devastating truth settled deep in my chest like a blade wedged between my ribs. And tomorrow, I would be killed at best, or at worst, tortured before being thrown back into this cage to rot.

But I would not let that happen easily. I would fight to my dying breath, the same as my mother.

Her face came to me in flashes—dark hair, fierce green eyes, the fire in them never fully extinguished, not even when they tied the rope around her neck. She had refused to be just another man's possession. Refused to let her daughter be treated with the same cruelty she endured day after day. And they had hanged her for it. I never understood why she didn't run, why she didn't try to escape before it came to that. Maybe, back then, I still believed there was some measure of honor in the system. That if you fought hard enough, proved yourself enough, they would see you as more than just a sword or a womb. But I knew better now. There was no honor. There was only control. And the moment a woman stopped being useful—whether in war or in a bed—she was discarded.

I stopped pacing, my breathing steadying. I realized then my mother may not have fought back with her fists that day they hung her, but she fought back with her strength. She didn't let them see her break. Didn't let them take even one more inch of her soul. I'd seen the look in her eyes as they put the rope around her neck. They'd made me watch. Made all the women watch as a reminder of what happens when we disobey. But my mother's eyes hadn't met mine filled with sadness and fear. They'd been a silent plea, a final command—never give up, never surrender. And I wouldn't. No matter what they did to me, like her, I would not break.

Heavy footsteps echoed down the stone corridor. I didn't turn. I didn't need to. I knew the sound of that smug, plodding gait anywhere.

Sir Roland.

"Well, well." His voice was thick with amusement as he came to a stop outside my cell. "The mighty Iron Rose, finally wilting."

I remained silent, glaring at the wall, refusing to give him the satisfaction of a response.

"You've caused quite a stir, girl," he continued, his fat fingers curling around the bars as he peered inside, his piggish eyes gleaming. "Killing three guards? Attacking a king? Tsk, tsk. If it weren't for your skills on the battlefield, you'd already be dead."

I turned then, slow and deliberate, my stare a dagger aimed at his throat. "Then do it," I said, my voice a low growl. "Kill me. Or are you too much of a coward?"

Roland laughed, a wet, hacking sound. "Tempting. But the king has other plans. You'll be made an example of. Tomorrow, you'll be stripped and whipped in the city square for all to see. Every man, woman, and child will witness the Iron Rose humbled at last." He leaned in, his breath hot and foul. "And after that, who knows? Maybe I'll pay you a visit. You're not so untouchable anymore. I can give you a taste of what's in store for your sister."

His gaze raked down my body, and I lunged for the bars, teeth bared. He jumped back with a startled chuckle. "Oh, I do hope you fight tomorrow," he sneered. "Nothing like watching a defiant woman scream."

My hands clenched so tightly my nails bit into my palms, drawing blood. I wouldn't give him the pleasure of seeing fear in my eyes.

A new set of footsteps approached, measured and precise.

Sir Asher.

He stepped into the torchlight, his expression as cold and unreadable as ever. If he was disturbed by Roland's words, he didn't show it.

"Enough," Asher said, his voice flat, as if he were bored of the exchange already. "You have your orders. The king wants her unharmed for the punishment. And you're wanted in the Warhold. Go."

Roland turned to him, an exaggerated sigh escaping his lips. "Oh, come now, Sir Asher. You're always so serious. Can't I have a little fun?"

"No." The single syllable carried enough weight to silence Roland's amusement.

Roland huffed but relented, rolling his shoulders. "Fine. I'm going." His beady eyes flicked back to me, a malicious grin curling his lips. "I'll see you tomorrow, Iron Rose. Though the next time I visit you in this cell, you won't be so pretty anymore. A shame, really. That scar on your face will be nothing compared to the ones that will carve you into something unrecognizable."

I didn't flinch as he turned and waddled up the stairs, his heavy footfalls fading into the distance. Only then did I shift my attention to Sir Asher, who still stood rigid outside my cell.

I exhaled slowly, forcing steel into my voice. "My sister. Where is she?"

Sir Asher settled his gaze on me. "That's none of your concern."

My blood boiled at his dismissive tone. My hands curled into fists, the iron chains rattling as I stepped toward the bars. "None of my concern? She is my sister! She is everything to me! She is my *only* concern!"

For the briefest moment, something flickered across his face—a tightening around his eyes, a slight shift in his jaw—so quick I almost thought I'd imagined it. But before I could decipher it, his eyes darted almost imperceptibly toward the guard before returning to mine, his expression hardening once more, carved from stone.

"And you are a prisoner. You have no concerns now outside these four walls."

"I had a deal," I spat. "She was supposed to be safe. She was never meant to be a breeder." My voice cracked with fury. "Send her back to the Warhold. Now."

He didn't even blink. "You are in no position to make demands."

The guard near the stairs let out a soft snort, as if surprised I'd been allowed to speak at all. Sir Asher must have caught it, because he shifted slightly, squared his shoulders, and when he spoke again, his voice was razor-sharp.

"You are a traitor who slaughtered three men," he said, his tone hard and deliberate. "You are lucky I didn't end you right there in the sand."

The words hit me like a slap, but I refused to recoil. I surged forward, my chains rattling violently, a beast caged but still baring its fangs. "I fought your wars," I snarled. "I led your armies. I followed every order you delivered from your pathetic king. And this is how I'm repaid? Like some common criminal?"

Asher's gaze was impassive, like he wasn't even seeing me. "What did you expect would happen?"

"I expected the deal I made to be honored. But honor means nothing to men like you." I spit, yanking at my chains so hard they cut into my wrists, fury overtaking reason.

His jaw tightened slightly, but his voice remained flat. "You are a woman. You have no bargaining power. You're lucky they agreed to it at all. But now the King has claimed her, as is his right."

Rage reverberated inside my chest thinking of my sister taken as some possession and not the strong, kind, wonderful woman she'd grown to be. I steadied my voice, my hardened eyes softening as I pleaded. "Give me my sister back. Without her, there is no life worth living."

"She's the king's now. Her fate is sealed."

I roared my agony as I hit the end of my chains again, desperate to be free. Desperate to have my swords back in my hands—to take his head and watch it roll to a stop at my feet.

He didn't move, didn't blink. He merely watched me as if I were an unruly beast throwing itself against its cage, waiting for exhaustion to take hold. And then, with a slow, deliberate step, he distanced himself further. Like I wasn't worth his time. Like I was nothing.

"Sleep while you can," he said coolly. "You'll need your strength tomorrow."

As he walked away, I sank onto the cold stone, my breathing ragged, my fists still clenched. My eyes caught a jagged piece of metal near the base of the torch holder on the wall. A sharp enough edge, long enough to do the job. I could end this now. Deny them the satisfaction of seeing me broken in the square. Stripped and sliced to the roaring of the crowd.

But Cassia was still out there. I couldn't abandon her. I needed to save her, and to do that, I had to survive.

Let them try to break me. Let them whip me until my flesh peeled from my bones. I would not kneel. I would not yield. And I would never stop until my sister was free and this kingdom burned to the ground.

CHAPTER FOUR
Reyna

The cold iron of the manacles bit into my wrists as the two Kingsguard led me from my cell. Though dawn had broken hours ago, the sky was dark with the looming threat of rain, a gloomy grey that matched my mood. The cloying scent of the oil they'd used to make my armor shine mixed with the musty odors of the dungeon. They'd dressed me in my formal battle gear—my polished armor gleaming, with special attention paid to shine up the thorned rose emblem emblazoned on my iron breastplate. The irony wasn't lost on me. They wanted me to look every inch the fearsome Iron Rose when they stripped me naked in front of the entire kingdom and broke me.

Or tried to. No matter how many lashes sliced into my skin, I wouldn't give them the satisfaction of seeing me break.

My stomach churned in anticipation of the pain and humiliation awaiting me if I reached the end of the walk through the streets. I'd seen other people whipped and could still hear their agonizing screams. But I forced my features to remain impassive. I refused to let them see my fear.

Two guards flanked my sides, with six more ahead and behind. Their faces all mirrored the same stern mask of determination, and when they'd glance at me with those wary eyes, their hands would twitch just above their swords.

Good. They were right to be scared of me.

We emerged into the cloud-covered morning light, and I blinked, taking in my surroundings. People scurried about rushing more than I'd expect at this hour. Then my jaw clenched with the heavy realization. They were excited for the spectacle of my punishment.

As we walked, I could barely contain my snarl seeing all the men in their fine clothing leering at me, smirking as I passed, no doubt excited to see me suffer to remind the beautiful submissive wives trailing behind them never to step out of line. Though the men stared at me openly, some spitting or shouting obscenities as I passed them, the women never looked up, their gazes firmly cast to the ground as they trailed behind their husbands. The only women who dared to look at me as we passed were the ones deemed neither beautiful nor strong, and instead they worked in the kingdom scrubbing laundry, cleaning houses, and emptying chamber pots. As I moved past them, they'd pause from their endless chores and give me a soft, sympathetic stare. The unluckiest of them lived in brothels, failed breeders condemned to serve many men a night since they couldn't get pregnant. A thought flashed through my mind thinking of Cassia there if for some reason she couldn't bear the king's children.

My stomach churned and I pushed down the vomit trying to creep up my throat, but that thought also invigorated my desperate need to somehow, some way, save my baby sister. To rip her from the hands of the king and take her away somewhere, anywhere, that would allow us to live a life away from the cruelties of our kingdom. But to do that, to make that fate a reality, I would need to be...

Free.

The Kingsguard pushed me along, but I kept my back straight and my chin high as we passed the leering onlookers, most never having seen the famous Iron Rose so close. My guards thought parading me down the busy streets and taking the long way to the site of my humiliation was a way to show their control.

Me? I saw opportunity.

The commotion surrounding us pulled their attention in different directions, and they started to lose their cohesive formation. A gap here, a moment of inattention there. My mind raced with lightning speed, cataloging every detail, every potential weapon, every escape route.

Then I saw it—the Warhold's stables, its doors wide open as grooms led out horses for the day's work. And there, standing in the crossties getting groomed, was Ember. My loyal mare, the horse I'd chosen as my mount in my first year as a warrior and forged a bond with as deep as a sisterhood. Our eyes met, and I swore I saw recognition in her gaze.

It only took a second staring into her deep brown eyes for a plan to crystallize in my mind. An out. It was reckless, probably suicidal. But it was a chance. And that was more than I'd had in that dank cell and more than I would have the moment they strapped me to the post and secured my wrists to the iron fastenings.

We approached a busy intersection, merchants setting up stalls, citizens gathering to watch the procession. The noise grew, a cacophony of voices and commotion.

Now or never, I thought, my stomach clenching with anticipation and excitement as I prepared myself.

I stumbled forward, appearing to trip on the uneven cobblestones. The guard on my right reached out instinctively to steady me, grabbing me from behind and catching me by the elbows. A smile quirked on my lips. That one moment, that one split second decision he made, was all I needed.

My muscles snapped at the ready, each nerve in my body crackling with anticipation, prepared to follow every split-second instinct. I slammed my head back, feeling the satisfying crunch of cartilage as my skull connected with his nose. He staggered backward, curse words tumbling from his mouth as he yowled in pain. I heard the distinctive ring of iron being drawn and glanced to see the guard to my left had pulled his sword. With a menacing snarl, he swung.

Time seemed to slow as the blade arced toward me. In that split second, I seized the opportunity.

Instead of ducking away and dodging the blow, I stepped into it. I raised my bound hands, positioning the chain between my manacles directly in the path of the descending sword. Gritting my teeth, I braced for impact.

The blade struck the chain, and a jolt of force ran up my arms as metal met metal. I felt the chain give way, snapping under the force of the blow.

Avoiding the final descent of the sword, I rolled to the side, the blade whistling past where I'd been standing a moment before. I glanced at my hands. They were still cuffed but no longer bound together.

Freedom.

The guard who'd swung his sword froze, eyes wide as he realized the error of his decision to attack me. I didn't give him time to process long. Still on the ground, I swept my legs out, catching him between his and twisting them out from under him. He let out a painted grunt as he hit the ground hard, his sword clattering to the cobblestones.

With a lightning-fast grab, I snatched it up, gripping it tight as a smirk lifted my lip.

I was unbound and armed. A potent combination for my escape and a deadly combination for the shocked guards surrounding me.

"The prisoner! She's free! Stop her!"

I didn't wait to see who had shouted. I was already moving, ducking under the swing of another guard's sword. I sliced through his calf as I rolled beneath him, and he cried out as he tumbled forward into a fruit vendor's stall. Fruit exploded into the air, and I snatched an apple as it started its descent, hurling it at the face of an approaching guard. It struck him square between the eyes, the sharp blow sending him stumbling backwards and buying me precious seconds.

My body sang with the thrill of combat, my joy unbound fighting against men, against my captors, instead of innocent women sent to the slaughter. Instead of dreading it, this time I ached to feel their warm blood across my skin as I sliced through them. I wanted to bathe in it, cover myself in the proof of their deaths. I ached to savor every single moment I spent sending another cruel, vile man from this world and down to the Depths of Oblivion where they all belonged. One less man to control us. Abuse us. This was what I was made for. Not to be some king's brood mare, not to be a broken thing for them to parade around, or an executioner of innocents. This — the dance of battle against my true enemy in the perfect harmony of body and blade.

A guard's spear thrust toward my midsection. I sidestepped, grabbing the shaft and yanking him off balance. As he stumbled past, I brought my knee up into his gut. He collapsed forward, and I let my sword sing as it sliced across his throat.

I spun, searching for my next opponent, but instead my eyes clapped onto a young woman cowering behind her market stall. When she looked at me, eyes wide, I saw not fear in them but a spark of admiration.

"Run," I told her, my voice course. "Get to safety."

She nodded, scurrying away. All around me, civilians fled the square, their screams echoing around me. Good. I had no quarrel with them, and I'd be damned if I caused the death of an innocent in my escape. I'd taken enough innocent lives. Today, the lives I'd take would be anything but innocent, and I vibrated in anticipation of their deaths.

I glanced to see more guards pouring into the square, a dozen at least now, and surely with more on the way. Though I wanted nothing more than to fight them all right here, right now, my escape had to take precedence. In order to save Cassia, I had to be free.

My lips lifted in a menacing smile, then I sprinted down a narrow alleyway, the clatter of armored boots following behind me. My lungs burned, but I pushed harder. I didn't know these streets like they did. I spent most of my time in the city locked in the Warhold, and they'd patrolled them countless times. But I let my instincts guide my feet and my muscles, and I twisted and turned making my way back toward the stable with my salvation inside.

Left, right, another left. I vaulted over a wall with my agile movements, hearing curses as my less nimble pursuers were forced to go around. Every second counted now.

I burst out of the alley onto a wider street, and my heart sank. More guards blocked the way, weapons drawn. Behind me, I could hear the others closing in.

A horn blasted from the city walls. The alarm. They were locking down the city.

I was running out of time.

I looked left and right and saw no escape from the guards closing in on me. With no time to think it through and seeing no other choice, I charged the guards before me. They braced themselves, expecting me to try to break through their line, swords drawn and ready to end my flee for freedom. Instead, at the last moment, I dropped, sliding between the legs of a particularly large one I assessed to be the slowest guard. With a roar of surprise, he swung his sword down, but I was already rolling to my feet behind him.

I launched forward, not even looking back to see how many guards had started their pursuit, instead focusing all my strength and attention on the one place I knew I had to get to. Each determined stride brought me closer to the stables, my salvation so close I could taste it. I let out a piercing whistle, our special call, praying to whatever gods might be listening that Ember would hear it and could find her way to me.

A loud whinny returned my call, followed by the sound of shouting stable hands and clattering hooves. Ember burst from the barn, a stable hand clinging to her lead as she dragged him, her powerful strides swallowing up the space between us as she galloped toward me.

My heart soared at the sight of her. Magnificent creature that she was, all sleek lines and rippling muscle. Most warhorses were stocky and stout, but Ember was tall and leggy, made for speed and agility, her coat jet black albeit the big white star on her forehead... the one I kissed each time I saw her. In that moment, I loved her more fiercely than I'd ever loved another living thing other than my beloved sister.

His grip slipped, and the stable boy tumbled to a stop as Ember closed in on me. I ran toward her, guards hot on my heels. Ember didn't slow, and neither did I. I would have only one chance at this, so I watched her strides closely and readied my muscles to spring into action. With a grunt of effort, I caught her swinging lead in my hand, leaping up, my hands finding purchase in her mane. I swung myself onto her back as she thundered past, clutching tight with my thighs as she wheeled around.

"Halt! In the name of the king!"

While her hooves clattered on the stones beneath us, I looked back to see a line of guards forming, shields interlocked to block our path. Beyond them, a flash of gleaming black and silver armor caught my eye, and my heart stuttered to a stop.

Sir Asher.

He stood apart from the others, his piercing gaze locking onto mine amidst the chaos. His face was impassive—no anger, no urgency, no surprise. Just cold observation, like a wolf watching a wounded deer struggle through the snow, already knowing how the hunt would end.

A fresh wave of fury burned through me. I wished I had a spear in my grip, wished I could drive it straight through his chest and pin him to the cold stone behind him. I wanted to carve that unreadable expression off his face, to see him bleed as I had bled, to take from him as he had taken from me when he'd stopped me from saving my sister.

But not now. Not yet.

Revenge would come later. Right now, escape was all that mattered.

He didn't move. Didn't shout for his men to stop me. He only stood there, silent, unyielding, as if my escape was inevitable. Or maybe meaningless.

I snarled under my breath, then forced myself to turn away, squeezing my mount's sides. Freedom lay ahead, and I would seize it with both hands.

Ember needed little encouragement, her legs dancing beneath me in excitement. We charged forward and she raced fearlessly into the wall of guards, her powerful body slamming through the shield wall. Men went flying as we raced through them then turned down the street toward the main gate.

The wind whipped at my face as we galloped through the twisting streets, her body responding to the smallest cues from my seat and my legs, the lead rope serving as a rein to help guide her. My smile broke free just as we were. Citizens dove out of our way, shouts of alarm rising in our wake. I could hear horses join the pursuit behind us, the thunder of the chase rumbling in our wake, but Ember was faster, her shoes striking sparks from the cobblestones as she swallowed the space with her lengthy strides.

The gate loomed before us, the massive portcullis already beginning to descend. My mind raced. We'd never make it under before it closed.

Fuck.

I felt freedom slipping away with each inch it came down. We'd be trapped between the wall of stone and the wall of guards behind us. No way to take them all. But then I looked up, and in those seconds, a different plan, another far more dangerous plan, snapped into place in my mind. I quickly surveyed our surroundings as we raced on and finally saw a slim chance of escape on my right.

A merchant's cart, piled high with sacks of grain, positioned perfectly next to a set of wide stone stairs leading up to the wall. It was madness, but it was our only shot.

"Come on, girl," I whispered to Ember. "I need you to trust me. I know you can do this."

As if she understood, Ember put on a fresh burst of speed. I aimed her at the cart, and she didn't hesitate for even a second, instead coiling back on her hind legs and leaping onto it, her hooves finding purchase on the pile of sacks. In a feat of incredible strength and agility, she launched us off the grain cart toward the stairs I knew held our path to freedom.

For a heart-stopping moment, I thought we'd fall short. But Ember's hooves clattered onto the stone steps, and she surged upward. Guards on the wall turned, eyes wide with disbelief as we thundered toward them.

"Hold on!" I yelled, though whether to Ember or me, I wasn't sure.

We burst onto the top of the wall, racing down the narrow stone walkway, shocked guards leaping left and right to avoid us. I could hear shouts of alarm, the clatter of weapons being drawn. But I ignored them, my attention focused sharply on what lay ahead—our one and only remaining chance for escape. There was one section of the wall that bordered the river below. If we could make it there, we could swim for freedom. But as I tried to picture the drop to deep water below, I struggled to remember how far it was. Too far? Could we survive it? I didn't have time to second-guess. A chance at survival was better than the certain death awaiting if we stopped now.

"Trust me," I whispered to Ember, leaning forward closer to her ear.

Arrows whistled past us as I urged her on. The edge of the wall rushed toward us. I threaded my fingers tighter into her long black mane, preparing for the final push of our escape. Ember gathered herself beneath me, muscles in her back tensing as she took the last stride, and then I felt the incredible surge of power as she trusted me enough to launch us into the unknown.

For a moment, we were flying. The wind rushed past, and my heart leaped into my throat as we sailed through the open air. I clung to Ember's mane, my stomach lurching as we dropped, those few seconds feeling like a thousand as we closed in on the blue-green water racing up to meet us.

We hit the water with a tremendous splash, the impact driving the breath from my lungs. The cold shocked me to my core, but I held on as Ember's powerful kicks brought us back to the surface.

With a sharp gasp as we broke through, I tried to regain my balance as Ember pushed toward the far shore. Arrows rained down around us, sending up small splashes where they struck the water. One grazed my arm, leaving a stinging trail of fire, but I gritted my teeth and pushed on.

Ember's powerful muscles worked tirelessly as she swam, and I could hear distant shouts from the walls, see soldiers rushing about in panic. But with each stroke, we got farther away, the current helping to carry us downstream and out of range quickly.

Finally, Ember's hooves touched the riverbed, and she scrambled toward the shore. We climbed onto dry ground, both of us soaked and puffing hard. I leaned forward on her neck, taking a moment to run my hands over her and look down at her legs, checking for injuries.

"You brilliant, brave, amazing girl." I pressed my face into her neck. "I knew you would get us out safely. I never doubted you for a minute."

Ember nickered softly, turning back and nudging my leg with her nose as if to say, "I never doubted you either."

I allowed myself one glance back at the city walls, now seeming small and insignificant in the distance. I saw tiny figures still rushing about, no doubt organizing search parties. Though we'd barely caught our breath, I knew we couldn't linger.

With a final pat to Ember's neck, I pulled myself back to sitting. We were both dripping and exhausted, but free. And right now, that was all that mattered.

"Let's go," I said, turning Ember's head toward the eastern horizon, a place I'd only been to fight battles, but the landscape I knew fairly well.

Wasting no time for the search parties to get moving, we set off at a gallop, leaving Ironheart and its chains behind us. We rode hard, putting as much distance between us and the city as possible. The adrenaline of escape surged through my veins, making every sensation sharper, more vivid. I could feel every brush of wind through my hair, every powerful stride of Ember beneath me, appreciate every inch of the meadows and trees surrounding me in Ironhold's kingdom as we put distance between us and Ironheart.

Only when the walls of Ironheart had long since disappeared behind us did we slow to a walk. My entire body ached, the exertion of the fight and flight catching up with me all at once. But under the pains of a hard battle fought coursed a fierce, wild joy.

I was free.

I threw my head back and laughed, the sound startling a flock of birds from a nearby tree and causing Ember to jump.

Free!

No chains, no cell, no looming threat of torture and humiliation. Just open sky above me and the steady rhythm of Ember's hooves below.

But as quickly as it came, the laughter faded, replaced by a sudden, overwhelming surge of emotion. I slumped forward, burying my face in Ember's mane as silent sobs wracked my body. Relief, exhaustion, fear—it all poured out of me in a torrent I couldn't control.

Ember seemed to sense my need. She slowed to a stop, turning her head to nuzzle at my leg. I wrapped my arms around her neck, clinging to her tightly and drawing comfort from the warmth and softness of her familiar body.

"Thank you," I whispered. "Oh, my brave, beautiful girl. I couldn't have done this without you."

As my tears subsided and the tornado of emotions inside of me settled to a quiet breeze, I straightened, taking stock of our situation. We were in open country now, rolling hills dotted with sparse woodland. Good for putting distance between us and any pursuers, but we'd need to find better cover soon. And supplies—I had nothing but my armor and the sword I'd swiped from a guard. No food. No water. No preparations for whatever lay ahead.

But those were problems for later. Right now, most importantly, I needed to decide where to go next.

The obvious choice was to run, to find some remote corner of the world where I could disappear. No city in the Seven Kingdoms of the Southlands would be safe for a woman, and I'd end up in chains and enslaved just as fast, but there were whispers of faraway lands across the ocean where women were free. They were likely fairytales, but still, a fairytale was better than the nightmare I knew awaited me in each of Southlands kingdoms. But even as the thought occurred to me to make my way to the shore and try to sail away to a distant land, I dismissed it. I couldn't abandon Cassia. My little sister, so brave and bright, now trapped in a nightmare I'd sworn to protect her from.

We'd seen what it meant to be a breeder— had lived it, breathed it, and seen it play out in bruises and broken spirits. Our father tormented both his wives—our mothers. After mine gave her life to protect me, Cassia's mother, Laila, became ours. She raised us like we were both hers, because we were.

For a few precious months, we knew peace. No orders barked. No hands raised. No begging whispered through locked doors.

Then Laila was reassigned to a new husband, and the torment began again.

And we could do nothing but watch as that strong, beautiful woman was forced to bend to his every demand.

And now, once wed to the king, my sister would find herself in that very same life.

And it would kill her.

No, running wasn't an option. I had to find a way to save her, to free her from this rotten kingdom that treated women as less than human. But how? I was one woman, alone and hunted. For now, I just needed to survive to plan my next move. I needed to get to safety, to regroup and organize. I had no idea where to go, but I knew I needed more distance between myself and the search parties certainly heading out after me. I gathered the lead rope as a makeshift rein and turned her north.

"I'm not sure where we're going yet, but I hope I'll know it when we get there. What do you say, girl? You with me?" I asked, patting her neck.

Ember tossed her head, as if in agreement. I smiled, grounded by her quiet partnership in this strange new world where I now stood alone. With a fresh surge of determination swelling inside my chest, I clicked my tongue and urged Ember into a canter.

All my life, I'd been a piece in men's twisted games. But as I rode toward freedom, I realized the true game was just beginning—and this time, I'd be the one moving the pieces.

Let them hunt me. Let them fear me. The Iron Rose had thorns, and by all the gods, I would make them bleed.

CHAPTER FIVE
Asher

The tension filling the air suffocated me as I approached King Lothaire on his large iron throne. His aged face, a thundercloud of barely contained rage, darkened as I approached. I steeled myself for the storm I knew was coming.

"Your Majesty," I began, dropping to one knee. "I regret to inform you that the prisoner, the Iron Rose, has—"

"Escaped," he finished, his voice a low, dangerous growl. "Yes, I'm well aware of that fact, Sir Asher. What I want to know is how in the Depths of Oblivion it happened!"

I kept my head bowed, eyes fixed on the stone floor, not daring to meet his gaze. "During transport, she overpowered her guards, Your Majesty. She—"

"Spare me the insignificant details of this embarrassment!" he roared, surging to his feet. "You were responsible for security, were you not? How could you let this happen?"

I swallowed hard, fighting to keep my voice steady as I lifted my eyes slowly. When I finally looked up at him, I saw his crown askew on his head, and his face flushed deep crimson with anger. "Your Majesty, I was inspecting the square as you ordered, to ensure it was secure for your presence and King Ruthio's. I was nowhere near the prisoner when—"

"Excuses!" Lothaire spat. He descended the dais with heavy, uneven steps. "You are the head of my Kingsguard. Everything that happens in this city is your responsibility. Or have you forgotten that?"

"No, Your Majesty," I said, my jaw clenching and gaze diverting back to the ground. The injustice of it burned as I hadn't been tasked with overseeing her transport, but I knew better than to argue. Instead, I held fast, absorbing the heat of his rage. "I take full responsibility."

Lothaire loomed over me, and I could feel his presence just above me. "Do you have any idea how this makes me look? Letting a girl slip through my guard? Kill them? Escape? And in front of King Ruthio, no less!"

I risked a glance up. Lothaire's eyes burned like wildfires, and his gaze darted around the room as if searching for hidden enemies. "Ruthio is up to something, I know it."

The old man's paranoia was sharpening again. He was convinced Ruthio was scheming, plotting against him. Maybe he was right. The young king had been traveling between the seven kingdoms of the Southlands for months flashing his charming grin and promising trade deals, peace talks, unity. He'd even brokered a treaty with Seastrand—something no king had managed in decades. That wasn't diplomacy. That was maneuvering. But behind those honeyed words, there was something colder. Calculated.

He didn't move like a man on a diplomatic tour. He moved like a man setting the board for war.

A war he would win.

It was enough to make even a wise king uneasy. And Lothaire... was not a wise king.

Lothaire paced, hands curling into fists. "He's up to something and now he sees me as weak, unable to control even one woman in my own damn army."

I should have told him the Iron Rose wasn't just any woman. That she was possibly the most skilled fighter in the Southlands, that her reputation among the armies was legendary. But Lothaire didn't want to hear about her prowess—he wanted someone to bleed for this insult.

I met his gaze evenly. "Your Majesty, I swear to you. I will make this right."

Lothaire's hand shot out, gripping my chin in his gnarled fingers. "Oh, you most certainly will," he hissed. "Dead or alive, I want that woman back, and then I want to smile as I stare at her head on a spike. And if you fail, Sir Asher, don't bother coming back at all. If I see you again without her head in your hands or her wrists bound in chains, I'll take payment with your head instead. Am I understood?"

A cold weight settled in my chest. This mission would define my future—not just my position, but my very survival. I'd spent my entire life working toward the Head of Kingsguard position, and now everything I'd built could crumble because of one woman.

I met his gaze, seeing nothing but cold determination there. "Yes, Your Majesty."

He released me with a shove, turning his back. "Get out of my sight. I'll assemble twenty-five of my finest Kingsguard to ensure you are successful. You'll all leave with haste before she can get any farther from our grasp. Go and prepare for this task."

I rose, bowing stiffly before turning to leave. As I reached the door, Lothaire's voice stopped me.

"Oh, and Sir Asher? Succeed in this, and that promotion you've been eyeing? It's yours. New quarters in the east wing, doubled salary. Fail, and... well." He let his voice hover with the looming threat of my demise.

I gave one sharp nod then spun on my boot and left the throne room.

The walk back to my quarters felt longer than usual, my mind racing with the task ahead of me. I'd never once faltered in my duty. This shouldn't be different. This was just another mission, another enemy to neutralize.

Yet something about it felt... wrong. Not the mission itself—my duty to king and kingdom had always been clear—but something about her. The Iron Rose. Reyna.

I'd watched her on the battlefield many times, had seen the way she commanded her Swordmaidens with a mixture of iron will and genuine care that few commanders possessed. I'd studied her techniques, her strategies. In another life, we might have compared notes, shared tactics.

But such thoughts were dangerous. She was a fugitive now. A traitor. And I had my orders.

I pushed open the door to my chambers and startled to a stop when I saw my brother, Erik, lounging in one of my chairs, a goblet of wine in his hand.

"So," he said, raising a dark brown eyebrow. "How'd it go?"

Instead of answering, I crossed the room and snatched the goblet from his hand, downing its contents in one long swallow.

Erik let out a long, slow whistle. "That bad, huh? What's the verdict?"

I collapsed into the chair opposite him, running a hand through my hair. "I'm to hunt down the Iron Rose and bring her back, dead or alive. If I fail, I'm not to return at all. If I do, he'll take my head as payment instead of hers."

"Well, fuck," Erik muttered. He leaned forward, concern etching his features that looked similar to mine. The same deep tan skin of our father with our mother's icy blue eyes, though his hair was lighter than my almost ebony locks and longer, half of it knotted on his head and the rest touching his shoulders. "And if you succeed?"

I flicked my wrist, gesturing to my chambers. "Promotion. New quarters. Doubled salary."

Erik's eyes widened. "You mean the east wing? Damn, Ash. That's..."

"I know," I said, my voice hollow as I contemplated the stakes.

The silence that fell between us was heavy, laden with unspoken understanding. Erik wasn't just my brother; he was my mirror, my confidant, the only soul in this gilded cage who truly knew me. We'd forged our bond as children with the clash of wooden swords, in shared dreams of Kingsguard glory, in whispered secrets under starlit skies. From little boys play-acting at heroism to grown men bearing the weight of real power, we'd walked every step of this path together.

My heart clenched remembering Reyna's face as they'd dragged her sister away. That raw desperation in her eyes, the primal rage—I recognized it because I'd felt it myself. If someone had tried to take Erik from me, I wouldn't have just killed three guards; I'd have burned the entire kingdom to ash. The bond between siblings ran deeper than any oath to king or country, stronger than iron and sharper than steel. In that one unguarded moment in the arena, I'd seen myself in her, and that recognition twisted something painful inside me that I couldn't afford to examine.

"You're troubled," Erik said finally. It wasn't a question.

I met his gaze. "She's one of our best warriors."

"Was," Erik corrected. "She's a traitor now."

"Yes," I agreed, though something in me hesitated. "Still, to waste such talent..."

Erik leaned forward. "This isn't like you, Ash. You've never questioned a mission before."

"I'm not questioning it," I replied quickly—too quickly. "I'm merely considering the tactical approach. She's not some common criminal. She's the Iron Rose."

"Exactly why you can't underestimate her," Erik said firmly. "She's dangerous. Maybe the most dangerous opponent you've ever faced."

"I went and saw her in the dungeon." I poured more wine into the goblet.

Erik arched an eyebrow. "And?"

"I saw Sir Roland heading down there. I had a feeling he was up to no good."

With an eyeroll, Erik snorted. "Up to no good is an understatement. He's the absolute worst. Like none of us know what that vile man does to those soldiers in the Warhold."

"Exactly." I took a swig of the wine, the bittersweet liquid warming my throat as it went down. "I know how much he hates her, and I knew with her chained up down there his intentions were foul. I went down to make sure she didn't succumb to his depraved temptations."

"Something tells me, even chained, he wouldn't have survived if he'd tried to have his way with the Iron Rose."

I chuckled, remembering how fierce she looked even chained up.

"This is true, but I didn't want to risk it. You know, she's in there because of him."

Erik furrowed his brow. "How so?"

"Her sister. He chose her for the games just to twist a knife in her gut. I'm not sure what happened that made him target her so much, but he thought her sister would fall in battle, punishing her. Instead, it was an even worse punishment."

Erik sighed. "Yes. Being one of Lothaire's wives is definitely a fate worse than death."

I pictured Reyna again, how fiercely she'd fought to get to her sister. "I can't say I blame her for what happened. If someone tried to take you from me, I wouldn't be able to stand aside either, King's order or not."

Erik smiled. "Well, I'd hope if Lothaire tried to take me as a wife you'd fight to the death to defend me."

I burst out laughing, my brother's humor always able to make me laugh no matter the circumstances.

"Well, I would. I will always honor my vows to the Kingsguard, but you're my brother. My blood. I would choose you over my vows anytime. And that's what Reyna did, and why our best warrior is now facing a punishment I can barely stomach. I mean, what the hell did they think was going to happen when they took the Iron Rose's sister? That she'd just step aside?" I snorted, the mere thought of someone as ferocious as Reyna simply waving goodbye while her sister was dragged away for a life I could barely fathom.

I stood and began pacing the spacious chamber that befit my rank. Fine tapestries adorned the walls and plush red rugs muffled my repetitive footsteps. It had all the trappings of the privileged life I'd been born into. As a man. As a Kingsguard. As revered, noble blood.

"I saw her, Erik," I said, keeping my voice level. "When she was escaping. Our eyes met, and... there was something there I can't explain. Not fear. Not hatred. Something that made me hesitate."

"You've always respected her as a warrior," Erik observed. "But remember what she is now—a traitor. Your respect for her skill can't cloud your judgment."

I nodded sharply. "Of course. The mission comes first. Always has."

Erik was quiet for a long time. Then he stood, placing a hand on my shoulder. "Maybe you could do with her what we did—"

"Stop," I cut him off sharply, knowing how he was going to finish that sentence. "We agreed never to speak of that again. Not a breath. Not a word." I looked around to ensure no one may have been listening even in the sanctity of my private quarters.

Erik's eyes widened slightly, but he quickly nodded. "Right. Of course. I just meant... maybe there's another way."

I shook my head. "The king assigned me twenty-five guards. And he said if I don't capture her dead or alive, I'm not allowed back, or he'll take my head in her place. And you know he will, Erik. He doesn't make idle threats."

With a heavy sigh, Erik softly shook his head, and his eyes lifted to meet mine with a silent plea. "I know this is a hard task at hand, brother, but if it comes to it, if you have to choose, then choose yourself. Come home."

His words landed heavily. If roles were reversed, I would want my brother to return no matter what. But the thought of hunting down a warrior of her caliber, ending her life for nothing more than trying to save her sister, it felt... wrong somehow. Not on a moral level—as a Kingsguard doing my duty to protect the king and keep order in Ironheart, I'd killed many times before—but on a tactical one. Wasting such skill seemed foolish.

But she'd sealed her own fate when she'd taken her blade to the Kingsguard, and powerful warrior or not, I would need to remember that when I finally caught up with her.

A knock at the door interrupted us. We exchanged a glance before I called out, "Enter."

A young servant stepped in, her small body thin and weak. Even though she must have been twenty, she looked no larger than a young teen. It was no wonder she hadn't been sent to the army. She'd have been crushed to bits with the slightest blow, and with her unattractive features, no man would want her as a breeder either. I hadn't seen her before, but I'd seen women like her coming and going into the Ironheart Castle my entire life.

She kept her gaze fixed on the ground as she bowed low. "Sir Asher, the king commands that you meet him in the courtyard immediately. He wishes you to inspect the men he's chosen."

"Very good. I will be heading out on a mission and I'm not sure how long I'll be gone. Please send word to the stablemaster to pack my horse with my usual necessities. Food, supplies, weapons. They know what I like."

She gave a curt nod to acknowledge me, bowed again, then backed out. When she was gone, I turned to Erik. "Hopefully the next time I see you, it won't be my bodyless head staring back at you."

"Just... be careful, alright? And remember, you're not alone in this. I can't be there in person, but I'm with you in spirit. Always, brother."

Erik gripped my arm tight, and I glanced at his wounded leg. If he hadn't injured it in that sparring match while training a clumsy new Kingsguard recruit, no doubt he would be assigned in my guardsmen to hunt her down. Though he was two years younger than me, thus unable to rank above me in title as Head of the Kingsguard, his fighting skills made him my equal in every way.

I managed a tense smile. "I know. Thank you, brother."

We made our way to the courtyard, walking slowly to accommodate his injury. When we arrived, Erik's demeanor shifted.

"So," he said, loud enough for others to hear. "Wish I could be there to watch the mighty Sir Asher hunt down the Iron Rose herself. Should be no problem for you, eh? She may be the toughest fighter in the Iron Swordmaidens, but she's got nothing on the Head of the Kingsguard."

I played along, forcing a confident smirk. "She may have gotten lucky once, but she won't escape us again."

We shared a quick look between brothers, same as the one we'd had as children when we'd have each other's backs avoiding father's wrath from some rule we'd gone and broken. Though we had over twenty half-siblings from our father's ten wives, we were the only two full brothers, our mother having passed away giving birth to Erik. We'd always been there for one another, an unbreakable bond that forged deeper each year.

We made our way to the center of the courtyard where King Lothaire stood, surrounded by his top advisors. To my surprise, King Ruthio was there as well, his piercing gaze sweeping over the assembled guards. Before them in tight formation stood the twenty-five men assigned to my mission, all hand-picked for their skill and loyalty.

Lothaire's eyes narrowed as he saw me approach. "Ah, Sir Asher. So good of you to join us. I trust you're preparing for your journey?"

I bowed low. "Yes, Your Majesty. They are packing my horse now and we will ride with haste."

He nodded, then addressed the assembled guards. "You men have been chosen for a vital mission. The traitor, the Iron Rose, must be brought to justice. Fail in this, and you will answer to me personally. Succeed, and you will be richly rewarded."

As Lothaire spoke, I couldn't help but notice King Ruthio's demeanor. He wore a slight smirk, his eyes glittering with an intelligence that made me uneasy. There was something predatory in his gaze, like a wolf sizing up its prey. King Lothaire had been uneasy about his visit, and I wasn't sure if it was his paranoia that King Ruthio was up to something making me look for signs to confirm it or if Lothaire was right and this young king truly was plotting something sinister. Whichever it was, the hairs on the back of my neck stood up when he looked at me, an instinct telling me he wasn't to be trusted.

King Lothaire's voice brought my attention back to him. "Remember, Sir Asher. Don't disappoint me again. Bring that vile woman back to me dead or alive."

"I will, Your Majesty," I said firmly.

As I finished speaking, King Ruthio stepped forward. "If I may, King Lothaire," he said, his voice smooth as silk. "I'd like to offer some of my own men to aid in this hunt. After all, we wouldn't want this... unfortunate incident to mar your reputation among the other kings in the Southlands. If word spreads your army is running amok, it could open you up to more aggression. You're already dealing with hostility from Stormspire. The quicker you bring her to justice, the quicker you can show your strength. Consider the gift of my soldiers a gesture of my friendship."

There was something in the way he said 'friendship' that sent a chill down my spine. I glanced at King Lothaire and saw a flicker of unease cross his face before he masked it with a grateful smile.

"That's very generous of you, King Ruthio," Lothaire said. "But I'm sure Sir Asher and his men are more than capable of handling one rebellious woman."

Though Ruthio's smile didn't waver, his eyes hardened slightly. "Of course, of course. I merely thought... well, considering the spectacular nature of her besting dozens of your men already, it might be prudent to have additional resources. But I defer to your judgment. This is your kingdom, after all. I'm just a guest here."

The tension in the air was palpable, and I had the distinct impression I was watching some greater game being played out. A game with rules I didn't fully understand.

King Lothaire cleared his throat. "Your concern is appreciated, King Ruthio. We'll certainly keep your offer in mind should the need arise."

King Ruthio inclined his head, his unsettling smile still in place. "As you wish. I look forward to hearing of your success, Sir Asher. It would be a shame if a simple woman were to outsmart and outfight your Kingsguard once again."

I gave him a small bow in response, then he turned and walked away, the black Nocturnium boots of his Kingsguard echoing as they fell into step behind him. I couldn't shake the feeling that there was some threat lurking just beneath the surface of his words, though I couldn't for the life of me understand it. He spoke like a friend, moved like a diplomat—but every instinct I had screamed he was neither.

King Lothaire stood and watched him go, then moved up close to me. "Hurry up and get that fucking woman back here because I don't trust that shite of a King. I don't know what he's up to, but I'm telling you, these past months he's been all over Southlands visiting each kingdom, and I have forty years of ruling under my belt. He's planning something. I'd bet my life on it."

Once again, I wasn't sure if it was his repetitive words that Ruthio was up to something causing me to see malice in his simplest gestures, or if Lothaire was truly right, but I had to agree that I, too, sensed something far more sinister happening beneath Ruthio's cool surface. He had the kind of charm that didn't disarm you—it drugged you. Left you smiling while he moved your pieces off the board.

Lothaire continued whispering, "Once you've handled this woman, return to me with haste and we can discuss the plan of going to retrieve the Aurorium. It's the only thing that can counter his fucking Nocturnium army, and if he attacks us, I want weapons and armor for my army that can withstand him. So, get going. Bring me that woman, dead or alive, and then as soon as that shite king is gone, we're marching north to Mistveil Mountains to claim that fucking Aurorium. Hurry up. Don't let me down."

He spun on his boot, marching away while mumbling under his breath, his servants and advisors all hurrying after him.

As I watched him go, my thoughts drifted to the formidable Cloudborn Clan, guardians of the Mistveil Mountains. These legendary warriors, born and bred high above the mists, were so feared that no one from the Southlands dared cross into the Northlands, and vice versa. Mistveil Mountain functioned as an impassable barrier between our worlds, and the Cloudborn Clan was the reason why.

Centuries ago, when magic was commonplace in the Southlands, the kings of the seven kingdoms deemed it too dangerous, sparking a brutal war against all magic users. Aurorium, a rare and radiant metal, became our greatest weapon. As strong as Nocturnium, Aurorium also possessed the unique ability to nullify magic upon contact. Desperate to combat the powerful witches, sorcerers, and other magic wielders, the kingdoms nearly exhausted the Mistveil Mountains mining for Aurorium to forge their weapons.

Their efforts succeeded; magic was eradicated, and it had been centuries since its last sighting. Now, the only remaining Aurorium lay deep within the caves of a small section of Mistveil Mountain, fiercely protected by the Cloudborn Clan. Facing them seemed a daunting task, but if the Iron Swordmaidens were ever to stand a chance against Shadestone's Nocturnium-equipped army, Lothaire was right. We needed superior weapons and armor. The Aurorium guarded by the Cloudborn Clan was our only hope.

But now wasn't the time to worry about King Ruthio and whatever game he was playing, or harvesting Aurorium or our Iron Swordmaidens facing the legendary, terrifying warriors protecting Mistveil Mountain. Right now, I had a mission to plan.

As I turned to prepare for the journey ahead, I found myself reviewing what I knew about the Iron Rose. Her fighting style, her tactics, the way she'd inspire loyalty in her Swordmaidens. Knowing your opponent was the first rule of battle, and I'd observed her many times, admiring her skill and ferocity.

And now I would be on the receiving end of it.

I would need to use everything I knew about her to complete this mission. My future, my position, my very life depended on it. I'd worked too hard, sacrificed too much to fail now.

As I gathered my men and mounted my horse, I pushed aside all thoughts except the mission. I'd always done my duty, followed my orders, served my king. This would be no different. It couldn't be.

Yet as we rode out through the gates of Ironhold, a single unwelcome thought slipped through my defenses: when I finally cornered her, what would I see in those fierce eyes that had met mine so briefly during her escape? And why did I find myself dreading that moment more than any fight I'd ever faced?

I shook the thought away. I was Sir Asher, Head of the Kingsguard. I had my orders. And I would fulfill them.

One way or another.

CHAPTER SIX
Reyna

A sharp gust of wind whipped through my hair as Ember and I wound our way up the narrow mountain path. Five days had passed since our daring escape from Ironheart, and though it was exhilarating to be free to live and breathe on my own terms for the first time in my life, exhaustion clawed at every fiber of my being. With the Kingsguard hunting me down, never far behind, sleep was a luxury I couldn't afford. Ember and I snatched mere moments of rest only when I knew she needed them. We needed to cover ground quickly, but I wouldn't risk her life to save mine and run her into the ground.

Instead, I just kept going, hoping eventually they'd give up. But each day I could see them as specks on the horizon, and the two of us would push on deeper into the vast kingdom of Ironhold, looking for any way to lose them. Their tracking abilities surprised me since I'd tried every trick in my arsenal to shake them. Their persistence was as impressive as it was infuriating. The Kingsguard were well-trained warriors to be certain, but they weren't as well-honed for survival as me and my Iron Swordmaidens. We were the ones who fought the wars out in the cold, harsh world while they merely trained behind the safe walls of Ironheart honing their skills only to protect their city and their rotten king.

I patted Ember's neck, feeling the sweat-slick muscles beneath my palm. "Just a little further," I whispered to her. "I'm sorry, girl. I see a place up there with some trees and grass where it will be safe, and we can get you some rest. It's not safe to stop here."

The path we traveled in my attempt to lose the Kingsguard was treacherous, barely wide enough for Ember to navigate safely. To our right, the mountain face rose in a sheer cliff, while to our left, a dizzying drop promised certain death with one misstep. Luckily, Ember was surefooted and brave, and she continued climbing up the track that spiraled slowly upward, each turn revealing more of the breathtaking—and terrifying—view.

As we rounded another bend, I glanced down to where we'd begun our ascent hours ago. When I saw the glint of armor in the sunlight in the distance below, my heart leaped into my throat. There, far below but unmistakable, was a group of riders.

"Fuck!" I spat as I saw them heading toward the path I knew would lead them straight to me.

Even from this distance, I could make out the royal standard of Ironhold. This time they weren't just small dots in the distance, and because of my height above them unencumbered by anything in my way, I could see them clearly far down below. But as I eyed them up trying to calculate how long I could let Ember rest and still keep ahead of them, my eyes locked onto the lead horse. A magnificent, dappled grey, its coat beautiful and distinctive. A horse I'd know anywhere...

Sir Asher.

There he was in all his Kingsguard glory leading the charge to hunt me down like an animal.

"Bastard," I hissed through clenched teeth.

I narrowed my eyes, my chest swelling back up with a renewed determination. If he thought I'd hand myself over and go quietly, he was in for a rude awakening. I may have been exhausted, hungry, and alone, but I was far from defeated and never going to give up this fight. My sister's life depended on my survival, so if Sir Asher wanted me, he'd have to catch me first, and I intended to make getting his hands on me the hardest task he'd ever face.

With a cluck of my tongue, I urged my tired mare faster, my mind racing for a solution to my current dilemma. Asher was the one they called when prey didn't die clean. I'd heard the tales—none ever escaped him. Though I was smarter than a wounded boar, I knew I'd never outrun them forever. No, I needed to change tactics. It was time to stop running.

It was time to turn from prey to predator.

As the path continued to wind upward and I surveyed my surroundings, a plan started forming in my mind. It was risky, borderline certain death, but then again, what part of my life lately hadn't been? By the time they started this treacherous climb, I estimated I had about a five-hour lead on my pursuers. Five hours to prepare for one of the most important fights of my life. A fight for my freedom. A fight for Cassia's freedom.

We pushed on, the path growing steeper as we climbed. Finally, we turned a bend, and it opened up onto a plateau, a stretch of mountain ripe with life that appeared to stretch far across to the other side where I hoped a safe descent awaited me. Relief whooshed out of my lungs as I surveyed my beautiful surroundings.

Trees stretched high overhead with little birds chirping above us. A small bunny hopped off through the tall patches of grass, disappearing beneath a bush covered in berries. Edible, I hoped. On one side, the mountain continued its ascent, but here it offered a reprieve from the never-ending climb. I walked to the edge, peering down at the winding path we'd spent hours climbing, and I had a commanding view of it from my perch on the plateau.

Perfect. This place was perfect for my final stand.

A soft gurgling drew my attention. Near the side of the plateau, water trickled down from the cliffs over moss-covered rocks, the thin waterfall forming a clear, shallow pool that continued emptying into another small waterfall disappearing off the edge below. Ember nickered softly, already moving toward the inviting water.

"Yes, girl." I gave her neck a pat. "This is our spot."

We both rushed to the water, and I slid off, dropping to my knees as Ember and I guzzled water like we'd never see it again. The crisp, cool liquid quenched my painful thirst, and I drank my fill beside her, pausing to make sure she didn't drink too much too fast. When I finished, I reached into the water and washed the sweat and grime off my face, then took my wet hands and rubbed them over Ember, washing the white sweat from her neck.

"There, girl. That's better, huh? Now you go find yourself some grass and fill your belly back up. I have work to do."

I kissed the star on her forehead and left her to dine, then my gaze swept the area, a plan forming as I took in all my resources. Scattered boulders provided natural cover, perfect for hiding should I have to fall back. The spring-fed pool ensured we wouldn't go thirsty, and along with the berries, I spotted a cluster of edible mushrooms growing in the damp soil nearby.

The dense forest stretched out around me in a sea of green that promised abundant materials for my plan. There'd be plenty of straight branches for arrows and flexible saplings for bows.

A satisfying smile tugged at my lips. This place was a gift—food, water, materials, and a tactical advantage all in one. The Kingsguard might be relentless, but here, I could make my stand.

Prepare yourself, Sir Asher. I am prey no longer.

I snacked on some berries and mushrooms to get up my strength, but then I turned my focus onto preparing my stand. First things first—I needed a ranged weapon. My stolen sword was fine for close combat, but for what I had in mind, I needed distance between me and my pursuers. I set about gathering long, straight branches, my eyes sharp and searching for any that might serve as a makeshift bow.

As I worked, my mind drifted to Cassia. My little sister. Was she married yet? Had he taken her to his bed and forced his old, saggy body on her? No. I shook my head, pressing the thoughts from it. Her beauty opened the door to her marriage, yes, but since she'd been trained for the army and not the bedroom, she'd need to go through the training meant for wives. Especially a king's wife. She'd need months of preparation to learn how to sit and speak and hold her utensils properly to make her a proper wife. Although all those greedy men truly cared about was what was between her legs, so I didn't know why they'd even bother with formalities. But I had to hope they'd follow their century's long structure of all breeders needing training in the art of submission and grace. It would buy me time to get back and rescue her before he had a chance to break her spirit. The thought of her in the clutches of that lecherous king made my blood boil. I channeled that rage into my work, using it to push through the exhaustion that threatened to overwhelm me.

I stripped bark from a flexible branch, twisting the fibers into a crude bowstring. Arrows came next—straight sticks hardened in a small fire I built, their tips sharpened to wicked points. I climbed a tree to retrieve feathers from a nest and bound them to the ends with strips of my own hair plucked from the root.

With the bow complete, I turned my attention to creating some spears. These would be easier to make and could prove deadly in the right circumstances. I selected several long, straight branches, stripping them of twigs and bark. Using my sword, I carefully sharpened one end of each to a lethal point. For good measure, I hardened the tips in the fire, the wood darkening and becoming more rigid as it smoldered.

When I finished creating my own armory, I had a bow, three dozen arrows, and a half a dozen crude but effective spears. I smiled, imagining how much joy it would bring me to see them penetrate the unsuspecting Kingsguard, their sprays of blood a welcome sight after my weapons found purchase in their jugulars.

I walked over to the edge of my fortress, peering down at the winding climb below. The twenty or more Kingsguard were a quarter of the way up the mountain, their large warhorses struggling along the path in single file.

Time for step two in my plan.

I walked back over and looked down, surveying the narrow path below, my mind racing with possibilities—many of them ending with a curse when I realized I had not the time nor the resources to make that plan a reality. My goal was to build a barricade that would stop the Kingsguard beneath me. While they remained trapped on the narrow path with no way forward and unable to turn back, I would have my fun from my perch above them, picking them off one by one. With any luck, none would be left, but if they broke down the barrier and made their push to get me, I should have no problem fighting the remaining guards in a hand-to-hand fight.

Finally, I located the perfect spot to build my barricade. I knew time was of the essence, and I couldn't risk Ember repeatedly traversing the treacherous path. This would have to be a one-woman job. With grim determination, I set to work. I gathered every branch, log, and rock I could carry, piling them near the cliff's edge above my chosen spot. My muscles screamed in protest, but I pushed through the pain. Cassia's face flashed in my mind, driving me onward.

When I had a sizable pile, I began the delicate task of creating my barricade. Peering over the edge, I focused on the perfect choke point on the path below—the narrowest section in my view with a sheer drop on one side and the cliff face on the other.

"Here goes nothing," I muttered, hefting a large branch.

Carefully, I lowered it over the edge, controlling its descent as best I could. But then I had to release it and let it drop the thirty or so feet to the path below. I held my breath hoping it wouldn't miss and tumble right off the mountainside. But it clattered down, landing directly on the path.

"Yes!" I grinned triumphantly.

It wasn't perfect, and certainly not a big enough barricade to stop them, but it was a start. I just needed to send down as many materials as I could so I could go down and fortify that barricade. One by one, I sent more branches and logs tumbling down, wincing at each crash and praying it wouldn't trigger a landslide and alert the men below to my plan.

Though initially creating a well-timed landslide was my original plan to wipe them all off the mountain in one swoop, I realized I'd be sending the horses to their death too. They didn't bear the same guilt as their riders, and I'd spilled enough innocent blood in my lifetime. I wouldn't harm them when there was another way. A more difficult way and at far greater risk to myself, but I deemed the risks worth it to try to spare their lives. Instead of sending the mountain down on their heads, even accidentally, as I dropped debris to build my barricade, I waited until they were on a part of the path not directly below me so each time I missed with my branches and logs, they bounced down the mountain without my determined hunters any the wiser of what awaited them above.

As the pile on the path grew, I finally had enough materials to create a truly impassable barrier. After I dropped the last branch down, I finally stepped back, allowing myself a satisfied smile. It wasn't pretty, but it would serve.

The barrier now spanned the entire width of the route, rising too high and wide for horses to jump on such a narrow path. Anyone trying to pass would have to climb through it on foot or dismantle it piece by piece—a time-consuming process that would leave them vulnerable to my arrows from my perfect perch above.

Satisfied with my work, I stared out from my vantage point. As the sun began its descent toward the horizon, I surveyed my work with pride. I looked past my trap to Sir Asher and the trail of riders climbing behind him, growing closer. Maybe a half hour before they reached me. Now, all that was left was to wait for my pursuers to climb right into my trap.

I led Ember further into the plateau of the mountain, finding a secure spot where she could rest unseen. "Stay here," I told her, pressing my forehead to hers. "I'll come back for you when it's done."

I stopped at the water's edge for another drink to prepare, and I smeared mud across my face and armor to help me blend into the rocky outcropping, making it harder for them to fire back if they couldn't find me.

With bow in hand, I made my way to my chosen vantage point where my arrows and spears lay waiting. A steep cliff rose about thirty feet above the barricade, offering a perfect perch from which to rain down death on my unsuspecting pursuers.

The sun sank lower, painting the sky in brilliant hues of orange and pink. In another life, I might have found it beautiful. Now, in this life, it was merely a countdown to the battle to come. As I settled in to wait, exhaustion tugged at me with iron fingers. I fought it off, knowing that to succumb now would mean death—or worse.

And then, I heard them. The distant clop of hooves, the jingle of tack and armor. My hands tightened on my bow, an arrow nocked and ready.

They were here.

I took a deep breath, steadying myself. This was it. The moment that would determine my fate—and Cassia's.

"I'm coming for you, little sister," I whispered, excitement and nerves gathering in my chest. "Just hold on a little longer."

The first riders rounded the bend, and I saw him. Sir Asher, his golden-brown skin catching the last rays of sunlight, those startling blue eyes scanning the path ahead. For a moment, I was struck by how handsome he was—all sharp angles and quiet strength. But then I remembered why he was here, and my resolve hardened.

My eyes narrowed at the man who had stopped me from saving my sister. The man who now hunted me like an animal.

I settled into position, nocking an arrow to my makeshift bow. Let them come. This time, I wasn't their prey. This time, I'd be ready.

The bowstring creaked as I drew it to full extension, my muscles trembling with the effort. Below, oblivious to the danger that lurked above, Sir Asher and his men approached the barricade.

I held my breath, waiting for the perfect moment to strike.

One heartbeat. Two.

The world narrowed to the point of my arrow and the unsuspecting targets below.

Any moment now...

CHAPTER SEVEN
Asher

The narrow mountain path wound ever upward, no doubt a tactical choice designed to give my pursued an advantage. Each turn revealed breathtaking vistas that I barely noticed, my mind consumed with the mission at hand. Finding the Iron Rose. Completing my assignment. Securing my future.

The woman had proven far more resourceful than anyone had anticipated. I'd expected her to be formidable—I'd seen her fight enough times to know her capabilities—but her ability to evade us for this long spoke to skills and smarts beyond mere combat.

My loyal stallion, Tempest, picked his way carefully along the treacherous trail. I gazed down at him, his dappled grey coat shimmering in the fading light. I remembered the day he was gifted to me, an awkward, leggy yearling with big brown eyes and a spirit as wild as a gale. It was during my first year in the Kingsguard, a reward for saving the king from a would-be assault. As I'd approached him in the royal stables, a sudden squall had broken out, rain lashing against the walls and thunder rumbling overhead. The noise had panicked the young horse, and he'd reared and spun wildly in his stall. But then his eyes had met mine with an intensity that matched the storm outside. His panic had ceased, and he'd walked over, touching me with his velvety nose, nuzzling against me as if he'd already known I would take care of him, and one day, when he was old enough, he would take care of me. In that moment, I'd known his name would be Tempest. Over the years, he'd lived up to it—powerful, unpredictable, yet steadfast in the face of any challenge. In Tempest, I found not just a mount, but a companion always willing to unleash his powerful storm for me once more.

A rock slipped beneath his hooves, and he scrambled back to sure footing. I exhaled a deep breath, then looked over my shoulder to check on the other Kingsguard all following in a single file line, the clinking of their armor and the clop of hooves on stone were the only sounds breaking the mountain's silence. Even after days on the hunt, I could still see the determination in their eyes, the King's promise of riches and rewards pushing them on in their relentless pursuit.

The hunt had been more challenging than I'd anticipated. Several times we'd lost her trail completely, only for Edmund to somehow pick it up again. They thought I was the best tracker in the Kingsguard, but it seemed the man was a bloodhound in human form. I'd found myself reluctantly impressed by her evasion skills—few could outmaneuver an entire Kingsguard patrol for this long.

Part of me—a part I refused to examine too closely—wondered what would happen if we never found her. If she slipped through our grasp despite our best efforts, would the king allow me to keep my head? Unlikely, as he was a man of his word, but perhaps eight years of loyal service since I'd joined on my sixteenth birthday would coax him into leniency if our tricky prey somehow just slipped away.

"It will be dark soon. We need to pick up the pace," Sir Edmund, who was my second-in-command on this ride, called from behind me.

I turned back, my jaw tightening with irritation as I looked at his rugged face, the lower half surrounded by a dark beard that matched his dark eyes. "I'm aware of the falling light. That's why I'm slowing down. This trail is treacherous enough in the daylight, and the setting sun is blinding me and Tempest up here. Unless you'd like for me to walk us all straight off the edge to our deaths, I suggest you quiet down and let me find the best way."

He muttered something under his breath that I couldn't quite catch, then fell silent. I could feel his eyes boring into my back, and it wasn't the first time I wondered if he suspected my reluctance to find our quarry. I'd known him for years. A strong warrior and ambitious, he always coveted my position as Head of the Kingsguard. I knew he'd seize any opportunity to discredit me—or perhaps even hoped I'd fall off this cliff, or push me if fate gave him the option, so he could challenge my brother, most likely my replacement, and step straight into my position.

As Tempest navigated another switchback, I found myself once again wrestling with the impossible choice before me. What would I do when we inevitably caught up to Reyna? Part of me admired her courage, her skill, her determination to fight for what she believed in. But I had my duty, my family's honor, my sworn oath to consider. To go against the king's command was treason, and with over twenty witnesses, there would be no way to let her go without condemning myself.

My brooding was interrupted when we rounded another bend. There, not fifty paces ahead, loomed a massive barricade of fallen trees and jumbled rocks spanning the entire width of the path.

I raised my hand, signaling the men to halt. "Hold!" I called out, my eyes scanning the obstacle and the cliffs above. I tipped my head as I stared at it, immediately noting something wasn't right. This was too deliberate, too perfect in its placement. This was no natural landslide in our path.

The realization hit me like a physical blow. "It's a trap! Take cov—"

My warning was cut short as an arrow flew toward me. I ducked my head left with just enough time it whistled past my ear, so close I felt the breeze of its passage.

"We're under attack!" someone shouted, and chaos erupted instantly. Men shouted in alarm, horses whinnied in fear. The narrow path became a frenzy of panicked movement as everyone tried to back away from the barricade and the unseen archer.

"Back! Get back!" I yelled, struggling to control Tempest as he danced nervously beneath me. The path was too narrow for the horses to turn, and we were frozen in place with a drop to our left and sheer cliff to our right; we'd have to back them out carefully or risk sending men and mounts plummeting to their deaths.

Tactically brilliant. I had to admit, I was impressed.

Another arrow found its mark, and one of my men cried out in pain. I looked up, searching desperately for our attacker.

A flash of movement on the cliff above caught my eye. For just an instant, I saw her. Reyna, her face smeared with mud for camouflage, her wooden bow already nocked with another arrow.

Our eyes met across the distance, and in that moment, I felt an unexpected jolt of recognition. Not just of her identity, but of something deeper—a warrior recognizing another warrior's resolve. Her eyes held the same determination I'd seen in battle, the same unflinching commitment to survival at any cost.

She released her arrow, and I ducked with just enough time that it pinged against the side of the cliff only inches from my head. The near miss sent a surge of adrenaline through me. Whatever respect I might have for her skills, while she was actively trying to kill me wasn't the time to admire them.

I heard another scream, and glanced to see one tumble off the side, an arrow in his neck. Though I understood that she was fighting for her life, knowing what fate awaited her if captured, I had men under my command—good men, many of them, who were simply following orders as I was. I couldn't let her slaughter them here on this mountain.

"Dismount!" I ordered, swinging down from Tempest's back. "Press yourselves to the cliff!"

As my men scrambled to obey, I pressed my back against the rocky wall, my mind racing for any way to get out of this trap alive. There was no way to get back down without eventually being in her arrow's path again, and the only way forward would take us too long to dismantle, and we'd be a pile of corpses added to the rubble before we finished. We were pinned down, with no way forward and a treacherous retreat. But there had to be a way out, a way to reach her...

My eyes traced the contours of the cliff face. It would be a difficult climb, but not impossible. If I could work my way around to where she couldn't see me, I might just have a chance.

"Edmund," I said, keeping my voice calm and low enough I knew she couldn't hear. "You're in command. Keep the men safe and stay in cover. I'm going after her."

Before he could protest, I was moving. I slid along the cliff face, using every inch of cover I could find, making sure she couldn't see me to take a shot or alert her to my plan. For all she knew we were all huddled together beneath the small ledge giving everyone just enough cover. When I was sure I was out of Reyna's line of sight for my climb, I began the slow, grueling work.

The rock was unforgiving, offering precious few handholds. More than once, I felt my grip slip, my heart leaping into my throat as I scrambled to regain purchase. But I pressed on, ignoring the rocks tearing into my flesh as I climbed and climbed.

As I neared the top, I paused to catch my breath. I still didn't know exactly what I would do when I reached her. The mission was clear—capture or kill—but something in me resisted the simplicity of that directive. This wasn't some common criminal; this was the Iron Rose, one of our kingdom's greatest assets. To destroy her seemed... wasteful.

With a final effort, I hauled myself over the edge of the cliff. There, not twenty paces away, was Reyna. She was focused intently on the path below, another arrow already nocked and ready. The fading sunlight caught her profile, highlighting the determined set of her jaw, the focused intensity in her stare.

I crept forward, my footsteps muffled by the carpet of pine needles. Just a few more steps and—

A twig snapped beneath my foot.

Reyna whirled toward me, her eyes widening in shock as they locked with mine. For a heartbeat, we stood frozen, staring at each other. Then, with a snarl of defiance, she sent her arrow whizzing toward my head. I ducked just in time, then she dropped her bow and launched herself at me.

I barely had time to brace myself before she slammed into me with the force of a charging bull. We went down in a tangle of limbs, rolling dangerously close to the cliff's edge. She fought with a desperate fury, all calculation and precision despite her obvious exhaustion.

I managed to gain the upper hand for a moment, pinning her beneath me. Our faces were inches apart, and I could see the flecks of gold in her green eyes, burning with a fury that was almost palpable. "Stop fighting," I ordered, trying to sound authoritative despite my ragged breathing. "You can't win this."

Her response was a knee to my groin that drove the air from my lungs. As I wheezed, trying to recover, she scrambled away and snatched up one of her makeshift spears.

"I won't go back," she spat, her eyes blazing with fury. "I'll die here before I let you take me to him."

She lunged at me with the spear, and I barely managed to dodge the thrust. We moved together in a deadly dance along the cliff's edge, neither of us willing to give ground. Her fighting style was impressive—efficient, adaptable, with none of the wasted movement I often saw in the training yards. Even exhausted and cornered, she was formidable.

I parried another thrust with my sword, the clash of steel on wood sending vibrations up my arm. "You're only making this worse for yourself," I said, though the words felt hollow even to my own ears.

"Worse?" she laughed bitterly, redoubling her assault. "There is nothing worse than what awaits me in Ironhold."

Wood met steel as we spiraled toward the cliff's edge, one misstep from the void below. I saw the danger an instant before Reyna did. The ground beneath her foot, weakened by our struggle, began to crumble.

Time seemed to slow. Realization flickered in Reyna's eyes, and I saw the flash of fear replace the anger. Without conscious thought, I lunged forward, my hand shooting out to grasp her wrist as the earth gave way beneath her.

For a heart-stopping moment, Reyna dangled over the abyss, her life quite literally in my hands. I could feel the strain in my arm, my shoulder screaming in protest as I held her weight.

I looked into Reyna's eyes, saw the mixture of fear and defiance there. But beneath that, I glimpsed something that made my breath catch—a fierce will to live, a determination that burned with such intensity it seemed to sear into my very soul.

And in that moment, something shifted inside me. Not a complete transformation, but a hairline crack in the foundation of everything I'd believed.

Her life hung by nothing but my grip, yet even dangling over death's abyss, she didn't beg. Didn't plead. Her eyes held mine with a challenge that said she'd fight to her last breath. I'd seen her same unyielding spirit on countless battlefields, but never this close—never close enough to feel it radiating from her like heat from a flame.

In her, I saw not just a fugitive or a soldier, but something rare and valuable—a fire that refused to be extinguished, no matter how fierce the storm that raged against it.

I could let go. One simple loosening of my fingers, and it would be over. Quick. Clean. Merciful, even, compared to what awaited her at Ironheart. Like a fierce wolf only protecting its pack, fighting to stay alive, I could barely stand the thought of such a creature being paraded through the streets, taunted and tormented, with a slow, painful execution at the end of the humiliating march. I could spare her that cruel fate. I could say she fell while resisting capture. No one would question it.

And with that single act, I would secure my future, fulfill my duty, claim my reward. I would remain the man I was raised to be.

My grip faltered for a heartbeat.

Her eyes widened slightly, understanding dawning in their depths. She knew what I was considering. Yet she didn't close her eyes in acceptance or surrender. Instead, her gaze became more intense, more demanding—not begging for life, but challenging me to make a choice that I could live with.

And I realized, with a clarity that terrified me, that I couldn't be the one to extinguish this rare fire. Maybe it was weakness. Maybe it was selfishness. But my hand tightened around her wrist with renewed determination.

I would not be the one to decide her fate—not here, not like this. And as I began to pull her up, I couldn't shake the unsettling feeling that in saving her life, I was irrevocably changing my own.

The sound of men climbing up behind me solidified my decision to let the Iron Rose live to fight another day. They'd found a way up, and now they were coming to join the confrontation. Whatever doubts I was feeling, whatever questions were forming in my mind, I couldn't act on them. Not here. Not now. Not with witnesses. They'd know I let her fall instead of bringing her home to face King Lothaire's judgment.

With a grunt of effort, I pulled Reyna up, dragging her away from the edge and back onto solid ground. As she regained her footing, I immediately moved to restrain her, grabbing her wrists and pinning them behind her back.

"Let me go," she hissed, struggling against my grip.

I leaned in close, my voice barely above a whisper. "Stop fighting. You'll only get yourself killed."

Something in my tone must have registered, because she stilled, her eyes searching mine with suspicion and confusion.

Before she could respond, Edmund and three other guards crested the ridge, their faces flushed from the climb but breaking into grins when they saw I had Reyna restrained.

"You got her!" Edmund exclaimed, striding forward with undisguised glee. "The Iron Rose herself, brought down by Sir Asher. The king will be pleased."

"Tie her up," I ordered, my voice carefully neutral as I handed her over to the guards. "Secure her properly. She's more dangerous than she looks."

As they bound her wrists with rough rope, Reyna kept her eyes fixed on me, as if trying to solve a puzzle. I looked away, unable to meet that penetrating gaze.

"What shall we do with her?" one of the younger guards asked, barely containing his excitement. "Kill her here? Make an example of her?"

"No," I said, perhaps too quickly. I cleared my throat. "The king's orders were clear. He wants her brought back alive if possible. He wants... he wants to make a public example of her."

Edmund's eyes narrowed slightly at my hesitation, but he nodded. "A wise choice. Her death here would be too quick, too clean. The king will want to ensure everyone sees what happens to traitors."

I felt my stomach turn at his words, now questioning my decision to keep her alive, but kept my expression impassive. "We'll make camp here for the night. It's too dangerous to attempt the descent in the dark. At dawn, we return to Ironheart."

As the men dragged Reyna away to secure her for the night, she glanced back over her shoulder at me. In that brief look, I saw something that would haunt me through the long night ahead—not just fear or anger, but a silent question that seemed to pierce straight through my carefully constructed armor.

Why did you save me just to condemn me to something worse?

I had no answer. At least, not one I was ready to acknowledge, even to myself.

Looking out over the darkening landscape, I tried to quiet the unwelcome thoughts circling in my mind. I was Sir Asher, Head of the Kingsguard. I had my orders. I had my duty. I had captured the fugitive, and soon I would deliver her to justice, claim my reward, and continue the life I'd always known.

So why did victory taste like ashes in my mouth?

CHAPTER EIGHT
Reyna

Pain shot through my shoulders as I shifted against the rough tree trunk. Hours of being bound with my hands behind my back had turned my muscles to fire, but I refused to show any discomfort. The Kingsguard had set up camp in a small clearing, their bedrolls arranged in a circle around a modest fire. Far enough from the cliff edge to be safe, close enough to keep watch over their prized prisoner.

Me.

I tested my bonds again, subtle movements that wouldn't catch attention. The ropes were tight, but not as tight as they should have been. Not tight enough to cut off circulation. Not tight enough to prevent the tiny movements I'd been making all evening, stretching the fibers bit by bit. A mistake? Perhaps. But the memory of Asher's eyes as he'd bound my wrists lingered. Something had changed in him when he'd pulled me from the cliff's edge. Something I couldn't name and didn't trust.

I flexed my fingers, keeping blood flowing as I scanned the camp. Twenty-five men had pursued me up the mountain. Now only twenty remained—five had fallen to my arrows before Asher reached me. And soon, if the gods favored me, the number would fall further.

All I needed was an opportunity.

"Look at her," a voice murmured from near the fire. "The great Iron Rose. Not so mighty now, is she?"

I kept my expression impassive as three Kingsguard approached. I recognized them immediately—the ones who had watched me most intently all evening, their eyes lingering in ways that made my skin crawl. The leader, a brutish man with a scar splitting his upper lip, crouched before me.

"You've led us on quite a chase," he said, his breath reeking of whiskey. "Cost us five good men."

I met his gaze without flinching. "They weren't good men. No man is, but especially a Kingsguard."

The blow came fast—an open-handed strike that snapped my head to the side. I tasted blood but didn't make a sound.

"Feisty," said another guard, leaner with a pointy nose like a hawk. "I like that. Bet she's still feisty when she's not playing soldier."

The third man, younger than the others with a patchy attempt at a beard, laughed nervously. "Sir Asher said not to touch her."

"Sir Asher isn't here," Scar-lip replied, glancing toward the edge of camp where Asher had disappeared to check the perimeter. "And what the king doesn't know won't hurt him. She's dead anyway once we get her back. Might as well enjoy the journey."

I spat blood at his feet. "Touch me and you'll lose the hand that does it."

He laughed, grabbing my chin roughly. "Big threats from a woman in ropes. The Iron Rose. What a joke. Nothing but a girl playing at being a warrior."

"I've killed better men than you," I said softly, my eyes raking up his frame. "Though that's not saying much."

His face darkened. "You think you're something special? You're nothing. Just another woman who forgot her place."

"And what place is that?" I asked, continuing to work at my bonds behind my back. I needed to keep him talking, keep him distracted.

"On your back," Hawk-nose snickered, emboldened by his companion's lead. "Or on your knees. Your choice."

The young one shifted uncomfortably. "We should go back to the fire. If Sir Asher returns—"

"Shut up," Scar-lip snapped. "The great Sir Asher. So concerned with his honor. Well, I've got other concerns." His hand moved to my face again, trailing down my neck. "King won't care what condition she's in when we bring her back, as long as she's breathing enough to scream when they put her on display."

I felt the rope give slightly. Just a little more.

"Maybe we should give her a taste of what's waiting for her at Ironheart," Hawk-nose suggested, his hand moving to his belt.

I was about to respond when a voice cut through the night like ice.

"Step away from the prisoner."

The men froze. Sir Asher stood at the edge of the firelight, his face a mask of cold fury. In that moment, he didn't look like the controlled, dutiful Kingsguard I'd known. He looked dangerous.

Scar-lip straightened slowly. "Sir Asher. We were just—"

"I know exactly what you were 'just' doing," Sir Asher cut him off, stepping closer. "The prisoner is to be delivered to the king unharmed. Those are our orders."

"With all due respect, sir," Hawk-nose said, not sounding respectful at all, "she's killed our brothers. Seems only fair we get some compensation."

Asher's hand moved like the strike of a venomous snake. His large fingers snatched the shocked man by the neck, tightening so quickly he couldn't even get in a single breath. With a cold fury swirling in those icy eyes, he pulled the man close to his face. His voice was smooth and slow as he squeezed even tighter. "The next man who touches her loses more than a hand. Am I understood?"

The younger guard nodded quickly, backing away. Scar-lip stumbled backward, his hands raised in submission. Hawk-nose, his face reddening by the second as he struggled to breath, tried to nod but Sir Asher's vice grip on his neck prevented any movement.

With a quick push, Sir Asher cast Hawk-nose to the ground. He gasped in a desperate breath then scrambled to his feet, hurrying to join his retreating friends, all muttering under their breath.

When they were gone, Sir Asher approached, crouching where Scar-lip had been moments before. His eyes met mine, searching. For what, I couldn't say.

"Are you injured?" he asked, his voice carefully neutral.

I laughed bitterly. "Why do you care? Taking me back to be executed with a clean face will ease your conscience?"

He didn't answer immediately. When he did, his voice was lower. "There are lines I won't cross."

"Yet you'll deliver me to those who will cross every line," I replied. "How noble of you."

Something flashed in his eyes—discomfort, perhaps guilt—but it vanished quickly. He stood, glancing back toward the fire where his men had gathered.

"You should rest," he said. "We leave at first light."

As he turned to go, I couldn't help myself. "Why did you pull me up?" I asked. "On the cliff. You could have let me fall. It would have been easier."

He paused, his back to me. For a moment, I thought he wouldn't answer.

"I don't know," he said finally, and then he was gone, walking back into the woods without looking back.

I watched him go, confusion warring with hatred in my chest. He was the enemy—the king's loyal dog. Yet twice now, he'd shown me... what? Mercy? Honor? Whatever it was, it didn't matter. I wouldn't be alive to see it happen a third time if I remained his prisoner.

The night deepened. The moon rose, casting silver light through the trees. Most of the guards had settled into their bedrolls, though three remained on watch—one at each edge of the clearing and one by the fire. Scar-lip and Hawk-nose had volunteered for the first watch, no doubt hoping for another opportunity.

Perfect.

I'd been working at my bonds steadily, the subtle movements hidden by the shadows. They'd tied me to the tree with one rope around my torso, with a separate binding for my wrists behind my back. The torso rope had been my first target, gradually creating enough slack, and finally, I was able to slip free.

My hands were still bound behind me, but carefully and quietly, I wiggled my legs through my arms until they were now before me rather than behind. Limited still, but far more dangerous than they knew.

Scar-lip had positioned himself closest to me, his back half-turned as he pretended to scan the forest. But I could feel his attention moving toward me, knew he was waiting for his companions to look away.

I didn't give him the chance to make the first move.

The moment he turned in my direction, I launched myself forward, driving my bound hands up into his throat with enough force to crush his windpipe. His eyes bulged in shock, hands clawing at his neck as he tried to draw breath that wouldn't come. Before he could make a sound, I grabbed the dagger from his belt and drove it into his throat, twisting to ensure no alarm could escape his lips.

As he choked on his own blood, I pulled his dagger free, a slight smile tipping my lips as I glanced at the hand that had touched me. The one I'd warned him he'd lose. His eyes flashed wide just before I swiped his blade down on it with enough force to sever the offending limb.

"I warned you," I whispered as I watched the life drain from his horrified eyes.

One down.

I twisted the dagger in my hands, preparing to work on my wrists, but from the fire nearby, Hawk-nose must have noticed movement because he turned to look at us. I saw the whites of his eyes when he saw me standing over his fallen friend, his mouth opening to shout a warning.

My throw sent the dagger spinning through the air to bury itself in his throat. He fell backward, his cry becoming a wet gurgle that was lost in the crackling of the flames.

Two down.

The third guard on watch shouted in alarm, drawing his sword as he ran toward me. In only seconds, the camp was stirring, men reaching for weapons as they scrambled from their bedrolls.

I met the third guard's charge, parrying his strike and countering with a sweeping blow that opened his abdomen. He fell, clutching at his insides as they spilled forth.

Three down.

"She's loose!" someone shouted.

The camp erupted into chaos. Guards rushed toward me from all directions, but I was already moving, cutting through the nearest man with a precise strike despite my bound hands.

Four down.

The next two came at me together. I ducked under the first swing, kicked out to knock one off balance, then spun to slice through the other's neck. As he fell, I completed my turn and drove the sword up through the first man's chin as he staggered forward.

Six down.

I fought like I was possessed, like every battle I'd ever won had just been practice for this moment. My bound wrists limited my movement, but I'd trained for worse. Every strike was economical, every defense fluid. These men might have been the king's elite, but I was the Iron Rose. I was made for this.

Another guard fell, then another. Blood slicked the ground beneath my feet. I spun to fend off an attack, and from the corner of my eye, I saw Sir Asher bursting from the trees, rushing back toward camp. When he saw me, our eyes locked for a brief moment, and he stopped—his face a mixture of shock and something else, something I didn't have time to interpret.

I cut down one more guard as he lunged for me, then broke from the fight, sprinting toward the edge of the clearing. I needed space, needed a moment to—

An arrow whistled past my ear. One of the guards had grabbed a bow. My time was running out.

I reached the perimeter of the camp and turned, bringing two fingers to my lips. The whistle that emerged was high and piercing, echoing through the forest like a bird of prey's cry. It was a signal Ember and I had practiced countless times, one she would recognize no matter the distance.

The Kingsguard hesitated, confused by the sound. All except Sir Asher, whose eyes widened in understanding just as the thunder of hooves broke through the night.

Ember burst into the clearing, her powerful legs carrying her straight toward me. I raised my bound hands and caught her mane as she passed, using her momentum to swing myself onto her back with a practiced move we'd perfected years ago.

"Stop her!" someone shouted, but it was too late. Ember was already turning, responding to the pressure of my knees as we charged back toward the forest.

An arrow struck the ground beside us. Another grazed Ember's flank, drawing a pained whinny but not slowing her stride. We raced between the trees, the sounds of pursuit fading behind us.

Just before the forest swallowed us completely, I glanced back.

Sir Asher stood at the edge of the clearing, sword hanging loosely at his side. He wasn't shouting orders. Wasn't giving chase. He was simply... watching. Our eyes met across the distance, and in that brief moment, something unspoken passed between us.

Then we were gone, Ember's powerful strides carrying us deep into the sheltering darkness of the forest.

As we rode, the realization of what had just happened settled over me. I'd been captured by the Kingsguard, by Sir Asher himself, and I'd escaped, leaving half his force dead or dying behind me.

The king would not forgive this. Sir Asher would not forgive this. The next time we met, there would be no mercy.

So why, when I closed my eyes, did I still see him standing there, watching me go, making no move to stop me? And why did the memory fill me not with triumph, but with confusion?

It didn't matter. I was free, and I had a sister to save.

I leaned forward, urging Ember faster into the night, toward the one place I knew they wouldn't follow.

Moonshadow Woods.

A place of legend and fear throughout the kingdom. The ancient forest that bordered the northern edge of Ironhold was said to be haunted by spirits and beasts that hunted any who dared enter. Monstrous creatures with gleaming teeth and claws that could tear through armor. Trees that moved in the absence of wind. Travelers who entered never returned, their screams echoing for days before silence claimed them forever. Most believed these were just stories to keep children obedient, but enough people had vanished over the years that even the bravest soldiers avoided its shadowy depths.

But I had nowhere else to go. Ironhold was lost to me. The other kingdoms would happily return me to King Lothaire for reward or favor. Moonshadow Woods offered the one thing I needed most—a place where the king's men feared to tread. Whatever dangers waited in those dark woods, they couldn't be worse than what awaited me in the king's dungeon.

CHAPTER NINE
Asher

I watched her from the shadow of a massive oak, a smile tugging at my lips. I'd successfully cornered my dangerous prey. The Iron Rose, the fearsome warrior who'd slaughtered nine of my men with bound wrists, now sat by a small stream, drinking water with her cupped hands. Her horse, Ember, grazed nearby, occasionally lifting her head to scan their surroundings. Smarter than her rider it seemed, as Reyna seemed wholly consumed by her task and unaware of my presence. Likely she thought she'd outrun us and had some time to relax, but she didn't realize I'd traveled alone.

Knowing my horse was far swifter than the others, I'd left my surviving men behind to tend to the wounded and pack up the camp with orders to follow as soon as possible. Sir Edmund would lead them, tracking my path. Without my men to slow me down, Tempest and I had covered ground quickly and quietly. Her trail was clear to someone with my training—broken twigs, disturbed undergrowth, occasional hoofprints in softer ground. She'd been moving fast, not covering her tracks. A mistake.

I shifted my weight, careful not to make a sound. She still had no idea I was here. After witnessing what she could do in combat, I had no intention of giving her a fair fight this time. I needed to capture her quickly. Efficiently. There could be no room for error.

Reyna stood, stretching her arms to the sky with a yawn. Her wrists were no longer bound—she must have cut the ropes at some point during her flight. She rolled her shoulders, wincing slightly. She was sore. Likely the remains of our last fight or having been tethered to that tree, and it startled me to see even the slightest weakness in the great Iron Rose.

Something about her movements, the efficient grace with which she carried herself even when injured, caught my attention. The warm rays of sunlight dancing across her skin gave it a golden sheen that seemed to soften her edges. With her guard down and those lethal eyes not burning into mine, she didn't look like the fearsome Iron Rose I'd seen slice through enemies with terrifying precision.

People said the scar that marred her right cheek diminished her obvious beauty, but I thought it only enhanced it. It was a badge of defiance, a testament to her warrior's spirit. The one small control she had over her own life where she could control entire armies and carry the weight of protecting our kingdom on her back, even if she couldn't choose her own next meal. I'd heard the whispers and rumors behind that scar, but no one could ever confirm the truth in how she'd attained the deep wound across her striking face. They say she'd done it to herself at fourteen to avoid being taken as a breeder. The thought made my stomach churn. A woman like Reyna—fierce, proud, unstoppable—would have withered and died in a breeder's gilded cage.

She was beautiful—there was no denying that—but until now, I had only ever seen her as the warrior, the commander, the enemy. For just a moment, I saw her simply as a woman. An intoxicating one at that. The realization was unsettling in ways I couldn't quite name.

I pushed the observation aside with sudden force. She was a target, nothing more. A fugitive to be captured. Admiring her was as foolish as admiring the deadly beauty of a drawn blade.

I moved silently toward her, keeping out of Ember's keen eyesight so she wouldn't alert her mistress. Three more steps. Two. One.

I lunged forward, wrapping an arm around her waist while the other pressed my dagger to her throat. Her body tensed, coiling like a spring ready to unleash.

"Don't," I warned, the blade pressing just firmly enough to dimple her skin. "I'd rather not hurt you, but I will if necessary."

A sound escaped her—half laugh, half snarl. "You again?" She spat the words with such venom it almost made me step back.

"Me again," I replied, keeping my voice steady despite our proximity. "And now you're going to come with me. I have orders to return you to Ironheart."

"Your orders can go to hell," she growled, her body vibrating with fury. "Along with you."

"Are we going to do this the easy way or the hard way?" I asked, maintaining the pressure of the blade against her skin. "Because I'm content with either."

For a moment, I thought she was going to fight. In fact, I expected nothing less from her. But then to my surprise, the fight seemed to drain from her. Not surrender—never that—but a cold calculation. I could almost hear her mind working, assessing options, planning her next move.

"Hands out to your sides," I instructed.

After a moment of defiant stillness, she complied, her movements deliberate. "So what now? You drag me back to Ironheart? To the king?"

"That's the plan." I reached for the rope at my belt, keeping the dagger firmly in place. "Though I'd prefer to do it without adding more scars to either of us."

"How considerate," she said dryly, but the rage still simmered beneath her controlled tone.

With practiced efficiency, I bound her wrists in front of her. Proper bindings this time—tight enough to hold, loose enough to prevent injury. I'd learned that lesson.

Once her wrists were secure, I stepped back, keeping my dagger ready but lowering it from her throat. She turned to face me, her expression hard as iron, eyes burning with a fury that was almost tangible.

"That was almost too easy," I said, studying her face for any hint of deception.

She smiled, the expression not reaching her eyes. "Don't worry. I'll make you work for it later."

I couldn't help but chuckle at that. "I don't doubt it."

Ember had approached during our exchange, standing protectively near Reyna. The mare's intelligent eyes seemed to assess me, ears flicking forward then back. I whistled softly, and Tempest emerged from where I'd left him hidden, his dappled coat catching the sunlight.

"We'll ride together," I said, gesturing toward Tempest. "I'm not making the mistake of letting you ride alone."

"And Ember?" Reyna asked, a hint of genuine concern breaking through her anger.

"She'll follow. She seems clever enough."

Something softened briefly in Reyna's expression as she looked at her loyal horse. "That she is."

I led her to Tempest. "Up you go."

With her bound hands, mounting required my assistance. I cupped my hands to boost her, and after a moment's hesitation, she stepped into them, allowing me to lift her onto Tempest's back. I swung up behind her a moment later, reaching around her to take the reins.

The position forced us together, her back pressed against my chest, her body fitted between my thighs. Every breath she took seemed to echo through me, each subtle shift of her weight sending an unwelcome awareness coursing through my veins. I felt her stiffen at the contact, her entire body becoming a line of rigid tension where it met mine. Heat bloomed where our bodies connected, a response so visceral and immediate it startled me. A soldier's discipline had never failed me before, yet I found myself fighting an inexplicable pull toward this woman—my enemy, my prisoner, my mission. I tightened my grip on the reins, white-knuckled, as if they might anchor me against this current threatening to sweep me somewhere dangerous. Somewhere forbidden.

"I hope my proximity doesn't offend your delicate sensibilities," she said acidly.

"I've endured worse hardships," I replied, hoping she hadn't actually noticed the physical response I seemed to be having to her body pressed so tightly against mine.

I clicked my tongue, and Tempest began to move. Ember followed without prompting, staying close to her mistress.

We rode in heavy silence for a time, the tension between us almost a physical presence. Finally, Reyna spoke, her voice tight with controlled fury.

"You stopped me from saving my sister."

The accusation hung in the air between us. I considered my response carefully.

"I didn't stop you from saving your sister," I said finally. "I stopped you from getting *killed*. You were grossly outnumbered, surrounded. You would have died before reaching her. And your sister would still be exactly where she is now. I stopped you because I didn't want to see you lose your life to a battle you couldn't win."

She twisted in the saddle to look at me, disbelief etched on her features.

I looked into her eyes, those fierce, hardened eyes, and I saw the pain flickering inside them.

"I know it's no consolation, but I'm sorry they took your sister. You reacted as I would expect you to, but I couldn't let you fight your way straight into death. You're a fierce warrior, probably the best I've ever seen, but even you can't survive against dozens of soldiers at once."

She turned away, but not before I caught the flicker of realization in her eyes. For perhaps the first time, she was considering that I might have been right.

"Why save me then, just to take me to be killed now?" she asked, her voice quieter but no less intense.

"Because then I was acting on my own choice, and now I have my king's orders," I replied simply.

She gave a bitter laugh. "Of course. You always follow orders, don't you? The perfect, obedient dog."

Something in her tone—the dismissal, the assumption—sparked an unexpected anger in me. "You think I'm the monster of your story. That I enjoyed delivering orders telling you to send those women to their deaths. You think I didn't know the plans were stupid and going to cause senseless slaughter? I'm not an idiot. Of course I knew. And I hated it. But what was I supposed to do, Reyna? Tell the king no? You really think he would have smiled and said, 'Oh, well thank you Sir Asher for letting me know I'm an arse. I appreciate it. By all means, let's go with your plan.'" I snorted at the thought.

"You did *nothing* to stop him!"

"Neither did you!" I shot back. "If I'm a monster, then so are you. Even knowing it would kill your fellow Swordmaidens, you followed orders in battle. How many women died following your command?"

Her body went rigid against mine. "That's different," she hissed.

"Is it?" I challenged. "You think I don't want to ignore orders too? You think men don't face consequences?"

She twisted in the saddle, eyes flashing with fury. "Consequences? What do you know of consequences? Will they send the poor little lordling to bed without his dessert if he doesn't do as he's told? My sisters *die* for disobedience. They *hanged* my fighters to punish me when I tried to ignore orders once. Women are beaten, starved, humiliated. What could you possibly know of real consequences?"

"If I don't bring you back dead or alive, I forfeit my head," I said flatly. "The king will execute me publicly as a traitor. My brother will likely lose his position. Everything we've built crumbles."

She fell silent at that, her righteous anger faltering as she processed my words.

"You see? Not all men are cruel," I continued, my voice lowering. "Some of us are just trying to survive in the same world you are. Does that make me a monster? Perhaps. Maybe choosing my own life over my conscience does make me guilty. But make no mistake, our cage may be gilded, but it's a cage nonetheless."

"Many of you are cruel though," she said after a moment, her voice quieter but no less intense. "I've experienced it more times than I can count."

I sighed, giving a slight nod of my head even though she couldn't see it. "Yes. Many men are cruel. There's no denying that. But not all of us choose to be."

"I've never met one who wasn't," she said, and there was something almost vulnerable in her admission.

"Well, I've saved your life twice now," I pointed out. "Doesn't that put me in the camp with the not-cruel men?"

She gave a bitter laugh. "You've saved my life only to deliver me to a far more brutal death. I think that still makes you cruel. Perhaps the cruelest of all."

"We don't know what fate awaits you in Ironheart," I said, trying to convince myself as much as her. "Perhaps the king will let you live after punishment for killing his men. If I let you die out here, I wouldn't be giving you any chance at survival."

She snorted, her contempt palpable. "If you think King Lothaire will let me live, then you're as foolish as you are cruel."

She wasn't wrong. Her chances of surviving King Lothaire's wrath were almost imperceptible, but still, somewhere deep inside me I had to believe otherwise. Had to hold on to the hope that by sparing her life I was giving her a chance. That I could keep my own head, my position, the rewards awaiting me upon my return, and somehow this powerful, incredible woman would survive to return to her rightful place as the Iron Rose.

I realized with unsettling clarity that I was lying to myself. Creating a fiction where I could fulfill my duty without blood on my hands. Where I could remain loyal without sacrificing someone who, against all reason, I had come to admire.

The silence that followed felt different—less hostile, more contemplative. I could almost feel the shift in her, subtle but significant. For the first time, perhaps, we were truly seeing each other beyond our roles as captor and prisoner.

"Where were you heading?" I asked after a while, changing the subject.

She hesitated, then apparently decided there was no point in hiding it. "Moonshadow Woods."

I nearly pulled Tempest to a halt in shock. "Are you mad?"

"Probably," she admitted with a shrug.

"Moonshadow Woods is a death sentence," I said, still processing her response. "The creatures that live there—"

"Can't be worse than what awaits me at Ironheart," she finished. "Besides, who knows if the stories are even true? Maybe they're just tales to keep people away."

"They are tales because so many people have vanished in those woods. The animals are said to kill anyone who sets foot there. They even say magic still exists in there. Giant beasts like ogres and cloakfang ursas are said to live in those woods."

"Yes, true," she conceded. "But that's why I was planning to go there. Because I bet the Kingsguard won't dare to follow me in. And though I highly doubt the woods are filled with magic and murderous creatures like cloakfang ursas, swiftclaw wolves, thornback boars. Ogres." She snorted, a laugh coming out her nose with it. "Unlikely."

I scoffed. "Why is it so unlikely? Those creatures all existed before magic was banished from the Southlands and they were hunted to extinction along with sorcerers and witches. It's not like they didn't exist. Who's to say they aren't still out there hiding in Moonshadow Woods? And even if they aren't, the woods themselves are said to be haunted."

She glanced over her shoulder, rolling her eyes. "Coward," she muttered.

My grip on her tightened. "I'm not a coward. I'm not scared of Moonshadow Woods. I was just pointing it out."

"Well, I was counting on the fact you and your Kingsguard were cowards because I doubted you would follow me in there."

She wasn't wrong, and I admired the brilliance of her plan. Even if I, myself, would brave the woods where they say no one ever returns, I knew the rest of my Kingsguard wouldn't dare set foot past the treeline where the ravens watch, like magical, mythical sentries guarding the woods.

She tilted her head slightly. "You don't really believe the stories, do you?"

"I've seen enough strange things in this world to not dismiss them entirely," I replied.

"Well, if there is any truth to the tales, then you know the rumors also say there is a tribe of free women living in those woods. I was hoping maybe they existed and would help me."

"Doubtful," I said with certainty. "If that tribe truly existed, the kings of the Southlands would certainly have hunted them down."

She arched an eyebrow. "Except they are all too scared to set foot in the woods to find out."

I pursed my lips, considering her words. Of course we'd all heard that sometimes escaped women had found refuge in those woods, but no one had ever survived to come back with proof of their existence.

"Well, it doesn't matter now, does it?" she said, nodding toward her bound wrists. "Since you're taking me back to a fate worse than anything those woods could offer."

The bitterness in her voice struck something in me, a chord of discomfort I couldn't quite ignore.

"Well, I think you're better off facing King Lothaire and hoping for mercy than whatever horrors may have been awaiting you in Moonshadow Woods."

She studied me, her eyes searching mine as if looking for deception. "Why do you care what happens to me?"

Another question I wasn't sure how to answer. Why did I care? She was the enemy. She'd killed my men. By all rights, I should hate her, should want to see her punished. Yet the thought of her execution filled me with a dread I couldn't explain. And something else—something I was even less willing to examine.

"I don't know," I admitted finally. "I just do."

We continued riding, the forest growing denser around us. I found myself increasingly aware of her presence—the warmth of her body against mine, the way she unconsciously shifted with Tempest's movements, the stray strand of dark hair that occasionally brushed my chin in the breeze. It was... distracting, in a way I hadn't anticipated.

"I understand, you know," I said after a long silence.

"Understand what?" she asked, wariness in her tone.

"Why you did what you did." I adjusted my grip on the reins, careful to maintain some distance between us despite our proximity. “I have a brother. Erik. He’s... he’s everything to me. I’d do anything to protect him.”

She was quiet for a moment. “Then you understand why I can’t stop. Why I won’t stop.”

“I do,” I admitted. “But it doesn’t change anything. You killed my men. I have my orders. I have no choice.”

“You do have a choice,” she said, her voice suddenly fierce. She twisted again to face me. “Let me go. Let me save my sister.”

I laughed, though there was no humor in it. “Is that your plan? Storm the castle alone? She’s a king’s wife now, Reyna. If not yet, soon. You’ll never get to her. Her fate is sealed.”

The moment I said it, I regretted my bluntness. Her face hardened, but not before I glimpsed the raw pain beneath her anger.

“Then I’ll die trying,” she said, each word like a blade.

I didn’t respond. What could I say? That I admired her determination? That I respected her loyalty? That some part of me, buried deep beneath years of training and duty, envied her clarity of purpose?

“Ember is a remarkable horse,” I changed the subject, watching the mare follow us with unwavering loyalty. “Most horses would have bolted for freedom by now.”

Reyna’s posture softened slightly at the mention of her mount. “She’s not like most horses.”

“I’ve heard stories about how you two found each other. Something about you sitting in a field for days?”

She glanced back at me, surprise flickering across her features. “You’ve heard that story?”

I nodded. “It’s one of the many tales that circulate about the great Iron Rose. I assumed it was exaggerated.”

“Two days,” she said, and I could hear a hint of pride in her voice. “I sat in that field for two days. She was deemed untamable—had thrown every rider who tried to break her. They were going to put her down."

"So instead of trying to break her spirit..."

"I respected it," she finished. "I knew she would never submit. So, I waited for her to choose me."

I watched Ember following us, her intelligent eyes never leaving her mistress. "And she did."

A small smile cracked Reyna's normally hardened face. "Yes, she did. But she isn't broke. She's my partner, and if ever she decides she doesn't want me on her back, then I'll respect that. But for now, she lets me ride her, and I'm grateful for every moment she gifts me up here."

I shook my head, another layer of the elusive Iron Rose peeling back to expose the person, the woman, behind the armor.

We rode in silence after that, each lost in our own thoughts. As dusk approached, I guided Tempest toward a small clearing.

"We'll camp here for the night," I announced, dismounting before helping her down.

Our eyes met as her feet touched the ground, our faces suddenly close. For a heartbeat, something passed between us—a current of understanding, of recognition. She was beautiful in that moment, fierce and proud despite her circumstances. The realization struck me with unexpected force.

I busied myself with securing the horses, needing the distraction. "You know I'll have to tie you to a tree for the night."

"You know it won't make a difference," she replied. "I'll try to escape again."

I nodded. "I'd expect nothing less."

"And you know you can't stop me forever."

I smiled despite myself. "I can try."

She studied me, her head slightly tilted. "You're a strange man, Sir Asher."

"I've been called worse," I replied. "Usually by you."

That earned a small, reluctant smile. "Don't get used to it. Tomorrow, we'll be enemies again."

I began gathering wood for a fire, considering her words. Enemies. Is that what we were? It seemed too simple a word for the complex web of duty, respect, and something else—something unnamed and increasingly undeniable—that had formed between us.

"Get comfortable," I told her, nodding toward a fallen log. "It's going to be a long night."

As I struck flint to steel, coaxing a spark into flame, I found myself watching her from the corner of my eye. The firelight caught the angles of her face, the determination in her jaw, the unexpected vulnerability in her eyes when she thought I wasn't looking.

I had my orders. My duty. My path laid out before me.

So why did it suddenly feel like I was lost in uncharted territory, pulled toward her by a force I neither understood nor could resist?

CHAPTER TEN
Reyna

Two days. Two days of riding pressed against the man I should hate with every fiber of my being. Two days of his arms encircling me as he held the reins. Two days of conversation that had, against all reason, begun to chip away at the wall I'd built between myself and every man who'd ever lived.

It was... unsettling.

The evening fire crackled between us, sending sparks spiraling into the darkening sky. My wrists were bound, but Asher had given me enough slack to eat the rabbit he'd caught and roasted. It wasn't half bad—the man knew his way around a cooking fire. Another unexpected discovery in a series of them.

I studied him across the flames as he tended to the horses. His movements were efficient, caring. Tempest nuzzled his shoulder while Ember—traitor that she was—allowed him to stroke her neck without pinning her ears or showing any signs of hostility. After two days, my faithful mare had apparently decided he wasn't a threat.

I wasn't so easily convinced.

"My horse doesn't tolerate just anyone being so close to her, much less touching her," I said, breaking the silence.

Asher glanced over, a half-smile tugging at his lips as he finished with the horses. "Is that a compliment, Iron Rose?"

"It's an observation," I replied, though without the bite such a comment would have carried two days ago.

"Neither do you, I imagine." He sat across from me, the firelight casting his face in gold and shadow. "Yet here we are."

"Not like I had much choice in the matter." I lifted my wrists, gently bumping against my restraints.

He conceded the point with a slight nod. "Fair enough."

I took another bite of rabbit, using the moment to organize my thoughts. This man confused me. The Sir Asher I'd known for years—the Head of the Kingsguard who barked orders on the battlefield, who stood stone-faced beside the king while women were punished for minor infractions—seemed a different person entirely from the one sitting across from me now.

"You're... not what I expected," I said finally, the words escaping before I could reconsider them.

His eyebrows raised slightly. "Not what you expected how?"

I shrugged, uncomfortable with having voiced the thought but unwilling to back down. "The way you speak. The way you move. Everything. The Sir Asher I've known for years was cold. Harsh. You sound... different."

He was quiet for a long moment, poking at the fire with a stick. When he finally spoke, his voice was low.

"Every time we've been near each other before now, another man has been present." His eyes met mine across the flames. "I couldn't very well show you kindness when others were watching. People would question my position. I had to rule with an iron fist, and that included how I treated you."

The explanation struck something in me—a memory from the dungeon. That brief moment when I thought I'd seen something like sympathy in his eyes, right before he'd glanced at the guard and his expression had hardened once more.

"In the dungeon," I said slowly, "when you came to see me. There was a moment when you seemed... different then too. But then you looked at the guard and suddenly became the cold Kingsguard again."

He nodded, something like relief crossing his features. "You noticed."

"I notice everything," I replied. "It's how I've stayed alive this long."

"And yet you didn't notice me when I crept up on you." A hint of teasing in his tone, so subtle I might have missed it two days ago.

"I was distracted," I said, refusing to give him the satisfaction.

"By what?"

By thoughts of my sister. By plans for reaching Moonshadow Woods. By exhaustion from days of hard riding. All true, yet not the complete truth.

"That's my business," I said instead.

"Admit it. You were thinking about me." His eyes sparkled with mirth as he flashed a playful smirk.

My face almost gave away the accuracy of his words, but I stilled my shocked response, countering with, "Thinking about what my sword would look like buried between your eyes? You're right. I was thinking about you."

He laughed softly, and as it did every time I'd hear it these past two days, the sound did something strange to my insides. As Kingsguard, I'd never heard him laugh before. Never seen anything but the stone-cold face of duty he wore so well. But here in the firelight, the smile lifting those lips transformed his face, softened the hard lines of authority into something warmer, more approachable.

Dangerous thoughts.

I looked away, focusing on the flames. "So, if we keep riding at this pace, we'll be back in Ironheart by week's end. I guess then it won't matter what I'm thinking about because, you know, I'll be dead."

"You don't know—"

"I do know," I snapped. "And so do you. You can pretend all you want that you're some noble, honorable man amongst a world of monsters, but deep down you know you're taking me straight to my death. And a brutal one at that."

He hesitated, his jaw working as if wrestling with something. "There might be another way."

I glanced up, wary. "What are you talking about?"

"I had a thought this morning. The king promised me a reward for capturing you." He spoke slowly, carefully, as if testing each word. "New quarters, doubled salary... and I've never married yet, much to his displeasure, so he will likely be happy to offer me my choice of brides."

The words hung in the air between us. My mind raced, trying to understand what he was suggesting. My first thoughts, infuriating as they were, were that he hadn't married yet. Strange for a man of his age and position, yet somehow it comforted me to know that he hadn't forced himself on some unwilling woman he claimed as his prize.

But beneath that comfort lurked something else—an inexplicable feeling that tightened my chest. The thought of him with another woman, any woman, sent an unexpected flare of... what? Possessiveness? Jealousy? Impossible. Absurd. Yet there it was, unwelcome and undeniable.

I shoved the feeling aside, focusing instead on the other impossible thing he seemed to be suggesting.

"Are you saying..." I couldn't even finish the sentence, the thought so unexpected.

"I could ask for you," he said, his voice dropping lower. "As my wife. It's not unheard of for warriors to claim enemy combatants as spoils."

A laugh escaped me, brittle and harsh. "You want to claim me as your prize? Make me your property to do with what you please?"

"No," he said quickly, leaning forward. "It would be in name only. I wouldn't... we wouldn't..." He struggled for words. "It would just be a way to keep you alive."

My heart hammered in my chest as I stared at him. Was he serious? For a wild, desperate moment, I actually considered it. Marriage to Asher wouldn't be freedom, but it would mean life. It might even bring me closer to Cassia. I could play the dutiful wife while plotting our escape together. There in the castle where he lived, no doubt she would reside as well.

Cassia. I could find her. Be near her. Save her.

"And the king would agree to this?" I asked, unable to keep the skepticism from my voice.

Asher's expression faltered. "I... I don't know."

"You'd do that? Claim me as your wife? But what...what would that mean?" I pressed, confused by the offer, and also equally confusing feelings I had about being in his bed. I should hate the idea, war against it, but somewhere, deep down somewhere, a little traitorous part of me wondered what it would be like.

"It would be different," he said, meeting my eyes again. "It wouldn't be... real. Just a way to keep you alive."

Even though his offer was intriguing, crazy, yes, but intriguing, I shook my head. "He may have promised you any bride, but he will never agree to me. I killed half a dozen of his Kingsguard," I pointed out. "I humiliated him by escaping."

He didn't answer, and in his silence, I found confirmation.

"You know it wouldn't work," I said quietly. "Lothaire will never spare me. Not after what I've done."

His eyes met mine across the flames, and in them I saw a truth he didn't want to acknowledge. "I have to try something. I can't just..."

"Take me to my death?" I finished for him.

He fell silent, and when I looked up, his expression had darkened. Not with anger, but with something that looked almost like grief.

"You know he won't spare me. So why didn't you kill me when you had the chance?" I asked, the question that had been burning in my mind for days. "On the cliff. You could have let me fall. It would have been clean. Quick."

"I told you, I don't know," he said, but his eyes said otherwise.

"I don't believe you."

He sighed, running a hand through his dark hair. The firelight caught the movement, highlighting the strong lines of his jaw, the curve of his lips. I cursed inwardly at my notice of such details. Two days of proximity had made me far too aware of him as a man, not just an enemy.

He looked up at me, his blue eyes reflecting the dancing flames. "You were defenseless on that cliff. It would have been murder, not combat."

"And what the king has planned for me—is that not murder?"

He flinched. "It's the law."

"Laws made by men to control women," I countered. "To keep us in our place. Fighting. Breeding. Serving. Tell me, Asher, have you ever questioned any of it? Ever wondered why things are the way they are?"

Again, that uncomfortable silence. I pressed on, sensing a crack in his armor.

"You have a brother," I said, remembering our conversation from yesterday. "Would you follow orders if they meant his death?"

"That's different."

"Is it? You say not all men are cruel, that some of you are just trying to survive in the same world we are. If that's true, then why uphold a system that treats women as expendable? That sees my sister as nothing but a womb to bear sons or a body to shield the men hiding behind walls?"

He stared into the fire, conflict etched across his features. For a moment, I thought he wouldn't answer. Then, so quietly I almost missed it, he said, "I don't know anymore."

The admission hung between us, weightier than any argument could have been.

I studied him in the silence that followed, truly seeing him perhaps for the first time. Not Sir Asher, Head of the Kingsguard, but simply Asher—a man caught in the same broken system as the rest of us, playing the role he'd been assigned since birth. The firelight softened his features, highlighting cheekbones that could cut glass and eyes that held more questions than certainties.

He was handsome. I'd always known that, of course. Any woman with eyes could see it. But I'd never allowed myself to acknowledge it, to truly look at him as anything other than an obstacle, an enemy. Now, with no one watching, with nothing but the crackle of the fire and the soft sounds of the horses, I found myself unable to look away.

The realization sent a jolt of panic through me. This was dangerous—far more dangerous than swords or arrows. I was developing feelings for my captor, the very man taking me to my death. The absurdity of it wasn't lost on me. And I knew, if I was going to succeed in my mission, it couldn't continue.

I had to focus on Cassia. Had to find a way to save my sister. That was all that mattered. Not the man across the fire who was becoming more human to me with every passing hour. Not the confusing feelings stirring inside me, feelings I had no name for and didn't want.

"We should rest," Asher said, breaking the charged silence. "We still have a few more long days of riding before we reach Ironheart."

The reminder sent a pang through me. Tomorrow we'd be closer to the king, closer to my execution. Closer to me failing at my goal of saving my sister. I pushed the thought away, refusing to dwell on it.

"Do you really have to tie me to a tree again? It's so uncomfortable. I can't get any real rest." I asked, keeping my tone neutral. I'd tried and failed at escape the past two nights, but hoped maybe tonight, he'd make a mistake and I could slip away.

He hesitated, then shook his head. "No. I'll bind you to that log tonight so you can lay down properly. But I'm a light sleeper. Don't try anything."

"I'll still be bound. It's not like I can do anything." I raised my bound wrists.

His dark eyebrow arched slowly upward. "I've seen what you can do even with your hands tied together."

"Well, so have your Kingsguard. It wouldn't be so unbelievable if you just let me go and I slipped away tonight. You can tell them I bested you. No doubt they've seen what I can do. They'll believe you."

Something flashed in his eyes—a consideration perhaps. But then his gaze dropped back to the flames. "I have my duty, Reyna."

"And I have mine," I replied. "To my sister. To myself. To every woman trapped in this cage you call society."

He didn't argue, just sighed and began preparing his bedroll. I did the same, awkwardly arranging the blanket he'd provided with my bound hands. After he secured me to the log behind me, we settled on opposite sides of the fire, the flames between us like a physical manifestation of the chasm separating our worlds.

"Goodnight, Iron Rose," he said softly.

"Goodnight, Sir Asher," I replied, deliberately using his title, reminding myself of who he was, of what he represented.

I closed my eyes, exhaustion from the day's ride washing over me. The last thing I saw before sleep claimed me was Asher's face in the firelight, troubled and pensive, as if wrestling with demons of his own.

The next thing I knew, a hand clamped tightly over my mouth. My eyes flew open, my body tensing to fight.

"Shh," Asher breathed against my ear, his voice barely audible. "Don't move."

I froze, momentarily confused. His face was inches from mine, his eyes reflecting pinpricks of the dying firelight. He wasn't looking at me, but past me, into the darkness beyond our camp.

Slowly, he removed his hand from my mouth, his finger pressing against his lips in a signal for silence. I nodded my understanding.

I knew in that moment, we weren't alone.

"Cut me free," I whispered, so softly the words were barely more than shaped breath.

He hesitated, conflict etched across his features.

"Asher," I urged. "There's someone out there. Cut me free."

He shook his head, his body positioned protectively over mine as he assessed the threat. Wolves? Innocent deer or...

A twig snapped in the darkness, followed by a muffled curse.

Humans.

And the fact they were sneaking up on us left no doubt they weren't the friendly kind.

Asher's head snapped toward the sound, his hand moving to the hilt of his sword.

"Cut me free so I can fight," I whispered, harsher now.

With a quick glance back at me, he made his split-second decision, using his sword and slicing through my bonds in one swift motion.

"Stay close," he murmured, and I wasn't sure if it was an order or a plea.

We rose silently, back to back, weapons drawn. I snatched up a fallen branch—not ideal, but better than nothing. The night pressed in around us, the forest suddenly alive with subtle movements and whispered commands.

"Bandits," Asher breathed. "At least six from what I could see."

"Seven," I corrected, my eyes better adjusted to the darkness. "One in the trees to your left."

Before he could respond, shadows detached from the darkness.

"Well, well," one of them drawled, stepping into the firelight. "What do we have here? A couple of weary travelers?"

Asher tensed beside me, his hand brushing mine in a silent signal. We barely knew each other, only traveling together for mere days, yet in this moment, it felt like we'd fought side by side for years. Wordlessly, I could sense his every intention, and I knew somehow, that he could sense mine.

"We don't want any trouble," Asher said, his voice steady. "Leave us be and move along."

The bandit leader laughed, a harsh sound that set my teeth on edge. He reached up, twisting the corner of his mustache with his free hand as he glanced at Ember standing at alert just outside of our camp. "Oh, we'll be moving along all right, but not until we take everything. Your money, your weapons, whatever you're carrying that I want, I'll be taking. Including those fine horses of yours. That black one is a pretty little thing. She'll fetch a nice price." His eyes moved to me and roved over my frame. "And you're a pretty little thing yourself. You'll fetch a nice price too."

I could almost hear the possessive rumble moving through Asher from the way he seemed to grow in size beside me, his shoulders swelling with his deep, controlled breath.

My own rage bubbled like a fiery inferno inside me, but it wasn't the leering glance at me that made my temperature rise to scalding, it was the mention of taking Ember.

I shared a quick glance with Asher, and I could see the fire in his eyes, the readiness for battle. We were both exhausted, but I knew without a doubt that we could take these men. Our eyes met in silent communication, and I gave him an almost imperceptible nod that I too was ready to show these men that though they outnumbered us four to one, they were about to find out exactly who they were dealing with.

Sir Asher of Ironhold and the Iron Rose.

The bandits moved closer, their circle around us closing in as grins spread across their dirty faces. They thought they had easy prey.

They couldn't have been more wrong.

In an instant, the peaceful night erupted into chaos. Asher and I exploded into action. My sword lashed out, the blade singing as it cut through the air. Beside me, Asher moved with shocking speed surprising for his muscular frame, his own weapon flashing in the firelight.

We fell into a rhythm, moving together as if we'd fought side by side for years. Back to back, we faced the onslaught of bandits. For every attack they launched, we had a counter. When one of us faltered, the other was there to cover the weakness.

A bandit's blade came dangerously close to my neck, but Asher was there, deflecting the blow and ending the man's life in one fluid motion. Moments later, I returned the favor, my sword finding a gap in his defense and felling an attacker he hadn't even seen.

A bandit lunged at me, his blade whistling through the air. I parried, the clash of steel sending vibrations up my arm. He was strong, but slow. I feinted left, then spun right, my borrowed sword finding the gap in his defenses. He fell with a gurgle, and I was already moving to the next threat. How good it felt to be slicing through the flesh of vile men instead of the women I was always sent to war against. I enjoyed every second of the sensations of my sword in their flesh, their warm blood on my skin. It invigorated me, fueled me more as I charged into the fight.

"Reyna, duck!" Asher's voice cut through the chaos. I dropped without hesitation, feeling the whoosh of air as a club swung where my head had been a moment before. Asher's sword flashed over me, and I heard a scream cut short.

Rolling to my feet, I saw a bandit sneaking up behind Asher, dagger raised. Without thinking, I hurled my sword. It spun through the air, burying itself in the man's chest just as he was about to strike.

Asher turned, his eyes widening as he saw the fallen bandit. Our eyes met, a silent acknowledgment passing between us. Then we were back in the fray.

The fight was brutal but brief. These men, for all their bravado, were no match for the former Head of the Kingsguard and Iron Rose. As their numbers dwindled, only one bandit remained. He started to tuck tail and run, but a smile lifted my lips as I saw the dagger one of them had dropped at my feet. I swiped it off the ground, then with practiced fury, sent it spiraling through the air. It landed in the back of his neck, dropping him to the ground in an instant.

In the sudden quiet, I became aware of my ragged breathing, the sting of sweat in my eyes. Asher stood a few paces away, his chest heaving, a streak of blood across his cheek. In his eyes, I saw the same wild exhilaration that coursed through my veins. Fighting alongside him had been... different. Intoxicating, even.

"Are you hurt?" he asked, stepping into my space, his gaze dropping to the blood dripping down my arm.

"It's nothing," I said, suddenly very aware of our proximity, of the heat radiating from his body in the cool night air.

He reached out, fingers gently probing the wound. "It needs binding."

"I heal quickly. I'll be fine," I said, but he shook his head.

"Let me tend to it."

I nodded, allowing him to guide me back to the fire. As he knelt to retrieve a clean cloth from his pack, his back to me, reality crashed down like a wave of cold water.

This was my chance. My only chance. He was distracted, guard down, trusting me in a way he hadn't before. One clean blow and I could be free, could make for Moonshadow Woods before the Kingsguard caught up to me. One hard night of riding and I could be there by dawn.

I gripped the hilt of the bandit's sword, steeling myself for what I had to do. This wasn't personal. It was survival. For me. For Cassia.

Asher turned back toward me, cloth in hand, concern etched across his features. Our eyes met, and in his, I saw something I'd never expected to find in a man—genuine care. Not possession. Not control. Just... care.

My grip tightened. I couldn't hesitate. Couldn't let these new, confusing feelings cloud my judgment. He was still taking me back to die. Still loyal to a king and a system that saw women as property.

"Reyna?" he asked, brow furrowing at whatever he saw in my expression.

I struck. Not with the blade, as I'd planned, but with the hilt. It connected with his temple with a dull thud, and surprise flashed across his face for an instant before his eyes rolled back and he crumpled to the ground.

I stood over him, breathing hard, the sword still clutched in my hand. I could kill him now. Should kill him. He would only come after me again.

But my hand wouldn't move. Something in me rebelled at the thought of driving the blade into his unconscious form. After fighting beside him, after seeing the man behind the Kingsguard mask, I couldn't do it.

"Damn you," I whispered, not sure if I was cursing him or myself.

I quickly gathered what supplies I could carry, whistling softly for Ember. She came immediately, sensing my urgency. I mounted in one fluid motion, glancing back at Asher's still form one last time.

"I'm sorry," I said, though he couldn't hear me. "But I have to save my sister."

With that, I turned Ember toward the north and urged her into a gallop. Moonshadow Woods loomed ahead, a darker shadow against the night sky. By dawn, I would reach its borders. By dawn, I would be beyond Asher's reach.

And beyond these dangerous feelings that had begun to take root in my heart—feelings that could only lead to disaster.

Or so I hoped.

CHAPTER ELEVEN
Asher

Pain pulsed behind my eyes as I urged Tempest forward, my head still pounding from the blow she'd given me last night. Dawn painted the sky in shades of fire and gold, but I barely noticed the beauty. My focus was singular, absolute: find her.

Why had I been surprised to awaken with my face in the dirt and Reyna gone? Had I truly thought that showing her trust by cutting her bonds, by fighting alongside her, that after that moment of connection—brief but undeniable—that we'd found common ground?

Fool.

What had I expected? That she would accept her fate because we'd shared a battle? That she would forget I was taking her back to a kingdom that had stolen her sister and would demand her own brutal death? The very thought was laughable. And yet, that moment of connection we'd shared haunted me still.

I touched the tender spot at my temple, wincing. Even knowing why she'd done it, something still ached beneath my ribs.

The blow to my head had been precisely delivered—enough to render me unconscious but not enough to do lasting damage. She could have killed me. And yet... she didn't. That mercy puzzled me. She knew my mission, knew what awaited her if I succeeded. A single decisive blow would have eliminated the threat permanently. Was it compassion that stayed her hand? Or perhaps a warrior's code she'd honored? The Iron Rose, feared for her ruthlessness in battle, had spared me when killing me would have been smarter. That contradiction lingered in my mind, unexplained.

Tempest's hooves thundered across the plain as we followed Ember's clear tracks. Reyna hadn't bothered with subtlety, choosing pure speed over stealth, the deep hoof prints evidence of her desperation. I didn't think I'd been knocked out for long, maybe minutes if I was lucky, and I hoped I was close behind her, following her tracks directly north to Moonshadow Woods.

I pushed Tempest faster, an unfamiliar urgency clawing at my chest. I had to catch her before she crossed into those shadowed woods. If she disappeared into that forbidden realm, my life would be forfeit. The King's orders had been clear—bring her back or don't return at all. But as the distance between us closed, I realized I was racing after her not just for my duty, my honor, my life—though all hung in the balance—but because something in me couldn't bear the thought of her disappearing into those trees, never to be seen again.

The edge of Moonshadow Woods appeared on the horizon, a solid wall of ancient, twisted trunks and dense foliage. At its border, a familiar figure on horseback paused, as if gathering courage for the plunge into darkness.

"Reyna!" I called, my voice carrying across the distance between us.

She turned, and even from here, I could see her shoulders tense. For a moment, I thought she would flee immediately into the woods. Instead, she waited, her expression unreadable as I closed the distance between us.

I pulled Tempest to a halt a few paces away, my breath coming hard, my hands tight on the reins. Now that I'd found her, the fury I'd been nursing ignited.

"You betrayed me," I said, the words drawn tight with anger.

Reyna straightened on her horse, chin lifting in defiance. "I could have killed you."

"Only because I trusted you." The admission burned like acid on my tongue.

"And I trusted that if I didn't escape, you'd take me back to be executed," she countered. "We both made choices."

"I was following orders—"

"And I'm trying to stay alive!" she cut me off, something raw breaking through her composure. "I didn't want to hurt you, Asher. But I can't go back to the king. I can't die that way."

She swallowed hard, and in that moment, I saw not the Iron Rose, the fearsome warrior, but simply a woman fighting desperately for her life. For her future.

"I have to live," she continued, her voice softer but no less intense. "I have to save my sister. Can't you understand that?"

The question struck me harder than the blow to the head she'd given me last night. Of course I understood. Had I not told her of my bond with Erik? Had I not admitted I would do anything to protect him? The secret, the one I shared with Erik, pushed into the forefront of my mind.

Yes, I would make sacrifices to protect the ones I love.

I already had.

"Say something," she demanded, but beneath the command, I heard a plea.

I looked at her—truly looked at her—sitting bareback astride her horse at the edge of doom, prepared to face unknown horrors rather than return to a death she knew awaited her. For her sister. For herself. For her conviction that women deserved better than the world had given them.

Her stern face softened for a moment, and I swore I saw a tear shimmer in those hardened eyes. I knew it wasn't for her own life but for that of her sister. The raw anguish in her voice made me want to break open the doors of my gilded cage, cast aside the years of loyalty to the king drilled into me. A cage created by duty, by tradition, by the weight of my family's legacy.

I thought of my father, and his father before him, and every man in my family who'd come before me. They'd all been proud members of the Kingsguard like me and my brother, Erik. From my earliest memories, I'd been groomed for this role. I could still hear my father's voice: "A Kingsguard's duty is to the realm, Asher. To the king. Personal feelings have no place in our calling."

But standing here, facing Reyna's fury and despair, those words rang hollow.

And something in me broke.

The wall I'd built between duty and conscience, between orders and morality—it crumbled with a force that left me breathless. In its place came clarity so sharp it was almost painful.

If I brought her back, she would die. Not quickly, not mercifully, but in pain and humiliation. There was no denying it. No pretending any longer that there may be another fate awaiting her. A happy ending for the fearsome Iron Rose. And I would have to watch her flame extinguished, knowing I had been the one to deliver her straight to her cruel end.

I couldn't do it. Gods help me, I couldn't do it.

"Go," I said, the word barely audible even to my own ears.

She stared at me, disbelief etched across her features. "What?"

"Go," I repeated, louder this time. "Into the woods. Now. Before I change my mind."

She didn't move, suspicion replacing shock. "Why would you let me go?"

"Because you're right," I admitted, the truth freeing me even as it damned me. "The king will kill you. And I... I can't be the one who brings you to that fate."

"But you said if you come back without me, he'll..." The concern in her voice twisted something in my chest. "He'll kill *you*."

"I'd rather lose my head than my conscience," I said, surprised to find I meant it. "I'll take my chances with his mercy. He's far more likely to show it to me instead of you. Now go, before it's too late for both of us."

She hesitated, as if struggling with something. Then, with a decisive movement, she urged Ember closer until we were side by side. Our eyes met, and in hers, I saw gratitude, relief, and something deeper I couldn't name.

"Thank you," she said simply, the words heavy with meaning.

I nodded, unable to speak past the tightness in my throat. For a moment, I thought she might say more, might reach out—but the moment passed, and she turned Ember toward the woods.

At the tree line, she paused, looking back once more. The rising sun illuminated her face, transforming her into something almost ethereal. Then she was gone, swallowed by the shadows beneath the ancient trees.

I sat there, staring at the spot where she'd vanished, a curious emptiness settling in my chest. It was done. I had betrayed my king, my oath, everything I'd ever known. For her. For the Iron Rose.

For Reyna.

And yet as I knew she was riding toward freedom, toward a future I only hoped held happiness for her, I couldn't bring myself to regret it. Not for a second.

A flicker of movement in the distance caught my eye, pulling me from my thoughts. I squinted, then my blood seemed to freeze in my veins.

Riders. At least a dozen, approaching from the south. The glint of sunlight on iron armor identified them immediately: Kingsguard. My men. Led by Sir Edmund.

They'd found me.

"Shit," I muttered, scanning the plains for any sign of how much they might have seen. How long had they been there? Had they witnessed my conversation with Reyna? My decision to let her go?

The grim determination on Sir Edmund's face as they drew closer answered my question. He'd seen enough.

I slid down from the saddle, my hand casually hovering over the hilt of my sword. Options raced through my mind. I could claim Reyna had overpowered me again. Could say she'd fled into the woods before I could stop her. But they were too close now, and no doubt had seen too much. Sir Edmund was no fool.

The riders pulled to a stop a few paces away, arranging themselves in a half-circle before me. Sir Edmund's eyes locked with mine, cold and calculating.

"Sir Asher," he said, his voice carrying a dangerous edge. "We witnessed your... interaction with the fugitive."

So there it was. No possibility of denial.

"You let her go," he said, not a question but an accusation. "You betrayed your king, your oath, your brothers-in-arms."

"I made a choice," I replied, my voice steady despite the turmoil within. "One I can live with."

A murmur ran through the gathered men. Some looked shocked, others angry. A few—the youngest, mostly—seemed uncertain, conflicted.

Sir Edmund's face hardened. "By the authority of King Lothaire, I place you under arrest for treason. Surrender your weapon and return with us to face the king's justice."

Two men dismounted and moved forward to flank me, hands on their sword hilts. I recognized them both—Thomas and Garrett, solid fighters, loyal to the core. Men I'd trained personally. Men who trusted me with their lives.

Garrett grabbed Tempests reins, my mount jerking his head in protest but quickly settling. In that moment, I saw my future with perfect clarity. If I surrendered, I would die—painfully, publicly, a warning to others who might consider defiance. If I fought, perhaps I could kill them all. Return to Ironheart with tales that the Iron Rose had slaughtered them, escaped and I was the only survivor. Though I would be berated for my failure, and perhaps even lose my head as promised, there was a solid chance King Lothaire would recognize my value as Head of the Kingsguard and show mercy. But to take that chance, I would have to kill men I'd lived alongside for years. Men who were simply following orders, as I had done for so long.

Though killing Sir Edmund, cruel and calculating as he was, wouldn't tear up my conscious, ending the lives of the other men was something my honor couldn't bear.

Or I could choose a third path.

My gaze drifted to the dark line of trees where Reyna had disappeared. Moonshadow Woods. A place of legends and nightmares. A place no sane person would enter willingly. A place I knew they wouldn't follow.

The moment I told Reyna to run, I'd chosen this path.

I'd already given up everything—my title, my future, my life.

And now, I would tempt the hand of fate.

"Surrender," Sir Edmund said, his eyes dancing with those delusions I knew filled his head about taking my place. The honor should go to my brother, but I realized in that moment, with a traitor in the family, he would likely also suffer from my choice. That reality pained me more than the loss of my status and comforts. With our family name tarnished, Erik would wear the badge of a traitor's brother and likely lose his place as next in line to my position.

But I knew without a doubt my brother, my most loyal companion, would be here cheering me on for my decision to release her. For following my conscience instead of my orders.

"I will not surrender," I said with renewed determination, drawing my sword in one fluid motion.

Sir Edmund's eyes widened, then narrowed. "Then you die here, traitor."

He nodded to the men beside me. Though there was conflict in his eyes, ever the dutiful soldier, Thomas lunged first, his blade arcing toward my shoulder. I parried, twisting to block his thrust with my arm guard.

I fought them defensively, parrying and blocking but never striking killing blows. These were my men. I would not have their blood on my hands if I could avoid it.

Sir Edmund watched for a moment, then drew his own sword and urged his mount forward. "Coward," he spat. "Too weak to finish what you've started."

His blade slashed toward my head. I ducked, countering with a strike that caught him across the thigh. He hissed in pain, blood darkening his breeches.

"I don't want to kill you, Edmund," I said, voice low and steady. "Any of you."

"Always the honorable one," he sneered. "Even in betrayal. But I have no such qualms."

He attacked again, more recklessly this time, rage making him sloppy. On the ground, he was as good with a blade as me, but on horseback, he'd never been as skilled. I blocked his sword and, with a twist of my wrist, sent it flying from his grasp. Before he could recover, I grabbed his mount's reins, and he reared, sending Sir Edmund flying through the air.

He hit the ground hard, the breath leaving his lungs in a pained gasp. I stood over him with my sword at his throat.

"You don't have to do this. Just let me ride away. No one needs to die here today," I commanded.

For a moment, I thought he considered it. Though he was a strong fighter, he was no match for me. Then his eyes shifted, looking past me, and I knew I'd made a mistake.

I spun, sword raised, to find three more men closing in. Seven against one now, with Edmund regaining his feet behind me. Terrible odds, even for the Head of the Kingsguard.

Or former Head, I supposed after the way I'd just betrayed my vows.

I had only one option left. One path forward.

I glanced out across the lands stretching out as far as I could see, and I knew Ironheart was just over the hills in the distance.

My home. My brother. My entire world.

And then I looked at where I'd last seen Reyna as she'd made her run for freedom, and I knew I'd made the right choice. Even if it meant I'd never set foot in Ironheart again. Or see my brother. Her freedom was worth every sacrifice.

Before the men could react, I was racing toward the tree line, toward Moonshadow Woods.

Toward Reyna.

Though they would call me a coward for running, I was doing it to save their lives. If forced to fight, I could only spare them so long before I would have to cut them down. End the lives of the men who I had trained. Had trusted me.

Shouts and curses followed me, but no hoofbeats. As I'd expected, none dared follow me into those cursed woods. Not even for the glory of capturing a traitor.

At the edge of the trees, I paused, looking back at the men I'd called brothers for so long. At the life I was leaving behind. The only life I'd ever known.

Sir Edmund had remounted, his face contorted with rage and humiliation. "You're a dead man, Asher!" he shouted. "If the woods don't kill you, the king will!"

Tempest struggled against the soldier holding his reins tight, and my chest tightened knowing I would have to leave him behind. My loyal mount. My friend. But these woods were no place for him, and though knowing my choice now meant parting with my loyal mount hurt as much as knowing I may never see my brother again, with one last look thanking him for years of partnership, I turned and sprinted into the gnarled ancient trees standing like sentries guarding the cursed woods. A murder of crows screamed from the branches above me, like a warning I didn't heed.

I had only one place to go now.

To her.

Taking a deep breath, I bolted into Moonshadow Woods alone, the shadows swallowing me as I ventured deeper. The light dimmed almost immediately, the dense canopy blocking the morning sun. Sounds changed too—muffled, distorted, as if the woods themselves bent the very air.

And yet despite knowing I could be racing toward certain death in these cursed woods, and that the life I'd worked so hard for was in shambles behind me, as the wind whipped past and the forest blurred into a green haze, I felt something I hadn't experienced in years: freedom. Whatever came next, whatever challenges I faced, I knew I'd made the right choice.

For the first time in my life, I followed my own code of honor and was forging my own path.

A path that would take me straight to her.

My strides slowed, and I moved carefully, following what I hoped were Reyna's tracks. The forest floor was soft with centuries of fallen leaves, making it difficult to be certain. I'd gone perhaps half a mile when a rustle to my left made me freeze, hand moving to my sword hilt.

"I wouldn't draw that if I were you," a familiar voice advised. "I'm already aiming at your heart."

Reyna emerged from behind a massive oak atop Ember, arrow nocked and bow drawn. When she saw my face clearly, her eyes widened in shock.

"Asher? What are you doing here?" She lowered the bow slightly, but didn't relax her arm entirely.

"The Kingsguard found me," I explained, suddenly aware of how mad this all was. "They saw me let you go."

"And now you're a fugitive," she said, understanding dawning in her expression.

I nodded. "It seems I chose your freedom over my own."

She stared at me for a long moment, as if trying to decide whether to believe me. Then, slowly, she lowered her bow completely and returned the arrow to her quiver.

"Why?" she asked simply.

I found I had no simple answer. "Because it was right," I said finally. "Because I couldn't be the man I was anymore and live with myself."

The admission hung between us, raw and honest in a way I'd never allowed myself to be before. I waited, unsure what came next. Would she send me away? Leave me to fend for myself in these dangerous woods?

Instead, she nudged Ember forward until she rode up beside me. Without a word, she extended her hand, palm up—an offering, an invitation.

"We should keep moving," she said. "These woods aren't safe to linger in."

I looked at her outstretched hand, then back to her face. In her eyes, I saw something I never expected to find—understanding. Acceptance. Perhaps even forgiveness.

I took her hand, and with one fluid motion, swung up behind her, settling into the space she'd made. As my arms encircled her waist to hold on, I felt a strange sense of rightness despite everything I'd lost. My position. My future. My entire world.

One moment we were a knight and the leader of a powerful army, and in the next, a hunter and the hunted, me the predator and her the prey. But now, in one split second decision, our fates became intertwined as we merged into two fugitives on the run. I wondered what the kingdoms in the Southlands would think of this when they heard that not only had the Iron Rose taken flight, but the Head of the Kingsguard had run off with her.

"Where are we going?" I asked as Ember began moving deeper into the woods.

Reyna glanced back at me, the ghost of a smile touching her lips. "To find help. To save my sister. To change everything."

And despite the darkness of the woods around us, despite the uncertainty that lay ahead, I found myself smiling back. For the first time in my life, I was following no orders but my own conscience. And somehow, that felt like freedom.

CHAPTER TWELVE
Reyna

The deeper we traveled into Moonshadow Woods, the more the world around us changed. Light filtered through the ancient canopy in scattered beams, illuminating dust that danced like tiny spirits. Sounds were muffled, as if the forest itself swallowed them—the crunch of leaves beneath Ember's hooves, the creak of branches overhead, even our voices seemed hushed by some unspoken command.

I was acutely aware of Asher behind me, his arms loosely circling my waist as we rode. The Head of the Kingsguard, now a fugitive because of a choice I still couldn't fully comprehend. It still felt surreal that he had chosen my freedom over his duty, my life over his.

His warmth pressed against my back, a stark contrast to the cooling forest air. It should have been comforting, but it only added to my confusion. This man who had hunted me relentlessly was now risking everything to help me. Part of me still wondered if this was some elaborate trap, but what would be the point now? He'd had countless opportunities to kill me.

"You're tense," he observed, breaking the silence that had fallen between us since we'd left the forest's edge.

"We're in Moonshadow Woods," I replied. "Being tense seems appropriate."

He made a sound that might have been a laugh. "Fair point. Though I thought you said they were just stories? What could you possibly be worried about?"

I caught the jest in his tone, turning to give him a brief look over my shoulder instead of answering. His smirk sent that now familiar flutter dancing around in my stomach.

I guided Ember around a massive fallen trunk, its surface carpeted with luminescent fungi that glowed faintly blue in the shadows. "Why did you really let me go?" I asked, the question that had been burning inside me since he'd appeared among the trees. "At the edge of the woods. You could have taken me back."

His silence stretched so long I thought he might not answer.

"I told you," he said finally. "I couldn't be the one to bring you to that fate."

"But why?" I pressed. "You've sent countless women to their deaths before. Following orders. Doing your duty. What made this time different?"

I felt him tense behind me, his breathing changing slightly. "You."

The single word hung between us, laden with meanings I wasn't ready to explore.

"I just gave up everything," he continued after a moment, his voice low. "My title, my home, my prestige, my brother... everything I've worked for. And to be honest, I'm still trying to understand why myself."

I twisted slightly, trying to see his face. "Do you regret it?"

His eyes met mine, steady and clear. "No. I don't regret choosing your life over delivering you to death. But it doesn't mean I can't be in shock that in the span of a breath, I made a choice that ended my entire life as I know it."

I turned back, digesting his words. Part of me wanted to scoff at his dramatics. His life over? He was a man, free to go anywhere, do anything. He could go to another kingdom, create a new identity and live free. Unlike me who would be chained for my existence as a woman no matter where I set food in the Southlands. But another part of me, a part I was trying desperately to ignore, understood. In saving me, he'd given up everything he'd ever known.

"You are running away from a completely shite life," he went on, "But me? I may have been in a cage same as you, but it was a gilded one to be sure. You were right about that. Now I'm a traitor to a kingdom, and I forfeited everything I have ever known. Just like that, it's all gone, and I don't even know what's next. I suppose I could head to another kingdom, find a job as a stable boy or something. I don't dare think I should join a Kingsguard again. Too risky I'll encounter King Lothaire or one of his Kingsguard one day. Perhaps Verdant. I've heard it's beautiful there. Or Seastrand. Maybe get a job on a ship." He let out a breath that twisted into an exasperated chuckle. "Fuck. I can't believe they saw me let you go. I can't believe my life is gone."

I rode silently, unsure of what to say. I felt guilty, of course, but also grateful. But mostly, still shocked that after all this time thinking he was a cold, heartless obedient hound to the king, there was a man beneath all that armor.

A good man.

"What about you?" he asked, his breath warm against my ear. "Where will you run to now? What's your plan?"

I gritted my teeth, determination flaring in my chest. "I'm not running away. I need to get my sister back."

I felt him stiffen behind me. "Wait. You're serious about that? That's crazy," he said, disbelief coloring his tone. "You'll never infiltrate Ironheart and the castle where your sister is. She's under the king's protection. It's not like you can just waltz in and take her back."

"I won't stop until she's free," I said, as much to myself as to him.

"That's suicide," he argued. "I know you want her back, but it's impossible. You need to keep running. Find some way to start over. Save yourself."

I shook my head, my jaw tightening with my resolve as I gritted my teeth. "I'm not stopping until my sister is free, and I'll slaughter every man I see who tries to stand in my way."

I felt him tense behind me.

"Don't worry," I added, a hint of dark humor in my voice. "Not you. I owe you one."

"You can't really plan on going back for her. I know you want to, but the reality is that it would be nearly impossible. You'll more than likely get yourself killed," he said, his voice a mixture of disbelief and concern.

"You must never have loved anything the way I love my sister," I retorted, "or you'd understand."

"I had a sister, and I loved her too," he shot back, and I could hear the pain threaded through his voice. I didn't know whether I should press, so instead, I let a heavy silence fall between us.

After we rode for a while, memories of my own sister playing through my mind, I wondered if she was married yet. Broken yet. "Do you think Cassia is married to King Lothaire?" I finally managed to ask.

Asher's grip on my waist tightened slightly. "No," he said softly. "I heard she was getting sent to the finishing school where women go to be trained as wives. It will be months before the wedding most likely."

Relief washed over me, so potent it made me dizzy. She wasn't with the king yet. He hadn't claimed her, forced her into his bed. He wouldn't. Not without a wedding. Though the men were vile, they still had their strange moral code, and to bed a woman they intended as a wife without wedding her was a shame on their honor. There was still time.

Our conversation lapsed into silence as Ember picked her way through increasingly dense undergrowth. The forest grew darker around us, the trees more twisted and ancient. I could feel Asher's warmth against my back, his arms steady around my waist, and despite everything, I found myself drawing comfort from his presence.

"Tempest. Where is he? I'm surprised you would leave him. I could see the bond between you two."

Asher went rigid behind me. "I had no choice. I had to leave him behind."

"I'm sorry," I said, my words true as I thought of how painful it would be to part with Ember. "I know what Tempest meant to you."

"He's a good horse," Asher said after a moment. "The best I've ever had. We've been through a lot together." He paused, and I could feel the grief in his words. "Another piece of my life gone."

I didn't know what to say to that. Instead, I reached down and stroked Ember's neck, grateful for her steadfast presence.

"What happened to your sister?" I asked, finally needing to know the answer to the question I wasn't sure he wanted to answer.

I felt him go still behind me, his arms tensing slightly around my waist. "Adira," he said after a long pause, the name soft on his breath. "She was my baby sister."

"Was?" I prompted gently.

He inhaled deeply. "She's gone now. At least, that's what everyone believes."

"Asher," I said softly, "what aren't you telling me?"

He was quiet for a long moment, his grip on me tightening slightly. When he finally spoke, his voice was barely above a whisper. "Can you keep a secret? I mean really keep it? Because what I'm about to tell you... it would mean death for me and my brother if anyone found out."

Intrigued, I nodded. "On the life of my own sister, I swear it."

Asher took a deep breath. "My father had ten wives, so I had a lot of half-siblings. We were raised in the same household, but it was so large, and each wife had their own section, that I was never really close to my twenty or so half-siblings. But my mother had three children. Myself, the oldest, Erik, the middle who is two years younger than me, and then..." He paused and I could hear the smile in his voice as he said, "I also had a younger sister, Adira. Our little baby sister. She was the light of our lives, and Erik and I loved her madly."

He stopped and after a lengthy sigh, he went on. "We had a good childhood, the three of us. She played swords with Erik and I, made us play dolls when we were done, and for the most part, our lives were happy. She wasn't a pretty child, which we were happy about knowing what becomes of the pretty ones in Ironhold. So, thinking she would be heading for the Iron Swordmaidens, Erik and I spent hours training her to be a warrior. She was quite good actually, and though we hated the thought of her being in danger, we knew she'd be well prepared for battle. Erik and I aged into the Kingsguard, and then when she was thirteen, suddenly she wasn't all elbows and knees anymore. The gawky, awkward little girl blossomed into a beauty, and much to our horror, she was chosen to be a breeder, a wife to a man we knew was vile and cruel to his other wives."

My stomach clenched, all too familiar with the fate that awaited such girls. His words hung in the air as he stopped talking, and I could feel his pain. It was as palpable as if he'd just been dealt the news of her fate moments ago.

"Adira also knew of his cruelty and what awaited her. She begged our father not to let him take her, to find her a different man, but even though he was her father, he still saw her as nothing more than a woman to be bred. My mother did everything to sway him, but he was cruel and vicious, and she paid dearly for stepping out of line."

Memories of my own mother stepping out of line crashed back into my mind. But my mother had lost her life for it.

"Adira, being strong and brave, wouldn't have survived what awaited her, so she told us that she was going to jump off the cliffs in order to spare herself a lifetime as a breeder married to a cruel and vile man."

Asher's voice cracked, and I found myself reaching out, placing my hand on his arm. The simple touch startled me, but I left my hand there despite myself.

"And Reyna, I agreed with her. Death was a far better choice than a lifetime of what awaited her."

"Asher, that's awful," I said, my heart clenching in my chest for not just his pain, but that of his brother, his sister and his mother. It only enraged me against men even further.

A branch snapped to our right, and we both tensed, hands moving to weapons. After a moment of silence, a small deer stepped into view, regarded us with wary eyes, then bounded away.

Asher went on. "But Erik and I loved her. We couldn't let her take her own life, and we couldn't let her marry him. So, we hatched a plan, the three of us, together. We told everyone she had thrown herself from the cliffs to avoid the marriage, that we'd run after her but couldn't stop her in time. That we'd seen her body land in the ocean and never come up again. And who wouldn't believe us? We were Kingsguard, loyal to king and kingdom. But in reality, she was never on that cliff. Instead, we got her passage on a ship sailing to a faraway land, one rumored not to enslave their women."

I froze in his arms, shock and admiration coursing through me. "Asher, that's... if you'd been caught..."

"We would have been executed for treason," he finished grimly. "That's why Erik and I vowed never to speak of it again. Not even to each other. But the truth is, I have no idea what happened to her. For all I know, that faraway land is just a myth, and she's enslaved somewhere else. But it was a chance we had to take. I couldn't let them destroy my sweet, strong baby sister."

I found myself seeing Asher in a new light. This man, who I'd been so quick to lump in with all the others, had risked everything to save his sister.

"Why tell me the truth?"

His eyes met mine, steady and clear. "Because I need you to understand that I've made sacrifices before too. Loved enough to risk my life for my sister, like you. But in your case, it's too dangerous, Reyna. Cassia's fate is sealed, and I'm sorry for that. Truly. But you don't need to die on a fool's errand to save her. You're free. Take this freedom and save yourself. If your sister loves you half as much as you love her, you know she would say the same."

"And would you truly have given up on your sister if odds weren't in your favor?"

He didn't answer, and though I didn't know him well, I knew enough about his tenacity, his strength, and his honor that he would have died trying to save her, like I was willing to lay down my life trying to save my own sister.

I studied him, this man who had been my enemy just days ago. Who had hunted me across the kingdom, yet refused to deliver me to death. Who had apparently risked everything once before to save a woman from a fate she didn't choose.

"You let me go because you saw me as Adira," I suggested.

He shook his head. "No. I let you go because I saw you as Reyna."

Something in the way he said my name made my heart beat faster. I turned away, urging Ember forward again, using the movement to mask my confusion.

As we traveled deeper into the forest, the air grew heavier, charged with something I couldn't name. The trees here were enormous, their trunks wider than ten men standing shoulder to shoulder, their bark black as midnight and twisted into shapes that sometimes resembled faces that seemed to watch us pass. The path ahead—little more than a game trail—split around a massive boulder covered in strange symbols I didn't recognize. I hesitated, then guided Ember to the right, following what seemed to be the more traveled route.

"Where exactly are we heading?" Asher asked.

I looked around at the woods surrounding us and answered honestly. "I don't know. I guess just far away from the Kingsguard for now. Find a place to lay low for the night and figure out our next steps."

"Solid plan," he answered. "As long as we don't get slaughtered by the creatures said to live in these woods."

"Do you think the stories are true?" I asked, my own confidence in dismissing them earlier wavering now that we were deep within the woods. "About the ogres and cloakfang ursas and swiftclaw wolves?"

"I didn't," Asher admitted. "But now... these woods feel... wrong somehow. Like we're being watched."

I nodded, understanding exactly what he meant. There was a presence here, an awareness that went beyond normal forest life.

As we rounded a bend in the path, Ember suddenly stopped, ears flicking forward, nostrils flaring. I tensed, scanning our surroundings. Asher's hand moved to his sword hilt.

"What is it?" he whispered.

I shook my head, listening intently. The forest had gone silent—no birds, no rustling leaves, nothing. Just a heavy, waiting stillness.

Then I heard it. A low rumble that seemed to come from everywhere and nowhere at once. Like distant thunder, but continuous, building.

"We need to move," I said, urgency flooding my veins. I nudged Ember forward, but she balked, hooves planted firmly in the dirt.

"Reyna." Asher's voice had gone taut. He pointed to our left, where the undergrowth trembled, parting to reveal—

"Are those..." I breathed, hardly daring to believe what I was seeing.

"Ogres," Asher finished, his voice a mix of awe and fear. "They exist. That means..."

This time I finished. "The rumors about Moonshadow Woods are true."

I sucked in a breath. Standing at twice the height of a man, their skin the gray-green of ancient stone, were two creatures long thought extinct that I'd heard of only in tales told to frighten children. Massive tusks protruded from their lower jaws, yellowed and sharp. Their eyes, small and dark in their enormous heads, fixed on us with unmistakable hostility.

The creatures let out ear-splitting roars and charged, their huge, muscular legs swallowing up the ground beneath them and shaking it beneath my very feet. Ember screamed, rearing up as I gripped her mane. But as Asher grabbed me to stay on, the heavier weight of his body started to take me with him, and he let go in order to prevent pulling me off my horse.

"Fuck!" he shouted as he slipped off my mare, landing on the ground with a thud. He was quick to his feet, and I spun her around quickly, reaching for his hand.

"Grab on! We have to run!"

But Ember was too scared, her feet dancing beneath her, and her body moving too much for him to make contact with my outstretched arm.

The ogres closed the distance, my heart pounding in my chest as I realized I couldn't escape without leaving him.

"Go! Get out of here!" he shouted, drawing his sword and placing his body between myself and the impending attack.

"Asher!" I shouted back, but he just lowered his eyes to the approaching enemy as if planning to hold them at bay while I got away. I knew he wouldn't survive a fight with two ogres, no one could, and in that moment, I knew I couldn't leave him to his death. Not after what he'd done to save me.

"Shit!" I spat, then jumped off my horse, landing on the ground beside him as I pulled my two swords from my back.

"What are you doing?" He spit out. "Get back on your horse and run!"

"I won't risk Ember," I said, slapping the mare's flank. Ember neighed and galloped off, leaving us to face the oncoming threat. "And I'm not leaving you behind."

"Damn you, woman," he growled. Our eyes met, and in them I could see his irritation I'd stayed but also admiration by my unwavering bravery even staring down certain death.

As I stood there, shoulder-to-shoulder with Asher, facing down creatures I'd thought were mere legend, I was struck by the absurdity of our situation. Here we were, two fugitives, about to fight for our lives against mythical beasts. And yet, when I looked at him, I knew there was no one else I'd rather have by my side.

In this moment, we were united, our bodies tensed and ready for battle.

"For what it's worth," Asher said quietly, "I'm glad I chose to follow you."

"Even facing certain death getting squashed by an ogre?" I asked, finding humor despite everything.

"Even then." He smiled, and damned if my stomach didn't flip having it aimed right at me.

"Ready?" I asked, my voice steady despite the odds against us.

He nodded, tightening his grip on his sword. "Ready."

As the ogres closed in, I steadied myself for the fight of my life, but as I glanced toward the powerful man beside me, I knew if any humans had ever stood a chance against these great beasts, it was us.

CHAPTER THIRTEEN
Reyna

I wasn't sure if it was my heart hammering against my ribcage or the rumbling of the ground beneath me that made my entire body feel like it vibrated as the ogres charged. I stood poised beside Asher, watching their massive feet slam into the dirt, each step bringing them closer to what could very well be our doom.

I'd heard the stories about them, of course. Everyone had. But I'd always dismissed them as just that – stories. Myths to scare children and keep people in line. Ogres were the stuff of legend, and though we'd been told they once existed when magic ran freely through our kingdoms, I still thought they were make-believe. It seemed impossible to see them with my own two eyes—creatures so fierce and powerful they could take on dozens of fighters and still walk away.

Now, faced with the terrifying reality of not one but two of these monstrous creatures not only being real but charging straight at me, a chill skittered down my spine that cooled the blood right in my veins. No matter how skilled Asher and I were with a blade, we stood little chance against such behemoths.

I glanced at Asher, his face set in fierce determination. In that moment, I was struck by how much I wanted him to survive this. It seemed days ago I wanted to snuff out his life, and now suddenly, I would need to fight harder than I ever had to save it. The thought of losing him now, after all he'd sacrificed for me, made my chest ache.

But I couldn't afford to dwell on that now. If I died here, Cassia would be left to her fate. My sister, my reason for fighting, would be lost. And now, as my eyes met Asher's one last time before the ogres reached us, I knew I had to fight for him too.

"Get ready," Asher growled.

My muscles twitched at the ready, prepared for what would be the hardest fight of my life. But I would fight for more than just my survival.

I would fight to get back to Cassia.

I would fight to save him.

The first ogre swung its massive club, aiming straight for Asher's head. He ducked, the whoosh of air above him a testament to how close it had come. I darted in, my swords flashing in the dappled forest light, but to my horror, the blades simply bounced off the creature's tough hide.

"Asher, watch out!" I shouted just in time. He rolled to the side as the second ogre's fist smashed into the ground where he'd been standing, leaving a small crater in the earth.

We fought with everything we had, ducking and weaving, striking whenever we could. But it was like fighting a mountain—our blows seemed to have no effect, while one hit from them could easily end us.

As we battled, a realization began to dawn on me. The ogres, for all their ferocity, never seemed to target me directly. Their attacks, devastating as they were, always seemed aimed at Asher.

"Asher!" I called out, parrying another blow. "They're focusing on you!"

He sidestepped another attack, glancing at me as he shouted back. "Yes, I'm becoming increasingly aware of that! Any ideas?"

Before I could respond, a particularly vicious swing from one of the ogres sent us both scrambling for cover and finding it behind a large boulder. We crouched there, breathing heavily, our backs pressed against the cool stone.

"This isn't working," I panted, frustration coloring my voice. "We could try to run."

Asher looked around us, then shook his head. "If we run that way, it's open fields with no cover to hide behind when they catch us. They are slow to start, but they seem to gain speed as they get going, and I have no doubt they'll overtake us. And over there is deeper woods. If the ogres are real, we have to assume more creatures await that way, and then we may be dealing with more than just two ogres. We're trapped."

I heaved a deep breath, agreeing with his assessment. "You're right. But we aren't winning this fight the way we're going. Our weapons aren't doing anything against their skin."

Asher nodded, his brow furrowed in thought. "I've heard stories," he said between breaths. "In the books my mother used to read me, it always said the only way to kill an ogre is through the eye. It's their only vulnerable spot."

I peered around the boulder, watching as the ogres lumbered toward our hiding spot, searching. "That's not going to be easy," I muttered.

"No," Asher agreed. "But it might be our only chance." He paused, his eyes meeting mine. "Reyna, I think I have a plan. It's risky, but—"

"At this point, I'm open to anything," I cut him off.

He nodded. "Alright. Here's what we do. You run over there to those tall rocks. I'll draw their attention and lead them over to you—shouldn't be hard, since they seem focused on me anyway. Hide on the rock, and you should be at about eye level. As they charge past you after me, you can leap out and get one in the eye with your sword."

I stared at him, my heart clenching at the thought of using him as bait. "Asher, that's too dangerous. If something goes wrong—"

"We don't have much choice," he said softly, his hand finding mine and squeezing gently. The touch sent a jolt through me, even amid our dire situation. "I trust you, Reyna. I know you can do this."

I swallowed hard, then nodded. "Alright. Let's do it."

Asher gave me one last look, a mix of determination and confidence, then darted out from behind the boulder. "Hey, you overgrown louts!" he shouted. "Come and get me!"

The ogres roared in response, charging after him. I waited until they'd passed, then scrambled across the open space to the rocks and scurried up them, crouching low to avoid detection.

I watched as Asher led the ogres on a deadly dance, always staying just out of reach. My heart was in my throat with every near miss, every close call. But he was buying me time, and I couldn't waste it.

His eyes met mine, a silent question asking if I was ready. I gave a sharp nod of my head, gripping my two swords tight as I readied myself for what felt like an impossible task. I had to time it just right, and I had to land a perfect blow directly in its eye.

And then I had to hope like hell his fairytale stories were right, because if it didn't go down, we'd never survive the aftermath.

"Holy shite! It's fucking fast!" Asher shouted as he sprinted straight at me.

The ogres charged after him, gaining speed with each step, their jagged teeth showing with their snarls as the one in front swung and missed. I crouched low, my muscles tightly coiled and ready to spring into action, and as Asher blew past me, I prepared for my attack.

Three, two, one... I counted its strides to time my leap, and then at the perfect second, I launched.

With a guttural roar, I shot through the air, my sword extended as I aimed for its eye. But before my sword pierced the tender flesh, it saw me, and with one massive swipe, knocked me out of the air.

I grunted, the wind expelling from my lungs with the force of the blow. But instead of landing on the ground, I reached out, catching a hold of its shoulder. My arms burned with the effort as I caught myself and swung onto its back. Though I couldn't get my breath to exhale, I still managed to fight, scrambling around its massive shoulders as I tried to reach its eyes. It swiped at me again, and as it did, it caught its foot on a rock, and with slow, ground shaking strides, it stumbled, falling first to its knees and then landing on its stomach with an earth-shaking *boom*.

Without hesitation, I leapt from my perch on its back and landed on the ground beside it, my sword aimed straight for its eye.

Time seemed to slow. I could see the surprise on the ogre's face as it noticed me, and for that brief moment, I thought I might actually pull it off.

Then, out of nowhere, a massive shape materialized beside me. One moment there was nothing but air, the next, I was face to face with an enormous bear. But this was no ordinary bear—its fur seemed to shimmer and shift, as if it wasn't quite solid.

What in the Depths of Oblivion?

Before I could process what I was seeing, I swung at it with my sword, but it blocked the blow with its giant paw, slicing my arm in the process. Pain exploded across my arm as its claws tore my flesh. I hit the ground hard, my breath knocked from my lungs.

As I lay there, struggling to move, to breathe, to do anything, realization dawned. This wasn't just any bear. This was a Cloakfang Ursid—another creature I'd dismissed as myth. And if the legends were true, those claws were poisoned, and I was going to be paralyzed in...

And just like that, my body ceased to respond as I lay there unable to do anything other than blink and breathe.

Cloakfang Ursids were another creature of myth they'd said existed in the days of magic, but I didn't believe such a creature could ever be reality. Huge, powerful bears with fur that captured the light around it, causing it to mirror their surroundings at will, changing to camouflage them until they could walk straight up to you undetected. If that wasn't enough, their claws were tipped with paralytic poison that rendered you unable to move and eventually left you unconscious. Which they say was a blessing because you'd be unaware while it killed you and ate you.

Which appeared to be my fate I realized since I couldn't fight back, and I was now at the mercy of the Cloakfang Ursid and the ogre now rising to its feet.

"Reyna!" Asher's voice seemed to come from far away.

"No, Asher! Leave me! Run!" I managed out, though I struggled to shout with the power I wanted. Instead, it was a weak attempt at saving him from certain death if he tried to reach me.

I watched, helpless, as Asher ran toward me, only to be caught by the bear's paw when it materialized in front of him. He crumpled beside me like his body had stopped working in only a second, his face a mask of pain and confusion. My heart pounded in my chest, profound loss coursing through me as I realized this was my end, and in my end came Cassia's doomed fate, and in my end also came Asher's.

My heart felt as if it was tearing apart inside me with not the sadness over my own impending death, but that I'd failed Cassia and I'd failed Asher. It was their fates that made hot tears burn behind my eyes as we lay there, side by side, the ogres and the bear looming over us. I could feel the poison working its way through my system, my consciousness starting to fade in and out. From the look on Asher's face, he was experiencing the same.

"Well," Asher managed to croak out, his voice strained. "This isn't quite how I imagined our adventure ending."

Despite everything, I felt a bubble of laughter rise in my throat. It came out as more of a wheeze, then I weakly answered, "No? Giant ogres and magical bears weren't part of your plan?"

He tried to smile, but it looked more like a grimace. "Strangely enough, no. I was thinking more along the lines of a quiet retirement somewhere in one of the kingdoms."

I tried to smile but my lips were slowly freezing up. As my eyelids grew heavy, I managed out, "I wouldn't have minded that. Of course, only after I overthrew a kingdom or two."

He gave a strained chuckle, then it faded out into a sigh. "Reyna," he said, his voice growing fainter. "I need to tell you—"

The ogres snarled above us, and I swallowed hard knowing any second they would end our existence. But as the one on the left raised its fist in preparation to finish Asher with a bone-crunching slam, a clear, calm, female voice commanded, "Stand down."

The ogres and the bear immediately backed away. I struggled to turn my head, to see who had spoken. Through my increasingly blurry vision, I made out a figure approaching from the shadows of the forest.

She was tall, with skin the color of rich earth and hair woven into intricate braids. She moved with a grace and authority that spoke of great power. Behind her, I could see more women emerging from the trees, all armed and watching us warily.

"The tribe," I whispered, realization dawning. "They're real."

Asher made a sound that might have been agreement. With the last of my strength, I turned to look at him. His eyes were on me, filled with a mixture of emotions that seemed to mirror my own.

The woman knelt beside us, her dark eyes studying us intently.

"Spare him," I managed to say, my voice barely audible. "Please."

At the same time, I heard Asher's weak voice: "Don't hurt her."

She said something in a language I didn't understand, and then the world began to fade to black.

The last thing I saw before unconsciousness took me was Asher's face, his eyes locked on mine. And then, nothing.

CHAPTER FOURTEEN
Asher

I awoke to the sensation of rough rope against my wrists. It dug into my skin as I struggled against it instinctually while my eyes fluttered open, adjusting to the dim candlelight of what appeared to be a large, circular hut constructed of sticks and leaves. The air was heavy with the scent of herbs and earth. As my vision cleared, I saw Reyna rising to sitting on a cot constructed of sturdy branches and woven sticks, similar to the one I was on. But unlike me, she was free of any restraints.

"Are you hurt?" I asked, my gaze raking her over for injury.

She shook her head. "No. Are you?"

"I think I've still got all my bits and pieces." I gave myself a mental check and didn't note any intense pain or injury points.

"Where are we?" she asked, surveying our surroundings.

"I don't know. The last thing I remember was being paralyzed beside you and thinking we were going to be eaten by a magical bear. But here I am, and unless this is some strange version of the Realms of Eternal Honor, I think we're still alive."

Before she could respond, the hut's entrance flap opened and a small procession of female figures stepped into the dim light, their presence commanding immediate attention.

At the forefront was the woman I'd seen just before losing consciousness. Tall and imposing, she carried an air of quiet authority. Long, dark braids cascaded down her back, adorned with beads and feathers that caught the light with every movement. Each step she took seemed deliberate, only amplifying her obvious strength and poise. It took a moment before I noticed the black raven perched on her shoulder, its head tilting as it seemed to appraise me.

Beside her a second woman, this one shorter in stature but no less fierce looking, stared at me with a set of sharp, intense dark eyes. Her hair was short and shaved at the sides, peaking in the center into a short mohawk. Her light tanned skin seemed to glow in the firelight. Her posture was confident, her demeanor unyielding, as she looked formidable and prepared for any challenge that might arise. Like the others, she wore clothing fashioned from leather and woven fibers in the natural colors of the forests.

The others in the group were no less striking, their presence filling the small hut with a blend of natural strength and the mysterious energy of their world. The way they carried themselves spoke of a life lived in harmony with the forest, yet with an intense edge that suggested they could be formidable adversaries if crossed.

"Welcome, Rebel Rose," the leader said, her voice rich and soothing.

Reyna's brow furrowed in confusion. "Rebel Rose? How do you know me? And why are you calling me that? Where are we?"

As Reyna fired off her questions, the woman's lips curved into a small smile. "I am Thalassa, leader of the Moonshadow Tribe and you are here safe in our sanctuary." She made a slight gesture to the iron rose emblazoned on her armor. "Word of the Iron Rose's rebellion and escape has traveled far and wide, even reaching us in our secluded hideaway. The women of Southlands have given you a new name—Rebel Rose—for your defiance against the oppressive system."

I watched Reyna process this information, seeing a mix of surprise and pride flash across her face.

Thalassa continued, "We hoped you might seek refuge here. You are welcome to stay, Rebel Rose. We can keep you safe. We have food, water, and everything you could need. You are free from the restraints of your former life here with us."

Her dark eyes shifted to me, narrowing ever so slightly in a silent accusation, and I felt a chill run down my spine. "The animals in these woods won't harm women. It's a safe haven for any who find their way in, but they will kill any man on sight."

I swallowed hard, suddenly very aware of my vulnerable position as she eyed me with a mixture of curiosity and caution.

Thalassa turned back to Reyna, her expression curious. "Why were you fighting to save this man? It's unprecedented. Usually, women who enter our woods with men are relieved to see them fall having suffered their cruelty for far too long. But you didn't want this one to die. You fought for him. Why?"

Reyna's eyes met mine, and as she stared at me for a long moment before answering, I felt a surge of emotion at the softness I saw there. "He sacrificed everything to save my life," she said quietly. "He's... different."

Thalassa studied me again, her long black braids moving against her rich, dark skin as she tipped her head slowly back and forth. "Do you trust him?" Thalassa asked, her tone serious.

There was a moment of silence that felt like an eternity. I knew how much Reyna had mistrusted me before, and I didn't think there would ever be a day when she would utter the opposite. But my breath caught in my chest as she held my gaze steady with hers, and I saw a certainty in her eyes when she whispered, "Yes. I do."

The simple words sent a wave of elation through me. After everything we'd been through, all the suspicion and wariness, Reyna trusted me completely. It was more meaningful than I could have imagined.

"Interesting," Thalassa said, still studying me like a strange curiosity along with her raven, then her attention moved back to Reyna. "Well, having a foreign man in our sanctuary is uncharted territory to be certain, but you, Rebel Rose, are welcome to stay here in the safety of our woods indefinitely. It would be an honor to have such a powerful warrior amongst our tribe of free women."

Reyna turned back to Thalassa. "Thank you for your offer, but I can't stay. I need to rescue my sister. She needs me. The King has her and I have to get back to Ironheart and save her, though I appreciate your aid." Reyna started to struggle to her feet, but wobbled and sat back down, her eyes blinking rapidly as if to stop her head from spinning.

Thalassa held up a hand. "This isn't the time for such discussions, and you aren't going anywhere right now. The poison from a Cloakfang Ursid will stay in your system for at least a full day as it works its way out. You need rest. We'll speak more later. For now, Gaia will take you to a hut of your own where you two can finish resting, and when you awaken, you'll feel much better, and we can talk."

She gestured to the shorter but muscular woman with the mohawk at her side, the one still staring at me like she wanted to snap my neck with her bare hands. I offered her a sheepish smile, but she remained frozen in her intense stare.

I knew Reyna wanted to argue and forgo any rest to try to free her sister, but her eyes, dark with circles beneath them, blinked heavy with the same sleepiness that weighed down on me.

With a nod from Thalassa, one of the women came forward and cut my bonds. I rubbed my wrists, relief flooding through me.

Gaia finally broke her stare and spun toward Thalassa. "I don't think we should allow him in our camp unrestrained. This is a mistake. Look at how he's dressed. He's Kingsguard from the kingdom of Ironhold. He's no ally. He's an enemy."

Thalassa softly shook her head. "He can't harm us here, and the Rebel Rose says he's trustworthy. We saw him fight to save her as she did for him, and I see no reason that we can't allow him comfort while we figure out what to do with him."

Gaia grumbled, her eyes narrowing again as they met mine.

"You're no longer deemed a threat," Thalassa explained as she turned her attention back to me, "but you cannot leave yet. We must decide what to do with you. No man has ever been allowed to leave alive with knowledge of our tribe." Her eyes met mine with a warning as she finished with, "And the animals in these woods won't let you leave if you attempt it. Am I understood?"

I nodded, understanding the gravity of the command.

"They will kill you on sight if you step outside of this encampment. They patrol the forests between here and the rest of the Southlands, and they will strike you down without mercy. Only a few men who have wandered in on the outskirts have ever escaped them. But their tales of dangers here help keep others at bay. But none have ever found the tribe itself. You are the first man not a child brought here with a fleeing mother to ever set foot in this camp. Don't make me regret allowing you in here."

I accepted her warning with a nod and a soft, "Thank you."

"You look weary from your journey," she said. "Now is the time for rest. You do not need to worry about your pursuers. If the Kingsguard dares to step foot in my forest, my creatures will make quick work of them."

"Ember!" Reyna sat straight up. "I had a horse. A black mare. When the ogres attacked, I sent her fleeing. Have you seen her?"

Thalassa smiled softly. "Yes, don't worry. She's safe. I called her in and told her you were safe and healing. She's at the stables getting a much-deserved rest and filling meal. It sounds like you had quite a long journey from what she told me."

"You... spoke with her? But I...?" Reyna paused, her eyes widening as they looked to the raven and then back at Thalassa. "Wait. Are you an... Animara?"

Thalassa nodded, a small smile playing at her lips.

My jaw slackened at the admission. Animara were thought to be extinct, their magical ability to commune with animals wiped out generations ago during the purge. "But... how?" I stammered. "I didn't think any Animara survived the magic purge."

Sadness played on her features. "I am the last of my kind," Thalassa said gently. "But how I came to be here is a story for later. For now, you must rest, and I will make sure the animals guard the boundaries extra hard tonight so you can sleep deeply and know that you are safe."

As if to demonstrate her power, Thalassa's eyes began to glow a brilliant gold. She whispered something in a language I didn't understand, and mere moments later, a beautiful wolf appeared, having run in so fast it almost seemed to appear out of thin air. Its eyes matched Thalassa's golden glow, and I realized with a start that I was looking at a Swiftclaw Wolf—another creature I'd thought long extinct.

"Impossible," I breathed, looking at the wolf's tall, lean, powerful form. Legends said Swiftclaws could move so fast they became nearly invisible.

"Only a handful of magical creatures survived the great purge," Thalassa explained, seeing our amazement. "Those that did found sanctuary here."

"But—"

A thousand questions raced through my mind, but Thalassa shook her head, forestalling them. "Later," she said again. "Now, you must rest."

She turned to the wolf, her eyes glowing that golden yellow once more. "Go, gather the others. Double the patrols at the forest's edge. No man sets foot in the woods tonight. Be on high alert."

The wolf disappeared in a blur of motion, leaving Reyna and me staring in awe.

"Go," Thalassa said, gesturing toward the door. "Rest. I'll show you everything later."

With a grumble, Gaia gestured for us to follow, and we didn't argue, moving through the village taking it all in as we went. The women all watched us, smiles lighting up their faces as they bid Reyna well wishes while we passed them by. But when their eyes would meet mine, that friendliness faded away into glares, and I'd never felt more unwelcome anywhere in my life.

As we made our way to the hut, my mind whirled with everything we'd seen and learned. Magical creatures, thought long extinct, were alive and thriving here. An Animara, the last of her kind, leading a hidden tribe of women. It was almost too much to process.

We reached our hut and Gaia pointed to a pitcher of water and two plates of food. Some cheese and fruits as well as fresh bread. My stomach grumbled at the sight of them.

"Your bodies are weak and need rest," Gaia said as she stepped back out the door. "Eat some food and sleep then tomorrow when you awaken, we'll show you all the wonders of our little village."

"Thank you for your kindness," Reyna said.

Gaia smiled.

"We appreciate it," I replied.

But instead of smiling back like she did with Reyna, her eyes narrowed, and she looked at me. "I will be watching you. If you try anything, you won't survive to your next breath."

Without a response from me, she spun on her bare foot and left the hut.

I cringed. "Yikes. Looks like they feel about men the same way you do."

"Can you blame them?" Reyna asked, finding a seat on one of the thatched cots placed side by side.

I walked over and sat on the other, then grabbed the plate of food on the small, rustic wooden table between us.

"Here. Eat." I offered her the plate, and she grabbed a hunk of bread and some cheese.

We ate in silence, both moaning over each bite of nourishing food, and when the last scrap was gone we sat back on our cots.

"Every muscle in my body aches," I said, rubbing my shoulder. "I'm not sure if it was from the journey, all the fighting, or if this is a side effect from the poison of that crazy magic bear." I glanced at the wound on my shoulder, noting that it had been covered with leaves and some strong-smelling black goo. I didn't dare disturb it to see the damage beneath.

"Probably a little of everything," she said, her own hands starting to rub her arms.

"I still can't believe this is real. All of the stories about magic and the Moonshadow Woods. Can you believe it's real? We're here. We've been attacked by ogres and Cloakfang Ursids. We've seen an Animara and Swiftclaw wolves. Is your mind spinning as much as mine?"

She let out a long puff of air. "It's all incredible. I have to admit I was making fun of you for being scared of coming here, believing in fairytales and all, but it turns out you were right to be worried. We would have died if Thalassa hadn't saved us."

I remembered that moment lying beside her thinking my time had come to an end. Though I hadn't relished the thought of my death, it was the thought of hers that had gutted me. But one powerful realization had crashed through my mind in those moments I thought would be my last: I would be leaving this world without ever knowing the taste of her lips. Those full, defiant lips that had captivated me from the moment she'd spat her first curse in my direction. The fierce curve of her mouth when she smiled, the way she bit her lower lip when deep in thought—all of it haunted me. To die without crossing that forbidden boundary between us seemed suddenly the cruelest fate.

I hadn't been ready to go. Not just for my own sake, but because every heartbeat I spent near her only intensified this maddening need. I wanted more time with her. More of her scent, her voice, her fire. I wanted to discover if her mouth would yield to mine with the same passion that fueled her in battle, or if she would challenge me even then.

I wanted more time with her. More of her.

All of her.

As I sat in the hut staring at her, I had to fight my need to storm over, pull her into my arms and claim her with that kiss I didn't want to die without. All I could think about was her kiss and what it would feel like. What other incredible pleasures could come from giving in to the passions for her I'd never felt before in my life. I envisioned our naked bodies, sweat-slicked and frantic as I buried my cock deep within her over and over again, her moans music in my ears as she writhed against me while I brought her pleasures like she'd never known.

"That was close." She lay back on her bed, and I had to force the powerful feelings back deep down inside me.

I mirrored the movement, propping my head on my arms, closing my eyes for a beat as I forced the images of her naked body from my mind.

"That bear just appeared out of nowhere. And it hit me so fast I didn't even have time to react. It was really awful lying there completely paralyzed."

I remembered the strange feeling of being unable to move, trapped in my body like an iron prison. "Yeah. Feeling powerless was not pleasant."

She gave a soft snort. "Well, I'm used to being powerless. I'm a woman. But I did hate not being able to move my body and being so vulnerable."

I returned the snort. "You? Powerless? Never. You're the most powerful person I've ever met. Think of everything you've survived, everything you've accomplished."

"Not powerful enough to stop my sister from being taken." Reyna's face darkened. "And what I've been through is nothing compared to what Cassia will have to survive."

Suddenly, she shot up from her cot, pacing the small confines of our hut. "I can't just lay down and rest, Asher. Now that the Kingsguard has lost our trail, I need to start working on getting back to free Cassia. I need to talk to Thalassa."

I sat up, frustration building in my chest. "You heard her. Rest now and we'll talk later. We're still feeling the effects of the bear's poison."

"I don't care," she snapped. "I can take it. The sooner I figure out my next steps, the sooner I can get back to Cassia."

"What's your plan?" I demanded, my voice rising. "You want to march out of the woods right now while the Kingsguard is likely still out there patrolling the area? We'll be on the run again within the day. You're not thinking like the strategist I know that you are. You're just reacting right now."

"I'm not just reacting!" she fired back. "I can't stop. I can't stand around doing nothing while my sister suffers. How long until her training is done? A week? A month? I have to get her back before that wretched King climbs on her and forces her to his will."

I took a deep breath, trying to calm myself. "Fine, then if you won't stay and rest for yourself or for me, then rest for Ember. She can't keep going like this. She deserves to get a few days of recovery for what she's been through for you."

That stopped her. I saw the recognition flicker in her eyes as she considered her loyal mount.

"Fuck," she grumbled, and I knew I'd stopped her from bolting out of this hut and the safety of the woods. Still frustrated, she started pacing again, but this time I noticed her wobble, the poison still affecting her system.

I jumped up, catching her before she could fall. Her body collapsed into my arms, and it amazed me how good it felt to have her in my embrace. As she leaned back, trusting in the security of my support, she looked up into my eyes. I saw the war of emotions in them. Anger. Fear. Frustration. Pain. And... lust?

Was I imagining it? Hallucinations from the poison coursing through my veins, or did Reyna's eyes flicker momentarily to my lips?

For a moment, we stood there, suspended in time. Her face was inches from mine, and all I could think about was what her lips would taste like and the warmth of her body against mine.

But as I gazed into her eyes, the most prominent emotion I saw in them was exhaustion, the weight of her worries and fears. As much as I wanted to lean down and claim those lips as my own and carry her to my cot to show her what pleasures a man could bring after only suffering their pains, I knew this wasn't the time.

Gently, I helped her back to her feet. "See? Even the invincible need rest," I said softly. "Just for tonight. We'll figure everything out in the morning."

Reyna nodded, the fight seeming to drain out of her.

"Okay, okay. You're right." She let out a defeated sigh then moved over to the small window, her gaze drifting out over the moonlit village in the direction of Ironheart... in the direction of her sister.

As I watched Reyna by the window, her face softly illuminated by the torch burning just outside, I felt a surge of emotion so strong it nearly took my breath away. This woman had turned my world upside down. She'd challenged everything I thought I knew, everything I'd been raised to believe. My choice to save her had meant giving up everything that I'd worked for. Everything I'd cared about. My title, my home, my prestige, my horse, my brother...

And yet, I couldn't bring myself to regret a single moment.

"She's out there you know," Reyna said, voice soft and vulnerable. "My sister is out there somewhere right now. And I can't stand thinking about what fate awaits her. I have to save her, Asher. I know you think it's crazy, but I have to. Or I will die trying."

It almost killed me hearing the pain in her voice, almost as much as it did thinking about her failing in her mission and losing her life. Suddenly my world didn't make sense without her in it. It felt hollow. Empty. Though I knew her plan was risky, crazy even, as I stared at the fierce warrior who had defied every odd stacked against her already, I knew that if anyone could do it, it was Reyna, the Rebel Rose.

"Okay, I'll help you," I said on a sigh.

She spun to look at me. "What? What do you mean?"

"If you're going to go back for your sister, you'll need someone who knows the ins and outs of the kingdom and castle. That's me. I can help you come up with a plan and together, we can try to free her."

"Asher, I—" she started, eyes wide with wonder.

I stopped her with a hand. "I still think this is madness. And there is an almost certain possibility that you're going to get both of us killed, but I'm willing to try to help you save Cassia as I know you'll never find happiness in any life knowing she suffers in hers."

"I... I can't believe you would do that for me," she said, stunned.

Almost as stunned as I was for uttering those treasonous words. Though I was already a traitor to the crown, it still felt strange beginning to plan on infiltrating the castle I'd once vowed to protect with my life. But as I looked into those eyes, so filled with gratitude and wonder, I knew that I would do anything for her. Even shatter the last of my vows to king and kingdom by stealing my king's new bride.

"Just promise me we can get some rest first before we go get ourselves slaughtered trying to break back into the very kingdom we are running from. I'd like to be well-rested before we march off to certain death."

She chuckled, and it warmed me straight to the center of my being. "Deal. We rest first, then we die."

I laughed as well, but deep down I knew that if there was ever a reason to sacrifice my life, it wasn't for some feckless king. Not for a broken kingdom. But for her. The woman who made me question everything. The woman who made me burn.

"Thank you, Asher," she said, turning to glance at me over her shoulder. "For everything. I know I can't begin to comprehend what you've given up for me, but I want you to know I appreciate it."

I crooked a smile, my chest tightening with emotion as she gave me a sleepy half-smile. Just seeing the way she looked at me now, no contempt, no hatred in those piercing eyes, made me know with absolute certainty that I would give up everything in my world a thousand times over just to have her looking at me the way she was now. The realization was both thrilling and terrifying. But instead of telling her that, all I said was, "You're welcome."

As those green eyes stared into mine, I saw a question dancing inside them. The vulnerability in her gaze made my breath catch. This was Reyna, the fierce Iron Rose, now the Rebel Rose, letting down her guard.

For me.

I moved closer to her, stepping to her side to get a better view out the window. It still felt strange being allowed in such close proximity when just days ago, she'd have skewered me with her sword given the chance.

"What are you thinking about?" I prodded, my voice soft, eager to know every thought in that brilliant mind of hers.

She peeked at me, opened her mouth to speak then closed it, turning her gaze back outside. "Nothing."

I gave her a little bump with my shoulder. "Come on. Tell me. I know you're thinking something. You said in there you trusted me, so trust me now. What?"

She gently chewed her lip as if to stop the words from coming out, and I found myself mesmerized by the gesture. Finally, she quietly asked, "When you left behind your life in Ironheart for me, did you leave behind any... wives? Children?"

"No," I answered quickly, my heart pounding at the implication behind her question.

She turned, her eyes widening a little. "Really? But you're Head of the Kingsguard and must be in your mid-twenties. I assumed you had several wives by now."

"I could," I answered honestly. "But I have no interest in forcing a woman to be with me. And if I take a wife and don't get her pregnant by respecting her wishes, they'll force me to replace her and send her to work as a prostitute for being infertile. I just couldn't bear either scenario, so I've been putting it off for as long as possible. I've just said I'm too focused on my duty to the king to be bothered with a bride."

Her face softened again as she stared at me, and I felt exposed under her gaze, as if she could see right into my soul.

"So, it's true then."

"What's true?" I asked, noting the way her eyes smiled as she said it.

"You are different."

I smiled down at her, moving a little closer. The new nearness to her let me feel the warmth of her skin just inches from mine. It sent sparks through my entire body. "Yes. I'm different."

"I still don't understand why you gave up your whole life. Everything you've worked for. For... me."

The question hung between us, suspended in the charged air like the moment before lightning strikes. The fierce warrior who'd challenged me at every turn—blade to blade, word for cutting word—now stood before me with vulnerability flickering behind those emerald eyes that had once promised nothing but contempt. She was searching for an answer to the question I hadn't, until this shattering moment, known how to voice aloud.

The answer came crashing over me like a wave breaking fiercely against cliffs. It washed away my carefully constructed armor piece by piece—armor forged of sacred vows and rigid honor, of blood-oaths and duty to king and kingdom. The torrent stripped away everything until there was nothing left but the raw, exposed man behind it all—the man I'd buried so deeply I'd forgotten he existed. The man who wanted her with a hunger so primal, so absolute, that he would set flame to everything standing between them—every sacred vow, every blood-sworn oath—and burn entire kingdoms to smoldering ruin for nothing more than the chance to surrender to the all-consuming fire raging between them.

"Isn't it obvious?" My voice came out rough, barely more than a whisper.

She stared at me, her fierce eyes burning into mine before they flicked to my lips. Her own parted, and her fingers—those same fingers that had once pressed a blade to my throat—now trembled slightly as they brushed against my jaw with a gentleness that undid me more thoroughly than any violence ever could.

That single, delicate touch ignited the sparks crackling between us, a fire raging so hot it nearly incinerated me from the inside. My breath caught as she leaned up, her lips hovering just a breath away from putting me out of my agony and quelling the need to taste her coursing through me.

When her lips ghosted across mine, it wasn't a kiss so much as a challenge. Like a question—uncertain, searching.

A question that demanded an answer.

And gods, did I answer.

Something primal tore loose inside me—the thing I'd chained and starved and denied for too long. As I surged forward, a sound ripped from my chest, raw and possessive like a growl. My hand shot into her hair, fingers tangling in those dark strands, silk against my calloused skin as I crushed my mouth against hers.

This wasn't soft. This wasn't careful. This was wildfire after drought, a dam breaking after centuries of pressure, every ounce of restraint I'd forced upon myself shattering all at once.

She made a sound against my mouth—half surprise, half surrender—before meeting my ferocity with her own. Her fingers slipped beneath my armor, yanking me closer until the hard metal clanked together as my body collided with hers. The unyielding plates between us only heightened my frustration, the barrier of steel and leather suddenly intolerable. All I wanted was to strip away the metal that kept me from feeling her skin against mine, to tear through every layer of protection we'd wrapped ourselves in—both physical and otherwise.

I kissed her like a starving man finally given sustenance. Like an enemy claiming his greatest victory. Her taste—sharp and sweet and addictive—flooded my senses until I could think of nothing else. When her lips parted on a gasp, I took the invitation, deepening the kiss until I was consuming her, being consumed by her, our breaths mingling as we tried to devour years of denial in seconds.

Her teeth caught my lower lip, the sharp sting followed by the soothing sweep of her tongue. I groaned, the sound dragged from somewhere deep and forgotten, a place inside me I'd never even known. My hand slid from her hair to cup her face, thumb tracing the high arch of her cheekbone with a softness that contradicted the ferocity of our kiss.

We pressed together like we were trying to erase the boundary between our bodies—like we could burn through iron and leather if we just got close enough, if we just wanted it badly enough. And gods, how I wanted it. The heat between us charged the air, making it thick and heavy, difficult to breathe anything but her.

A crash from outside the hut jolted us apart. We froze, our ragged breathing the only sound as we listened for danger. Our senses still on high alert. After a moment, we heard laughter—just someone in the village dropping something.

"It's nothing," I said, my gaze flicking back to her from where it had darted to my sword.

Her lips were swollen from my kisses, a flush spreading high across her cheeks. She took a step and stumbled, catching herself against the wall. The flush I'd taken for passion now looked fevered against her too-pale skin.

"The cloakfang venom," I said, moving to her side without thinking. "It's still in our blood."

"I'm fine," she insisted, but her eyes told a different story.

"Reyna," I said, noting the venom still affecting me as well. Though I would have ignored it happily for a night in her arms. Gods, I'd have swam in it straight to my death if it meant I could feel her naked, sweat-slicked body moving against mine. But she'd been on the run for so long. Fought so hard for this freedom. This safety. I knew now wasn't the time to try to press this incredible connection between us. "You need to rest."

She tried to straighten, to summon that iron will that had kept her fighting long after others would have fallen. But the poison, the exhaustion of our journey, and perhaps the aftermath of what had just happened between us seemed to finally catch up with her. She swayed again, and this time I caught her, my arm slipping around her waist.

"I don't need your help," she muttered, but she leaned into me, nonetheless.

"Of course you don't," I agreed, guiding her toward her cot. "The mighty Rebel Rose never needs anyone's help. But humor me anyway."

The ghost of a smile touched her lips, and something in my chest bloomed under the small warmth of her softness.

I helped her to her cot, surprised when she allowed me to tuck her in beneath the blanket—an intimacy entirely different from our kiss, yet somehow just as profound. She watched me through half-lidded eyes, her usual walls and defenses temporarily lowered by exhaustion and the lingering effects of the venom.

"Goodnight, Asher," she whispered, then closed her eyes as much-needed sleep quickly claimed her.

I sat there, stunned and transformed, the ghost of her kiss burning on my lips like a brand. In that moment, I knew with absolute certainty that whatever happened next, I was irrevocably changed.

I watched her drift off to sleep, my heart full to bursting with emotions I couldn't even begin to name. In that moment, I knew that whatever challenges lay ahead, whatever battles we might face, I would face them all gladly as long as Reyna was by my side.

I allowed myself to acknowledge a truth that still stunned me to core of my being, but a truth I could no longer, nor wanted, to deny.

The dutiful Head of the Kingsguard had died in that kiss, and I would gladly burn it all down for her again... and again... and again.

I gently stroked her hair, marveling at how this fierce, beautiful woman had completely upended my world. When I finally lay down on my own cot, the memory of her kiss lingered on my lips, a promise of something more, something I had never dared to hope for before.

As sleep began to claim me, I found myself marveling at how quickly life could change. A week ago, I was the head of the Kingsguard, my path seemingly set in stone. Now, I was in a hidden, magical forest with the woman who had turned my world upside down.

Whatever tomorrow brought, I knew one thing for certain—I would do anything to keep her safe, to help her save her sister, to see her smile again.

CHAPTER FIFTEEN
Reyna

It was nothing like I'd imagined my first kiss would be—not that I'd allowed myself to imagine it often. It was better. Warmer. More real. And it had awakened something inside of me. A need I'd never known, didn't understand. Yet I enjoyed every second of the way my body tingled for more, begged for the attention my lips had received.

I touched my lips, still tingling from our kiss. The very idea of having intimate relations with a man had always repulsed me, knowing what most men were like. But now, I found myself curious. What would it be like to be with someone like Asher? Someone who saw me as an equal, who respected my strength? I'd heard rumors that sex could be more than just a woman getting humped for breeding, and that it could be the most incredible feeling in the world.

The women of the Warhold had certainly figured out how to please each other in ways I hadn't experienced myself. My position as the Iron Rose kept me elevated from such romances that bloomed in the darkest corners of our prison. But I'd never believed those rumors about passion with men being possible as well until I'd felt his lips on mine. If a kiss felt that good, what other pleasures awaited at his touch?

I'd never known a kind man before. Never allowed myself to see them as anything but the enemy. But Asher... he was different. He'd risked his life to save his sister. He'd given up that same life to save *me*. And now he'd agreed to help me save *my* sister. And gods help me, he was more handsome than any man I'd ever seen.

What the hell is wrong with me?

I jerked my gaze away from his sleeping form, pressing my palms against my eyes as if I could physically push away the thoughts. This was exactly what I couldn't afford—getting distracted by a man when my sister was suffering gods-knew-what fate. Every moment I spent mooning over stolen kisses was another moment Cassia was trapped, probably being "trained" for her wedding night with the king.

The thought made bile rise in my throat. While I was here having romantic fantasies about handholding and tender touches, my sister was being broken down, piece by piece, shaped into the perfect submissive bride. The guilt crashed over me like a physical blow.

I was the Iron Rose. The Rebel Rose. I didn't get distracted by men, no matter how different they claimed to be. No matter how his eyes made my stomach flip or how his smile sent heat coursing through my veins.

Focus, I commanded myself. *This isn't about you. This is about Cassia.*

But even as I tried to push the feelings away, my treacherous gaze drifted back to Asher. In sleep, he looked younger somehow, vulnerable. The hard lines of duty and rigid honor that usually defined his features had softened. This was the man who had risked everything for me. Who had chosen my freedom over his own life.

The man whose kiss had awakened something in me I'd never known existed.

Stop it. I clenched my fists, nails digging into my palms. *You don't have time for this.*

As if sensing my gaze, Asher's eyes flickered open. For a moment, we just looked at each other, and I saw something warm and searching in his expression that made my pulse quicken. Then he smiled, a soft, sleepy thing that made my heart skip a beat despite my internal warnings.

"How long did we sleep?" he asked, his voice still rough with sleep.

"Judging by the light, I'd say most of the day. It's nearly nightfall again." I kept my voice carefully neutral, trying to ignore the way his morning voice sent shivers down my spine.

Asher sat up, stretching his arms above his head. "It feels like it. Wow. I was really out."

I nodded, surprised at how rested I felt despite the tumultuous thoughts. "I can't remember the last time I slept so deeply."

"Me neither," Asher agreed. "I guess we needed it more than we realized. I'm sure that poison still in our blood didn't hurt either."

Two stacked piles of clothing on the small chair in the corner caught my eye. "Are those for us?"

Asher pushed up and walked over, examining the simple cloth, leather and wool pieces. "I think so. Probably so we can get out of this armor and be more comfortable."

The thought of taking off my protective armor during our journey had made me feel too vulnerable, and instinctively I bristled against the idea. But then I remembered how safe I felt in the village. How safe I felt with him.

Too safe, warned a voice in my head. *You're getting comfortable. Soft. While Cassia suffers.*

"Yes. I think we can put them on," I said finally, accepting that I didn't need my armor here. For the first time in my life, I could truly let my guard down.

But should you?

Asher and I each took the clothing made for us, him leather pants and a thin tunic and me a soft leather skirt that finished just above my knees and a sleeveless tunic woven from soft, durable plant fibers. We got dressed with our backs turned toward one another, and I had to force myself from peeking back to catch a glimpse of him without his clothes on.

When we finished, we turned to face each other.

"Wow. You look like you belong here," he said, his eyes roving up the length of my legs and torso before finishing when they met mine.

The appreciation in his gaze made warmth pool in my stomach, and I had to fight the urge to step closer to him. Instead, I crossed my arms and tried to keep my voice steady. "You do too."

He gave me a little turn, opening his arms when he finished. The movement pulled his borrowed tunic tight across his muscular chest, and I had to force myself to look away. "Comfy. And well made."

"Yeah. Mine is comfortable too. Feels strange to be out of my armor after so many days." And it did feel strange—not just physically, but emotionally. Without my armor, I felt exposed, vulnerable in ways that had nothing to do with physical protection.

"I'm not complaining. And hopefully by getting out of my Kingsguard armor, these women will stop glaring at me so much."

He pulled a face, and despite my internal turmoil, I laughed. The sound surprised me—when had laughing with him become so natural?

"Well? Should we go out?" I asked, suddenly feeling a bit nervous about facing the tribe again. Nervous about what Thalassa might see in my eyes when she looked at us together.

Asher nodded, stepping toward the door and gesturing for me to follow. "Might as well. I'm starving, and I'm sure they have questions for us. I know I have questions for them."

As we stepped out of the hut, I was momentarily overwhelmed by the scene before us.

The village was alive with activity. Women of all ages moved about, some carrying baskets of food, others tending to small gardens or mending clothes. A few children, both males and females, darted between the huts, their laughter ringing out in the evening air. And everywhere I looked, I saw smiles. Genuine, carefree smiles.

"I've never seen so many happy women in one place," I murmured, more to myself than to Asher.

"This must be what freedom looks like," he replied quietly.

The words hit me like a physical blow. Freedom. This was what freedom looked like—and here I was, getting distracted by a man instead of fighting to give this same freedom to my sister. Instead of using every moment to plan her rescue.

Before I could respond, a familiar face came around the corner.

"Hello, Gaia," I said as she approached.

"You're awake," she responded, her tone friendly but with an undercurrent of caution when her eyes fell on Asher. "I'm glad you slept well. Thalassa would like to see you both. Come, I'll take you to her."

As we followed Gaia through the village, I tried to focus on the tactical advantages this place could offer for my mission. Safe haven. Potential allies. Information about the outside world. But my treacherous mind kept drifting to the way Asher moved beside me, the way his presence made me feel simultaneously safe and completely off-balance.

We arrived at a large, circular hut near the center of the village. Gaia ushered us inside where we found Thalassa seated on a cushion, various wooden bowls and plates arranged before her.

"Ah, our guests are awake," Thalassa said, her dark eyes twinkling as they moved between Asher and me with unmistakable knowing. "Come, sit. You must be hungry. How did the Rebel Rose sleep?"

"Just Reyna is fine," I answered, still unsure how I felt about my new title, and suddenly very aware of how Thalassa was watching us.

"Very well. Reyna," she said, smiling.

As we settled onto the cushions across from her, Gaia took a seat on the chair off to the side. Thalassa began filling plates with an array of fruits, nuts, and what looked like some kind of dried meat. The smells made my stomach growl embarrassingly loud.

"Eat," Thalassa encouraged, pushing the plates toward us. "Then we'll talk."

As we ate, I couldn't help but think of Ember. "My horse," I said between bites. "Is she alright?"

Thalassa nodded, her smile reassuring. "Your mare is well cared for, I assure you. You can see her after you've eaten."

Satisfied for the moment, I returned to my meal. The food was simple but flavorful and delicious, unlike the tasteless slop they fed us in the Warhold. As we ate, Thalassa watched us with curious eyes—eyes that seemed to see far too much.

"The Kingsguard in pursuit of you gave up last night and is headed west," she said, my mouth too full to answer.

"You're certain?" Asher asked.

She nodded. "Yes. My birds are watching them as they go and reporting their movements. They spent a few hours arguing outside the woods about coming in, but in the end, they decided not to try."

Asher snorted. "Cowards."

I arched an eyebrow. "You weren't too keen on coming in here either."

He shrugged. "And I was right. We nearly got killed."

Thalassa chuckled. "The animals are watching them closely, and if they change their mind and attempt to enter, the ogres, swiftclaws and cloakfangs are positioned all throughout the borders. They won't reach you here. You're safe."

A swell of relief lifted my shoulders with my sigh, followed immediately by a stab of guilt.

Safe. We were safe here. An odd feeling I don't think I'd ever truly experienced before. But safety was a luxury Cassia didn't have.

"Now, you must have questions," she said as if she could read my mind as much as the animals.

I nodded, swallowing my last bite. "Many. But... perhaps you could start by telling us about you? About this place?"

Thalassa leaned back, her eyes taking on a faraway look. "I am what's known as an Animara. The last of my kind, as far as I know. My magic allows me to communicate with animals. I can share their minds, their thoughts and their feelings, and they can share mine." The raven on her shoulder let out a *caw* as if agreeing with her. "Some people think that we can control animals, forcing them to attack or protect us, which isn't the truth. We can only communicate with them, ask them for help if we need it, but their decisions are always their own."

I'd heard whispers of such abilities in old stories, but to hear it stated so matter-of-factly was astounding.

"And how does it work? How do you... communicate with them?" I asked.

"Well, there are multiple ways, really. For the easiest communication that takes the least energy from me, it's with eye contact. If I can see an animal, I can easily share its mind."

"But you can call in animals from a distance, right? Like you did with the wolves?"

She nodded. "Once I've made a connection with an animal, it's fairly easy for me to access them again, and them me. But usually, they have to be within a mile, maybe two if we are well connected. The only one I can connect with over great distances is Rhaska, here."

I looked at the raven perched on her shoulder, noting his intelligent eyes fixed on mine.

"He is my Kindrion, a soul-bonded companion. In our language, we call such beings Kindrions because they are more than just animal companions. They are kindred spirits, bound to us by a deep, unbreakable connection. I can see through his eyes and communicate with him over great distances. Our bond is special, and it allows us to share thoughts and experiences no matter how far apart we are. Every Animara has one Kindrion."

"That's incredible," Asher said, staring at the beautiful bird. "But other animals you have to be within range of?"

She nodded. "Yes. I can communicate with animals at a greater distance, or even animals I've never made eye contact with before at a distance, but it takes a significant amount of energy out of me. If I try to communicate with a large group of animals, say a flock of birds a mile away that I've never seen, it can drain me so much I can barely stand. Even kill me if I go too far. But if I know those birds, it is much easier on me to communicate."

"This is just fascinating," I said, shaking my head. "I love my mare with all my heart, and I wish so much that I could communicate with her the way you can with Rhaska. What a wonderful gift. I'm so sorry your people were wiped out by ignorant, fearful kings."

Sadness clouded her eyes as she gave me a faint smile. "During the great magic purge, when the kings decided magic was too dangerous and must be extinguished, my people were hunted nearly to extinction. My great-grandparents and my parents were among the few who escaped, fleeing here to the Moonshadow Woods with a small group of survivors."

She paused, a shadow of old pain crossing her face. "My kind has a lifespan of over two hundred years. I'm approaching one hundred myself, though I know I don't look it." She smiled wryly. "But my parents were the last two of our kind, and now, as their only child, I am all that remains. It takes two purebred Animara to produce a magical child, so..."

"You're the last," I finished softly, my heart aching for her loneliness.

Thalassa nodded. "When my grandparents were still alive, they began finding women in the woods—escapees, mostly. Some were pregnant. They took them in, sheltered them. Then my parents did the same. Over time, more came, and they built this sanctuary. Now I have taken over the mantle of caring for all the refugees, and we have a thriving community of women, and the few men who were babies or young children when they arrived with their mothers."

As I sat there listening, my mind filled with visions of what life must have been like during the purge and how amazing it was that this place existed.

"Reyna?" Thalassa's voice brought me back to the present. "Are you alright? You seemed far away for a moment."

I nodded, exhaling a long breath. "Yes, sorry. It's just... a lot to take in."

Thalassa's eyes glinted with understanding. "Of course. Now you know a little about me, and I would like to know a little more about you."

Her eyes moved to Asher quickly, and I knew she wanted to understand why I was fighting to save a Kingsguard... the greatest oppressors of them all. Before I knew it, I launched into the story, Asher piping in to add to it as we told her our tale. She listened with wide eyes and a shocked expression until we finally reached the part where she found us.

"And that is the whole story," I said, blowing out a breath as I finished.

"And quite a story it is." She mirrored my breath with an exhale. "Well, I am so glad you trusted your instincts to bring you here. You're safe with us."

"About that," I started. "Though I appreciate it, I really do need to get back to save my sister."

Thalassa gave me a gentle nod. "I understand. And though I won't stop you, I do hope you know that this sanctuary is the safest place for you. I think you could be happy here."

I thought about the smiling women and how happy they looked. Thought about how easy it would be to just give up my fight and settle into this amazing little part of the world where I could be free. But then Cassia's face flickered in my mind, and I shook away the pleasant notion of a life in Moonshadow Woods. I couldn't stop my traitorous eyes from glancing at Asher wondering if he'd also be part of my happy existence in this new life she promised. But as much as I relished the thought of spending more peaceful nights tasting those lips I couldn't stop craving, I shook the notion from my head.

"I know that I would be happy here," I answered, my voice thick with emotion. "But I have to save my sister. I can't just pretend she doesn't exist and stay here in this paradise. Though I would love to."

As I spoke, I noticed Gaia's reaction from the corner of my eye. Her face contorted with pain, a flash of what looked like guilt crossing her features. Our eyes met briefly before she cast her gaze to the ground, unable to hold my stare. There was a story there, one I was suddenly desperate to know.

Thalassa's face registered disappointment, but she nodded. "I understand. Well, once you're healed up and rested, we'll make sure you have everything you need for your journey. First things first, let me look at those wounds Olaf gave you."

"Olaf?" Asher asked.

"The cloakfang you met." Thalassa smiled. "He packs a punch."

"I'll say." Asher looked down at his muscular bicep wrapped in the cloth.

"Let me see," Thalassa gestured for him to remove it, and he did.

The wound was covered in black ointment, but it was deep and angry. Four slash marks that left wide channels of torn flesh in his skin.

"It's healing nicely, but you should stay here at least a few more days while we treat it so it doesn't get befouled. We will keep it clean and use our special ointment to prevent it from festering."

"Thank you," he said.

Thalassa gestured for me to remove my bandage. I did, and when she looked at my wound, now almost completely healed, her eyes flashed wide and then looked up into mine, searching. "It's almost healed. That's... impossible."

I shrugged, suddenly uncomfortable from the way her eyes probed mine. "I've always been a fast healer."

"Hmm," Thalassa mused, then her eyes seemed to change as if a great idea had popped into her head. "Perhaps there's more to you than meets the eye, Reyna. You might have some latent magical abilities yourself. There are a people who were fast healers. The Aegisari."

I stiffened at her words. "No," I said firmly. "That's not possible. Magic was purged from our lands generations ago."

But even as I spoke, a tiny part of me wondered. Could it be true? Could I have magic? The thought was both thrilling and terrifying. All my life, I'd been told that magic was dangerous, that it had been purged for good reason. But seeing Thalassa, seeing this peaceful village... maybe what I'd been told wasn't the whole truth.

"Yes, it was purged, but that doesn't mean you couldn't have Aegisari in your bloodline. Unlike my people, you don't need to be pureblood Aegisari to pass on the healing traits. It's very possible you have lingering Aegisari in your blood. It would explain your healing."

"Wait," Asher said, lifting his finger. "Are you saying that she may have magical powers?"

Thalassa nodded. "Rapid healing is an innate ability in an Aegisari. It just happens. I can't say I know a lot about them having spent all of my life here, but I do remember hearing stories that some of them can heal others and cast protection shields. The power of the Aegisari is not just in their abilities, but in their spirit and determination to protect and heal those around them."

"I think I remember hearing about them in some of the books I used to read," Asher said, his eyes looking me over as if trying to see the Aegisari in me. "There's no one who wants to protect people more than you, Reyna. And you do heal unbelievably fast. Maybe Thalassa is right. Maybe you do have this Aegisari blood in your veins."

My whole life I'd been told magic was evil and dangerous, and thinking I could be one of them set my nerves on edge. "No. I'm not magic. I can't be. I'm just... me. A fast healer. That's all."

"But Reyna," Asher started, his voice gentle but insistent.

I raised my hand, cutting him off. "I'm not an Aegisari. Let's drop it." The words came out harsher than I intended, but the idea of having magic... it was too much to process right now.

Asher and Thalassa shared a look, and then Thalassa didn't press the issue, but I could see in her eyes that she wasn't convinced by my denial. "Well," she said, changing the subject, "you are certainly healed enough to start your travels without risk, but Asher here needs a few days."

The words hit me like cold water.

A few days.

A few more days Cassia suffered in that finishing school, learning to be the perfect submissive wife.

Asher's eyes met mine, and in that moment, I could read every thought, every fear in his gaze. He didn't need to speak for me to hear his question: *Are you leaving without me?*

The question tore through me like a blade. Every instinct screamed at me to grab Ember and ride hard for Ironheart. Every moment we delayed was another moment stolen from my sister. Another day of her spirit being slowly crushed.

But looking at Asher—really looking at him—I saw the truth that made my chest ache. He'd sacrificed everything for me. His position, his future, his very identity. He was injured because of me, because he'd chosen to follow me into these woods instead of delivering me to my death.

And if I was being brutally honest with myself, it wasn't just gratitude keeping me here. The idea of leaving Asher, of continuing this journey without him by my side, felt wrong in a way that terrified me. Not because I needed his help—though I did—but because somewhere along the way, he'd become... important. Too important.

This is exactly what you can't afford, the voice in my head warned. *You're choosing a man over your sister.*

But was I? Or was I choosing the partner who gave me the best chance of actually succeeding in my impossible mission?

I took a deep breath, forcing myself to think strategically instead of emotionally. Asher knew the castle layout. He knew the guards' rotations, their weaknesses. He understood the political landscape in ways I never could. Taking him with me wasn't just about sentiment—it was about giving Cassia the best possible chance of rescue.

At least, that's what I told myself.

"I'll stay here until he's ready to travel again," I said finally, the words feeling both like surrender and betrayal.

The relief that flooded Asher's face was palpable, his entire body seeming to relax as his eyes lit up when they met mine. But beneath his relief, I caught something else—something that looked suspiciously like the same dangerous warmth I'd been fighting all morning.

But the decision was made. I would stay. I would help Asher heal. And I would try very, very hard not to think about why that decision had felt so inevitable.

"Well, that's great news you're staying because you two have arrived just in time for our monthly feast," Thalassa continued, and I forced myself to focus on her words instead of the way Asher was still looking at me. "Tonight, we take the sacrifice of the eldest gryphhorn and have a feast in his honor, eating his meat and nourishing our tribe. We celebrate his life with a great party. Dancing, drinking, and laughter."

I paused. "But you're an Animara. You can talk to animals. How can you... eat them?"

She glanced at the raven on her shoulder. "I don't eat just any animal. You're right. It would feel wrong to consume my friends. But meat is important for survival for many creatures. It's part of the cycle of nature and life. The wolves, bears, and other predators need it for sustenance, but they only consume what they need for survival. The same goes for us. Our ways are deeply rooted in balance and respect. Tonight, we honor the eldest of the gryphhorn herd. It is a sacrifice, yes, but it is also an act of compassion."

I frowned, still not fully grasping the concept. "How can taking a life be compassionate?"

"Come. I'll show you."

She rose and gestured for Asher and me to follow. We did as she asked, and the three of us walked through the village to the outskirts, stopping when we reached the edge of a large clearing.

My jaw dropped at the sight of the beautiful herd of majestic creatures moving gracefully among the trees. The gryphhorns were a stunning blend of power and elegance, their massive bodies reminiscent of moose or elk, but their coats were a striking pattern of black and white stripes, each animal unique in its markings. Some bore predominantly ebony hides with thin white streaks, while others were nearly pale as snow with just a few dark stripes accenting their forms.

Their most distinctive feature was the impressive set of antlers crowning their heads. Unlike the branching antlers of deer, these were more akin to curved horns, spiraling upward and slightly forward, lending them an almost regal appearance. The horns varied in size with the largest horns on the beasts with the whitest of fur.

The gryphhorns' muscular bodies rippled with strength as they moved, their long legs carrying them with surprising grace for creatures of their size. Their thick necks arched proudly, supporting heads that seemed almost too delicate for such powerful beasts. Large, intelligent eyes surveyed their surroundings, alert yet calm in their forest home.

It was a breathtaking sight, one that made me feel privileged to witness such rare and magnificent creatures in their natural habitat.

"Wow," Asher said, stepping up beside me. "I've heard of them in old stories, but gods. What a sight. They're huge."

"And beautiful," I said in awe. "I thought they were hunted to extinction in the Southlands."

"Almost," Thalassa said. "But this herd found sanctuary here with us and has been thriving in Moonshadow Woods for centuries now."

"They are so beautiful. And their coats are all so different."

Thalassa pointed to the largest one, pure white instead of striped and the size of a large draft horse with antlers so large I wondered how it could lift its head. "You see him how he is pure white?"

I nodded.

"Baby gryphhorns are born black and develop their striping as they age. The older they get, the more white stripes cover their bodies. When a gryphhorn loses its stripes, it indicates its advanced age. The gryphhorns are our partners," Thalassa paused, her gaze fixed on the elder beast. "We protect them from predators and ensure they have ample food, even in harsh conditions. In return, they sustain us. When a gryphhorn reaches the end of its life, it turns white like that one. This is a sign that it only has a few weeks left to live. Rather than letting it suffer a slow, painful death, it sacrifices itself so that its strength can continue to nourish the tribe."

I watched the white gryphhorn with a mix of awe and sorrow. "But it must be hard for you," I said softly, "to see a creature you can communicate with die."

"It is never easy," Thalassa admitted, her voice tinged with sadness. "But this is the natural order of our world. The gryphhorns understand this balance. They accept it, and in doing so, they honor their own lives by ensuring their bodies do not go to waste. Their sacrifice allows the herd to thrive and keeps our people strong. It will feed us for a month, give us warm furs for bedding and clothing. Its bones and horns will be turned into tools and weapons. No part of it will go to waste, and the death is quick and painless instead of a slow suffering as its body fails. It is a kindness to give him the honor tonight."

Asher nodded slowly, beginning to see the wisdom in Thalassa's words. "I suppose it's a way of maintaining harmony," he said thoughtfully.

"Exactly," Thalassa agreed. "It is a cycle of life and death that sustains us all. Tonight, we will honor the white gryphhorn's sacrifice with a feast. We will use every part of its body, ensuring that nothing is wasted. Its spirit will live on in the strength it gives us."

In that moment, I felt a profound connection to the cycle of life in the Moonshadow Woods and the wisdom of Thalassa and her people. If only the rest of the Southlands could be so kind and compassionate.

"We'll leave him to say his goodbyes now. It's part of our tradition." She gestured for us to walk with her, and I gave the beautiful creature one last look before turning and moving along after her.

"Would you like to see your horse now? I'm sure she'd be happy to see you."

I nodded eagerly, grateful for the distraction. "Yes, please. I miss her terribly."

"And she misses you," Thalassa said, and it was strange to think Thalassa could communicate with Ember as easily as she and I talking, but also comforting to know that even though I knew our connection ran deep, that she did truly love me too.

A flicker of pain crossed Asher's face, and without needing words, I understood. His thoughts had turned to his own horse, Tempest, left behind during our journey.

Left behind for me.

Before I could process the thought, my hand moved of its own accord, reaching out to slip into his. The moment our skin touched, a jolt of lightning shot through me, and I saw the same shock mirrored in Asher's eyes. This wasn't a conscious decision, just as the kiss we'd shared hadn't been planned. It was as if my body had a will of its own around him, constantly seeking connection, constantly yearning for his touch.

But as quickly as I'd touched him, I pulled my hand away. I'd made my choice. I would stay with Asher until he healed. But

I couldn't—wouldn't—let myself get any more distracted than I already was. No more stolen kisses. No more lingering looks. No more letting my heart make decisions my head knew were dangerous.

Cassia was counting on me. And I'd already wasted too much time on feelings I couldn't afford.

As we prepared to see Ember and then bathe before the feast, I made myself a promise: I would keep my distance. I would remember why I was here. And I would not—absolutely would not—let myself fall any deeper under Asher's spell.

Even if every cell in my body screamed in protest at the very thought.

CHAPTER SIXTEEN
Asher

As we left the stables, the moonlight cast a warm glow over the village. After our visit with Ember, Reyna's face was alight with joy, her smile more radiant than I'd ever seen it.

"I'm so glad she's happy and well-rested," Reyna said, her voice soft with affection. "If it weren't for Ember, I wouldn't be here. I never even would have made it out of Ironheart without her. You're right. She's earned a good rest after everything she's been through for me."

I nodded, feeling a pang in my chest as I thought of my own horse, Tempest. I missed him fiercely, but as I looked at Reyna, I knew without a doubt that I'd made the right choice. I'd give up a thousand beloved horses in exchange for her life... for the chance to be here with her.

"She has," I agreed. "And so have you."

Reyna's eyes met mine, and for a moment, I forgot how to breathe. The urge to pull her into my arms, to kiss her until we were both breathless, was almost overwhelming. I could see something flickering in her gaze—want, need, the same desperate hunger I felt clawing at my chest—but then it was gone, shuttered behind those walls she kept rebuilding between us.

It was maddening. Every time I thought we were getting closer, every time I caught a glimpse of the woman beneath the armor, the one I'd kissed senseless just last night, she pulled back. Retreated. Left me aching for more.

Gaia appeared then, breaking the moment. "If you'd like to freshen up before the feast, there's a river nearby where you can bathe," she said, gesturing toward a wooded path. "It's about a five-minute walk that way. The feast starts in an hour."

"Thank you," Reyna said, and I echoed her gratitude.

As we walked down the path, I was acutely aware of Reyna's presence beside me. She was being careful—too careful—to keep space between us. But occasionally, when the path narrowed, the back of her hand would brush against mine, sending jolts of electricity through my body. Each time it happened, I saw her tense, saw her deliberately step away.

She was fighting this thing between us as hard as I was surrendering to it.

Gods, what was happening to me? I'd never felt this way about anyone.

There'd been flings in my youth—brief, clumsy things with girls my age before they were shipped off to become breeders for some man who never saw them as anything more.

But this felt different. Wilder. Sharper. More desperate.

Every time I looked at Reyna, my thoughts turned dark and possessive. I wanted to pin her against a tree and kiss her until she forgot every reason she had for holding back. I wanted to hear her moan my name, to feel her powerful body arch beneath mine.

Nothing in my youthful lust had ever come close to the way my body responded when I imagined myself between her powerful legs.

The sound of running water grew louder as we approached the river. When we reached the bank, we stood beside the softly rippling water, and I wanted to rip off my clothes and jump into it, washing away the stench of our long journey. I could see the same yearning in Reyna's eyes, but we both hesitated.

"I, uh... I'll turn around," I offered, seeing the uncertainty etched on her face. "You can get in first."

She nodded gratefully, but I caught the way her eyes lingered on me for just a moment too long before I turned my back. The knowledge that she wanted to look, that some part of her was fighting the same battle I was, made my blood run hot.

I heard the soft rustle of fabric, envisioned her naked body just within my reach, wondering what her breasts would feel like in my hands, or the warmth between her legs. My cock pressed against my pants as I envisioned my fingers dipping into her, listening to her moan into my ear as I worked her until she came apart for me.

I heard the quiet splash of her entering the water.

"Okay," she called, her voice slightly breathless. "Your turn."

I began to undress, hyper-aware of Reyna's presence behind me and angling myself so she couldn't see my rock-hard cock standing at attention for her. As I pulled off my shirt, I couldn't resist the temptation to glance back.

My breath caught in my throat as I saw Reyna quickly averting her gaze, a flush creeping up her neck. She had been watching me. The knowledge sent a surge of primitive satisfaction through me.

In that brief moment, I caught a glimpse of her in the water, her skin glistening in the moonlight. She was breathtakingly beautiful, and I had to force myself to look away even though all I wanted to do was stare at her for eternity, soaking in the sight of that beautiful, powerful woman so soft and vulnerable in the dimly lit waters.

I quickly finished undressing and entered the water, the coolness a welcome relief for my overheated skin. We stayed at a respectable distance from each other, the darkness of the water providing some modesty, but I could feel the tension crackling between us like lightning before a storm.

"This feels amazing," Reyna sighed, tilting her head back to wet her hair.

I watched a droplet of water trail down her neck, disappearing beneath the water's surface. The sight of her like this—unguarded, sensual—made my mouth go dry.

"It does," I agreed, my voice rougher than I intended as I choked on the simple words. I wanted to lick that drop of water off her skin, to taste every inch of her.

As I started washing myself off, I closed my eyes, trying to push the tantalizing visions of Reyna's body from my mind. But when I opened them again, I caught her staring at my chest, her lips slightly parted. Our eyes met, and the heat in her gaze nearly undid me.

She looked away quickly, but not before I saw the want there. The same desperate need that was eating me alive.

Attempting to lower my body's feverish temperature, I struck up a benign conversation as we bathed, talking about everything and nothing. Despite the intimacy of our situation, or perhaps because of it, I felt more relaxed than I had in days. There was something freeing about being here with Reyna, away from the pressures and expectations of my old life.

My old life.

The thought hit me like a war-hammer to the gut, stealing the breath from my lungs. I could never return to it. What would Erik think when he heard about what I'd done? Would he be proud that I hadn't sacrificed my honor by killing Reyna? Probably, but I knew he'd also be devastated, knowing I could never return, forced to live with the shame of my dishonor to our family name. My heart ached at the thought of never seeing him again.

But this was my life now. I'd chosen it the moment I set her free, even if I hadn't been aware of it at the time. But I didn't regret it. I couldn't as we floated beneath the moonlight together. And then I started to envision a new future, one that made my heart sing just picturing it. I would help Reyna rescue Cassia because

I knew she could never be truly happy without her sister safe by her side. But once Cassia was free, maybe, just maybe, I would convince Reyna to return here with me, to the safety and joy of the Moonshadow Woods. Together, we could build a life here, away from the dangers and cruelties of our old world.

Here, we could be free.

Together.

I gazed at Reyna, her skin gleaming in the soft moonlight, and felt something powerful swell in my chest. She was fierce, determined, and utterly captivating. As we talked more, I couldn't help but notice the way her eyes lingered on me when she thought I wasn't looking, the way she seemed to lean toward me unconsciously before catching herself and pulling back.

The air between us was charged with unspoken desire, and more than once, I found myself moving closer to her, drawn by an invisible force. Each time, she would tense, her breathing growing shallow, and I could see the war playing out on her face—want battling against whatever walls she'd built in her mind.

But each time we got too close, she would pull back, not quite ready to cross that line. The tension built with each near miss, until I felt like I might combust from the sheer want of her.

Finally, aware that our time was running short and hearing the music starting up in the nearby woods, we reluctantly left the river. We dressed with our backs to each other, though I was acutely aware of every movement she made. More than once, I felt her gaze on me, and when I caught her looking, she would flush and turn away quickly. Each stolen glance felt like a small victory, proof that she wanted me as much as I wanted her, even if she was fighting it with everything she had.

As we made our way back to the village, the sounds of music and laughter grew louder. When we arrived, the celebration was in full swing. A large bonfire burned in the center of the clearing, casting flickering shadows over the partygoers.

Thalassa stood near the fire, her voice rising above the crowd. "Tonight, we honor the gryphhorn who gave its life so that we might live," she proclaimed. "Let us celebrate its sacrifice and the continuation of our community!"

A cheer went up from the crowd, and the music swelled. People began to dance, their movements wild and joyous.

Reyna hung back, watching the festivities with a mixture of curiosity and apprehension. I could see the tension in her shoulders, the way she held herself apart from the crowd—and from me.

"Come on," I said, stepping closer to her, close enough that I could feel the heat radiating from her skin. "Let's join in."

She hesitated, her eyes darting between me and the dancing crowd. When she looked at me, I saw that flicker of want again, quickly suppressed. "I don't know, Asher. I'm not much of a dancer. Celebrations and parties weren't exactly part of life in the Warhold."

"Neither am I," I admitted with a grin, letting my hand hover near hers without quite touching. "But that's not going to stop me from trying. Come on, live a little. Just for one night."

After a moment's hesitation, she nodded. "Okay. Just for one night."

But instead of taking my hand, she stepped toward the crowd, maintaining that careful distance between us. The message was clear—she would participate, but she wasn't going to make this easy for either of us.

I followed her into the crowd, where we were immediately swept up in the rhythm of the music. The women, and a few men, greeted us with smiles, introducing themselves as they danced around us. Someone pressed cups of sweet, fermented berry juice into our hands, and we drank deeply, the alcohol warming us from the inside out.

At first, Reyna's movements were stiff and uncertain. But as the music flowed through us, she began to loosen up. With each beat of the drum, more and more of her rigid structure seemed to slough off like a snake shedding its skin, until finally, she looked exposed and raw.

Free.

I watched in awe as she gave herself over to the rhythm, her body moving with a grace that took my breath away. The firelight played across her skin, highlighting every curve, every powerful line of her body. She was intoxicating, mesmerizing, and I found myself moving closer, desperate to be near her.

We danced together, our bodies moving in perfect synchronization, but never quite touching. It was torture—exquisite, maddening torture. Every time the dance brought us close, I could feel the heat of her skin, could smell the scent of her hair. But she always managed to spin away before we could make contact, leaving me aching for more.

The heat of the bonfire, the pulsing rhythm of the music, the intoxicating presence of Reyna—it all combined to create a heady, dreamlike atmosphere. As the night wore on, I found myself moving closer and closer to her, drawn by an irresistible force. And despite her attempts to maintain distance, I could see her resolve weakening with each hypnotic beat of the drums.

At one point, Reyna stumbled slightly. Without thinking, I moved to catch her, my arms wrapping around her waist. She looked up at me, her eyes wide and illuminated in the firelight, her lips parted in surprise.

For a moment, the world around us seemed to fade away, leaving only us. I was acutely aware of every point where our bodies touched—her hands gripping my shoulders, my arms around her waist, her breasts pressed against my chest. I could feel her heart racing, matching the frantic beat of my own.

This close, I could see the war playing out in her eyes. Want and fear, desire and determination battling for control. Her gaze dropped to my lips, and I felt her body sway toward mine.

"Reyna," I breathed, hardly aware I was speaking. "I—"

But before I could finish, she seemed to remember herself. Her body went rigid in my arms, and she stepped back quickly, breaking the spell. A mix of emotions flashed across her face too quickly for me to decipher—desire, regret, frustration, and something that looked almost like panic.

"Asher, I—" she started, then shook her head.

Before I could press her to go on, the music changed, a faster, more energetic tune filling the air. The women around us hooted and hollered, and Reyna used the distraction to slip away into the crowd.

I stood there for a moment, my body still thrumming with the memory of her closeness. Part of me wanted to follow her, to corner her somewhere private and demand an explanation for the walls she kept building between us. Demand she admit she wanted that kiss to happen again as much as I did. But after a lifetime of having men dictate her every move, I knew I had to give her the space to choose.

Even if it was killing me.

I'd never felt this way about anyone before. It wasn't just desire, though gods knew there was plenty of that. It was something deeper, more consuming. In the short time we'd known each other, Reyna had become essential to me in a way I couldn't fully articulate.

She challenged me, frustrated me, inspired me. She made me question everything I'd ever believed about myself and the world. And despite the danger we were in, despite the uncertain future that lay ahead, I found myself looking forward to each new day with an eagerness I'd never known before.

Because each new day meant another day with Reyna. Another day to learn more about her, to uncover new facets of her strength and her vulnerability. Another day to try to break through those walls she'd built around herself.

Another day to burn for her.

I spotted Reyna across the clearing, standing alone and watching the dancers with a pensive expression. Even from this distance, she took my breath away. The firelight played across her features, highlighting the strength of her jawline, the curve of her cheek, the intensity of her gaze.

As if feeling my eyes on her, she turned, her gaze meeting mine across the crowd. For a long moment, we just looked at each other, the rest of the world fading away. Even at this distance, I could see the conflict in her eyes, the same battle between want and whatever force was holding her back.

Then, slowly, Reyna began to make her way toward me. My heart rate picked up with each step she took, until I thought it might burst from my chest.

When she reached me, we stood in silence for a moment, the air between us thick with unspoken words and unresolved tension.

"Asher," she said finally, her voice soft but strained. "I—"

But whatever she was going to say was interrupted by Thalassa's voice, rising above the crowd. "Come, friends! Let us end the night with a traditional dance of gratitude!"

Reyna hesitated, looking torn between staying with me and joining the others. I could see the relief in her eyes at the interruption, and it stung more than I cared to admit.

"Go on," I said, forcing a smile despite the disappointment that coursed through me at another near miss. "We can talk later."

She nodded, returning my smile with a small, uncertain one of her own. As she turned to join the others, her fingers brushed against mine—whether by accident or design, I couldn't tell. But the brief contact sent electricity shooting through me, and I saw her shiver in response.

I watched her go, my skin tingling where she'd touched me. Whatever was happening between us, whatever this thing was that was growing and evolving with each passing day, I knew she felt it too. The question was whether she would let herself surrender to it, or if she would keep fighting us both.

As I watched Reyna join the dance, her movements graceful and sure, I made a silent vow. I wouldn't push her—I couldn't, knowing her past. But I also wouldn't give up. Whatever was holding her back, whatever walls she'd built around her heart, I would find a way through them.

Because what I felt for her was too powerful, too consuming to ignore. And deep down, beneath all her defenses, I knew she felt it too.

The night stretched on, filled with music and laughter and the warmth of community. And through it all, my eyes never left Reyna, my body burning with need, my heart full of determination for the battle that lay ahead—not just the one to save her sister, but the one to claim her heart.

Even if it took everything I had.

CHAPTER SEVENTEEN
Reyna

The music pulsed through me, a living thing that set my blood on fire and made my body move in ways I'd never imagined. I twirled and swayed, my arms raised to the star-studded sky, feeling lighter than I had in years. Perhaps lighter than I'd ever felt in my entire life.

Some of the women from the village that I'd met grabbed my hands, pulling me into a circle with them, and I let their joy, their freedom, wash over me like soft waves. How magical that they had carved out this safe place for themselves in a world where nowhere was safe for a woman. But here... here they were free. Here I was free.

Free while Cassia suffers in captivity.

The thought hit me like a splash of cold water, but I pushed it away. Just for tonight. Just this once, I would let myself feel this lightness.

As I spun around once again, my eyes landed on Asher. He was leaning against a tree at the edge of the clearing, a cup of fermented berry juice in his hand, watching me with an intensity that made my skin tingle. The firelight played across his features, accentuating the strong line of his jaw, the curve of his lips. He looked impossibly handsome, and for a moment, I forgot how to breathe.

Don't. Don't go to him. You know what happens when you get close.

But without conscious thought, I found myself moving toward him anyway, drawn by an invisible force I couldn't resist even if I'd wanted to. It seemed my need to be near him grew with every moment we spent together, and even the small distance between us now seemed too much. As I approached, Asher straightened, his eyes never leaving mine.

"Having fun?" he asked, a smile playing at the corners of his mouth.

I nodded, suddenly breathless. "I can't remember the last time I danced like this. Or if I ever have."

Asher's smile widened. "I know what you mean. In the Kingsguard, there wasn't much time for... frivolity."

"And in the Warhold, every moment was about training, about being ready for the next battle." I leaned against the tree next to him, our shoulders almost touching. The brief contact sent electricity through me, and I had to fight the urge to lean closer. "I never realized how much I was missing."

We stood in comfortable silence for a moment, watching the dancers around the fire. The joy on their faces, the freedom in their movements—it was intoxicating.

"It would be so easy to stay here," I murmured, more to myself than to Asher. "To just... forget about everything else."

But even as the words left my mouth, I felt a familiar weight settle over me. Cassia's face flashed in my mind—her bright smile, her infectious laugh. And then I imagined her as a wife, as a breeder, that light in her eyes extinguished forever.

Guilt crashed over me in waves. How could I be here, feeling this happiness, this freedom, while my sister was trapped? How could I have chosen to stay here with a man—even *this* man who had given up everything to give me a chance at winning her freedom—when every moment I delayed was another moment bringing her closer to a lifetime of suffering?

Asher must have sensed the change in my mood. He turned to me, his eyes soft with understanding. "Hey," he said gently, "I know what you're thinking. But there's nothing you can do tonight,

Reyna. For once in your life, can you just... let go? Have fun for once?"

I looked up at him, ready to argue, to insist that every moment I wasn't working toward saving Cassia was a moment wasted. But something in his eyes stopped me. Something warm and understanding and... dangerous.

You can't save her tonight. It's okay to just... breathe. Be happy. Just for one night.

"Okay," I said finally, the word slipping out before I could stop it. "One night."

Asher's face lit up with a smile that took my breath away. He set down his cup and held out his hand to me. "In that case, my lady, may I have this dance?"

I stared at his outstretched hand, knowing I should refuse. Knowing that every step closer to him was a step further from my purpose. But the fermented berries had loosened my resolve, and his smile was so warm, so inviting...

Slowly, I reached out, and the moment my fingers slid into his, that charged electricity crackled straight through me, a rush warming every inch of my body as his fingers closed around mine.

He stared at me, that look of want heating up in those eyes. A look I knew I mirrored back at him despite by best efforts to control my desires burning like wildfire.

With a crooked smile, he tugged me behind him, leading me back to the dancing crowd. A chill ran through me at his touch. His hand was warm and strong, callused from years of swordplay, yet gentler than I'd ever imagined a man's hand could be.

We reached the edge of the dancers, and Asher pulled me close, one hand on my waist, the other still holding mine. For a moment, I tensed, such strangeness to be so close to a man, but as we began to move to the music, I felt myself relax into his embrace despite every warning voice in my head.

It felt... right. Safe. As if I'd found a piece of myself I didn't know was missing.

Wrong. This is wrong. You have a mission. A sister to save.

But the voice in my head—the one forged in blood and duty—was drowned out by the thrum of my heart, the warmth of his hands, the way his eyes stripped me bare and didn't flinch.

For the first time in my life, I wasn't a soldier. I wasn't a symbol. I wasn't a blade to be wielded.

I was just... Reyna. A woman. A woman unraveling in the arms of the man sent to destroy her.

And gods help me, I didn't want to resist.

Because here, beneath the stars, there were no chains. No crowns. No kingdoms dictating who I had to be. Just him. Just me. Just this dizzy, dangerous gravity between us.

He wasn't my enemy tonight—the man sworn to claim my head.

And I wasn't the warrior determined to destroy him.

I was just a woman with desires for a man I couldn't deny.

Didn't *want* to deny.

And maybe this desire burning like wildfire for him would consume me.

Destroy me.

Maybe letting go would cost me everything.

But for one stolen heartbeat, I let myself fall—into the fire, into his arms, into the only place I'd ever felt truly safe.

We danced for what felt like hours, sometimes wild and energetic, other times slow and intimate. Through it all, Asher never let me go, his touch a constant anchor that kept me grounded even as the music and the dancing made my head spin.

With each song, each step, I felt my carefully constructed walls crumbling. The warrior, the mission-focused leader—she was fading away, replaced by something softer, more vulnerable. It terrified me as much as it thrilled me.

As a slower song began, Asher pulled me closer. I rested my head on his chest, listening to the steady beat of his heart. I breathed in his masculine scent, feeling more at peace than I had in my life.

Peace. While Cassia knows no peace at all.

I tried to summon the guilt, the anger at myself for this distraction, but Asher's warmth, his solid presence, seemed to chase away everything but this moment.

I looked up at him, and the world seemed to stop. His eyes, usually a clear blue like a cloudless sky, were dark with an emotion I'd never seen before but that made heat pool in my belly. His gaze dropped to my lips, and I found myself leaning up, drawn by that invisible force that kept pulling me to him.

Closer... *closer.*

Our lips met, and even though we'd kissed once before, it still amazed me how such a simple thing such as touching lips together could transcend the whole world. Soft and gentle at first, then growing in intensity as years of pent-up longing and desire poured out of us both. It was as if he'd been waiting for permission to unleash his powerful emotions on me, and the moment my lips touched his, the floodgates broke free. Asher's hand came up to cup my face, his touch reverent, as if I were something precious and fragile. Then it gripped me tightly, and his tongue moved into my mouth, the force of his kiss causing an intoxicating blend of pleasure and pain.

I moaned into his mouth as he pulled me tight against him, my need growing with each sweep of his tongue against mine. I became unaware of anything and anyone around us, the world fading into fog as I lost myself in his kiss, in his touch. My body pressing against him in a need I didn't understand, but instinctually knowing he was the only thing that could ease the ache growing inside of me. He spun me around behind a tree, pressing my back into the bark with such strength it forced the breath from my lungs. I clutched the hard muscles of his back, gripping him tightly as I threaded my fingers into his hair.

"Reyna," he moaned into my mouth, and I caught the words with my tongue.

The music grew louder, and it seemed to match the thumping of my heart against my chest. I reached down and slid my hand along his torso, my fingers tracing the carved muscles of his stomach.

"Gods, Reyna," he breathed, his body tensing to my touch.

For a moment I wasn't sure if he was tensing because he enjoyed the touch or because he didn't, but the way his kiss deepened gave me my answer. I continued my exploration of his body, my fingers greedy as I stroked over the swell of his chest, moving back down to the flat planes of his stomach, stopping just at the top of his pants.

Asher pulled back, and when I looked into his eyes, I saw a fierce passion that reflected my own. A need that could only be quenched in the body of the other.

He smiled, his thumb tracing the curve of my cheek. He glanced around, seeming to suddenly remember where we were. "Come with me," he said, taking my hand once more.

I hesitated, my last thread of rationality screaming at me to refuse. To go back to the celebration, to focus on what mattered and not get distracted by the lips I wanted to kiss again and again. But the heat in his eyes, the way my body sang at his touch...

"Lead the way," I whispered, sealing my fate as if I'd launched off a cliff headfirst and had no cares on the aftermath of when I'd eventually hit the ground.

I let him lead me away from the celebration, into the quiet of the forest. The sounds of music and laughter faded, replaced by the gentle rustling of leaves and the distant murmur of the river.

With every step away from the safety of the crowd, my heart pounded harder. Part of me wanted to turn back, to stop my treacherous feet from leading me away from the mission-focused woman I'd always been. But a larger part—a part I was only beginning to understand—craved whatever awaited us alone in the darkness.

After a few minutes of walking, we emerged into a small clearing. I gasped at the sight before me. A natural pool, fed by a small waterfall, glimmered in the moonlight. Fireflies danced above the water, their soft light reflecting off the surface like fallen stars.

"It's beautiful," I breathed.

"Not as beautiful as you," Asher said, and when I turned to look at him, the intensity in his gaze took my breath away.

He stepped closer, his hand coming up to cup my face once more. "Reyna," he murmured, my name a caress on his lips.

Last chance. Last chance to remember who you are and why you're here.

But those words faded from my mind like the last gasps of breath of a dying warrior, my desire for him drowning out everything else—duty, fear, the voice that had kept me alive for so long. For just this one perfect, stolen moment, there was only him.

In answer, I rose up on my toes, pressing my lips to his. This kiss was different from before—even deeper, more urgent, like I was trying to pour my very soul into him. Asher's arms wrapped around me, pulling me flush against him, and I melted into his embrace.

My hands found their way into his hair, marveling at its softness. Asher groaned, the sound sending a shiver down my spine.

His tongue traced the seam of my lips, asking for entrance, and I opened to him willingly.

As our tongues met, I felt as if I were falling and flying at the same time. Every nerve in my body sang with pleasure, with a need I'd never known before. I pressed closer, wanting—*needing*—to eliminate any space between us.

Asher's hands roamed my back, leaving trails of fire in their wake. When they slipped under the hem of my shirt, touching bare skin, I gasped into his mouth.

He pulled back immediately, concern replacing the desire in his eyes. "I'm sorry," he said, his voice rough. "I got carried away. We don't have to—"

I silenced him with another kiss, pouring all my longing, all my newfound desire into it. When I broke us apart, I met his gaze steadily. "I want this," I said. "I want you."

The look of awe on Asher's face made my heart swell. "Are you sure?" he asked, his thumb tracing the deep scar across my face. "We can wait, if you're not ready."

All my life I'd only heard that breeding men was a duty a wife must endure. The only pleasures I'd heard of had been women in the Warhold finding pleasure in each other. But here, now, in his embrace, I instinctively knew that pleasure deeper than anything I'd ever imagined was waiting for me in his touch.

I shook my head. "I've never been more sure of anything in my life."

With a groan, Asher captured my lips once more. This kiss was passionate, all-consuming, and I lost myself in it completely. His hands returned to my skin, and this time I arched into his touch, craving more.

Slowly, reverently, Asher began to undress me. He paused after each piece of clothing removed, his eyes asking for permission to continue. I nodded each time, my breath catching at the look of adoration on his face as more of my skin was revealed.

When I stood before him, bare and vulnerable, I expected to feel exposed and uncomfortable. But the way Asher looked at me, like I was the most beautiful thing he'd ever seen, made me feel powerful in a way I'd never experienced before. I didn't feel like a possession as men considered women. I felt... cherished.

"You're perfect," Asher breathed, his eyes roaming my body with a hunger that made heat pool between my legs.

I reached for him then, my fingers fumbling with the laces of his shirt. Asher helped me, and I bit my lip as his shirt came off, exposing his smooth skin. I took a moment to admire him—the broad planes of his chest, the defined muscles of his abdomen, the trail of dark hair that led lower. He was beautiful, and for a moment I couldn't believe that this man, this warrior, wanted me as much as I wanted him.

Asher pulled me close once more, and I gasped at the feeling of skin on skin. He kissed me deeply, then trailed his lips along my jaw, down my neck. Each press of his lips sent sparks through my body, igniting a fire I'd never known existed within me.

We sank to the ground together, the soft grass cool against my heated skin. Asher hovered over me, his weight supported on his forearms. "Are you sure?" he asked again, his voice strained with the effort of holding back.

In answer, I pulled him down to me, kissing him with all the passion I felt. Asher groaned, his control finally snapping. His hands and mouth explored my body, finding places I never knew could bring such pleasure. I wasn't idle either, my own hands mapping the contours of his body, reveling in the way he shuddered at my touch.

His lips moved to my neck, then drifted lower to my breasts. His hands, rough but warm, cupped them and lifted them to his mouth. As his tongue flickered across my stiffened nipple, I gasped. He looked up at me, his eyes flickering with passion as he took it between his lips, giving it a gentle nibble.

"Asher," I breathed out, arching my back to push myself deeper into his mouth.

He followed my lead, his lips and teeth working harder on my sensitive skin. It felt like every nerve in my body joined between my legs with the need building up between them. And as if he could read my mind and my body, while his tongue continued circling my nipple, his fingers made a soft trail down my stomach to the wet skin between my legs.

He brushed his fingers down the length of me, and I whimpered when he touched the little swollen bud between my legs.

"Oh, Gods," I breathed out, my knees falling open to give him better access.

My words and my moans encouraged him on, and he moved his fingers against me, sliding up and down over my sensitive spot over and over before a finger slipped inside of me.

I gasped, and he paused, his eyes lifting to meet mine as if searching for permission. I gave it with a breathless nod, before collapsing back into the grass, my body vibrating with need as he began moving in and out of me. I pressed my hips against him, grinding against his hand trying to extinguish the ache and the heat I'd never experienced before.

His mouth left my breast, and the cool air, a stark contrast to his warm breath, brushed across my nipple, causing it to stiffen in a mix of pleasure and pain. I opened my eyes, glancing down my body to watch him kissing his way to my stomach, my hips, my thighs, and finally, with his eyes lifting to meet mine, he kissed me between my legs where I needed him most.

The pleasure of his tongue against me caused my body to shudder, and I whimpered as I collapsed backwards, my eyes slamming shut as it felt like the world spun beneath me. He pressed my legs open wider with his shoulders, settling between them as his tongue gave me the tantalizing attention he'd given my nipples. Soft circles, gentle flicks, each movement making me moan and cry, shudder with need and desire. The pleasure mounted as I writhed in the grass, my hips moving in rhythm with his fingers thrusting inside of me as his tongue worked against my most sensitive spot.

"Oh, Asher!" I cried out as I felt every muscle in my body tighten, a wave of pleasure building, building, building, as it pulled me up to the top with it, holding me there as the breath trapped in my lungs, my eyes squeezing shut while I waited for the release. Finally, with a cry, he took me over the edge, and my body shuddered and trembled as wave after wave of ecstasy washed over me. His touch lightened as he remained between my legs before slowly kissing his way back up my body.

I lay panting below him, sensations I'd never known still causing me to struggle for my next breath. Then when I opened my eyes to see his beautiful ones staring down at me, I struggled to breathe once again.

I swallowed hard, my mouth dry as I tried to form words. But instead, nothing came out and I just reached up, slid my hand behind his head and pulled his lips against mine.

"Reyna," he whispered against my mouth.

I kissed him deeper, my hands moving to the small of his back and drawing him against me. His hard cock pressed into my hip, and he moaned.

"Fuck," he breathed, as he slid it against me, slipping the length of it against the wetness between my legs.

"Are you sure?" he asked, his cock sliding against my entrance but not going in.

Though I didn't even know what I was agreeing to, having only heard horror stories about what pain men caused women, my gut, my instincts, that things would be different with Asher came pouring out in one word. "Yes."

He held my gaze as he pushed inside of me with one firm thrust. There was a flash of resistance, of pain, but then when we finally joined, it was with a tenderness that brought tears to my eyes. Asher moved slowly, carefully, always watching my face for any sign of discomfort. But there was no pain, only a fullness, a rightness that I'd never known before.

We moved together, finding a rhythm as natural as breathing. I'd always thought of intimacy as something clinical, a duty to be performed. I'd never imagined it could be like this—a dance, a conversation without words, a merging of bodies and souls.

As the pleasure built, I clung to Asher, overwhelmed by the intensity of what I was feeling. Between kisses both soft and passionate, he whispered words of encouragement, of adoration, his voice rough with emotion. When I finally peaked again, it was with Asher's name on my lips, my body arching into his as waves of ecstasy washed over me.

Asher followed soon after, burying his face in my neck as he pulled out then shuddered above me. For a long moment, we lay there, our hearts beating in tandem.

Finally, Asher rolled to the side, gathering me into his arms. I rested my head on his chest, listening to the steady thump of his heartbeat as it slowly returned to normal.

"Are you okay?" Asher asked softly, his hand tracing patterns on my back.

I nodded, not trusting my voice just yet. I felt... different. Changed in some fundamental way I couldn't quite articulate.

"I never knew it could be like that," I said finally, my voice barely above a whisper.

Asher pressed a kiss to the top of my head. "Neither did I," he admitted. "Reyna, I—"

But whatever he was going to say was cut off by a distant shout. We both tensed, years of training kicking in. Then the shouts turned to laughter and we both slumped back into each other's arms.

"Even though it's safe here, I don't think I'll ever feel that. Safe, I mean," I said.

Asher stroked the hair from my face. "You're safe with me, Reyna. Always."

Though I was a warrior, a woman capable of slicing through flesh and steel, getting to feel safe and protected in his arms was something that meant more to me than anything. For the first time in my life, I let myself be vulnerable, let someone see all of me—not just the warrior, but the woman beneath. And instead of feeling weak, I felt stronger than ever.

But as we lay there listening to the soft lapping of the water and sounds of the forest, reality began to seep back in. The contentment I felt in his arms warred with the growing voice of guilt and responsibility.

This was selfish. While you found pleasure, Cassia learned submission.

I tried to push the thoughts away, to hold onto this moment of peace, but they grew stronger with each passing second.

"I could just stay here with you in my arms forever," Asher whispered, pulling me closer, kissing my forehead and filling me with a warmth that made my heart soar.

But as I sank deeper into his embrace, I felt something crack inside my chest.

Stay here with you in my arms forever.

Those words, as beautiful as they were, as right as they felt, were impossible. This peace. This safety. It was built on borrowed time and my sister's suffering.

It wasn't real.

None of this could be real. Not while my sister suffered.

How could I know such beauty, such safety, when she prepared for a life of unimaginable torment?

I buried my face deeper into Asher's chest, breathing in his scent, memorizing the feel of his arms around me. Because this perfect moment was just that... a moment. Tomorrow, I would have to remember who I was and why I was here.

Tonight had been a gift. A glimpse of something I'd never known I wanted.

But it couldn't distract me from my mission.

Cassia.

Because I could never be free until she was free.

Until they were *all* free to live as I'd just lived.

Be safe as I'd been safe.

To have found peace like I'd never known in the arms of this man who should have been my undoing.

The truth settled over me like a shroud, and I closed my eyes, trying to hold onto the last moments of this stolen peace before the inevitable dawn brought me back to reality.

CHAPTER EIGHTEEN
Asher

I awoke in the morning to Reyna's warm body curled against mine. For a moment, I simply lay there, savoring the feeling of her in my arms, the quiet sound of her breathing, the scent of her hair.

Last night had been... incredible. More than incredible. It had been a revelation. I'd known Reyna was strong, fierce, unstoppable on the battlefield, but to see her soft, vulnerable side, to be allowed to touch her, to cherish her... it was a privilege I never thought I'd have.

As if sensing my thoughts, Reyna stirred, her eyes fluttering open. When she saw me watching her, a smile spread across her face, softer and sweeter than any I'd seen before.

"Good morning," she murmured, stretching languidly against me.

I couldn't resist leaning down to kiss her, marveling at how natural it felt. "Good morning," I replied when we finally parted. "Sleep well?"

Reyna nodded, her fingers tracing patterns on my chest. "Better than I have in years," she admitted. "I feel... safe here. With you."

My heart swelled at her words. "I feel the same," I said softly.

She snuggled up against me, and the way she sighed contentedly sent a warmth flooding through me.

"I could get used to this you know." I kissed the top of her head.

"To what?" she asked, coyly.

"To waking up with you every morning." I kissed her head again, my hand drifting down and tracing the outline of her breast. "To touching you here whenever I want." I smiled against her hair, and she sighed. My fingers started to drift lower, tracing the soft skin of her stomach. "To tasting you there every night."

"Oh, yeah?" she asked, her voice practically purring.

"Mmmhmm," I murmured, my cock already starting to rise in anticipation of what I hoped was next.

"Just you and me here in this little hut for eternity. That's what I want. Other than popping our heads out to eat and bathe, I don't see any reason to leave this bed." My fingers drifted lower, just above the soft curls of hair between her legs.

But before I could reach her sweet spot, a shadow passed over her face. "Asher," she said, her voice tight with sudden tension. "You know I can't stay here."

I sighed, the bubble of contentment bursting. "I know," I said. "But can't we just... stay here for a while? Enjoy this peace we've found?"

Reyna sat up, the blanket pooling around her waist. Even now, I couldn't help but admire the strength of her body paired with the soft, feminine curves of her breasts and her waist. "We can't," she said firmly. "Cassia. We can't just stay here. We need to free her." She paused, and I saw a dark determination cloud her features. "In fact, we need to free them all."

My eyes went wide as I sat up beside her. "What do you mean we need to free them all?"

"Last night as I watched these women living wild and free, as I lived wild and free myself, I realized how selfish it would be if I just save Cassia and leave the rest to languish. Jaila. My swordsisters. All the women trapped in the grips of cruel men. I don't just want to stop with Cassia. I want to free them all."

"You can't be serious," I said, a laugh stirring in my chest with the absurdity of her words. "That's... impossible, Reyna."

"It can't be impossible, Asher. I... I think I have a plan."

I held up my hand, stopping her before she could go on. "I agreed to help you save Cassia. And I will, even though it's likely certain death for us both. But if you think I'm going to watch you try to upend an entire kingdom and *guarantee* your demise, you've gone insane. This is madness to even speak of it."

"But Asher," she started, and I just shook my head.

"Reyna, it's too early to be arguing about this. Can we just... talk about it later when you're thinking more clearly?"

Her eyes flashed with anger at my words. "I *am* thinking about it clearly. I want to save them *all*."

I sighed, running a hand down the back of my neck as I considered my next words carefully. Though I appreciated her desire to end the cruelty I agreed needed to cease, there was no way she could ever accomplish it. No way one woman and one man could erase centuries of tradition, cut through thousands of soldiers, and change the entire fabric of our kingdom. So instead of arguing against her knowing there was no way this plan could ever come to fruition, I let her win this battle so she could believe in her dream a little longer before the reality sank in that there was nothing she could do to save them all. We could save Cassia, at best.

"I need to talk to Thalassa," she said, starting to rise. "I have a plan."

I quickly caught her arm, gently stopping her. "Okay, okay. We will," I said quickly. "But maybe we could just enjoy this morning together before we go make plans to die in an almost impossible attempt to save every woman in the kingdom?"

She smirked, and I saw the fire blaze in her eyes prepared to battle me until she got her way, but instead she just gave me a little nod.

"Fine. But we'll talk to her soon."

Glad I'd bought myself some time to get her to think with a cooler head, my thoughts returned to wanting to lay her back down on the cot and spread her legs open once again, but all the voices outside our little thatched hut gave me pause.

"Sounds like the whole village is awake. Maybe we should go out and get some food," she said.

As I looked at her sitting on the bed, those beautiful eyes staring back into mine, my desire for her overrode my hesitations about fucking her while the entire village passed by.

"I'm hungry for something else," I said, and when I saw the same desire ignite in her eyes, despite the commotion happening around us, my cock immediately sprang to life.

With a grin, I rolled over, grabbing her by the knees and pressing her legs open. She squealed with playful delight, but I lifted my finger to my mouth to remind her to be quiet, nodding to the movement and voices just outside our hut. She bit her lip, her eyes igniting with that heat as she nodded her understanding.

I looked down at the wet, pink skin between her legs, and my cock throbbed desperate to be back inside of her. But she'd only known men to bring her pain and suffering in her life, and I vowed to make sure she understood just how much pleasure I could bring as well.

She watched me with hooded eyes as I knelt down between her legs, my fingers parting her flesh as I rubbed her with my thumb. She started to whimper, but I playfully silenced her with a slight shake of my head. Watching her struggle to suppress her sounds only increased my own arousal. Her breaths quickened as I worked her with my fingers, enjoying the sight of her glistening skin growing slicker by the minute. I dipped a finger inside her, first one, then two, and she pushed herself against me, a needy thrusting of her hips that brought her closer to my mouth.

I accepted the invitation, reaching out my tongue and tasting the warmth of her heat. A small cry escaped her lips, but she cupped her hand over her mouth, and I smiled as I watched from between her legs as she struggled to stay quiet. Her hips moved faster, and I followed her lead, my tongue working quicker against her as my fingers moved in and out, pressing deep inside her to fill her need as I felt her tightening around me.

Suddenly, she shuddered as I licked her, my fingers deep within. Her cries muffled in the nook of her arm brought a smile to my face knowing how much pleasure I'd brought her. When I felt her finish, she looked up at me, eyes half closed and face soft and satiated. I grinned a triumphant smile then grabbed her behind the knees and pushed myself between them. Holding her gaze and seeing the invitation in it, I pressed the tip of my cock to her wet entrance. I was so aroused the light touch nearly sent me spilling myself onto her already. But I fought the urge and instead I thrust myself deep inside of her.

She gasped, and I suppressed my own groan. Silently, while women and children laughed and rushed past our little hut in the village unaware of what was happening inside, I sank myself deep inside of her. I kept her legs pressed open wide, looking down between them and marveling at the sight of my cock sheathed inside of her, watching as she moved her hips with need while I pressed myself in and out of her.

She started to whimper, so I leaned forward and closed her mouth with a kiss. Thrust after thrust, I struggled to keep from grunting and groaning, announcing our interlude to the world around us. The need to be quiet only heightened my pleasure, and soon I couldn't contain the need for my own release.

"Reyna," I moaned into her mouth as I pumped inside her again.

"Asher," she breathed back, her fingers digging into the flesh on my back, her body tightening I felt her body grip tight around my cock, the pulsing of her entrance pulling me over the edge with her. I pulled out just in time, my seed spilling onto her stomach as I swallowed down the guttural moan I wanted to roar. When I finished, I collapsed beside her.

"If this is how we end arguments, then we need to argue more often," I said, catching my breath.

She chuckled, and I reached down and found a small piece of fabric and cleaned her off.

"Why do you?" she gestured to her belly. "You know."

"So I don't get you pregnant," I answered, surprised she didn't know. But then I realized that as formidable as she was on the battlefield, she'd been raised in the Warhold where things like birth control and the realities of sex weren't common knowledge.

"There are things you can take to prevent pregnancy, certain tonics and berries. When we have access to those, I can finish inside of you, which I think we'll both enjoy. But until we get some, I don't want to risk getting you pregnant."

She looked at me, her mind making sense of everything I said.

"It's not that I don't want to have your kids someday. Because I do," I said, surprised with the words coming out of my mouth. I'd never even thought about kids before, but now all I could envision was a life here in these woods with Reyna at my side and a gaggle of children conceived from our love. "But right now, we have to save your sister, and it's going to be difficult to fight with a baby swelling inside your belly. So, I'm just trying to be careful."

"Thank you," she said, smiling softly. "I wouldn't know how these things work, so I'm glad you're being careful for my sake."

"I'll ask Thalassa about a tonic or some berries," I said. "Because as much as I enjoyed that, I can't wait to do it while I'm still inside you."

I grinned and leaned down to kiss her, pausing to enjoy the softness of her lips and the sensation of her touch.

Eventually, we dressed and made our way out to join the rest of the tribe. The village was already bustling with activity, women going about their daily tasks with a cheerfulness that still amazed me.

Thalassa approached us, a warm smile on her face. "Good morning," she said. "I trust you slept well?"

Reyna nodded. "Very well. What a wonderful celebration that was. I've never seen anything like it."

"I imagine you haven't in the Warhold," Thalassa said. "I've heard many stories from women who were raised in the armies. There was no room for dancing and celebration."

Reyna shook her head. "None at all. It was amazing to be part of it and to honor the sacrifice. Thank you for allowing us to join you."

"Of course," Thalassa said. "This is your home now if you want it to be. You are always welcome here and at our celebration.

"I appreciate the offer," Reyna said, but I could see the determination in her eyes. "But Thalassa," she paused, searching "I need to ask you something. I need your help."

Thalassa's smile faded, replaced by a wary expression. "Go on," she said, opening her arm and gesturing for us to come and sit with her on the small bench beneath the swaying branches of the tree on the outskirts of the village.

We settled down beside her, and then Reyna took a deep breath. "I initially escaped so I could be free to go back and save my sister. Something I still intend to do. But last night, seeing all of you free here in this woods, what life can be like for women, I realize I can't stop with just Cassia. All women deserve this freedom. This amazing life denied to us on the day of our birth."

I furrowed my brow, unsure where this conversation was heading but knowing instinctively, I wouldn't like where it ended.

"I used to lead an army, and I've fought countless battles. I am known for my ability to strategize and plot for success" She paused and glanced at me. "Though often it was ignored by the king."

I swallowed knowing how many times I'd had to deliver King Lothaire's ridiculous orders to supersede her brilliant strategy.

"Last night while I lay in bed after such a magical evening, an idea formed in my mind. And if you can help me, I know it can work."

"What do you need? What is this idea?" Thalassa asked, and I too sat wondering what she had concocted in that beautiful brain of hers while I slept holding her in my arms.

"Several times in our history, the Iron Swordmaidens have tried to revolt. To lead an attack against their oppressors. But they have always attempted from inside the Warhold where we are unarmed. Each attempt has ended in failure, with the punishment being severe enough to tamp down any more rebellious ideas for decades."

We listened, and still I wondered where this was heading. A pool of dread settled in my belly when I heard her next words.

"I'm going to build an army." She said the words as if it was such an easy thing to do. "I'm going to build an army big enough to draw out my swordsisters from the Warhold. And with your help, with the strength of your tribe, we could do it. With a large enough threat marching on Ironheart, the entire army will come out. Armed. I will then confront Jaila, my second-in-command, who should be the Iron Rose now, and I know she'll join us and turn her army to march on the king himself. With the two armies combined, ours and theirs fully armed, we could slaughter every man in Ironheart. Every man who has oppressed us. Raped us. Beat us. We can kill them all and free every woman in Ironheart. Then all women can enjoy the same freedom that you have here."

Air turned to stone in my lungs as her words sank in. This wasn't just vengeance talking— words said in anger that she would soon realize was an impossible dream. This was a meticulously crafted strategy for rebellion. I struggled to wrap my head around the horrifying feasibility of it all. If she secured this army, drew out the Iron Swordmaidens and turned them... Gods, I could see it unfolding with military precision.

The cold realization washed over me like ice water: If I chose to stand by her side, the side I never wanted to leave, I might soon stand on a battlefield facing my brothers-in-arms—men I'd trained with, fought beside, broken bread with. Men who didn't believe in this system but were slaves to it none-the-less. Good men. Loyal men.

Men like... Erik.

Her plan was no longer just to sneak in and save her sister. It was to overthrow an entire kingdom, and it would force me to choose between the woman I was falling for and everything—everyone—I'd ever known. If Reyna could somehow enact this dangerous dream of hers, if I chose to remain at her side and fight, I would see Erik again—across the battlefield. The image of my brother, sword in hand, facing me as an enemy, made my stomach churn. Would he honor his Kingsguard vows and go to war against me, or would he turn and fight at my side? The thought of him getting hurt or killed in Reyna's war made me question my loyalties.

With bated breath awaiting her answer, I watched Thalassa's face, seeing the conflict play out in her eyes. But when she spoke, her voice was firm.

"No," she said. "I'm sorry, Reyna, but we've worked too hard for this peace. I can't risk my people in your war."

I had to swallow my sigh of relief so Reyna wouldn't hear it. Though I felt sad for Reyna that her plan was already starting to crumble, the sooner she gave up on it, the sooner we could rescue Cassia and come back here to start our life of peace.

"But don't the other women deserve peace too?" Reyna argued, her voice rising. "Don't they deserve the same freedom you have here?"

Thalassa's expression softened with sympathy, but her resolve didn't waver. "They do," she agreed. "But my obligation is to my people, and my people alone. I can't ask them to die for your cause, no matter how just it might be. We have spent centuries building this sanctuary, and these women, many whom have suffered those same fates, deserve their peace. Most of them aren't warriors, and I won't ask them to risk their lives and their freedom for anything. I'm sorry, Reyna, but I can't help you with this."

"But most wouldn't even need to fight. Just gather a force intimidating enough to draw out my army. The Kingsguard are no match for the Iron Swordmaidens, and once I have them on my side, your people could run for safety."

Thalassa just shook her head again. "It's too risky, Reyna. Not only would they have to leave the safety of our woods, risking exposing our very existence, but what if your army doesn't turn? What if they instead cut every last woman down?"

"Jaila won't allow that to happen. I know it," Reyna said quickly.

But Thalassa, sadness filling her eyes, simply said, "No. It's too risky. I'm sorry."

I saw the disappointment and frustration on Reyna's face, and my heart ached for her. But despite her disappointment, my body flooded with relief. Without Thalassa's support, surely Reyna would see that her plan was impossible. Surely now she'd agree to focus on just rescuing Cassia, on building a life here in the safety of Moonshadow Woods.

A life with me.

But before I could say anything, offer her some comforting words in the face of her disappointment, another voice spoke up.

"I'll help you."

We all turned to see Gaia step forward from behind a hut. Her eyes burned with a fierce determination that reminded me of Reyna.

"Gaia," Thalassa said, her tone cautionary. "Think carefully about what you're offering."

But Gaia shook her head. "I have thought about it," she said. "For years. My family is still out there, Thalassa. My girlfriend is an Iron Swordmaiden, like I was. My blood sisters are breeders. My mother... if she's still alive..." Her voice broke, and she took a moment to compose herself. "I can't sit here in safety anymore while they suffer. I abandoned them when I found sanctuary in these woods. I could have healed from my wounds and gone back to fight beside them, but I was too happy here. I was selfish, and I stayed, leaving them to their fates. The guilt of that decision has torn me apart for the past decade, and now I have a chance to atone for my selfish sin. I need to do something."

Reyna stepped forward, hope blazing in her eyes. "You were an Iron Swordsmaiden?" she asked. "When?"

"Ten years ago." Gaia's gaze drifted off toward the woods. "I was in a battle not far from Moonshadow Woods. I was gravely injured and left for dead. I lay there for over a day just waiting to die, but then bandits came along to pick the bodies for valuables and found me alive." Her eyes clouded with fear and disgust. "They took me with them to use me for..."

She paused, and we didn't need her to finish the sentence we all knew the answer to.

"That night, even though my wounds were severe, and I was barely alive, they got drunk around the fire and one of them came to me. I fought him. Hard." Her jaw clenched. "As hard as I could in my condition anyway. I was able to get away, though barely. I made it into the woods before he caught up to me, and I was in too much pain, too injured, to fight him anymore. As I lay there prepared to accept my fate and hoping death would take me first, a cloakfang appeared beside us. With one swipe of its paw, it sent him flying off me."

"Gaia. That's so awful that happened to you." Reyna reached out a hand and pressed it to her arm. "I'm so glad you were saved."

My stomach lurched thinking about what had almost happened to her... what happened to so many women in the Southlands. Gods men were cruel. Was I wrong in hesitating to get behind her plan? Perhaps Reyna was right, and men needed to be extinguished from the kingdom so women could finally be safe. As I heard Gaia's story, I started to see the anger toward my kind in a new light, but still, I remembered the kindness of many men and knew that though many deserved their ire, there were just as many who were innocent of such cruelty.

"I was saved." Gaia nodded. "I watched that bear eat him alive, paralyzed but still able to feel every shred of his flesh. I reveled in his pain and celebrated his last breath. That's when Thalassa appeared and brought me back here, nursing me back to health."

She and Thalassa shared a smile.

"She was badly injured," Thalassa said. "I didn't know if she was going to make it."

"But I did make it," Gaia said. "And I healed for months until I was finally strong enough that I could have left. Could have gone back to the Warhold and helped fight with my swordsisters. Been there for them. But instead, I chose the easy way, and I stayed here and left them."

"You chose peace," Thalassa said, her voice comforting. "All you would have done is go back to die beside them if you'd left."

"But at least I would have been beside them," Gaia said, and I saw the pain in her expression. "I was a swordsister, sworn to protect each other. And I just left them to their fate and have lived here happily ever since while they suffered. I understand why Reyna can't stay, and I envy her for having the strength to walk away from this paradise when I couldn't. Because if she chooses my path and forgoes her beliefs to choose this easy life, the guilt will tear her apart from the inside. It has for me."

"I'm sorry you're feeling guilty," Reyna said. "And you're right. I know if I don't go back and do everything I can to free them, I'll never forgive myself. Even if it gets me killed, I'll die fighting for what I believe."

My heart stalled out thinking about her death. Thinking about my life without her.

"I want to get back there and tell Lorna I'm sorry. Free her. Beg my love's forgiveness for not returning to her and bring her here and start a life with her. I want to find my sisters and my mother and free them as well. And I'll die trying." Gaia lifted her chin. "I'm done hiding. I want to fight with you, Rebel Rose."

Reyna's face froze, and I saw a flash of deep pain in her eyes. "Did you say Lorna was your girlfriend?"

Gaia's face lit up. "Yes. She's my love, and I've never forgiven myself for abandoning her. Do you know her? Is she... is she still alive?"

As Gaia's eyes searched Reyna's, filled with hope, I saw sadness returned in Reyna's gaze.

"I'm so sorry, Gaia. She fell in the battle against Stormspire just weeks ago. She died bravely, protecting her sisters. She was a strong and courageous woman, and I was honored to have fought beside her. I'm so sorry," she said softly.

Gaia let out a strangled sob, her knees buckling. I moved to catch her, but Reyna was faster, wrapping her arms around the devastated woman.

"I should have been there," Gaia wept. "It was so peaceful here, so safe... I never went back. I've felt guilty every day since, wondering what happened to her, to all of them. Maybe if I'd gone back, I could have been there to save her. And now..."

As I watched Gaia fall apart in Reyna's arms, that nagging feeling that I was wrong and they were right chewed apart my insides. Seeing how much pain men had caused them, pain *I'd* caused since I was the one who'd brought the order that had gotten so many women killed in that battle. I'd known it was foolish, and I'd known Reyna's plan was better. But yet I'd followed my king's orders, and now I saw the harsh reality of that decision even clearer. Lorna had lost her life because I hadn't stood up for them, and Gaia had lost her love.

After Reyna held her for a while, she softly said, "I'm so sorry you lost her. But now you can help us save the others," Reyna said fiercely. "You can honor Lorna's memory by fighting the men who sent her to die for them."

Gaia nodded, wiping her eyes. "Yes," she said. "Yes, I will. And I know others who might join us too. There are other swordsisters from more kingdoms here. Let me talk to them. If they agree, we'll march with you."

"I cannot stop any of you from going," Thalassa cut in. "But I want you all to think about what you're giving up if you go. You could be marching those women straight to their deaths when they could live a long, happy life right here."

"I know that," Reyna said, firmly. "And I don't take that lightly. But if any woman feels the way I do about justice for those still enslaved, feels guilt for being here enjoying this freedom while others suffer, then they can choose to follow me if they want. I won't force anyone, and I just ask that you not stand in their way if they choose to come."

Thalassa stared at her for a long moment and then gave a soft nod of her head, an understanding between the two women. Then

Thalassa walked away, and I could sense her quiet concern at the dangers heading toward her peaceful community.

As Reyna thanked Gaia profusely and the two of them joined in their cause, my heart sank like a stone cast into the ocean. Instead of realizing the impossibility of this plan and abandoning it for one with reason, Reyna's impossible dream was gaining traction, and I could see the fire of determination burning even brighter in her eyes.

How could I make her see reason? How could I convince her that this path would only lead to more bloodshed, more pain? That the men she wanted to slaughter weren't all evil, that many of them were my friends, my brothers-in-arms? Or was I wrong, and these women had every right to demand the lives of every one of us that had harmed them... failed them?

But I thought of Erik, of the other good men I knew in the Kingsguard. Men who were kind to their wives, who treated the women of the kingdom with as much respect as they were allowed. Men who, like me, had been born into a system they didn't create and were just trying to survive. The thought of them dying at Reyna's hand made me feel physically ill.

No. Though their pain and suffering was vast and their anger warranted, I couldn't... wouldn't... stand aside and let them slaughter every man that crossed their paths or get themselves killed in the process. But as I watched Reyna comforting Gaia, saw the passion and conviction in her eyes, I realized something that terrified me even more: she wouldn't stop. No matter what I said, no matter how impossible the odds, Reyna would keep fighting for her cause until she succeeded... or until it killed her.

And I couldn't live without her. The realization hit me like a battering ram to the gut. In the short time we'd known each other, Reyna had become as essential to me as breathing. The thought of losing her, of watching her throw her life away in a futile quest for vengeance, was unbearable.

I had to find a way to convince her. To show her that there was another path, one that didn't require the slaughter of many innocents. One that would allow us to save Cassia, to free as many women as we could, without destroying everything in our path.

But how? How could I reach her when she was so consumed by her rage, her pain?

"Don't worry, Gaia. Together we will get justice for Lorna and all the other women who have died and suffered at the hands of men. Go talk to the others and see if anyone else wants to join our cause."

Gaia wiped her tears, and the pain and sadness on her face transformed to match the same rage I often saw on Reyna's.

"I will, Rebel Rose. You have my sword."

"Iron in our blood." Reyna started their mantra.

Gaia's eyes narrowed. "Iron in our bones."

They locked arms, and with a firm grip, they parted. Gaia marched away to gather more fighters for Reyna's cause.

As if sensing my turmoil, Reyna looked up, her eyes meeting mine. For a moment, I saw a flicker of doubt, of vulnerability. Then it was gone, replaced by that steely determination I both loved and feared.

She made her way over to me, slipping her hand into mine. "What's wrong?" she asked softly.

"You really need to ask that?" Anger flared in my chest, hot and sudden.

She looked away. "It's what I must do. I'm sorry if it's hard for you to understand."

"Reyna, you can't plan to kill every man in Ironhold. Not only is that an impossible task, and one certain to get you killed, but just because some are bad, there are plenty of innocent men that don't deserve your sword in their gullet," he protested.

A bitter laugh escaped her. "Please. An innocent man? Other than you, I've never met a man worthy of anything other than my sword. They are vile, cruel, selfish and they've treated women worse than the shite on the bottom of their boots. We're raped, beaten, humiliated, forced to fight and die at their pleasure. Men have controlled us long enough, and now I am going to find a way to exact my justice and slaughter them one man at a time until none are left to *ever* control us again. And when I succeed, you can be relieved that it's going to be very hard for the king to take your head for this betrayal when I'm holding his in my hands." She grinned.

"So your plan is to slaughter every man in the kingdom?" My voice had hardened. "Even those who've never harmed a woman? Even boys who've yet to become men? Would you kill Erik? My brother?"

She didn't answer, and I took the small opening to try to reason with her. To point the sharp tip of her vengeance away from the ones who didn't deserve it.

"Revolution doesn't have to mean genocide," I argued. "Change can come without wholesale slaughter."

"Easy words from someone who's never been on the receiving end of the system's cruelty," she shot back.

"And what about me?" I challenged. "Do I deserve death too? Having served the king faithfully for years? Having followed orders that sent women to their deaths? Orders I gave *you?*"

She fell silent, unsure how to answer.

I ran a hand through my hair in frustration. "Reyna, I understand your desire to save them. But your plan... it's too risky. Too many innocents could be hurt or killed."

Her eyes flashed with anger. "Innocents? What innocents, Asher? Are you referring to the *men* again? My whole life, men have treated me and my sisters like property. We've been violated, tortured, used as disposable fodder in their wars. They don't deserve to live."

I flinched at the vehemence in her voice but pressed on. "Many of them are just as much prisoners of the system as you were," I argued. "They'll be beheaded if they disobey orders. Should they be punished for the circumstance of their birth? For being born into a society they didn't choose?"

For a moment, I saw doubt flicker in Reyna's eyes. But then her jaw set, her expression hardening. "They made their choice when they decided to follow those orders," she said. "When they stood by and watched us suffer."

"You hated me once," I reminded her. "And I'm not so bad, am I? Or am I just a means to an end for you?"

Those words seemed to get through to her. Reyna's face softened, and she reached out to cup my cheek. "No," she said softly. "Of course not."

"I swore to help you save your sister, a vow I did not make lightly. But you can't expect me to march against my friends. My own brother!"

"And you can't expect me to choose you over my sister! My swordsisters! Whatever this is between us," she said, pausing to gesture toward our chests, "I can't let it stop me from my mission. I won't let you deter me, Asher. I can't."

Her pointed, callus words cut me deeper than a sword to the gut.

I couldn't hide the pain that flashed through my eyes. "I see. So you're just going to ignore everything happening between us, everything you've learned about me and men, and just head down this path of vengeance. I vowed to help you save your sister, but I didn't vow to help you destroy good men like my brother."

"Then I relieve you from your vow. You do not need to follow me down this path. You're a man. You can start your life over somewhere else. But me? I can't stop, I won't stop, until all the women of Ironhold get to experience the freedom I felt last night."

Her words hit me like a slap to the face. "How the fuck can you even say that?" I growled, my voice low and dangerous. "You want me to go? To leave you? Are you so blinded by your own rage that you can't even see what's right in front of your face? Can't see how I feel about you? Can't see that I can't even breathe thinking about losing you? Can't understand that your plan is doomed and you're probably going to die?"

"So then I die!" She spat back.

"And then your sister gets stuck as the king's whore!"

Her anger flashed to fear for only a moment then it slipped back behind the mask of rage she wore so well. "I won't fail!"

"Or we can go and save Cassia. Together. We have a far greater chance at succeeding than an all-out revolution. We can bring her here to live a happy, safe life. With us. There is no reason for you to die trying to fight a war with an entire fucking kingdom, Reyna! And a war that threatens to kill my brother!"

"If he stands against us to protect his vicious king, then he deserves his fate."

I ran my hands through my hair, grasping it in pure frustration. "You know how you love your sister? How you'll do anything for her? You know how I've vowed to help you rescue her because she's important to you? Can you even *try* to comprehend that I love my brother that much too? How is it that you expect me to throw away my entire fucking life to save yours and then march on my own fucking brother to save your sister? Has it even occurred to you how selfish you're being? How narrow-minded and cruel?" I snorted, a maniacal laugh starting in my chest. "At this point, I may as well just call you King Reyna because that's what you're behaving like. Acting like someone's sex determines their worth and not the individual person."

"I am not like King Lothaire!" she spat back.

"But aren't you? He thinks all women are slaves. You think all men should die. Neither of you are looking past what sex someone is born with." I drew my sword from my belt, flipping it to show her the hilt. "You want all men dead? I'm a man. Here. Take it. Kill me now."

"Asher," she warned, her eyes still flaming with anger, but now I could also see her confusion.

"Go on, Reyna. Kill the big, bad man. And while you're at it, there are some men over there in the village. Better slaughter them too. And the little boys. Better drop them now before they grow up. Go on, Reyna. Have at it."

She stared at my extended hand, and her mouth opened to argue but then finally, *finally*, I saw reason start flickering in her eyes.

"This is why I didn't want to let myself go with you. I knew I would regret it. I knew you would try to use this connection we have to control me. To stop me from what needs to be done. I won't let you stop me from saving my sister, Asher! From saving *all* my sisters."

"I'm not trying to stop you from saving them," I said, trying to keep the calm in my voice though it trembled. "I'm trying to stop you from destroying yourself. Even if you survive this, which I doubt you will, you'll be a monster when it's over if you follow this plan. Can't you see that I'm trying to *help* you, Reyna? This connection we have that you're so scared of, the one you think is weakening you, if you'd just stop for a second and *trust* me, then maybe you could see I'm right about this. That you don't have to become a villain in place of being a victim. You can become something else entirely if you'd just take a step back and think this through."

I softened my voice, stepping forward. "I know that many men have done many terrible things. I've seen it. I can't even begin to imagine the rage burning inside you. *Valid* rage. Rage that is blinding you to reason. You have one narrow viewpoint. You've only seen the world from inside the walls of your captivity. And it's a terrible world. One I can't imagine. I truly understand why you think you need to destroy them all. That all men are evil. I do. But you aren't seeing the whole picture. You have to stop painting every man with the same brush. No one holds you to blame for killing those women you were ordered to kill. You didn't like it, but you did it anyway."

She looked at me, tears glistening behind her eyes.

"Many men feel the same way about this system, but just like you, they followed their orders. They are no more to blame for the way women were treated than you and your swordsisters were for slaughtering other women by the thousands. If you want to go through with this plan, which I still hate by the way and think we should go and get Cassia and come back here to live out our lives in peace, then at least promise me this."

I took her hand in mine, my eyes boring into hers and hoping, praying, that she would finally start to see past the anger and start to see reason.

"Promise me that you'll at least try to let me help come up with a plan that saves any man who is worthy of saving. Men like my brother, my friends, and other men that I know don't deserve this cruel fate. Reyna, I want to help you save Cassia, to free as many women as we can. But this... this crusade to kill every man in Ironhold? It's not right. And it's going to get you killed."

Reyna's face softened, and she reached up to cup my cheek. "I understand your concern," she said. "But Asher, I can't just abandon my sisters. I can't leave them to suffer while I live in peace. Can you understand that?"

I nodded, leaning into her touch. "I do," I said. "I do understand. But there has to be another way. A way that doesn't involve the bloodshed of every man, innocent or not. Please, Reyna. Let me help you find it. Vow to me you'll do everything you can to help me protect my brother the way I've vowed to help you save your sister. If you can't even do that, if you can't even show me that you're not so consumed with hate and vengeance that you would slaughter my own blood without a second thought, then... then you're not the woman I thought you were. You're no better than the men you hate."

For a long moment, she was silent, her eyes searching mine. Then, finally, she nodded. "Okay," she said softly. "I'm sorry, Asher. You're right. I... I'm just so angry. I just want them to pay."

Relief flooded through me, so intense it made me dizzy. I pulled Reyna close, burying my face in her hair. "Thank you," I whispered. "And they will pay. But only the ones that deserve it. Not the men just following orders trying to keep their heads on their neck. We'll figure this out. Together. Even though I know it may feel impossible to trust me, I need you to do it anyway. Trust me, Reyna. Please. You don't have to shoulder everything alone. I'm here. And I'll help, but only if we do it the right way."

She let out a long sigh and sank into my arms. "Okay. I'll do everything in my power to protect your brother while I fight to save my sisters. You have my word."

As we stood there, holding each other in the morning light, I allowed myself to hope. Hope that we could find a path forward that would save Cassia and the other women without destroying everything in our wake. Hope that Reyna and I could build a future together, one free from the shadows of our past.

I just had to make sure that her desire for vengeance didn't blind her to the cost of it. It would be a delicate balance, but one I was determined to help her find.

For now, though, I was content to hold her, to feel her heartbeat against mine. And somehow, someway, we would find a path to freedom that didn't require us to become the very monsters we were fighting against.

We had to find a way to destroy the system without destroying ourselves in the process.

CHAPTER NINETEEN
Reyna

I spent the night in Asher's arms, but sleep eluded me, my mind churning with the weight of our earlier conversation. My plan to overthrow the kingdom and slaughter all the men had seemed so clear, so righteous before. But now, Asher's words echoed in my thoughts, casting shadows of doubt on the certainty I'd clung to for so long.

The hatred I harbored for all men was a fire that fueled me, kept me going through the darkest times. It was simple, clean-cut. All men were the enemy. But life, as I was beginning to realize, was rarely so black and white.

Asher's question haunted me: How were the men, forced to follow orders, any different from us? I thought of the countless battles I'd fought, the women I'd killed on our king's command. I hadn't relished it, but I'd done it. Was I so different from the men who controlled us, who were similarly bound by duty and fear?

I closed my eyes, picturing the faces of the cruel ones, the ones who took pleasure in our suffering. My blood still boiled at the thought of them, my hands itching for the feel of my blade sinking into their flesh. But for the first time, I forced myself to look beyond them, to consider the others—the ones who might be trapped, just as we were, in a system they didn't create and couldn't escape.

Asher was right. If I truly wanted to be different from our oppressors, if I wanted to break the cycle of cruelty and injustice, I needed to think differently. The path forward couldn't be paved with indiscriminate bloodshed. I needed to find a way to free my sisters, to liberate all the women of Ironhold, while still offering a choice to the men: to lay down their arms, to fight beside us, to be part of the change rather than its victims.

It wouldn't be easy. Years of pain and anger couldn't be erased overnight. But as I lay there, feeling the steady beat of Asher's heart against my cheek, I felt a glimmer of something new.

Hope.

Hope for a future where we could break the chains of oppression without becoming oppressors ourselves.

I didn't have all the answers yet. The path ahead was still shrouded in uncertainty. But for the first time, I was open to the possibility that there might be another way. A way that didn't require me to sacrifice my humanity in the name of vengeance.

As dawn broke, I made a silent vow. I would fight, yes. For Cassia, for my sisters-in-arms, for all the women suffering under the yoke of tyranny. But I would fight without losing sight of the very thing we were fighting for—a world where everyone, regardless of gender, could live free.

I would rally my army, but I would carry with me this new seed of understanding. It was time to redefine what victory truly meant.

Asher awoke and pressed a kiss to my lips, another reminder that for every cruelness of man there could be tenderness and kindness.

"Good morning," he said, his voice sleepy and slow.

"Good morning," I answered back, then kissed him again, taking my time to enjoy the softness of his lips and the flutters in my stomach that erupted every time we touched.

"Did you sleep well?" he asked, wrapping his arm around my shoulder and squeezing me tight against his bare skin.

I splayed my fingers across his muscular chest, pressing my head into him as I sank into his embrace. "Actually, barely at all."

"What?" he looked down at me, and I peered up at him. "What's wrong? I figured after what we did before I fell asleep that you'd be out too."

I smiled thinking of the pleasures he'd brought me before we'd gone to bed, and that ache started between my legs again, like a need he'd awakened that couldn't be extinguished no matter how many times he brought me over the edge.

"No, it's not that. It's just that I did a lot of thinking last night about what you said, and you're right. I've been letting anger and vengeance guide me when it should be justice. And to do that, I need to give everyone an equal chance to live free of tyranny. Both men and women, and only slaughter those who truly deserve it."

Asher smiled and pressed a kiss to my head. "You have no idea how happy it makes me to hear you say that."

"Thank you for helping me see reason. I was blinded by rage."

"We're partners in this thing now. Even though I'll admit, selfishly, that I still want you to just rescue Cassia and forgo this whole grand plan of freeing the women, I know now that you'll never be happy here. You'd rather die fighting than make the same choice Gaia did."

I traced my fingers along the defined muscles on his chest, marveling at how easy it was to soften into him when everything in my past screamed that trusting a man was dangerous. But here, in the quiet morning light, those warnings felt distant. I had carried everything on my shoulders for so long, I didn't know how to share the burden, but here, with the sun's rays peeking in through the cracks, I felt... lighter.

Though I wasn't sure if I was ready to tear down my walls and trust him completely, though Gods knew I wanted to, I did know with certainty that Asher was trying to look out for me, and I had to find a way, some way, to let him help me. But despite my feelings for him, the ones growing stronger each moment in his arms, I still had to cling to my vow to save the women in Ironheart. All of them. And I prayed I would find a way that would mean I didn't have to choose between him and the women depending on me to save them.

"I'm glad you can understand that now. I don't want to die. It's not that. But I also can't live with myself knowing my sisters still suffer."

He sighed, and the motion lifted my head on his chest. "I know. So, I'll fight with you."

We lay there in silence for a moment, finally united in our understanding.

His stomach grumbled, and I chuckled as I felt it as much as I heard it. "Are you never not hungry?"

He paused then laughed. "No. I'm always hungry. What do you say we get up and get some breakfast. Thalassa wants to check my wound, but I think it's safe for me to travel now."

I glanced up at his wound, still wrapped in the bandages Thalassa put on him twice daily. Then I glanced at my own, almost completely healed now. Thalassa's words rang in my ears about having magical blood in my veins, but I shook them from my mind. I had far more pressing concerns right now than worrying about why I healed so quickly.

We rose and dressed, and the morning sun made me squint against it as I emerged from our hut. Asher followed close behind, his hand resting lightly on the small of my back. The simple touch sent a warmth through me that had nothing to do with the early morning heat.

As we approached the center of the village, Gaia stood with a group of women I didn't recognize. Their stance, the fierce look in their eyes—I knew immediately they were warriors.

"Rebel Rose," Gaia called out, a hint of pride in her voice. "I've found some allies for our cause."

As we drew closer, Gaia introduced the group. "These are former battlemaidens from different kingdoms. They've all found refuge here in Moonshadow Woods, but like me, they are haunted by the fact they have found peace here while others still suffer under the oppressive rule of men. They no longer wish to turn away from those left behind. Other women in need. They're ready to fight again. For freedom."

The women all gave me nods of solidarity, and I felt a surge of hope as I looked at the determined faces before me. "Thank you so much for joining our cause. How many of you are there?" I asked.

"Thirty," Gaia replied.

My heart sank a little. Thirty was better than nothing, but it was far from enough. "Thank you all for your willingness to fight," I said, trying to keep the disappointment from my voice. "But I'm afraid we need more."

Asher stepped forward. "How many do you think we need?"

I sighed, running a hand through my hair. "My army—the Iron Swordmaidens—they're a thousand strong. We need to look threatening enough to draw out the full force. If only half come out to meet us, then half are still inside and can be trapped there. To take on the Kingsguard and storm Ironheart, we need the entire army on our side. If some are still stuck inside, they could also be forced to fight us. It would be a slaughter on both sides. I won't fight my own people."

"And if we draw out the whole army as you plan, there is still the question... What if you're wrong?" Asher asked gently. "What if your army comes out and fights us instead of siding with us? We need to be prepared for that reality."

I shook my head vehemently. "They won't. I know it. They hate the oppressive men with everything they have. Jaila will help me. She'll jump at the opportunity to join us and revolt."

Asher and I argued this point with him making valid concerns, but I knew Jaila. I knew my swordsisters. Given the chance to fight, and even die, for a chance to take their freedom, they would gladly bleed beside me.

We started discussing our strategy options, and the other battlemaidens chimed in with ideas and their experience of battle.

As we spoke, more of the Moonshadow Woods tribe started gathering around us, listening to our plans. Soon, most of the village seemed to be surrounding us, and I could see the conflict on their faces, hear the murmurs of disagreement rising.

"We should join them," one woman called out. "It's time we did something to help our sisters beyond these woods."

"Are you mad?" another countered. "We're not warriors. It's a crazy plan. Why would we give up our peaceful existence here?"

The argument grew louder, women taking sides, voices rising in passion and fear. I watched, feeling helpless, as the community that had welcomed us began to fracture.

Suddenly, Gaia stepped into the center of the crowd. "Enough!" her voice rang out, silencing the quarrel. All eyes turned to her.

"Listen to me, all of you," she began, her voice thick with emotion. "We have been blessed here. We've found safety, peace, a life free from the oppression that plagues our sisters beyond these woods. But in our comfort, we've become selfish. Blind to the realities of the world outside the trees."

She paused, her gaze sweeping over the crowd. "I know, because I am one of the selfish ones. I found this paradise and I stayed, leaving behind my love, my family, my sisters-in-arms. I told myself I deserved peace, that I'd fought enough. But every day, every moment of safety we've enjoyed here has been bought with the suffering of those we left behind."

I saw tears in the eyes of many women as Gaia continued. "Now we have a chance to make a difference. To fight not just for ourselves, but for all women. Yes, it's dangerous. Yes, we might fail. Yes we might die. But can you look into your hearts and truly say you're content to hide here while our sisters suffer?"

A hush fell over the crowd. I held my breath, watching as women exchanged glances, as silent communications passed between them.

"Not everyone is a trained fighter like us, but that doesn't mean you can't learn. That we can't teach you how to wield a sword and defend yourself. And if the Rebel Rose's plan works, you won't even need to fight. You just need to be there making our army look large enough to pull off this plan. Because if it works, you'll have a thousand trained warriors to fight at your side and protect you while we take back what's ours and grant freedom to the women still trapped in this cruel system! We fight for us. We fight for them. We fight for freedom!"

Silence settled over the women for only a moment before one woman stepped forward, raising her hand in the air. "I'll fight," she said simply.

"And me!" another called out, stepping to her side.

One after another, voices rose from the silence. Another. And another.

My heart swelled to see them rally to our cause—rally to the cause of *all* women. These women weren't warriors, and yet they were willing to risk their lives to make sure the peace and safety they'd found could be felt by every woman in Ironhold.

In the end, a quarter of the village—two hundred women—agreed to join our cause. It was more than I'd dared hope for, but still...

"I'm not sure if it's enough," I said, voicing my doubt aloud.

That's when Thalassa, who had been silent throughout the debate, stepped forward. She closed her eyes, and when she opened them again, they were glowing with shifting colors—blue, yellow, red. I knew now that this meant she was communing with animals, her eyes reflecting the colors of theirs as she spoke to them.

"What is she doing?" Asher whispered to me as we watched her.

"I think she's talking to the animals."

Within moments, creatures starting filtering into the village. First the birds came and then the wolves appeared almost instantaneously. The woods around us shook with the familiar sounds of ogre footsteps, and then the trees parted, and I saw the two ogres who'd attacked us step through. Then the bears appeared, six of them, larger than any I'd ever encountered. They gathered around Thalassa, awaiting her command.

While we stood in awe, she seemed to be speaking to them, their eyes shifting to each other and then back to her. Finally, with a smile she looked at us, her eyes returning to their natural color.

"What you have said has moved me. And you're right. We have been selfish in our safety and peace of these forests. I'm with you, Rebel Rose" Thalassa said, her voice resonating with power. "And so are they."

As if on cue, the bears roared, the wolves howled, the birds chirped... all the creatures seemed to dance with excitement.

Thalassa smiled as she waved a hand over them. "Now are we enough?"

My throat tightened. This was no longer just a rebellion. It was a revolution.

I looked at the intimidating crowd before me—two hundred fierce women and an array of magical creatures that defied belief. A smile spread across my face as hope swelled inside my chest. "Now we're almost enough. If we can find a few hundred more, there's no way my whole army won't come out to face us. Together, we can overpower the Kingsguard, kill the king, and free every woman in Ironhold."

The women all smiled, excitement flickering in their eyes as they looked at each other, my dream now theirs.

"What about the guardians of Mistveil Mountain?" Asher suggested. "The Cloudborn Clan."

A collective gasp went through the crowd. I turned to Asher, shock evident on my face. "Are you serious? They kill anyone who sets foot on their mountain. There's a reason no one tries to cross over to the Northlands and they never try to come here. And why would they fight for us?"

Asher's face was grim as he explained. "I know for a fact that King Lothaire has plans to conquer them and enslave them. He wants to force them to give up their mines of Aurorium."

"But why would he do that? Not only would it be practically suicide for the Iron Swordmaidens to take them on, but why does he want their Aurorium?" I asked.

"What's Aurorium?" a young woman in the crowd asked.

"It's a rare and almost unbreakable metal," Asher explained. "Only the Cloudborn know how to mine and smith it. It's the only metal that can compete with the strength of Shadestone's weapons and armor made from Nocturnium."

Thalassa nodded, her eyes now back to their normal brown hue. "I know of Aurorium. It's how humans won the magical wars during the purge. It has the unique ability to absorb and stop magic."

"Exactly," Asher continued. "King Lothaire wants it to outfit the Iron Swordmaidens. With Aurorium weapons and armor, they'd be nearly unstoppable, and King Ruthio would no longer have the most powerful army in the Southlands."

"And you're sure of this?" I asked.

Asher nodded. "Yes. He feels King Ruthio is up to something, though he doesn't know what. But he thinks it's worth the risk in fighting the Cloudborn Clan to get ahold of Aurorium to bolster Ironhold's strength. He's even in talks with Gold Coast to join armies so they can defeat the Cloudborn Clan, splitting the Aurorium as reward. If they can get claim on those last mines of Aurorium, they could pose a serious threat for King Ruthio. As it sits now, with his Nocturnium, he's stronger than all the kingdom's armies combined."

He paused, then added, "But I don't think Ruthio's just waiting to be challenged. Kings don't travel the Southlands this often unless they're rallying allies—or choosing which kingdom to strike first. But if we have Aurorium..."

"Then he loses that power," I whispered, understanding now why King Lothaire would be willing to take such a risk as to attack the powerful, legendary Cloudborn Clan.

"Exactly," Asher continued. But if we tell the Cloudborn Clan of King Lothaire's plans, they might be willing to fight with us. It's in their interest to stop him before he can mount an attack on their mountain."

A heavy silence fell over the group as we all contemplated the dangers of this plan. The Cloudborn were known to be some of the fiercest warriors ever born. Approaching them was a risk that could very well end in all our deaths.

But as I looked around at the faces of the women who had pledged to fight with me, at the magical creatures that stood ready to battle at our side, I knew we had to try. With the Cloudborn's strength added to ours, my plan had a real chance of success.

"We'll do it," I said, my voice firm with resolve. "We'll take a smaller group through Moonshadow Woods to the base of Mistveil Mountain. From there, we'll attempt to make contact with the Cloudborn Clan."

Murmurs of agreement—and fear—rippled through the crowd.

"I know it's risky," I continued. "We could be marching to our deaths. But with the Cloudborn Clan at our side, we'll have a real chance of freeing not just my sister, not just the women of Ironheart, but all the women of the Ironhold kingdom. It's a risk worth taking."

Asher stepped closer to me, his hand finding mine. "I'm with you," he said softly. "Whatever happens."

I squeezed his hand, drawing strength from his touch. "Thank you," I whispered.

As the crowd began to disperse, people moving to prepare for our journey, I took a moment to breathe. The enormity of what we were about to attempt threatened to overwhelm me.

But then I thought of Cassia, of all the women suffering under the cruel rule of men like Lothaire. I thought of the strength and courage of the women who had pledged to fight with me, of the magical creatures ready to battle at our side.

And I thought of Asher, who had given up everything to stand with me, who continued to support me even when my plans seemed impossible.

With all of them behind me, how could I fail?

CHAPTER TWENTY
Asher

The fifth day of our journey brought us to the end of Moonshadow Woods. We'd stayed inside the protection of the forests as we made our way toward Mistveil Mountains, which bordered the northern edge. Reyna and I traveled with Gaia, the former battlemaidens, and Thalassa joined along with her pack of swiftclaw wolves.

I rode behind Reyna on Ember, and when the mare stepped out of the woods and into a meadow, my mouth slackened at the sight of Mistveil Mountain looming ahead, its peak shrouded in mysterious clouds, both enticing and forbidding. The perilous mountain range stretched the entire length of the Southlands, an impenetrable wall of stone and snow that separated our known world from the mysteries of the North.

"Wow," Reyna breathed. "I've never seen them before. They seem to go on forever."

"There's a reason no one crosses it. Now I can see why." I stared at it in awe.

For centuries, the Mistveil Mountains had stood as more than just a physical barrier. They were the edge of our understanding, the boundary beyond which lay only rumors and half-forgotten legends. The Northlands, with their supposed vast cities, magic, and strange customs, might as well have been on another world for all we knew of them.

It wasn't just the treacherous peaks that kept our lands divided. The seas that flanked the mountain range were equally impassable, plagued by violent storms, deadly sea creatures, and unnatural mists that swallowed ships whole. Many a brave, or foolish, sailor had attempted the journey, lured by tales of Northern riches and magic. None had ever returned.

But it was the warriors of the Mistveil Mountains that truly kept the two realms apart. The Cloudborn, they were called—fierce, almost mythical figures that guarded the few passable routes through the mountains. Stories of their prowess in battle were told in hushed whispers around campfires throughout the Southlands. They were said to be giants among men, with strength to rival the mountain itself and weapons forged from the mysterious Aurorium that could cut through steel like butter.

These were the warriors we were marching straight toward, the legendary guardians we hoped to recruit to our cause... or the warriors who would give us swift deaths if Reyna was wrong about winning their loyalty.

Tales spoke of entire armies being turned back by just a handful of these mountain warriors. Some said they could control the very mists that gave the mountains their name, using them to confuse and disorient intruders. Others claimed they had the strength of ten men, and skin as tough as the Aurorium they wielded. No one had faced them and returned, so whether these legends were myth or fact was anyone's guess. But whatever they were, they were perilous because entire kingdoms quaked in their boots at the thought of facing them. King Lothaire must have gone mad thinking he could take them on, but he wouldn't care if he sent a thousand women to their deaths as long as he could get his hands on some of that Aurorium.

Our group crossed over the meadow until we reached the base of the mountain, and then after spending the night there to regain our strength, Thalassa communicated with the horses, telling them to stay behind and relax in the meadow because the climb would be too dangerous for them. Reyna bid Ember goodbye, and then we began our ascent on foot. One step after another, we climbed for hours. The air grew noticeably thinner, each breath a little more labored than the last. Above us, the mists swirled ominously, obscuring the peak and whatever—or whoever—awaited us there. We were about to step into legend, to confront myths made flesh. And all on the slim hope that these fearsome warriors might listen to our plea, might join our seemingly impossible quest.

As I watched Reyna forge ahead, her determination unwavering, I couldn't help but admire her courage. She was willing to risk everything on this gamble, to face down legends for the sake of her cause. It was terrifying and awe-inspiring in equal measure.

"What are you grinning about?" Reyna asked, catching me staring at her for what must have been the hundredth time that day.

I shrugged, trying and failing to appear nonchalant. "Just admiring the view."

She rolled her eyes, but I caught the blush that colored her cheeks. "Keep your eyes on the trail," she muttered, but there was no bite to her words.

As we climbed higher, the air grew thinner, the path steeper. But Reyna never faltered, her determination seemingly limitless. It was one of the many things I admired about her.

That night, we made camp in a patch of woods halfway up the mountain. Thalassa came to check my wound, nodding her approval at how well it was healing, but then giving Reyna a knowing glance when she looked at her arm, which had healed as if weeks had passed. It made me wonder again about her words that Reyna may be an Aegisari. But any time I tried to bring it up, she immediately shut down the idea.

I had to admit thinking Reyna was a magical being was a lot to process, but I couldn't shake the feeling that there was more to Reyna than even she realized. The stories of the Aegisari's abilities, their drive to protect others—it all fit too well. But for now, those questions would have to wait. We had more immediate challenges to face, and I knew it wasn't the time to press Reyna about her healing abilities again. She needed to focus on the task at hand... confronting the Cloudborn Clan.

As we sat around the fire, some of the battlemaidens who'd joined our cause came and sat with us. Curious, Reyna began to ask them about their experiences, their reasons for fighting.

A woman named Myra, her face etched with old scars, spoke up first. "I was from Thornvale," she said, her voice tinged with bitterness. "Our king... he sees us as nothing more than tools. When I was injured in battle, he discarded me like a broken sword."

Reyna's fists clenched at her sides, her jaw tightening. "I'm sorry," she said softly. "No one deserves to be treated that way."

Another woman, Helga, chimed in. "In Seastrand, if we didn't perform in a battle, they would strap us to the sides of our ships and leave us there to try to survive the waves while they sailed. As many women died a horrible, slow and painful death as survived."

A tall, lean woman with a thick head of red hair introduced herself as Brenna from Stormspire. "Our kingdom prides itself on our ability to fight in any weather," she said, her eyes haunted. "To train us, they make us climb the mountains until the ground is covered with snow and the air so cold it bites your lungs with each breath. We have to stand for days in the freezing temperatures. No sleep. No food. No shelter. Those who survive are deemed worthy. The rest... well, they say the mountain claims its due."

Each story seemed to fuel Reyna's determination, her eyes growing harder, more focused. But I could also see the weight of responsibility settling on her shoulders.

A younger woman, barely more than a girl really, spoke up next. "I'm Kira, from Goldcrest," she said, her voice barely above a whisper. "They... they were going to make me a breeder. Said I was too pretty to waste on the battlefield. I ran the night before my... my wedding." She spat the word like a curse.

Reyna reached out, squeezing Kira's hand. "You're safe now," she said fiercely. "And we're going to make sure no one else has to go through what you did."

An older woman, her hair streaked with grey, nodded in agreement. "I'm Vela, formerly of Verdant," she said. "I've seen too many young girls forced into breeding chambers, too many women worked to death in the fields. I may be past my fighting prime, but by the gods, I'll die before I see another generation suffer as we have."

With each story, I felt a growing sense of shame. How long had I stood silent, a cog in the very machine that perpetrated these atrocities? The sadness in Reyna's eyes was mirrored in my heart.

"And you?" Reyna asked, turning to a quiet woman who had been listening intently. "What's your story?"

The woman, her honeyed skin marked with intricate tattoos, met Reyna's gaze steadily. "I am Zeyna, once of Shadestone," she said, her accent thick. "I was a shadow assassin, trained from childhood to kill in the name of our king. But when I was ordered to eliminate a group of women planning escape... I couldn't do it. I helped them instead and fled with them."

Reyna nodded, a mix of respect and sorrow in her eyes. "You're all so brave," she said, looking around at the group. "To have endured so much, and still be willing to fight..."

"We fight because we must," Myra said firmly. "Because if we don't, who will?"

Helga nodded in agreement. "I'd rather die on my feet, fighting for freedom, than live another day under their rule."

"For our sisters," Brenna added. "For those who couldn't escape."

"For the future," Kira said softly. "So that other girls don't have to live in fear."

"We won't let you down," Reyna vowed, her voice ringing with conviction. "Together, we're going to change everything. I promise you that."

The women nodded, their faces set with grim determination. In that moment, I realized that these weren't just followers or allies. They were a sisterhood, bonded by shared pain and a common goal. And Reyna, my Reyna, was at the heart of it all.

The next morning, we continued our ascent. I couldn't help but marvel at the strength of these women, at their resilience in the face of unimaginable hardship. They had survived things I'd never even imagined, and I swore to myself that I would do everything in my power to help them, to atone for the years I'd spent as part of the system that had caused them so much pain.

As the day wore on, we entered the misty part of the mountain, and as we climbed higher, we entered a thick bank of clouds, the mist so dense it was hard to see more than a few feet in any direction.

"I can see why they're called the Cloudborn," I muttered, wiping moisture from my face.

Reyna, walking beside me, nodded. "It's like we're walking through the sky itself," she marveled.

"Let's just hope we don't walk off a ledge we can't see." I glanced down at my feet, hoping they were still on solid ground.

"Stay close," Reyna called out to the group, her voice muffled by the thick fog. "We don't want to lose anyone in this."

After what felt like hours of climbing through the mist, we suddenly broke through. The world around us was transformed. Instead of stepping out of the mist onto the top of a snowcapped mountain like I'd expected, we were still only part of the way up. Meadows of lush grass stretched in all directions to the edges of the jagged peaks stretching toward the heavens, their snow-capped tops gleaming in the sunlight. The air was crisp and clean, filling our lungs with each breath. Green trees gathered together in small forests, and I was startled by how much life was here above the clouds. I'd expected snow and dreary rock, but this was anything but.

For a moment, we all stood in awe of the beauty surrounding us. Then Reyna's voice cut through our wonder, sharp and urgent.

"Stop," she commanded. "We're being watched."

Instantly, our group tensed, hands moving to weapons. I stepped closer to Reyna, my eyes scanning the rocky outcroppings around us.

For a long moment, nothing moved. Then, so quickly I almost missed it, a figure stepped out from behind a boulder. My eyes widened as they processed the sight of the man larger than any I'd ever seen. Within seconds, I knew that the myths were true.

The Cloudborn Warriors were huge and formidable... and one of them was staring right at us.

He was enormous, easily two heads taller than me and built like a mountain himself. His skin was deeply tanned, covered in intricate tattoos that wrapped around his arms swollen with muscles stretching his skin. Bold stripes of black paint streaked his commanding face, giving him a fearsome, otherworldly appearance. But what truly caught my eye was his armor—gleaming Aurorium that captured the sunlight and almost glowed with how radiant its reflection was. In his hand, he held a spear of the same material, its tip wickedly sharp.

He drew a bow from his back, and I tensed, ready to fight, to protect Reyna with my life if it came to that, though I couldn't imagine how I could take on a man with muscles so large they looked like boulders plucked from the mountains.

With a snarl from beneath his black, braided beard, he snatched an arrow from his back with lightning-fast movement surprising for his size. He launched it at us before we even had time to take our next breath. The arrow struck the ground at her feet, embedding itself in the dirt with a loud thud.

I reached for my sword, rage swelling inside me that anyone had threatened her.

"He didn't miss," Reyna quickly whispered, her voice tinged with awe. "It's a warning. Don't."

She caught me by the hand, stopping me from pulling my weapon and gave a soft shake of her head. Slowly, deliberately, she began to remove her weapons, laying them on the ground before her.

"Reyna," I hissed, "what are you doing?"

She turned to me, her eyes blazing with a mixture of fear and determination. "Trust me," she said softly.

As Reyna straightened, weaponless and vulnerable, the powerful warrior took a step forward. His green eyes, lined with kohl that matched the long, black hair braided down his back, studied us intently. The tension in the air was palpable, thick enough to cut with a knife.

For what felt like an eternity, no one moved. No one spoke. We stood on a knife's edge, balanced between peace and violence, life and death.

And as I watched, helpless, unsure whether to reach for my weapon or follow Reyna's lead, I realized that everything—our mission, our rebellion, perhaps the fate of the entire Ironhold kingdom—hung on what happened in the next few moments.

The mountain air, thin and cold, seemed to hold its breath along with us, waiting to see whether this encounter would end in blood or understanding.

And in that suspended moment, with Reyna standing tall and unarmed before the towering figure, I had never been more terrified—or prouder—in my entire life.

CHAPTER TWENTY-ONE
Reyna

Thump. Thump. Thump.

My heart hammered in my chest as the intense eyes of the huge warrior bore into mine. It wasn't just his massive size and powerful muscles that stole the breath from my lungs, it was the sheer power radiating off him in waves. I'd been in countless battles, and never once had I stared into a face knowing, with certainty, that death stared back at me.

As I watched him, waiting, from the corner of my eyes I caught small flickers of movement. Figures began to emerge from hiding places all around us. From behind rocks, from crevices I would have sworn were too small to hide a person, even seeming to materialize out of the mist itself, warriors appeared until we were completely surrounded.

Their armor was like nothing I'd ever seen before, gleaming with a silvery-white light that looked delicate, but I knew from legend to be incredibly strong. Each warrior carried weapons of the same material—swords, spears, bows, each weapon pointed at me and my tribe of followers, all frozen as we surveyed the dangers surrounding us.

Aurorium. This was the metal Lothaire coveted so desperately. Seeing it now, I understood why. It radiated power, seemed alive in a way no ordinary metal could be.

I tensed, my instincts making me ready to fight, but not only did I know we wouldn't survive a battle with these fierce warriors in the position we were in, but I also knew if I wanted peace, I had to be the one to hold steady and resist the urge to defend ourselves.

"By the gods," I heard Asher mutter beside me. "How did they..."

I shared his amazement. These warriors, despite their impressive size, had managed to conceal themselves with a stealth that bordered on supernatural. The Cloudborn warriors remained as still as the mountain itself, and as I looked closer, I noticed something else that surprised me—there were both men and women among the warriors, fighting as equals.

A low growl broke through my thoughts. Thalassa's swiftclaw wolves appeared, their speed making them seem to materialize out of thin air. Hackles raised and teeth bared at the Cloudborn warriors, I felt the power of these creatures ready to strike. For a moment, I feared we were about to witness a bloodbath.

The Cloudborn Warriors looked startled for only a moment, and then their faces clouded with anger as they bared their teeth in response, their hands tightening on their weapons.

"Thalassa," I said quickly, not taking my eyes off the large warrior standing before me. "Tell them it's okay. We're not here to fight."

I saw her nod from the corner of my eye, her eyes flashing the same gold as theirs, and a moment later, the wolves backed down, though they continued to watch the Cloudborn warily. The tension in the air was palpable. I could feel the others behind us, their fear and anticipation a living thing.

Gathering my courage, I stepped forward. "I am Reyna," I called out, my voice steadier than I felt. "Once known as the Iron Rose, now called the Rebel Rose."

"I am Thorun, warrior of the Cloudborn Clan," he said, his booming voice carrying easily across the distance between us. "You have courage to come here uninvited. Or perhaps it is merely foolishness."

"We've come seeking your help."

Thorun's laugh was like thunder rolling across the mountaintop. "And why," he asked, his deep voice tinged with amusement, "would we care about your people or your problems? Why should we not just kill you now?"

I steadied myself, weighing my next words carefully. "Because King Lothaire plans to conquer your mountain and enslave your people. He wants your Aurorium, and he'll stop at nothing to get it."

A ripple went through the assembled warriors at my words. The amusement vanished from Thorun's face, replaced by a flash of shock that quickly hardened into anger. But then he smiled, a fierce grin that sent a shiver down my spine. "Let them try," he growled, tapping his Aurorium spear and touching his chest armor. "They will not succeed."

He looked truly ferocious, a warrior born and bred. But I couldn't back down now.

"You may be strong," I conceded, "but the Ironhold army is a thousand strong. And if any of the other kingdoms join them, as they are planning, they'll number in the thousands."

Anger blazed in Thorun's eyes, but I pressed on before he could speak. "But that's not what I want. I'm here to prevent that from happening. To ask you to work with us, to free my people and stop Ironhold before they can march on the Mistveil Mountains. Together, we can stop King Lothaire and put an end to his tyranny."

His dark eyebrow arched slightly. "A bold claim. If true, these words would indeed be cause for concern. But why should we believe some lowlander? Why would you, a stranger, care about our fate?"

I took a deep breath grateful he'd let me get this far without sending one of those arrows through me. "Because I believe that all of us—women, men, Cloudborn and lowlanders alike—deserve to be free. Because I'm tired of seeing the strong prey on those they deem weak. And because I think that together, we might have a chance to change things. To build a world where no one has to live in fear of being conquered or enslaved."

Thorun studied me for a long moment, his expression unreadable. Then, slowly, he nodded.

"You speak well, Rebel Rose," he said. "But words are easy. Actions are what matter."

"I stand ready to back my words with action," I declared, my voice ringing with conviction. "I'm prepared to fight with you, and for you, if you'll extend the same loyalty to us. All I ask is an audience with your leader. Give us the chance to plead our case, to forge an alliance that could change the fate of both our peoples. Even if you choose not to march alongside us to reclaim our kingdom and halt King Lothaire's advance, you'll at least be armed with the knowledge to defend your home when he comes."

As the words left my mouth, a chilling realization struck me. In warning the Cloudborn, I was potentially condemning my own swordsisters to a brutal fate. By robbing Lothaire of the element of surprise, I might be sentencing even more of my sisters-in-arms—perhaps all of them—to a merciless death at the hands of these formidable warriors.

The weight of this truth settled on my shoulders like a mountain, but instead of crushing me, it forged my resolve into something harder, more unyielding. I knew then that I would do whatever it took to win the Cloudborn's support. The stakes had never been higher, and failure was not an option.

For a long moment, Thorun studied me, his expression unreadable. Finally, he spoke. "You ask much, Rebel Rose. I must converse with our leader. No outsider has been allowed into these mountains in centuries. You wait here and I will return with an answer."

"That's all we can ask. Just a chance to be heard."

He narrowed his eyes at me, and with a grunt, he nodded to the warriors surrounding us. They seemed to communicate without words, and then Thorun took off running, his powerful strides covering vast amounts of ground until he disappeared around the jutting rock of the mountain, leaving us surrounded by his silent, watchful warriors.

As we waited, my companions and I spoke in hushed tones, marveling at the power and honor we'd witnessed in these mountain people. Even Thalassa, usually so composed, seemed awed by the Cloudborn.

After several hours, Thorun returned. His face was stern as he addressed us. "Our leader will see you," he announced. "But only if you prove yourselves worthy of her presence."

Her? The leader of the Cloudborn was... a *woman*?

This strange revelation, a woman in power, set me back for a moment, but I had no time to dwell on it because Thorun continued on.

"Only the two strongest warriors are allowed into our sacred land. Choose your partner."

The moment he said I needed a partner, my gaze shifted to Asher. For a brief moment, it stunned me how far we'd come from predator and prey, the hunter and the hunted, two enemies destined to destroy each other, and now, in this moment, I realized... I trusted him.

Completely.

He was the person I trusted most with my life... the *man* I trusted most with my life.

The thought should have terrified me. Everything I'd been taught, every hard-won lesson carved into my soul by years of cruelty, screamed that trusting a man—any man—was absurd. But as I looked at Asher, standing ready to face whatever challenge awaited us, I felt something I'd never experienced before: absolute certainty that he would protect me as fiercely as I would protect him.

When had that happened? When had this man, who once represented everything I despised, become the first person I'd reach for in a crisis? The realization sent a tremor through me that had nothing to do with fear and everything to do with how completely he'd dismantled every wall I'd built around my heart.

I'd spent my entire life learning to stand alone, to never depend on anyone, to trust only in my own strength. But here, faced with the most dangerous challenge yet, there was no question who I wanted beside me. Not because I needed his protection—I was the Rebel Rose, after all—but because I wanted his partnership. His steady presence. His unwavering faith in me.

The trust I felt for him was bone-deep now, undeniable, and it both thrilled and terrified me in equal measure.

He gave me a nod of solidarity before stepping forward to my side. "I'm with you."

We shared a look, one that spoke volumes with no words, then I turned back to Thorun. "We can face any obstacle you put in our path," I declared, gesturing to Asher and myself.

Thorun's lips lifted into a predatory grin. "Good," he said, and I could have sworn he looked excited at the prospect of our potential demise. "But know this—if the test doesn't kill you first and you fail, we will kill you ourselves."

I swallowed hard but nodded my acceptance. What choice did we have?

"To earn entrance to the trial, you must first defeat two warriors and prove yourselves worthy. Fail, and die. Succeed and you can move on."

I took a stilling breath, sharing a look with Asher and seeing the ferocity fill his eyes.

Thorun gestured, and two Cloudborn stepped forward, a man and a woman, their brilliant Aurorium weapons shimmering and catching the light in an almost otherworldly glow. The warriors, both with dark hair and green eyes like Thorun, and covered in tattoos with black paint streaked across their features, looked more lethal than any warrior I'd ever encountered.

Asher and I shared a look, and I knew he would fight for me the way I would fight for him.

"Begin," Thorun commanded.

The Cloudborn warriors wasted not a second and attacked as one, their movements fluid and devastatingly fast. I barely managed to parry the first blow, the impact sending shockwaves up my arm. The Aurorium blade seemed to hum with energy, its edge glinting with a ghostly light that made my own sword look dull in comparison.

Beside me, I heard Asher grunt as he fended off his own attacker. A quick glance showed him holding his ground, but just barely. His opponent was a whirlwind of deadly grace, each strike of his spear precise and powerful.

I refocused on my own fight just in time to dodge a vicious swipe at my midsection. The Cloudborn warrior pressed her advantage, forcing me back step by step. Her Aurorium weapon left trails of light in its wake, each near-miss making my skin tingle with residual energy.

"Reyna, duck!" Asher's voice cut through the chaos.

Without hesitation, I dropped to the ground. Asher's opponent sailed over me, having been thrown by a clever maneuver. The distraction gave me the split second I needed to regain my footing and counterattack.

We fell into a rhythm, Asher and I, covering each other's blind spots and creating openings where we could. A cry of pain snapped my attention to Asher. His opponent had landed a blow, a thin line of red blossoming on his arm. Anger and fear surged through me. Without thinking, I threw myself between Asher and the advancing Cloudborn, my sword meeting their Aurorium spear in a shower of sparks.

"I'm okay," Asher panted behind me. "Watch your left!"

I spun, bringing my sword up just in time to deflect a blow from my own opponent. The force of it numbed my hand, but I gritted my teeth and held on.

The fight seemed to stretch on for an eternity. My lungs burned in the thin mountain air, and my arms felt like lead. Sweat stung my eyes, and more than once, I tasted blood from a split lip or cut inside my cheek.

But we refused to give up. Every time one of us faltered, the other was there, offering support, creating a distraction, or landing a crucial blow. We moved as one unit, our deep connection and trust in each other evident with every motion.

Finally, I saw my opening. As my opponent launched a powerful overhead strike, I ducked under his guard, using his momentum against him. With a move I'd perfected in countless battles, I twisted my body, my sword creating a perfect arc that caught his weapon at just the right angle. The Aurorium blade, for all its power, was wrenched from the Cloudborn's grasp, clattering to the ground with a ringing sound that echoed off the mountainside. I was on him instantly, my knees pressed to his shoulders, pinning him with my blade to his throat.

At almost the same moment, I heard a clash of metal and turned to see Asher standing over his own defeated opponent, the tip of his sword pointed at her, a warning not to move. His chest heaved with exertion, a sheen of sweat making his skin glisten in the fading light. But his eyes were clear and determined as they met mine.

We had done it. Against all odds, we had bested the Cloudborn warriors.

For a moment, silence reigned on the mountainside, then Thorun stepped forward, his face unreadable. "Finish it," he commanded.

I looked down at my fallen opponent, then back at Thorun. The Cloudborn warrior met my gaze steadily, no fear in his eyes, only acceptance. It would be easy, so easy, to end it now. But the thought made my stomach turn.

"No," I said firmly, surprising myself with the strength in my voice. "I've spilled enough innocent blood at the command of men, and I won't take another life in vain. The fight is over."

Asher left his opponent and moved to stand beside me, his sword lowered but his stance ready. "We refuse," he echoed, his shoulder brushing mine in silent support.

Thorun's eyes narrowed, and I braced myself for his anger. But to my surprise, he simply nodded. With a gesture, he dismissed the defeated warriors, who rose and melted back into the mist without a word.

"You have passed the first test," Thorun said, his voice betraying no emotion. "The true trial begins at dawn. Rest now. You'll need your strength."

As Thorun and the other Cloudborn disappeared, leaving us alone on the mountainside, Asher and I sagged against each other, exhausted but relieved.

"We did it," Asher breathed, a smile tugging at his lips despite his evident fatigue.

I nodded, too tired to speak. We had passed the first test, but I knew the real challenge was just beginning. Whatever dawn would bring, we would face it together, just as we had faced this trial.

As night fell over the mountain, we settled in to rest, my mind racing with possibilities and fears about what the next day would hold. The fate of our mission, of our people, perhaps of the entire kingdom, hung in the balance. And as I drifted off to sleep, I sent a silent prayer to whatever gods might be listening. We were going to need all the help we could get.

CHAPTER TWENTY-TWO
Asher

The first rays of dawn were just beginning to paint the sky when Thorun's imposing figure materialized at the edge of our camp. I was already awake, my body tense with anticipation for whatever challenge the day might bring. Beside me, Reyna stirred, her warrior instincts bringing her to alertness in an instant. Our crew of women all stirred, one after another rising from their sleep around the dwindling fire, nervous eyes darting between each other as they took in the powerful man standing silently staring at us.

Thorun's eyes swept over us, his expression unreadable. "The second trial begins now," he announced without preface, his deep voice carrying easily in the crisp mountain air.

Reyna and I rose to our feet, exchanging a quick glance. Whatever was coming, we would face it together.

Thorun turned, pointing to a distant peak that seemed to pierce the very sky. "There," he said. "You must reach the summit before nightfall."

I followed his gaze, my heart sinking. The peak looked impossibly far, its upper reaches shrouded in mist. There appeared to be no path to the top, and instead sheer cliff face we would have to scale.

"If you fail," Thorun continued, his tone matter-of-fact, "you die. If you succeed, you earn the right to speak with our leader."

I looked at Reyna, seeing my own determination reflected in her eyes. We had come too far to turn back now.

"We accept," Reyna said, her voice steady.

Thorun nodded, a hint of respect flickering in his eyes. "Then begin. Time is already against you."

With that, he melted back into the landscape, leaving us alone to face the daunting task ahead.

"Well," I said, trying to inject some levity into the daunting situation, "at least we'll get a good view."

Reyna's lips quirked in a small smile. "Let's go, funny man. We've got a mountain to climb."

We said our goodbyes to our group who all gave us wishes for success, and then we set off at a brisk pace, our eyes fixed on the distant peak. We crossed through the woods and the meadows quickly, making good time and feeling confident about our success. But as we drew closer to the base of the mountain, the true scale of our challenge became apparent, and it wasn't the summit itself. A raging river cut across our path, its waters churning and frothing as they cascaded over rocks.

"We have to cross that?" I asked, eyeing the rapids warily.

Reyna nodded, her face set with determination. "Together," she said, holding out her hand.

I took it, drawing strength from her touch. "Together," I agreed.

As we approached the raging river, the roar of water filled our ears. The current was far stronger than we had initially thought, churning violently over hidden rocks and debris.

"We can't just wade through this," I said, having to raise my voice to be heard over the din. "Look there." I pointed downstream where the river disappeared over the edge of a cliff. The distant thunder of falling water sent a chill down my spine. "If we get swept away, we're going over that waterfall, and we're dead."

Reyna nodded grimly, her eyes scanning the riverbank. "We need to find another way over."

We looked left and right, and as far as the eye could see, there was no safe place to cross. "We could keep heading that way down the river and try to find a spot without the rapids," I said.

She shook her head, pausing to point at the falling sun. "We don't have that kind of time. If we're going to make it by sunset, we have to cross here. Now."

A long swallow slid down my throat. "That's easier said than done."

"Just look for ways across. There must be one," she said, determination tightening her jawline.

As we scoured the river for any weakness, Reyna's eyes lit up. "Look," she said, pointing to a series of jagged rocks jutting out of the water. "If we can make it to those rocks, we can use them to jump on and cross."

I looked at them, my head tipping as I envisioned the test of balance and timing it would take to leap across the river churning around each jagged stone step. "Those are not flat and easy to balance on, plus they will likely be wet and slippery."

"It's the only solution I see unless you have a better one."

Her eyes met mine, and I saw that familiar determination building in their green depths.

I sighed. "Well, if we can get to them, it's possible. But they are halfway across. How are we going to reach them." Then I looked at the woods behind us, noting a fallen log. "Wait. Together, I think we could move some logs to make a bridge to reach them."

Reyna's face lit up at my suggestion and she was already moving toward the first log. Working together, we managed to strip it of its branches and roll it toward the rocks starting in the center of the river. It was backbreaking work, but finally, we had it positioned, and as we pushed it in, I held my breath that it wouldn't get washed away.

When it settled into place, a grin split my face. "We did it!" I said triumphantly, but then my face fell. "It's not long enough." I saw the log fall short of a jumpable divide to the first rock step by several feet.

"Then we go get more wood."

We scrambled quickly, grabbing branches, rocks and logs, working tirelessly to carry them across our log bridge and drop them in the river to extend our path. Some of them washed away, breaking against rocks as they swept down the river before plummeting over the edge of the waterfall ahead. It served as a dooming reminder of our fate if we lost our balance and went in. But finally, our path grew to the point we could reach the rocky ledges and finish our trek across the perilous river.

"I'll go first," I said, and though I knew she wanted to argue, we didn't have the time.

"Be careful," Reyna said, her hand lingering on my arm.

I nodded, took a deep breath, and started across. The log and stick bridge we'd built was slippery, and I had to fight to keep my balance as I inched my way across. When I reached the end, I gauged the distance to the first rock and leaped.

My feet hit the slick surface, and for a heart-stopping moment, I thought I would fall. But I managed to regain my balance. From rock to rock I jumped, the spray from the river soaking me, until I reached the last one.

A deep breath of relief whooshed from my lungs as I reached the final rock. "Your turn!" I called back to Reyna.

She started across the log, moving with that feline grace that never failed to amaze me. But as she reached the end of our hastily built bridge of sticks and debris and prepared to jump to the first rock, disaster struck. Part of the bridge we'd built gave way in the current as she started her leap to the first rock, causing her jump to fall short, and suddenly she was in the water.

"Reyna!" I shouted, my heart in my throat.

For a terrifying moment, I thought the current had swept her away. My eyes darted around the waters, looking for her heading toward the waterfall crashing nearby. But then I saw her, clinging desperately to the side of the rock, the raging river threatening to tear her away at any second.

Without hesitation, I leaped back across the rocks. Each jump was a risk, the wet surfaces treacherous, but all I could think about was reaching Reyna. As I landed on the rock she clung to, I reached down and grasped her arms.

With all my strength, I pulled her up. As soon as she was secure, I wrapped my arms around her, holding her tight against me. We clung to each other, our hearts racing, the river surging around us.

"I've got you," I murmured into her hair. "I've got you."

Reyna looked up at me, eyes wide with a mix of fear and something deeper—something that hit me like a punch to the chest.

"Thank you," she whispered, breathless.

I gave her a crooked smile. "You're very welcome. Actually, I'm just glad you finally gave me the chance to save you for once. You're usually too busy saving yourself and everyone else. Let a man feel useful, will you?"

She blinked, a small smile tugging at her lips. "Asher, you've done plenty of saving me."

"Maybe," I said, "but I'll never stop relishing every moment I get to feel like the unstoppable Rebel Rose actually trusts me with her life."

A breath of laughter escaped her—but then her smile faltered, and something shifted in her expression. She looked down for a moment, then back up at me, her voice quieter. Thinner.

"I haven't let myself trust you. Not really. Not completely. I've wanted to, but it's just..."

I stayed still, letting her take a moment before continuing.

"I couldn't," she went on. "I've spent my whole life surviving men who used, betrayed, or broke me. And with you... even after everything... part of me kept waiting for the moment you'd turn. Like you being so good, so perfect, it just couldn't be true. I couldn't let down my guard with you. Not completely."

Her throat bobbed as she swallowed.

"But now... now I see. You're not going to turn, are you? You've never let me down. Not once. And I finally get it. You never will."

I felt something tighten in my chest at her words—something warm and aching and impossibly tender.

"Congratulations," I said with a soft grin. "Took you long enough."

She laughed—a real, surprised, *rare* laugh—and it was the most beautiful sound I'd ever heard.

"Don't worry," I murmured. "I'm a very patient man. It may have taken you a while to get here—to understand that I'll be here for you, Reyna. Always. Through everything. But you were worth the wait."

I brushed a damp strand of hair from her cheek, letting my fingers linger for just a breath. "You've been surviving on your own for so long, Reyna, you don't even realize you don't have to anymore. Not with me. You've carried a thousand battles on your back. You've bled and broken for people who never once deserved your loyalty. You've shattered yourself to protect the people you love. And you've done it all impossibly alone. But that ends here."

Her eyes searched mine, guarded still—but I didn't flinch. I didn't look away.

"You're not alone anymore. You don't have to carry the weight of the world on your back. I'm here now—to help you shoulder whatever burdens you need to carry. To be your safe place to rest. To carry you when you're tired. To be your shield when you're hurting. Your sword against anyone who would dare to harm you. I don't need your armor. I don't need your surrender. All I need is you—exactly as you are. Every scar. Every fury. Every wall you'll try to build up between us when you get unsure. Because you will. I know you, Reyna. But I'll still be here anyway. Because you're worth it. You always were."

I leaned in slightly, my voice dropping lower, softer. "You don't have to trust the world. But knowing you trust me now—that's not something I take lightly. I'll be here through every fight, every storm, every time you try to push me away. I'll still be standing. You're strong enough to stand alone. I'm just strong enough to stand beside you."

And then... she kissed me.

There was no desperation in it this time. No fear. No panic. Just us—finally choosing each other, finally letting go.

It was fierce, yes, but sure. Built on everything that had come before—every fight, every scar, every look that said *maybe*. And in that moment, balanced precariously on a rock in the middle of a raging river, wrapped in the arms of the woman I would follow into fire, I felt more alive than I ever had before.

When we finally broke apart, she looked at me. Really looked at me.

And in her eyes, I saw everything she still couldn't say.

She didn't need words.

I already knew.

As we stood there together atop the slippery rock with the raging river crashing past us, reality came rushing back. We were still in danger. Still had a mountain to climb. And time was not on our side.

"Ready to finish this?" I asked, not loosening my hold on her.

Reyna nodded, a new determination burning in her eyes. "Together."

"Always," I said with a smile she matched.

One after another, we made our way across the remaining rocks. Each jump was a challenge, but when we finally reached the opposite bank, we collapsed onto solid ground—exhausted, soaked, but triumphant.

For a moment, we just lay there, catching our breath and marveling at what we'd accomplished. But we couldn't rest for long. The sun had climbed higher in the sky during our ordeal, reminding us of the challenge that still lay ahead.

"You up for a climb?" Reyna asked, a smile on her face that made my heart skip a beat.

I nodded, getting to my feet and offering her my hand. "After that, a cliff should be easy."

We made it to the base of the cliff, each straining our necks as we stared up at the top.

"We can't make any mistakes or we'll run out of time," Reyna said.

"Yes, or fall to our deaths, so there's that, too."

She quirked a smile, then rose up on her toes, planting a soft, sweet kiss on my lips. "Then we'd better not fall."

I couldn't help but smile back, despite the challenge that still loomed before us. "Let's go."

Side by side, we began our ascent. The cliff face was steep, with few obvious handholds. We climbed slowly, carefully, each movement calculated to conserve energy and maintain our grip on the treacherous surface.

As we climbed higher, the wind picked up, its icy fingers seeking to pry us from the mountainside as if the mountain itself wanted us to fail the challenge. But still, we pressed on.

We were about halfway up when I heard it—a faint cry, barely audible over the wind. At first, I thought I had imagined it, a trick of the mind brought on by exhaustion. But then I saw Reyna freeze, her head cocked to one side.

"Did you hear that?" she asked, her voice tight with concern.

I nodded, scanning the area below us. That's when I saw him—a small figure clinging desperately to a rock in the middle of the river we had crossed earlier. It was a black-haired boy, no more than ten or eleven years old.

"Help!" his cry reached us again, weak but unmistakable.

My blood ran cold. The boy was in imminent danger of being swept away by the raging current. But if we went back to help him, we would certainly fail to reach the summit before nightfall.

I looked at Reyna, seeing the conflict in her eyes that I felt in my own heart. Then I glanced at the sun, already well past its zenith. Time was running out.

"Reyna," I started, not even sure what I was going to say.

She cut me off, her voice firm. "We have to help him."

"But the trial—" I began, even as I hated myself for the words. "If we go back down, we'll never make it to the top in time. You heard Thorun. If we fail, they kill us."

"I don't care," she said fiercely. "I'd rather die than let that boy drown."

In that moment, looking at Reyna's determined face, I knew she was right. Whatever the consequences, we couldn't abandon a child to die.

"Okay," I said, already turning to begin our descent. "Let's go get him."

We climbed down as quickly as we dared, our muscles protesting the strain. By the time we reached the ground and rushed to the river's edge, the sun was sinking dangerously low on the horizon.

The boy was still there, his small form shaking with cold and fear. The rock he clung to was slick with spray, his grip visibly weakening.

"Hold on!" Reyna called out to him. "We're coming!"

We leaped across the same rocks we'd come across, dancing above the dangerous waters below once more, desperate to reach him before he was swept away but careful not to lose our footing and go in ourselves.

Finally, we reached the boy. His green eyes were wide with terror, his lips blue with cold.

"It's okay," Reyna soothed, even as she fought to maintain her position above the rushing water. "We've got you."

Together, we managed to pry the boy's stiff fingers from the rock. I took him in my arms, his small body feeling fragile against my chest. Reyna positioned herself in front of us, leaping back across the rocks one at a time, pausing to help catch me as I followed with the boy in my arms.

When we finally reached the bank, we collapsed onto the ground, all three of us gasping and shivering. The boy clung to me, his fingers tightly gripping my drenched Kingsguard armor.

It was only then, as the adrenaline began to fade, that I looked up at the mountain peak. The sun had set, its last rays fading from the sky.

We had failed the trial.

Reyna followed my gaze, understanding dawning in her eyes. For a long moment, we just looked at each other, the weight of our failure settling over us. But then Reyna smiled, a small, sad thing that nonetheless warmed my heart.

"We did the right thing," she said softly.

I nodded, hugging the boy closer. "We did."

As we sat there, steeling ourselves for whatever punishment our failure might bring, a sound broke through the gathering darkness. It was... cheering?

Suddenly, figures began to emerge from the surrounding woods. Cloudborn warriors, dozens of men and women, all smiling and whooping, weapons jutting into the air in victory. I stared in disbelief, wondering if I had somehow slipped into a dream.

Then Thorun stepped forward, a grin splitting his usually stern face. "Well done," he boomed. "You have passed the true test."

"But... we didn't reach the summit," Reyna said, confusion evident in her voice.

Thorun's grin widened. "The climb was never the real trial," he explained. "We wanted to see what you would do when faced with a choice between your goal and an innocent life. You passed the first test by choosing to spare my warriors instead of killing them needlessly. You showed mercy. By choosing to save the boy, even at the cost of your own lives, you have proven your moral character. You have shown us that at your core, you are a protector. You will save others even if it means sacrificing your own life."

I felt a wave of relief wash over me, followed quickly by a surge of respect for the Cloudborn. He was right. This test had revealed more about us than any feat of physical prowess could have.

As the Cloudborn warriors surrounded us, offering words of congratulation, I felt a wave of relief wash over me. But beside me, I could feel Reyna tense up.

"Wait. If this was a test, then you put that boy's life in danger," she said, her voice low and tight with anger as she addressed Thorun. "He could have died!"

To my surprise, Thorun laughed, a deep, rumbling sound that seemed to shake the very ground. "The boy was never in any real danger, Rebel Rose," he said, his eyes twinkling with amusement. "Had he slipped, we had ropes ready to catch him and haul him out."

Reyna's anger seemed to deflate slightly, replaced by confusion. "Then why...?"

"This wasn't just a test for you," Thorun explained, his voice taking on a more serious tone. "It was also a test for him." He gestured to the boy, who was now standing proudly among a group of Cloudborn warriors, accepting their congratulations with a beaming smile.

"In our clan," Thorun continued, "a boy becomes a man not just through age, but through trials of strength and endurance. By holding on for so long, by facing his fear and persevering, Heiden has proven himself ready to begin his training as a warrior of the Cloudborn Clan."

I watched as understanding dawned on Reyna's face. Her anger faded, replaced by a look of respect and curiosity.

The boy approached us then, his chest puffed out with pride. "Thank you for coming to save me," he said, his voice steady despite the ordeal he had just been through. "Even though I didn't need saving, your willingness to risk everything for me proves you are true warriors, as I will be someday too."

Reyna knelt down to his level, a soft smile on her face. "You were very brave," she said. "I'm sure you'll make an excellent warrior."

The boy beamed at her words before being swept away by his fellow clan members, all eager to celebrate his achievement.

As we watched the scene unfold, I could see Reyna taking it all in—the way the Cloudborn interacted, the care they showed for one another, the pride they took in their traditions and in nurturing the next generation.

"It's impressive," she murmured, almost to herself. "They're not just warriors, they're a true community."

I nodded in agreement. "It's a far cry from what we're used to in Ironhold," I said.

Reyna's eyes met mine, and I could see a new determination there. "This is what we're fighting for," she said softly. "Not just freedom from oppression, but the chance to build something like this. A place where people support each other, where strength is balanced with compassion."

Before I could respond, Thorun's voice boomed out again. "You have earned the right to speak with our leader," he announced. "Rest now, and in the morning, we will take you to our village."

The Cloudborn went to work building small fires, their efficient and harmonious teamwork mesmerizing. Reyna and I made our own small fire just outside their lively camp, and Heiden trotted over and gave us some freshly cooked meat. Reyna and I thanked him, ate our fill then curled up on the ground together, our exhaustion making the hard ground seem as welcoming as a feather bed.

As I held her in my arms listening to the laughter and stories coming from the Cloudborn camp, I felt a sense of peace settle over me. We had made the right choice, the human choice, and in doing so, we had also glimpsed a vision of what our own kingdom could become.

No matter what the next day would bring when we met their leader, together, we had proven that we were worthy of the trust placed in us. Now, it was time to see where that trust would lead.

CHAPTER TWENTY-THREE
Reyna

The next morning, we followed Thorun for an hour, slowly climbing farther up the mountain. When we reached a narrow fissure in the mountain face, he paused in front of it.

"This way." He gestured toward the opening barely wide enough for a horse to pass through, its edges rough and uninviting. I exchanged a glance with Asher, seeing my own skepticism mirrored in his eyes.

As we entered the crevice, the world seemed to close in around us. The walls of the passage rose high on either side, blocking out most of the sunlight. It twisted and turned, seeming to go on endlessly. As I started to feel like we may never reach the end, the passage widened, and suddenly...

I gasped. We emerged into a hidden valley, a verdant paradise nestled high in the mountains. Lush green grass carpeted the ground, swaying gently in the breeze. A majestic waterfall cascaded down one of the encircling cliff faces, feeding a clear river that meandered through the valley floor.

But what truly caught my eye were the horses. At least a hundred of them grazed peacefully throughout the valley, their coats gleaming in the sunlight. They were unlike any horses I'd seen before—sturdy and compact, with thick feathering on their legs and long, flowing manes and tails. Their coats came in a variety of colors—deep blacks, rich chestnuts, dappled greys, splotched paints, and even some with coats that seemed to shimmer with an almost metallic sheen.

"Beautiful, aren't they?" Thorun said, a note of pride in his voice. "Our mountain breed. Strong enough to weather the harshest winters and sure-footed on even the most treacherous mountain paths."

I nodded, unable to take my eyes off the magnificent animals. Something about them called to me, stirring a feeling deep in my chest that I couldn't quite name.

Looking around, I realized the valley was entirely encircled by sheer mountain walls, rising so high their peaks were lost in the clouds. The narrow passage we'd come through appeared to be the only way in or out.

"It's a natural fortress," Asher murmured, clearly impressed.

Thorun nodded. "The mountains protect us, as we protect them. Come, the entrance to our halls is this way."

We walked through a village with some scattered huts and children racing through the meadows. Sheep grazed in the distance, villagers seemed relaxed and happy as they carried on about their day. Thorun led us toward the base of the cliff where the waterfall tumbled down. As we drew closer, I realized there was an opening in the rock face, partially hidden by the cascade of water. Thorun led us through, and we entered a world of wonder.

The passages were carved directly into the mountain, smooth and polished, with veins of Aurorium running through the stone like rivers of starlight. The metal seemed to pulse with a gentle, warm light, bathing everything in a soft glow. It was beautiful, yes, but more than that—it felt alive.

As we moved deeper into the settlement, the corridors opened up into vast caverns, each one a marvel of nature and artistry. In one, a portion of the river had been diverted into a series of stone channels and pools, creating a tranquil, flowing water garden. The soft sound of water echoed through the cavern, soothing and harmonious. In another, gardens of strange, luminescent plants thrived, casting an ethereal glow. Their leaves shimmered with iridescent hues, lighting the caves with a soft, magical radiance.

Stalactites and stalagmites formed natural sculptures, some of which had been gently shaped and polished by the Cloudborn into intricate designs, honoring their ancestors and the spirits of the mountains.

But it was the people who truly caught my attention. The Cloudborn moved with a poise that seemed almost supernatural, their steps silent even on the stone floors. Even the men, most of them larger than any man I'd known, moved with a quiet grace that seemed unnatural for beings their size. I'd have expected ground-shaking, lumbering footsteps like the behemoth ogres we'd met, but they glided like shadow-hunters, with the same lightness of the mist moving over their mountains. With their imposing stature, Aurorium weapons and armor, and preternatural stealth, it was no wonder they were considered the most powerful warriors in the land.

Most of the Cloudborn we passed wore clothing woven with threads of Aurorium, the fabric shimmering with every movement. Warriors passed us, their Aurorium weapons and armor gleaming, while others went about their daily tasks, all with a sense of purpose and serenity.

Something about them struck me as familiar, but I couldn't quite place it. It wasn't until we passed a group of young warriors that it hit me—their eyes. Every single Cloudborn we encountered had the same unique shade of green eyes as mine. I'd always thought my eye color was unusual, but here it seemed to be the standard.

"Asher," I whispered, nudging him. "Have you noticed their eyes?"

He nodded, a small smile playing on his lips. "I was wondering when you'd catch on. They're just like yours."

Before I could ponder this further, we arrived at a set of intricately carved doors. The carvings, sweeping lines of stone and metal, depicted scenes of battle and peace, of healing and protection—the story of the Cloudborn, I realized.

Thorun, who had been leading us, pushed the doors open, revealing a spacious chamber that took my breath away. The ceiling arched high above us, a dome of polished stone inlaid with Aurorium in patterns that mimicked the night sky. The walls were lined with tapestries and weapons of exquisite craftsmanship.

At the center of the room stood a woman who could only be Aria. She exuded an aura of power and wisdom that made me stand a little straighter. Her long silver hair was twisted into a long braid that cascaded over her shoulder and finished almost down to her waist, and her green eyes—the same as mine—seemed to pierce right through me. She wore the same Aurorium armor as the other Cloudborn, but on top of her head was also an Aurorium crown.

Surrounding her were other Cloudborn, clearly members of some kind of council. Their elderly eyes seemed to hold immeasurable wisdom, and they each radiated strength and authority in their own way. They watched me in silence, their aged eyes searching mine as I approached.

"Welcome, Reyna," Aria said, her rich voice filling the chamber with warmth. "And you, Asher. You've both shown great courage and compassion in our trials."

I bowed my head slightly, unsure of the proper Cloudborn greeting but hoping it would show my desire for respect. "Thank you for seeing us, Aria," I said, my voice steady despite the awe I felt. "We've come seeking your help."

Aria gestured for us to sit at a low table of polished stone, its surface inlaid with swirling patterns of Aurorium. As we settled onto the cushions, I noticed the ache in my muscles from our recent ordeal beginning to ease, as if the very air in this place had healing properties.

"Tell me," Aria said, her gaze intense but not unkind, "what brings the Rebel Rose to our mountain?"

Taking a deep breath, I steeled myself. This was it—the moment that could change everything. As I began to speak, I felt the eyes of every Cloudborn in the room upon me, waiting upon my words. The fate of my people, of the Cloudborn, perhaps of the entire realm, hung on what happened in this chamber. And as I launched into my tale, I silently prayed that I would find the right words to convince them.

Aria listened intently, her expression giving nothing away. When I finished, she was silent for a long moment, her eyes studying me. Then, suddenly, her gaze sharpened.

"Your hands," she said, reaching out to take them in hers. "These cuts were from your climb up the cliffs, were they not?"

I looked down, startled to see that the cuts and scrapes from our climb were already healing, far faster than normal even for me. "Yes. But how? They are almost healed?"

Aria looked at me, her eyes searching deep into mine, and I could practically feel her probing deep inside of me.

"It's the Aurorium," she said, a note of amazement in her voice. "It's speeding up your healing as it does for us. We, the Cloudborn Clan, are Aegisari, and I believe you, Reyna the Rebel Rose, are Aegisari too."

I pulled my hands back, shaking my head.

Aegisari.

That's what Thalassa had called me back at her village. But still, the thought of having magic inside me still felt impossible. "But how? I'm not Cloudborn. I don't know of any Aegisari in my family."

Aria's eyes softened. "Tell me about your family, Reyna. Your father, your mother, your grandparents."

Confused but seeing no reason to refuse, I began to recount what little I knew of my family history. My mother had died when I was young, and I didn't have much memory of her, but she did share my green eyes and dark hair, as did every Cloudborn I looked at. Aria pressed me more, asking about my grandparents and great-grandparents. I told her as much as I knew, recounting their names I'd heard my mother speak in telling me stories about our family. As I mentioned my great-grandmother's name, I saw one of the Cloudborn elders present stiffen.

"Lyra?" the elder said, his voice trembling. "Lyra was your great-grandmother?"

I nodded, surprised. "You knew her?"

The elder approached, his aged body making his steps slow and deliberate, his eyes wide with a mix of emotions. "I was a small body when she left here. Lyra was Cloudborn, and the keeper of the horses. Every few years we take the oldest horses in our herd down the mountain to be retired at a farm with a family we've had an understanding with for centuries. They help us breed our mountain horses, making sure we have fresh blood in the bloodlines to avoid interbreeding. Lyra went down with the herd... and never returned. We sent search parties looking for her. The horses were found grazing in the wild, and she never made it to the farm with them. We never knew what became of her." He reached up, tracing his weathered hands across my face. "Gods you look just like her. I can see it now."

The implications of his words stuck me like a sharp arrow to the gut. My great-grandmother, a Cloudborn? And if she never returned...

"Then that means... she must have been captured by someone in Ironhold and taken as a breeder," I whispered, the words tasting like ash in my mouth.

A ripple of outrage went through the gathered Cloudborn. Aria's face hardened, a flash of anger in her eyes quickly replaced by determination.

"We must be certain," she said, standing. From a nearby pedestal, she retrieved a small Aurorium pendant. "Reyna, if you are indeed Aegisari, this will react to you. Are you willing to try?"

I hesitated, suddenly afraid. If this was true, it would change everything I thought I knew about myself. But I'd come too far to back down now. Slowly, I nodded.

Aria placed the pendant in my palm. For a moment, nothing happened. Then, suddenly, it began to glow. A warm energy surged through me, starting from my hand and spreading throughout my body. I gasped as I felt my fatigue melt away, my remaining scrapes and bruises healing in an instant.

When the glow faded, I felt stronger than I ever had before. I looked up to see Aria smiling broadly.

"Welcome home, sister," she said softly.

The chamber erupted in cheers. Cloudborn warriors approached, clasping my shoulders and welcoming me to the clan. It was overwhelming, this sudden acceptance, this sense of belonging I'd never known I was missing.

Through it all, Asher stood by my side, a steady presence amidst the chaos. When our eyes met, I saw pride and something deeper, something that made my heart race.

As the excitement began to die down, Aria raised her hands for silence. "Tonight," she announced, "we feast to welcome Reyna the Rebel Rose to our clan!"

More cheers followed this proclamation. As the Cloudborn began to file out, making preparations for the celebration, a thought occurred to me.

"Wait," I said, turning to Aria. "My people—the ones who came with me. They must be worried. Can they join us?"

Aria smiled warmly. "Of course. They are your family, which makes them our family as well."

Thorun stepped forward. "I'll go fetch them," he offered. "All are welcome to our celebration."

"Thank you, Thorun," I said, still reeling that somewhere, somehow, he and I shared ancestors.

"I have so many questions," I said, turning to Aria.

"Of course you do. And we will answer them all. For now, rest and recover from your trials, and tonight we will welcome you home and tell you all about your Aegisari bloodline."

She leaned forward, pressing a kiss to my cheek, then after a soft look into my eyes, she said, "Follow Layana to a chamber where you can rest and recover. I'll see you tonight. We'll discuss everything, including your request for our assistance."

"Thank you, Aria," I answered, still struggling to find any words that weren't a barrage of questions.

A beautiful Cloudborn woman approached, her smile kind and wide as she gestured for us to follow her. Asher took my hand, seeming to understand how disoriented I felt, and he led me along with him to a chamber inside the mountain fortress.

Layana guided us through winding corridors, each turn revealing new wonders. We passed chambers where Cloudborn artisans worked with Aurorium, their hands dancing as they shaped the magical metal into intricate designs. The air hummed with energy, a tangible reminder of the power that permeated this place.

Finally, we reached a set of carved wooden doors inlaid with swirling patterns of Aurorium. Layana pushed them open, revealing a chamber that took my breath away.

The room was circular, carved directly into the rock of the mountain. The walls were smoothed to a polish, with veins of Aurorium running through them like frozen lightning. These veins converged at the center of the domed ceiling, forming a starburst pattern that seemed to pulse gently with an inner light.

A large, circular bed dominated one side of the room, piled high with furs and blankets that looked softer than anything I'd ever seen. The frame was crafted from a pale wood I didn't recognize, etched with symbols that I somehow knew were protective runes.

On the opposite side, a natural hot spring bubbled up from the ground, steam rising in lazy spirals. The pool was lined with smooth river stones, and the air was thick with the scent of mineral-rich water and some herb I couldn't name—something crisp and clean that reminded me of mountain air after a rainstorm.

Near the spring, a low table was set with an array of fruits, breads, smoked meats, and a carafe of water beside two metal goblets.

"This is... incredible," I breathed, turning in a slow circle to take it all in.

Layana smiled. "This chamber is reserved for honored guests. It seemed fitting for you, Reyna."

As she spoke, I noticed something I had missed in my initial awe—a small alcove near the bed. Within it stood a statue of a Cloudborn woman, her features sharp and proud.

"Who is that?" I asked, drawn to the statue.

Layana's smile softened. "That is Galania, a great warrior from our past who ruled our tribe as Aria does now. In fact, if Lyra was your great-great-grandmother, I believe that would make her your great-great-great-great-great-grandmother. This was her chamber, long ago."

The weight of history, of belonging, settled over me like a physical thing. This room, this place—it was part of my heritage. A heritage I was only just beginning to understand.

"Rest now," Layana said, moving toward the door. "Someone will come to fetch you for the celebration tonight."

As the door closed behind her, I turned to Asher, feeling overwhelmed. He squeezed my hand gently, his presence a comforting anchor in this sea of new experiences.

In the span of a minute, everything I'd ever known had been challenged. I was Cloudborn. I was Aegisari.

I was... magic.

And I had no idea how to process this new reality.

CHAPTER TWENTY-FOUR
Reyna

"Wow. This is a lot to take in," Asher said softly.

I nodded, moving toward the statue of Galania. As I stood before it, I felt a connection to this woman I'd never known, this ancestor whose blood ran in my veins.

"I have so many questions," I murmured, more to myself than to Asher.

He came up behind me, his hands resting lightly on my shoulders. "I can't imagine how you must be feeling. Are you okay?" Asher asked softly, his hand finding mine.

I looked up at him, emotions warring within me. "I don't know," I admitted. "It's all so much to process. I've spent my whole life thinking I was one thing, and now..."

"Now you know the truth," Asher finished for me.

But a new worry gnawed at me, one I couldn't shake.

"Asher," I began hesitantly, my eyes searching his face, "does this... change things between us? My being Aegisari, I mean. Magic has been banished from our lands for so long. Is it... is it a problem for you?"

His brow furrowed, and for a heart-stopping moment, I feared the worst. But then his expression softened, and he cupped my face gently in his hands. "Reyna, this doesn't change who you are. It just... expands it. You're still the same fierce, compassionate woman I've come to... to care for deeply. Now you just have a better understanding of where that strength comes from."

Asher's words hung in the air between us, his reassurance a balm to my tumultuous thoughts.

"You're sure? You've already given up so much for me. If word got out in the kingdom that I had magic in me, I..."

"Reyna," he stopped me, his voice low and intense, "Don't worry about that. We're fighting to change this kingdom, and maybe we aren't just fighting to free the women. Maybe it's to free everyone from a tyrant. Women, men, people with magic. Maybe there are more hidden than we know. If there's one thing you've taught me, and one thing I've learned on this incredible journey we've been on, is that everyone is unique, more so than I even knew existed, but each one deserves the same freedoms. You being Aegisari doesn't change who you are at your core. If anything, it helps me understand you even better. Your strength, your compassion, your unwavering determination—they're all part of your heritage, yes, but they're also uniquely *you*. Learning about your Aegisari blood doesn't change how I feel about you. If anything, it makes me love you even more."

His eyes widened suddenly, and I felt my breath catch in my throat. Had he just said...?

Asher's face froze for a moment, realizing what had slipped out. But then, instead of backtracking, a look of resolve settled over his features. He took a deep breath and met my gaze steadily.

"I love you, Reyna," he said, his voice clear and certain. "I've known it for a while now, but I was waiting for the right moment to tell you. I suppose there's no time like the present, especially when we're standing in a magical mountain fortress surrounded by your long-lost kin." A slight smile tipped his lips, as he stepped closer, brushing a piece of hair from my face. He looked into my eyes, my heart melting as he whispered, "They sent me for your head, Reyna. But it seems you took my heart instead."

A laugh bubbled up from my chest, equal parts joy and relief. I wrapped my arms around his neck, pulling him close.

"I love you too, Asher," I whispered against his lips. "Through all of this madness, you've been my constant. My rock. I don't know what I'd do without you."

He smiled, pressing his forehead to mine. "Well, lucky for both of us, you won't have to find out. Whatever comes next—whatever we learn about your past or face in our future—we'll face it together."

As we stood there, wrapped in each other's arms in the chamber of my ancestor, I felt a surge of strength. The Aurorium in the walls seemed to pulse in response, as if acknowledging this moment, this declaration of love. And in that instant, I knew that no matter what the future held, this—Asher's love, my newfound heritage, the strength we found in each other—would be our guiding light.

His words warmed me, chasing away some of the confusion and fear. I squeezed his hand, grateful for his unwavering support.

"Thank you," I said softly. "For everything. I don't think I could have made it this far without you."

Asher's eyes softened, and then he leaned in and kissed me. This kiss was soft, tender, and it took no words this time to feel his love for me as his lips brushed against mine. I sank into his kiss, a deeper need than just to feel his love for me rose up inside of me.

My fingers started working on his armor, and as he whispered against my lips, I could feel his smile. "Really? You're not too tired?"

"No," I whispered back, then seeing the threads of Aurorium surrounding me, I realized why. "It's this place. The Aurorium. It has reinvigorated me completely. It's amazing how good I feel right now.

He quirked a smile. "If you feel good now, then just wait until I'm done with you."

I lost my breath when he bent me back into a knee-quaking kiss.

Our kisses only broke long enough for us to rip off our armor before we were back in each other's arms again, his tongue meeting mine in deep, passionate kisses. Then Asher took my hand, leading me to the small pool of water. I followed him in, moaning as the warm water enveloped my body, soothing every muscle as I sank into it.

"This is incredible," he said, dunking himself in before coming up, the droplets of water cascading down his face and muscular shoulders, only amplifying the heat between my legs.

I floated forward, wrapping my arms around his neck and my legs around his waist, his cock brushing against me and sending pulses of excitement between my legs. I didn't hesitate, not wanting to prolong my desire, prolong the connection to the man I loved, the man who loved me, for another second. I slid down on his cock, a low moan escaping my lips when he filled me completely.

"Reyna," he breathed into my ear, then slipped his hand into my hair, pulling my head back and pressing kisses to my neck.

I moved up and down on him, my hard nipples brushing against his chest only amplifying the sensations coursing through my body. It wasn't just the Aurorium surrounding us connecting with my body and my soul, it was him. The sensation of him inside of me while Aurorium flowed around me was overwhelming as I lost myself in the moment with Asher in this place that invigorated the very essence of my being.

He pulled me tight against him, his hips lifting up to match my motion, pushing himself deeper and deeper inside of me. I leaned back in the water, and he slid his hands along my stomach and up to my breasts, cupping them firmly. His fingers played with my nipples, then his hand drifted south and he found that sensitive spot between my legs. I whimpered as he rubbed me with his fingers while he slid himself in and out of me. His breathing quickened along with mine, and I pulled myself back up to sitting, wrapping myself tightly around him as I moved quicker, rubbing myself against him and feeling the passion swelling up inside of me.

"Reyna," he breathed against my skin as his lips trailed down my neck. "You brave, beautiful, impossible woman. And you're mine. All mine."

I laughed, the sound turning into a gasp as he found a particularly sensitive spot. "I'm yours am I? Aren't we trying to put an end to men owning women?" I teased, even as I arched into his touch.

He pulled back slightly, his movements stopping. Gently, he slipped a hand alongside my face, his eyes dark with desire but also shining with an emotion that made my heart skip. "Yes," he said simply. "You're mine. You are mine as I am yours. Always."

The intensity of his gaze, the weight of his words, sent a shiver through me. This was more than desire, more than the heat of the moment. This was a promise, a vow as binding as any made before gods or men.

Mine.

He said the word not as if he wanted to own me or to control me. Not like I'd been claimed as property my whole life. But that he wanted to possess me completely, body and soul.

And Gods did I want to be his. Only his. Always his.

He started moving against me again, his cock sliding deep inside, sending a sharp jolt of need straight through my core. A deep growl rumbled from his chest as his hands slid down my back, gripping my ass and holding me against him, exactly where he wanted me.

"You feel so fucking good." His voice was rough, guttural, like he was barely holding himself together. Like I was his undoing.

I rolled my hips, reveling in the way his body shuddered beneath me. He was holding back again. Barely. But I could sense it.

Not tonight.

I leaned in, my lips brushing against his ear as I whispered, "Don't hold back."

A fire ignited in his eyes as he held my gaze. "I don't think you know what you're asking of me."

I bit my lip, knowing that there was so much more buried beneath his surface. So much raw power that he held back from me, always touching me with only tenderness and love. Like he never wanted me to feel out of control after a lifetime of it. But I trusted him, and I didn't just want to give him control, I wanted to feel him take it from me. Show me what kind of man he was. The one that made his enemies tremble in his presence.

"Make me yours, Asher. Don't hold back. I want to feel that power I know you're withholding from me."

His eyes darkened. "I don't want to hurt you."

A smile tipped my lips. "Don't worry. I don't break easily."

He smirked, and I saw the passion crackling to life in his eyes. "Tell me to stop, and I will. But if you don't... I won't hold back."

"Try me."

Something snapped in him.

A wicked grin flashed across his face before his hands tightened like iron around my thighs. "You want me to ruin your petals, little rose?"

My breath hitched. *Gods.*

Before I could answer, he grabbed me around the waist, spinning me around in one breathtaking move, bending me over the edge of the pool. His hand grasped my wrists, his grip unrelenting as he pressed my hands into the stone, his large body pressing down on mine.

With one devastating thrust, he slammed himself inside of me.

A sharp cry tore from my lips. Pleasure and pain mixed, an exquisite stretch that sent me spiraling.

Asher didn't wait.

He drove into me hard and deep, each movement claiming me, owning me.

And I loved every excruciating, intoxicating second of it.

Raw power radiated from him as he let go of my wrists, grabbing my hips and forcing me to take every inch of him.

"Mine." The word was a growl, a vow, his lips pressing hot and demanding against my ear.

I arched back, my bare breasts scraping against stone, but I didn't care. If it caused pain, I didn't feel it. My world narrowed down to only the powerful man consuming me with each punishing thrust.

My breath quickened coming out in sharp pants as I closed in on the edge of the abyss he dragged me to. But just before I cried out his name, he stopped, pulling out of me and leaving me gasping for air.

"You'll come when I'm ready for you to come."

He spun me around and there, in the depths of those blue eyes, I finally saw the warrior who could command anyone in his presence. And he was fierce and mighty and so powerful I could have come just from looking at him.

His mouth found my nipple, his teeth scraping, tongue flicking, sucking. My moan was his reward, and gods, he devoured it.

He grabbed me by my hips, propping me on the edge of the pool's ledge. He coaxed my legs open, his scalding gaze landing between them, licking his lips as he stared at what I offered him. What he could take. The way his eyes filled with hunger as he watched his finger move in and out of me only ignited the need for him making me writhe against the stone.

"Do you want to come for me, little rose?" he asked.

I bit my lip, swallowing my cry as the palm of his hand rubbed up against that sensitive place sending white-hot pleasure bursting behind my eyes while his fingers drove in deeper.

"Yes," I breathed out.

"Do you like being mine?" he asked, his voice deep and possessive.

"Yes," I breathed out again. I spread my legs wider.

"Say that you're always mine and I'll make you come so hard you'll never forget it."

I leaned back, my eyes slamming shut as I neared my peak again. In that moment, I would have sworn to anything just to get the sweet release I knew he could deliver me. But it wasn't just the heat of the moment that had me crying out the words, "I'm yours!"

It was because they were true.

I'd never felt so safe. Never felt so protected. After a life of fighting for every second of existence, I now had a partner that I trusted completely. A man who consumed me. Cherished me. Worshipped me. A man who respected me. And a man who could make me unravel in ways I never knew existed.

"Yes! I'm yours, I'm yours!" I cried out on repeat. "Please. Let me come. Please, Asher."

"Good girl," he rumbled, and suddenly his cock was pressed against my opening.

"And I'm yours," he whispered against my lips, then with a powerful kiss to match the powerful thrust between my legs, Asher drove inside of me.

A low growl vibrated from his chest as he gripped my hips, pulling me into him, deeper, harder. I gasped, my nails digging into his shoulders, but he didn't stop. He wouldn't stop.

His breath was hot against my throat, his lips teasing the sensitive skin there. "You feel so fucking good wrapped around me."

He pulled back, just enough to make me whimper at the loss. His smirk deepened.

"I want to hear it." His words drifted across my lips. "Tell me how much you love this. Tell me how much you love me."

He rolled his hips, slow and punishing, dragging every ounce of pleasure from me. I arched against him, my breath ragged, but he wasn't done with me yet.

He caught my wrists, pinning them above my head, completely at his mercy.

"Say it." His voice was pure sin, pure dominance, pure desire.

And gods help me—I did.

"I love you, Asher," I barely managed, my chest tight from the sharp inhales trying to get past my lips.

My eyes opened for a moment to see his boring back into mine. His perfect lips arched in a smile. His voice was low, rough, dripping with need. "I love you too." He tilted my head back, baring my throat to him. "Look at me."

I obeyed. And gods, the thrill of it sent heat spiraling through me.

"Come for me, Reyna." A demand. A command. A promise.

I shattered.

I cried out, wrapping my arms around his muscular back, clinging to him for dear life as I opened the flood gates I'd been holding back, waves of euphoria pouring out of me on my cries. Pleasure crashed through me in wave after wave, my body convulsing around him. Asher snarled, burying himself so deep it felt like I'd never be without him again.

He thrust one last time, a broken sound escaping his lips as he lost himself in me, his release triggering another pulse of heat through my body.

We didn't move. Couldn't.

His forehead pressed against mine, our breaths ragged, our bodies still joined, still tangled, still completely and utterly owned by one another.

He cupped my jaw, his thumb stroking over my lips as he murmured, "Never again."

I swallowed hard, barely able to form words. "Never again what?"

His grip tightened, and the rawest emotion I'd ever seen burned in his eyes. "Never again will you ever be alone in this world. Never again will I let you doubt that you're mine."

I had no fight left. Not against this. Not against him.

Because I was his. And he was mine.

We lay on the rock floor next to the pool in a tangled pile of limbs, panting and boneless. He slipped an arm around my shoulders, pulling me into his chest. Even though he had been so rough, so raw, just moments ago, I felt cherished in his embrace.

"Gods, woman. You're going to be the death of me if you keep letting me fuck you like that. I hope I didn't hurt you."

I peeked up at him, my eyes hooded and heavy. "I told you. I don't break easily. I don't ever want you to hold back on me. I may have spent my life as a prisoner to men's wishes, but they weren't you. You aren't forcing me to do anything I don't want to, and you don't have to treat me like some precious thing that will panic if you look at me the wrong way. I trust you, Asher. Completely."

"But you are precious." He tucked a piece of hair behind my ear. "To me, you're precious. But you're also powerful, fierce, unstoppable, and downright lethal, and I love every single part of you. I love you, Reyna. Always."

I slumped forward, my head resting on his chest as I lay boneless and satiated in his arms.

"I love you too, Asher."

"And I also love those herbs from Thalassa. There is nothing more amazing than releasing with you at the same time," he said, his sigh lifting his powerful chest.

I smiled, giving a slight nod though I had no energy for anything else.

"Well, I don't know about you, but now I'm *really* ready for a rest."

I nodded, and after clinging together for a few long moments, we dragged ourselves to our feet and dried off. He pulled me toward the bed, and I sank into his softness, our naked bodies tangled together as I felt the exhaustion of the past days catch up with me all at once.

The truth of my identity washed over me in waves: Aegisari. Cloudborn. Words that had been merely legend now coursed through my veins, as real and vital as my own heartbeat.

And his. Now being his became as much a part of me as the magical blood coursing through my veins.

I felt Asher's breathing slow beside me, his chest rising and falling in the steady rhythm of deep sleep. A warmth bloomed in my chest as another truth crystallized within me: I'd found not one, but two places where I truly belonged.

In the span of a day, my world had expanded beyond measure. I was no longer just Reyna, the outsider, the Rebel Rose. I was Reyna, Aegisari warrior, Cloudborn daughter, and—my eyes drifted to Asher's peaceful face—I was his.

For the first time in my life, I felt whole. I was home.

CHAPTER TWENTY-FIVE
Reyna

I inhaled a breath of the invigorating, crisp night air as Asher and I stepped out of the mountain halls and into the hidden valley. The sky above was a tapestry of stars, more brilliant than I'd ever seen them. Bonfires dotted the landscape, their flames reaching toward the heavens, casting flickering shadows that danced across the faces of the gathered Cloudborn.

The beat of drums filled the air, a primal rhythm that seemed to pulse in time with my own heartbeat. All around me, my newfound kin moved in fluid, graceful motions, their bodies swaying to the music. The firelight glinted off their Aurorium armor, creating an incredible spectacle.

"Reyna!" a familiar voice called out. I turned to see Thalassa approaching, a wide smile on her face. She pulled me into a warm embrace. "We were so worried when we saw Thorun returning without you. I'm so glad you're safe."

I hugged her back, feeling a rush of affection for this woman who had become such an important part of my journey. "Thalassa," I said as we pulled apart, "I'm so glad you're here. Is everyone okay?"

"We're all safe and here." She pointed, and I scanned the crowds of Cloudborn and finally saw the Moonshadow people I'd traveled with gathering at the celebration with them.

"Your trial. Thorun says you succeeded. Did you get an audience with Aria then? Will they commit to your cause?"

I realized she wasn't aware yet of the startling revelation I'd been made aware of earlier. I took a deep breath and shook my head. "We're going to discuss more about the rebellion tonight, and I hope to gain their support. But, Thalassa, I discovered something amazing. You were right. I'm Aegisari. When we met Aria, she noticed something about me, and it turns out all the Cloudborn are Aegisari, and I'm one of them. My great grandmother, Lyra, ended up being taken as a breeder in Ironhold, but my heritage, my people... they are Cloudborn."

Thalassa's eyes widened. "The Cloudborn are Aegisari? I... I had no idea. I've heard of the Aegisari of course, but no one has ever known much about the Cloudborn. What an amazing thing to discover that you have a whole people here. I'm so happy for you, Reyna. You've found your clan, your heritage." There was a touch of sadness in her voice as she continued, "As the last Animara, I will never get to experience that. Cherish it, Reyna. Cherish your people and this gift you've been given."

I nodded, feeling a mix of joy for myself and sympathy for Thalassa. "I will," I promised. "And you'll always have a place with me, Thalassa. You're family too."

"Reyna! Join us!" Gaia called, and I looked to see all the previous battlemaidens laughing and dancing.

"I can't wait to hear more about what you've discovered, but I fear Gaia will be most disappointed if we don't join her. Come on."

Before I could protest, she took my hand, pulling me into the swirling mass of bodies. I glanced back at Asher, who just gave me a wave, smiling as he watched me join our friends in their dance. At first, I felt awkward, unsure of the steps. But as the rhythm of the drums seeped into my bones, I found myself moving instinctively, my body remembering steps it had never learned.

The dance went on, a whirl of motion and music that seemed to take on a life of its own. When at last the drumming slowed, I found myself breathless but exhilarated. Aria appeared at my side, offering me a cup filled with a sweet-smelling liquid.

"Aurorium wine," she explained as I took a sip. The taste was unlike anything I'd experienced—cool and refreshing yet warming me from the inside out. "Made from berries that grow only in the presence of Aurorium. Now come. Let us discuss our past and our future."

As we moved away from the dancers, Aria led me to a quieter area where a group of elders had gathered. They welcomed me warmly, their eyes—so like my own—filled with a mixture of joy and sorrow.

"We have much to tell you, young one," one of the elders said, his voice gravelly with age. "About your heritage, and about the duty that comes with it."

Over the next few hours, as the celebration continued in the distance, I learned more about my people and my own history than I ever thought possible. They told me of the Aegisari, protectors and healers, whose connection to Aurorium gave them their power. They spoke of the great purge centuries ago, when the Southlanders, fearing the power of magic, had stripped the Mistveil Mountains of almost all its Aurorium to forge weapons to fight the magic. Though Aurorium fueled our magic and enhanced our powers, it rendered all other magic useless with a simple touch. It had allowed the human kings to wage a war on everyone with magic, rendering them powerless as they eradicated them one by one.

"The parts of Mistveil Mountain that weren't guarded are now void of any Aurorium, but we never allowed them onto this part of the mountain that we guard with our very lives," Aria said, her voice growing solemn. "The Aegisari need Aurorium to manifest our full power, so it is our duty, our very nature, to protect it. And now, it is your duty too."

I listened, awestruck, as they recounted tales of my great-grandmother, Lyra. She had been a respected member among the Cloudborn, known for her skill with horses and her fierce protective instinct.

"To learn of her fate, to know she was forced to become a breeder..." Aria's voice trailed off, her eyes flashing with anger. "It is an insult that cannot go unanswered."

"We will help you, Reyna," another elder added. "Not just to protect our Aurorium from Lothaire's greed, but to free your people. To honor Lyra's memory and to right the wrongs done to her descendants. To our family."

"Thank you," I said, my heart filled with a mixture of gratitude and determination. "I know it's asking a lot, but we can't stand by and let King Lothaire and the vile men of Ironhold continue enslaving women. They deserve the same freedoms and respect as men, and I won't stop until we achieve it. And now, knowing my heritage, I will protect this mountain, this clan, with every ounce of my strength until my dying breath."

I clenched my fist and pressed it to my chest.

They smiled back at me, mirroring my gesture.

"And we will protect you, Reyna of the Cloudborn Clan."

Everyone stood and took turns pulling me into their embraces, and I held each one tight, a familiarity in each one of them I couldn't explain. It felt like coming home, but to a place I'd never been.

After we finished our private meeting, we all rejoined the festivities. I danced with Thalassa and Gaia, laughed with the Cloudborn warriors, and shared quiet moments with Asher. With each passing hour, I felt more and more connected to these people - my people.

During a lull in the music, Thorun approached me, his imposing figure softened by the flickering firelight. "Reyna," he said, his deep voice carrying even over the ambient noise of the celebration. "There's something I want to show you."

Curious, I followed him to the edge of the valley, where the herd of mountain horses grazed peacefully. Asher walked beside me, his presence a comforting constant. As we approached, one of the horses—a magnificent black stallion with a long tail and a mane that flowed in waves down past his knees—lifted its head and trotted over to us.

"This is Stormrunner," Thorun said, a note of pride in his voice. "He's a descendant of the horses your great-grandmother used to breed. I think... I think he's meant for you."

I reached out, running my hand along his muscular neck, feeling a connection I couldn't quite explain. But then I thought of Ember, my loyal companion who had carried me through so much.

"Thorun," I said, my voice filled with gratitude and hesitation, "I'm incredibly honored. But... I already have a horse I'm deeply bonded to. Ember. She's been with me through everything."

Thorun nodded, understanding in his eyes. "The bond between a Cloudborn and their horse is unbreakable. I understand."

Then an idea struck me, and I turned to Asher. "You gave up your own beloved horse to save me. Perhaps... perhaps Thorun could let you ride Stormrunner? Just for now, since I know he belongs with the Cloudborn and his herd."

Thorun hesitated for a moment, his eyes moving between Asher and Stormrunner. Then, slowly, he nodded. "Very well. Asher, you may ride Stormrunner during our siege of Ironheart and fight by Reyna's side. It is a great honor to ride a Cloudborn stallion, so take good care of him."

As Asher approached Stormrunner, tentatively reaching out to touch the horse's muzzle, I found myself standing beside Thorun. We watched in companionable silence as Asher and Stormrunner seemed to size each other up, the magnificent stallion eventually lowering his head to allow Asher to stroke his neck.

"He is a good man?" Thorun's deep voice rumbled beside me, a thread of distrust mixed with the words.

I turned to look at him, surprised by the protective tone in his voice. His eyes, so similar to my own, were fixed on Asher, his expression a mix of curiosity and wariness.

"He is," I replied, my voice soft but firm. "The best I've ever known."

Even though he didn't make a sound, I could practically hear the growl rumble in his chest as he said, "I know enough about your land to recognize the emblem on his armor. Isn't he a Kingsguard? One of the men who has oppressed your people for generations? One of the men who would have taken our Lyra and forced her into their beds?"

"He *was* Kingsguard. But he left it for me." Thorun's powerful glare remained fixed on Asher, so I continued. "He didn't choose to be born into that harsh, horrible system, and he never committed any atrocities himself, you should know. He never took wives or treated us with anything less than respect. He's different, and he chose to save my life in exchange for giving up everything and everyone he's ever known. He may not be Cloudborn, but he's as much of a protector as I am. He protects me, and I protect him. He's... important to me."

Thorun nodded slowly, his gaze still on Asher. "You should know, Reyna, that traditionally, the Cloudborn only... bond with other Cloudborn. Our connections run deep, tied to our very essence as Aegisari."

I felt a flicker of understanding. This wasn't about romantic interest—this was about protection, about preserving the Cloudborn way of life. I turned to face Thorun fully, making sure he could see the sincerity in my eyes.

"I understand, Thorun. And I respect the Cloudborn traditions. But just as my bond with Ember means I can't be with another horse, even one from my own people, the same goes for Asher. He's... he's part of me now."

Thorun's eyebrows rose slightly at this, his gaze finally shifting from Asher to me. "You feel this strongly about him?"

I nodded, feeling a warmth spread through my chest as I glanced back at Asher, who was now running his hand along Stormrunner's flank, a look of awe on his face.

"I do. I trust him completely, Thorun. Even though he's not Cloudborn, he's risked everything for me. He's stood by my side through all of this. I love him. He's..." I paused, searching for the right words. "He's my partner, in every sense of the word."

Thorun was quiet for a long moment, his eyes moving between Asher and me. Finally, he let out a deep breath, his shoulders relaxing slightly.

"I see," he said, his voice softer now. "Your great-grandmother, Lyra, they talked about her a lot today and say she had a similar spirit. Always pushing the boundaries of our traditions." A small smile tugged at his lips. "Perhaps it runs in your blood."

I felt a surge of affection for this man, this kinsman I'd only just met but who already cared enough to worry about my well-being. "Thank you for your concern, Thorun. It means a lot to know that you're looking out for me."

He nodded, reaching out to clasp my shoulder in a gesture that felt both foreign and familiar. "You are Cloudborn, Reyna. We protect our own. Always."

As we stood there, watching Asher and Stormrunner begin to form their own bond, I felt a sense of peace settle over me. I had found my people, my heritage. But I hadn't lost the connections I'd made along the way. Somehow, I knew, there would be a way to bridge these two worlds—the one I'd come from and the one I'd just discovered.

Asher finished bonding with Stormrunner and returned to my side. Thorun continued giving him a wary gaze, but then he looked to me, and I took Asher's hand, letting him see me choose to trust this man. A silent understanding passed between us as he gave me a slight nod, then the three of us returned to the party.

As the night wore on, Aria called for everyone's attention. The music died down, and all eyes turned to her as she stood atop a large boulder, her silver hair gleaming in the firelight.

"My people," she began, her voice carrying easily across the gathered crowd. "Tonight, we celebrate the return of one of our own. Reyna, daughter of Lyra's line, has come back to us. But she has also brought us a call to action."

A hush fell over the crowd as Aria continued. "For too long, we have hidden in our mountain, content to protect our own. But the world beyond our borders grows more dangerous. Lothaire of Ironhold seeks our Aurorium, threatening not just our way of life, but the very essence of who we are."

Murmurs of anger rippled through the crowd. Aria raised her hand for silence. "But we will not cower in fear. We are Cloudborn. We are Aegisari. Protection is in our blood, and it is time we extended that protection beyond our borders."

She turned to me then, her eyes blazing with determination. "Reyna has asked for our help in freeing her people, in stopping Lothaire before he can threaten us. I say we give her more than help. I say we join her cause fully."

The crowd erupted in cheers. When they quieted, Aria gestured for me to join her. As I climbed up onto the boulder, my heart pounding, Aria turned to address the crowd once more.

"As Reyna leads us into this new chapter of our history, it is only fitting that she does so as a true Cloudborn warrior." She nodded to Thorun, who stepped forward carrying a bundle wrapped in a white cloth.

Slowly, Thorun unwrapped the bundle, revealing a set of armor that seemed to glow in the firelight. The crowd gasped in awe.

"This armor," Aria announced, "forged from our sacred Aurorium, will protect Reyna in the battles to come. And these," she said as Thorun revealed a pair of curved swords, "are the khopesh, the same style weapons Lyra and her family before her used. With these, Reyna will carve a path to freedom for her people and ours."

Aria turned to me, her eyes shining with pride. "Reyna, daughter of the Cloudborn, will you accept these gifts and the responsibility they carry?"

Tears stung behind my eyes as I struggled to process this great honor. Over the lump tightening in my throat, I answered, "I will, with honor and gratitude."

What followed was a ceremony unlike anything I had ever experienced. Each elder came forward, helping me to don the armor piece by piece. From the gauntlets to the chest piece to the pauldrons, every piece was meticulously placed. They secured the armguards around my forearms and the greaves around my shins. The intricate vambraces were fastened next, followed by the sturdy Aurorium skirt and the carefully molded cuirass. Each piece seemed to hum against my skin, as if awakening some long-dormant part of me.

As the final piece was secured, I felt a surge of energy course through me. The armor, far from feeling heavy, seemed to make me lighter, stronger. When Thorun handed me the khopesh, they felt like extensions of my own arms.

I turned to face the crowd, fully armored, the khopesh gleaming in my hands. For a moment, there was silence. Then, as one, the Cloudborn erupted in cheers, their voices echoing off the mountain walls.

Aria's voice rose above the din. "Behold, Reyna, the Rebel Rose, daughter of the Cloudborn!"

The cheering intensified. As I stood there, feeling the weight of my new armor and the responsibility it represented, I was overwhelmed by a sense of belonging, of purpose.

When the cheers finally died down, I stepped forward, my heart pounding but my voice strong. "My people," I began, the words feeling right in a way I had never experienced before. "I stand before you not just as a warrior, but as a sister. The battles ahead will not be easy, but with your strength behind me, I know we can triumph. Who will stand with me?"

The response was immediate and overwhelming. Warrior after warrior stepped forward, pledging their swords to our cause. Thorun was among the first, as were others I had met throughout the night and some I hadn't seen before.

As I watched them come forward, my heart swelling with gratitude and determination, I knew that this was more than just a rebellion. It was the beginning of a new era. And we, the Cloudborn, the Moonshadow tribe, and my beloved Asher would be the ones to usher it in.

After the last warrior pledged himself to my cause, overwhelmed with gratitude and emotion, I made my way to Aria's side. "Thank you," I said, my voice thick with emotion. "I... I don't know what to say."

Aria placed her hand on my shoulder, her touch warm and comforting. "You don't need to say anything, child. You are Cloudborn. You are family. Your cause is our cause."

As the night wound down, I found myself standing at the edge of the valley, looking out over the moonlit landscape. Asher joined me, his presence a comforting warmth at my side.

"It's really happening, isn't it?" I said softly. "We're going to do this. We're going to free Cassia, free all of them."

Asher nodded, taking my hand in his. "We are. And we're going to win, Reyna. With you leading us, with the Cloudborn at our side, how can we not?"

I turned to him, seeing the faith in his eyes—faith in me, in our cause. In that moment, looking out over the valley where my ancestors had lived for generations, surrounded by the strength and spirit of the Cloudborn, I felt invincible.

Cassia, I thought, my heart swelling with determination. *Hold on, sister. We're coming for you. We're coming for all of you.*

As I stood there, with Asher by my side and the strength of my newfound family behind me, I knew that we were ready for whatever challenges lay ahead. The time for hiding, for surviving, was over. Now was the time to fight, to reclaim what was ours, to build a world where all could be free.

And we would do it together.

CHAPTER TWENTY-SIX
Asher

The sun glinted off Reyna's Aurorium armor as we approached Ironheart, the metal seeming to pulse with its own inner light. Her new khopesh swords were strapped to her back, their curved blades a testament to her newfound heritage. I couldn't help but stare, marveling at how she'd transformed from the fierce but isolated warrior I'd first met into this radiant leader, fully embraced by her people. She looked so beautiful, so powerful, up there on her black mare that it nearly took my breath away.

As if sensing my gaze, Reyna turned to me, a small smile playing at her lips. "Something on your mind, Asher?"

I shook my head, trying to dispel the mix of awe and unease that had settled in my chest. "Just... taking it all in," I said, gesturing to the impressive array of forces surrounding us.

And it was impressive. The Cloudborn warriors, resplendent in their Aurorium armor, marched alongside the determined women from Moonshadow Woods. Interspersed among them were creatures I'd once thought were mere legend—ogres lumbering along, wolves darting between legs, even the occasional cloakfang ursa padding silently at the edges of our group.

It was a sight that would have been unimaginable to me just weeks ago. And yet here I was, riding toward my former home at the head of this magical army.

Thorun rode up beside Reyna, his massive form dwarfing me even as I sat astride Stormrunner, the magnificent Cloudborn stallion I'd been entrusted with.

"We're nearing the city," he rumbled, his eyes fixed on the distant walls of Ironheart.

The city looked so small from this distance, barely recognizable as the massive thing it was. That it held tens of thousands of people inside those high walls... people who would know soon that the Rebel Rose's army was coming straight to their door.

"Your orders, Reyna?" Thorun asked.

I felt a twinge in my chest as Reyna leaned in close to Thorun, discussing strategy in low voices. Their easy camaraderie was evident, born of shared heritage and mutual respect. For a moment, I felt like an outsider looking in—a feeling that had become all too familiar since we'd joined the Cloudborn. Before that, it was me and Reyna together, a partnership that seemed impenetrable to the rest of the world. But now I shared her with countless others, and it was hard not to miss those days where it was just us against the world.

"Asher?" Reyna's voice snapped me out of my brooding. "What do you think? You know the city better than any of us."

Her words warmed me, a reminder that even though it wasn't just the two of us anymore, I was still a valuable part of her plan. As I began to outline the city's defenses, I caught Thorun eyeing me with a gruff stare riddled with wariness. It was clear he still had reservations about trusting a former Kingsguard.

As we continued our approach, still staying well away from the city to prevent drawing out the Iron Swordmaidens too soon, the reality of what we were about to do hit me full force. This was Ironheart—the city I'd sworn to protect, the home I'd left behind. Faces flashed through my mind—fellow guards I'd trained with, servants I'd exchanged friendly words with, even the pudgy old baker who'd always slipped me an extra sweet roll when I was on patrol.

How many of them would be caught in the crossfire of our rebellion? How many might die never understanding why their world had been turned upside down?

The weight of it all threatened to overwhelm me. But then I felt a hand on my arm. Reyna was looking at me, her green eyes full of worry.

"My sister," she said, her voice softer than usual. It sounded almost meek, and nothing like the powerful woman who was prepared to tear down an entire kingdom. "Do you think she's still unmarried and he hasn't taken her yet? I can barely stand the thought of him forcing himself on her. I don't want to be too late."

I saw the worry flickering in her eyes, and I tried my hardest to quell it. "If he followed tradition, she'll be in training to be a wife for a while. Most girls go in at fourteen and aren't married until they are sixteen. Even if they rush her schooling, I can't imagine he's married her yet. I'm sure she's safe in there right now and untouched by Lothaire. We'll find her, Reyna. And we'll save her. We'll save them all."

Her eyes flooded with gratitude, and she gave me a slight nod as I saw that same resolve replace the worry on her face. I knew that look well by now—it was the face of the Rebel Rose, the leader who had united disparate groups under a single banner of freedom. "We will save them all. We won't stop until every woman in Ironheart is free, and I'm reunited with Cassia again."

This was why I'd chosen to follow her, to leave behind everything I'd known. Because Reyna, the Rebel Rose, for all her fierceness, cared about others far more than she cared about herself.

The life I'd left behind lay just beyond those stone barriers. But my future—uncertain, dangerous, but filled with purpose—was right here, riding beside me in gleaming Aurorium armor.

Whatever came next, I knew one thing for certain: there was no going back. The only way was forward, into the storm we were about to unleash.

"Someone will have spotted us by now," I murmured, leaning in close so only she could hear. "They are likely riding back to

Ironheart at a gallop to tell them of the strange army coming their way. We shouldn't get any closer if we don't want to risk pulling out your army too soon."

She nodded, her eyes never leaving the distant walls. "Though I'm glad they've seen us, and I hope it makes them tremble with fear, you're right. We have to play things carefully to time everything just right."

I knew this area outside Ironheart well, so I led our army to a spot I knew would make a good place to camp. It gave us tactical advantage on the off chance we were attacked, and it had water nearby for us and the horses, plus lots of meadows to graze our herd and ample hunting for our army. We worked quickly to set it up, knowing that now we'd been seen without question, we'd have to move fast to make sure we remained in control of the way things played out. Reyna assured us that though we'd been spotted, no doubt, her army wouldn't come out in full force until we marched closer to Ironheart with a menacing intent. Tonight, they would send scouts to secretly investigate us and get an idea of the strength of our forces.

"Come. We should plan our assault," Reyna said to me, gesturing for me to take her hand.

I followed her back into her tent where Thalassa, Gaia, and Thorun were poring over a crude map of the city. The city we were about to siege. My old city. The one I'd sworn to protect.

These thoughts weighed heavily on me as we gathered around together.

"We should march our army here." Reyna pointed to a spot on the map just west of the castle gate. "It's close enough to Ironheart that Lothaire will be threatened enough to send out the full force of his army, and it's close enough that when we convince Jaila to turn and march with us, we'll be at the castle gate in full force within minutes, giving the men inside less time to prepare for the assault."

Thalassa pursed her lips, concern etched on her features. "And you're sure these Iron Swordmaidens will turn and march with us?"

"Yes. I am," Reyna said with certainty. "Every woman in there is always plotting for ways out, but there is no option that doesn't involve certain death. But this plan... with our army and theirs combined, it is enough of an advantage that they'll see we can do it. We can take the city and claim the freedom that every single one of them has dreamed of her whole life. Yes. I'm certain. They'll march with us."

Thorun nodded, his eyes scanning the map. "And once we have them, we turn and march on the castle itself. Here."

Reyna nodded. "Yes. We go in with our joined forces and take control of the city."

I saw Thorun's jaw clench, his eyes burning with a fury I'd come to recognize. "We leave no man alive," he growled. "Not after what they did to our Lyra. To our Reyna. Not after centuries of oppression."

Gaia's eyes blazed with hatred. "I can't wait to feel my sword slice through them. See their eyes as they die the way my Lorna died."

To my dismay, I saw several heads nodding in agreement. Even Reyna seemed to be considering it.

"No," I said, my voice louder than I'd intended. All eyes turned to me. "We can't just slaughter every man inside those walls. There are innocent people in there—people who've never raised a hand against a woman, people who are just trying to survive. I've trained with them, laughed with them, shared meals with them. There are men who, like me, had been born into a system they didn't create. How many of them, given the chance, would choose a different path? We can't slaughter them all. It's not right."

Thorun's eyes narrowed, his voice so deep I could feel it rumbling inside my chest. "And how many innocents have suffered because of their inaction? How many women have been enslaved, abused, killed while these 'innocent' men stood by and did nothing? Men like you." His accusatory eyes narrowed as they locked onto mine. "As Cloudborn, we would never stand by and watch one of our women suffer. We would have fought to free them centuries ago. Unlike you, who merely stood by and did nothing."

Though I wanted to shrink beneath his accurate accusation and the force of his powerful glare, I stood firm.

"You're right. I was one of those men. I stood by silently and watched the horrors inflicted on the women of our kingdom. I did nothing while they were enslaved, forced into marriages, died in our armies. Like every other man in Ironhold, I stayed silent to keep my own head. Do you know the punishment for speaking out for a woman? Defending her against a man? Death. If any man so much as lifts a finger to stop a man from abusing his wife or says aloud that this system is disgusting, his own life is forfeit. So yes, I stood by, and so do many other men that I *know* will understand and even support our cause."

Thorun's imposing figure seemed to grow even taller. "A Cloudborn would have chosen death."

I'd always considered myself an honorable man, but beneath the weight of his stare, I felt my certainty crumbling.

Gaia's eyes met mine, narrowing into slits of rage. "You have no idea what we have been through. You think you have it bad having to remain quiet and watch? Imagine how we felt having to *endure* the pain, the rapes, the torture while you stood there silently. Forgive me for not feeling sorry for the men who allowed us to be abused. Killed. The men who sent the orders that got my Lorna killed just weeks ago." Her voice cracked, and sadness filled her eyes for a moment before she swallowed hard and straightened tall. "If we go in without showing our absolute power, the men will take it back from us the minute they see an opportunity. The safest way to ensure no woman in Ironhold is enslaved again is to slaughter any man in our path and rid them from this kingdom like removing a befouled limb to save a life."

"She has a point, Asher," Reyna said softly. "We can't afford to be soft. Not now. What if we spare men's lives and they betray us? What if there aren't as many men sympathetic to our cause as you think? If we fail and the men take power again, they will take it out on the women tenfold. I can't risk that happening. I won't let more women suffer."

I turned to her, my heart pounding. This was the moment I'd been dreading—the moment when the weight of her mission might overshadow her compassion.

"Reyna," I said, meeting her gaze. "Think about the men you've met since we left Ironheart. Think about the men in Moonshadow Woods. The men in the Cloudborn clan. Hell, think about me. We're proof that not all men are the enemy. It's the *system* that is our enemy, not just anyone with a cock. You've made friends with men. You know there are good ones inside those walls who don't deserve this fate." I stopped, crossed my arms over my chest and straightened my spine. "I could have been one. When I was sent to hunt you down, I tried to turn the Kingsguard off your trail so you could get away. If I had been successful, I would be behind those walls right now, and with your plan, I would be killed. Do you believe I deserve that fate knowing now what you know about me."

"Of course not," she said, "But you're different."

I pointed in the direction of Ironheart. "You have no idea how many men inside may think and feel like me but are too frightened to stand against the system. Against soldiers and kings. When those gates open, some men will fight us. Of course, sure.

Some men are as evil as you believe them to be. But some are not. If we can get those men to lay down their weapons, why would you think it's okay to murder them? If you slaughter them out of spite... out of a vicious hatred that paints all men in one light, then you're no different than they are. And I can't, I refuse to be part of that. If you plan on slaughtering every man in Ironheart, I won't march at your side because I won't feel that you're worthy of my loyalty."

As the words came out of my mouth, I froze, wondering if I'd gone too far. But as much as I wanted to shove them back into my mouth, I realized that they were true. The woman I had come to know, the woman I respected, cared for... loved... she would never kill an innocent person out of spite. If Reyna chose to let the hatred and anger of her council drive her to slaughter even innocents, then I couldn't march with her because then she'd no longer be the woman I thought her to be... the woman I knew she was deep inside.

I saw the conflict in her eyes, the battle between her desire for vengeance and her inherent compassion. For a moment, I feared I'd lost her to her anger. But then, slowly, she nodded.

"You're right," she said. "We can't become the very thing we're fighting against." She turned to the others. "If we just go in there killing every man we see, we're no better than them enslaving every woman they see. Asher has a plan. We should hear him out."

Relief washed over me, but it was short-lived. Now came the hard part.

"The biggest obstacle we face is getting into the city," I began. "Even with our combined forces, we'll be sitting ducks for the archers and catapults on the walls when we march on the city itself. We need the gates open."

"And how do you propose we manage that?" Gaia asked, skepticism clear in her voice.

I took a deep breath. "My brother. Erik. I can convince him to open the gates for us."

The tent erupted in protests. Thorun's voice rose above the others. "You want us to stake our entire plan on the word of a Kingsguard? A man sworn to protect the very king we're trying to overthrow?"

"Erik is more than just a Kingsguard," I argued. "He's my brother. He'll listen to me. And he can help us convince the good men in Ironheart not to fight. To lay down their arms."

"And if he doesn't?" Thalassa asked quietly. "If he betrays us to Lothaire? Our entire plan will be ruined before it begins."

The gravity of what I was proposing hit me full force. I was asking them to risk everything on my faith in my brother. If I was wrong, if Erik chose duty over family... I pushed the thought aside. I couldn't afford to doubt him now.

"I know my brother," I said, my voice firm. "He won't betray us. And think of the advantage we'll have if he's on our side. He can open the gates, rally support from within. It could mean the difference between a bloody siege and a swift end to Lothaire's reign."

Reyna was quiet, her brow furrowed in thought. "It's a big risk, Asher. If Erik doesn't come through, we'll be trapped outside the walls, easy targets for Lothaire's forces."

"What about the ogres?" Gaia asked. "Can they break down the gates? The arrows should bounce off them as they charge it, right?"

Thalassa shook her head softly. "They are strong. Very strong, but I don't know if they have that kind of strength for iron gates. And they are still vulnerable if they get shot in the eyes. Every archer in Ironheart will be shooting at them as they rush in alone, and I feel that's too great of a risk. Plus, they have catapults on the walls. One of those could injure or kill them. I can ask them, however, if they would be willing to try, but it shouldn't be our main plan."

"The Cloakfangs," Thorun said, crossing his arms over his expansive chest. "They can camouflage themselves and walk right past men unaware. With the gates open during the day, could they go in inside and hide, then you communicate with them on how to open the gate?"

I shook my head. "A don't think a Cloakfang can open it. It requires human hands to manipulate the mechanisms, and two sets at that. It's a good idea, but they would have to be able to work fast as we're approaching with an army, and I just don't see two bears being able to get it done. We need humans at the gate."

He frowned, frustrated.

"What if during the day we slipped in a couple of the men from the Moonshadow Tribe," Thalassa suggested. "The Cloudborn won't blend in, but our men, the ones born and raised in the woods, they look just like your average citizen. Could they go in pretending to be merchants or something, hide out and then take the gate at the right time?"

"Can they fight?" Reyna asked, considering this proposal.

Thalassa and Gaia shared a look, then Gaia shook her head. "No. They've never been trained for warfare."

Reyna and I shared a look, and I shook my head. "There is no doubt with the sight of this army nearby, the guards on the gates will be doubled. Or tripled. That means whoever opens the gate needs to be able to walk right up to the mechanism and trigger it without detection. There's no way the guards will let some random merchants walk up there. It will be a fight, and if they can't take on a dozen or more guards, it will be over in seconds."

I stepped forward. "Erik can do this. He's Kingsguard, and likely Head of the Kingsguard by now if my betrayal to Lothaire didn't get him stripped of that position. He can walk right up from the inside and find a way to open those gates. He'll know who to trust in the Kingsguard to help him. Before anyone knows what's happening, the gates will be opening."

"This is a huge risk, Asher, to trust him with our plan. To trust him *and* another man not to betray us." Reyna's eyes met mine.

"I know," I said softly. "But it's a risk we have to take. If we go in with force alone, how many innocents will die in the crossfire? Can the ogres get those gates open eventually if they don't fall first? Maybe. Can our Cloudborn archers and the Iron Swordmaidens lay down cover to keep the men stationed on the wall busy while they work? Yes. But that should be our last resort. There will no doubt be far more casualties on both sides with that plan. With my plan, we have a chance to minimize casualties on both sides. Erik opens the gates, and we can flood right in and spread the word any man who lays down his arms that he will be spared. I think you may be surprised how many guards and citizens simply step out of our way. And some may even surprise us, and like me, and like I know Erik will do, fight at our side."

The tent fell silent as everyone considered my words. I could see the doubt on their faces, the fear. But I also saw something else—a glimmer of hope. The possibility of ending this with less bloodshed was tempting, even to those who thirsted for vengeance.

Finally, Reyna spoke. "Okay," she said. "We'll try it your way, Asher. But you understand what's at stake here? If this goes wrong..."

"I know," I said, meeting her gaze. "I won't let you down, Reyna. I promise."

She nodded, then turned to the others. "Asher will infiltrate the city tonight. He'll speak with his brother and attempt to secure our entry."

"And this entering your city is so easy?" Thorun stiffened. "How are you going to do this without getting caught?"

"I know the city like the back of my hand. There are ways for a person to sneak in and out."

Worry flickered in Reyna's eyes. "And if you get caught?"

"I won't. But if I'm not back by dawn, then you can assume I'm taken, and you'll have to figure out another plan to get the gates opened."

"I'll send Rashka with him." Thalassa gestured to the raven on her shoulder. "He's my kindrion, meaning he's the one animal that I can see through his eyes and communicate with him anywhere at any time. Distance doesn't matter. He can help by moving ahead of Asher warning him of threats, and if something happens, I'll know it instantly because I'll be here watching through his eyes."

"And spying to make sure I'm honest about what happens with my brother?" I arched an eyebrow.

She raised hers in return. "Ensuring that I'm not sending my tribe from Moonshadow Woods to an ambush by the Kingsguard at the castle gate? Yes. You're right."

I chuckled, nodding my head. "Well, thank you for sending Rashka with me. I'll welcome the help."

As the others began to discuss the details of the assault, Reyna pulled me aside. "Are you sure about this?" she asked, her voice low. "You're *sure* Erik won't betray us? You're asking me to put a lot of faith in someone I've never met."

I took her hand in mine, marveling at how natural it felt now. "I'm sure," I said. "Erik is a good man, Reyna. Remember how he did the right thing for our sister? He'll do the right thing again. Trust me. I trust him the same way we're putting all our trust in your bond with Jaila. Both plans mean taking a risk, but I believe in him as much as you believe in her."

"Yes, but Jaila will be fighting for her own freedom. Erik will be risking his cushy future for our cause."

"That's true," I noted, her point valid, "but I know him. He helped me free our sister. He hates this system. He won't want to be on the opposite side of a fight as me. Just like Jaila, I know he'll help us."

She squeezed my hand, a worried smile playing on her lips. "Let's hope we're both right."

I pulled her against me, pressing my lips to hers as I kissed her deeply. When our lips broke apart, I brushed my fingers against her cheek and pressed my forehead to hers, staring into those eyes I loved so much. "I won't let you down, Reyna. I promise."

As I prepared to leave, gathering the few supplies I'd need for my covert entry into the city, I couldn't shake the weight of responsibility that had settled on my shoulders. So many lives hung in the balance. If I was wrong about Erik, if he chose duty over family...

No. I couldn't think like that. Erik was my brother. He would listen. He had to.

As night fell, I made my way to the edge of our camp. Reyna was there, waiting to see me off. Without a word, she pulled me into a fierce embrace.

"Come back to me," she whispered. "Whatever happens in there, just... come back."

I held her tight, breathing in her scent, drawing strength from her presence. "I will," I promised. "And when I do, it'll be with the key to our victory."

With one last kiss, I bid her goodbye. Rashka flew just ahead of me prepared to caw and warn me of any dangers ahead as I slipped into the darkness, heading toward the city I once called home. I sent up a silent prayer to whatever gods might be listening. Not for my safety, but for the strength to do what needed to be done. For the wisdom to find the right words to convince Erik. And for the courage to face whatever consequences my actions might bring.

The fate of Ironheart, of Reyna's rebellion, of countless lives, now rested on my shoulders and on the bond between two brothers.

CHAPTER TWENTY-SEVEN
Reyna

The sun hadn't yet risen when Asher left, melting into the shadows with a raven as his guide. I watched until he disappeared from sight, my heart heavy with worry. It was the first time we'd been apart since this journey began, and his absence felt like a physical ache.

What if he was caught? What if his brother betrayed him? The possibilities swirled in my mind, each one more terrifying than the last.

Sleep wouldn't come. I sat by the fire, watching embers rise into the dark. Around me, scattered across the camp, dozens of smaller fires glowed softly—pockets of warmth where our army slept. Cloudborn and Moonshadow warriors lay side by side, no longer divided by tribe or blood. Over the past week, since reuniting in Moonshadow Woods, they'd marched as one—fighting, training, laughing together. Friendships had formed fast, forged by a shared cause and a common enemy. Curiosity had replaced suspicion, and the lines between them had blurred with every mile toward Ironheart. Now that we'd arrived, I was grateful for the quiet. The stillness. The few hours of rest before the storm broke.

I glanced out into the trees surrounding us, wondering if any of my sisters from the Iron Swordmaidens were out there, watching us, counting heads and wondering what kind of horror may be coming their way. How shocked they must be seeing ogres and bears and wolves mixed with this strange army of huge Cloudborn men and women. If I was still the Iron Rose, I would be having us monitored at all times, preparing to defend against this unknown force but not engaging them, just hoping they were just passing by, moving on to leave us in their wake. I wondered what Jaila must be thinking now, not knowing it was me leading this strange army and invading the territory Lothaire would certainly command her defend. What would I have been thinking when I was in her boots not long ago?

Gods, it felt like ages had passed since I was the Iron Rose, and yet it had only been a month. How my life had changed so drastically in those fleeting days. I'd escaped from Ironheart, a fugitive on the run. I'd discovered the Moonshadow Tribe with their magical creatures and women hiding amongst the safety of their woods. I'd learned I was Aegisari, a descendent of the Cloudborn Clan, and I'd met my people and found a welcoming community embracing me with open arms.

And Asher.

My heart ached not seeing him here by my side.

I'd forged a bond with a man so deep that it felt unbreakable, and I'd found something in him that I'd never dreamed possible for someone like me.

Love.

I glanced at the woods where I'd last seen him, praying to the gods for him to be successful in his mission and return to me soon.

"You look troubled, Reyna," Thorun's deep voice startled me from my brooding.

I turned to find him studying me, his green eyes—so like my own—filled with concern. "I'm worried about Asher."

He grumbled, and I knew he still didn't trust the man I'd given my whole heart to. He wasn't Aegisari. Wasn't Cloudborn. And he'd been Kingsguard, the very man that had partaken in this system we now vowed to end. Thorun didn't seem to find forgiveness, or trust, an easy task.

Instead of arguing with him again about how Asher wouldn't betray us, I pushed up off the ground. "I need to work on my shielding. It would be really nice if I could finally get it to work *before* we go into battle against the entire Kingsguard. We've been practicing for days and nothing," I admitted, frustration evident in my voice.

Thorun stepped up beside me. "The Aegisari abilities take time to master. Months. Years even. You're already doing remarkably well with the healing and enhanced strength."

Shielding was one of the most valuable Aegisari abilities, allowing us to generate a protective energy barrier that could deflect attacks. Most Aegisari could shield themselves with practice, while a rare few could even extend their shields to protect others. But despite days of trying, despite mastering the enhanced healing and strength that came naturally to me, I couldn't summon even the faintest flicker of a shield. Every blow Thorun had thrown at me had landed, and the battle ahead wouldn't be fought with sticks.

"But the shield is what could save lives when we march on Ironhold," I said, touching my Aurorium chestplate. The metal seemed to warm beneath my fingers, responding to my touch in a way no ordinary armor would. In the week since discovering my heritage, I'd grown more attuned to the subtle ways the Aurorium interacted with me—how it accelerated my healing, how it made me faster, stronger when I wore it.

"Let's try again," Thorun suggested. "A different approach this time."

Grateful for his patience, I followed him to a small clearing away from the camp. As we walked, Thorun continued explaining the intricacies of our shared heritage—knowledge I was still absorbing.

"Remember, Aurorium is most potent when it's still in the mountain," he said. "Once harvested, it slowly loses its magical energy over time. Each time you activate your shield, you drain a little more. In about two years, your weapons and armor will be no stronger than regular steel."

I frowned, sliding my hand across the beautiful armor they'd created for me. "I hate that this is temporary."

Thorun nodded. "When it's time, you'll get new armor. New weapons. Unless we can find magic out in the world to recharge them with, they'll fade in time. But for now, they're incredibly strong—even more so than Nocturnium. But only the Aegisari can harness the magical energy within. For other people with magic, it steals their power temporarily, which then fuels the Aurorium back up again. For us, it expands our power, merging with our essence to make us stronger. Faster. More resilient."

"I've felt that part," I acknowledged, recalling how effortlessly I'd moved in our last skirmish, how my reflexes had quickened beyond what should have been possible. "And the healing—I've never recovered so quickly before."

"But never forget that we're not invincible," Thorun warned. "A killing blow is still fatal. And the more wounds you take at once, the slower you heal as the power in our bloodline must split focus. Too many wounds and you can still bleed out before you repair yourself. And the ability to heal others I can't teach you as I don't possess that power, and I'm not sure if you do. It's something you'd have to explore with Aria when you return to the mountain. She has that power."

"And then there's the shield," I said, returning to my primary concern. "You make it look so easy."

Thorun tapped the armor at his chest. "When you are truly connected with it, one with it, then all you have to do is think about deflecting a blow, and it is done."

"But *how*? You say if an arrow is coming toward me, I can just think about stopping it and it will bounce off me. But we've tried. It doesn't work for me."

As we reached a small clearing in the woods, he turned to face me, those intense eyes locking with mine. "We've been too gentle."

"What do you mean?" I asked.

"Spar with me," he said, his voice taking on an edge I hadn't heard before. He drew his sword—not a practice stick, but his actual Aurorium blade that gleamed dangerously in the dappled moonlight of the clearing.

"Wait, what?" I stared at him in disbelief. "With real weapons?"

His eyes hardened. "Go ahead. Try to strike me. As hard as you can. Miss, and I'll make you pay." His voice was playful, but the steel in his eyes told me he wasn't entirely joking.

My heartbeat quickened. This wasn't our usual training session. He was genuinely threatening me—or at least wanted me to believe he was. I drew my blades, suddenly uncertain.

"Don't hesitate," he warned. "In battle, hesitation means death."

Swallowing my fear, I lunged forward, swinging my blade with genuine intent. The result was immediate and powerful—a golden burst of energy erupted from Thorun's armor, sending me flying backward with much more force than ever before. I hit the ground hard, skidding several feet before coming to a stop.

For a moment, I just lay there, stunned by the raw power of his shield. This wasn't the controlled demonstration I'd felt before—this was the full force of an Aegisari warrior's protection.

Before I could fully recover, Thorun was advancing, sword raised. "Get up!" he commanded. "Your enemy won't wait!"

I scrambled to my feet, barely raising my blade in time to deflect his strike. But my shield didn't activate, and his blade sliced across my forearm. I gasped as blood welled from the cut—shallow but real.

"I'm sorry," he said, genuine regret in his eyes as he stepped back. "I thought perhaps your shield would activate facing a true threat."

The cut was already healing, the edges of the wound knitting together as my Aurorium armor worked its magic, but that didn't lessen the sting or shock.

"Again," I said, gritting my teeth.

"Reyna—"

"Again!" I insisted, dropping into a fighting stance.

Thorun nodded, his expression grim, and came at me once more. We exchanged blows, real ones this time, and though I managed to deflect some with my swords, others found their mark. A slice across my thigh. A nick on my shoulder. Each one healing almost as quickly as it was delivered, but each one hurting nonetheless.

"Focus!" Thorun shouted as his blade came down. "Feel the energy in your armor! Channel it! Make it part of you!"

I tried with everything in me, visualizing a shield, willing the energy to flow outward rather than inward. I could feel the Aurorium responding to me, warming against my skin, but the shield wouldn't come.

In desperation, I launched myself at Thorun, blades swinging in a flurry of strikes. Once again, his shield flared to life, the golden energy throwing me backward like I was nothing more than a rag doll. I crashed into a tree trunk, the air driven from my lungs.

Thorun was at my side instantly, his face etched with concern as he pulled me to my feet. "Enough," he said firmly. "It's too much. I thought this would help, but I won't hurt you anymore. We'll figure out another way."

I wanted to argue, to demand we continue, but my body ached from the multiple cuts and impacts. Even with the accelerated healing, I was exhausted.

"Maybe," I panted, leaning against the tree, "maybe I just can't do it. Maybe I don't have that ability."

"Nonsense," Thorun said, his voice gentler now. "You have the blood of the Aegisari. The shield will come when you need it most." He squeezed my shoulder. "The coming battle will be challenge enough without wearing yourself down today."

Finally, admitting defeat, I nodded. He reached down and pulled me up to standing, brushing the dirt off my shoulders.

"You'll get it, Reyna. But like I said, this takes time. Let us rest now."

As we walked back to camp, I found myself curious about Thorun's life. "Do you have a wife?" I asked. "When we were on Mistveil Mountain, you mentioned that Cloudborn have very strong connections with their partners. Do you have one back home?"

His face darkened, pain flashing in his eyes. "I had a love," he said softly. "She was killed in an attack from one of the northern tribes."

My heart ached for him, and a flash of worry about the realities of losing Asher pierced my gut. "I'm so sorry, Thorun."

He nodded, his voice growing wistful. "Among the Cloudborn, men and women are equals in all things. But there's something special that happens when you meet your true partner. You balance each other perfectly, your strengths and weaknesses merging into a perfect whole. We had that." His face hardened. "One day, I'll hunt down the tribe that killed her."

"What happened?" I asked gently.

"A tribe from the north wanted Aurorium to combat the magic attacking them. They are not Cloudborn or Aegisari, so we denied them. They refused to take no for an answer, and they struck at us to get it." His voice grew tight with anger and grief. "She fell in battle fighting bravely."

"I'm so sorry, Thorun. That must have been awful."

"It was two years ago, but it still feels like yesterday. I miss her. And I *will* avenge her."

I reached out and pressed a hand to his oversized arm. "I have no doubt you'll avenge her. This tribe. You said they live in the north? I don't know anything about what's north of the Southlands." Then I frowned, confused. "Wait, did you say the north has magic?"

Thorun nodded. "North of the Mistveil Mountains, magic is still alive and well. When they learned of the Southlands' attacks on magic, they decided they didn't want to befall the same fate. They knew the Mistveil Mountains were impassable because of the terrain and us, so to prevent Southlanders from sailing around and reaching them by sea, they had a powerful sorcerer magically seal the oceans on either side to prevent Southlanders from coming after them."

My eyes widened in surprise. "Is that why the seas are impassable? Magic?"

"Yes. Sorcerers cast powerful spells, creating the fogs, sea monsters, and turbulent waters surrounding their half of the continent. No one can reach them now. The only way through is the Mistveil Mountains."

I marveled at this new information, my mind reeling with the implications. But seeing the sadness in Thorun's eyes as I knew he thought about his lost love, I didn't press further.

As we returned to camp, my thoughts drifted back to Asher. I stared at the horizon, willing him to appear, safe and successful.

"He'll return," Thorun said softly, following my gaze.

Even though I knew that Thorun didn't trust Asher, and deep down thought a Cloudborn shouldn't be with a Kingsguard, especially one who'd been upholding the system for so long, I appreciated his support. I nodded, hoping desperately that he was right. As night fell and there was still no sign of Asher, I retreated to my tent, my worry gnawing at me. I touched the Aurorium pendant at my throat, drawing comfort from its warm glow.

"Please," I whispered into the darkness. "Please come back to me, Asher. Be safe."

The fate of our mission—and my heart—hung in the balance, waiting on Asher's return.

CHAPTER TWENTY-EIGHT
Asher

The familiar streets of Ironheart lay before me, shrouded in darkness. As Head of the Kingsguard, I had memorized every hidden passageway, every nook and cranny of this city. Now, those same secrets would aid in my infiltration.

Rashka flew silently ahead of me. I still couldn't believe I was working with a bird, but I had to admit, the creature's ability to help me infiltrate the city was invaluable. As we approached a narrow alley, Rashka let out a soft caw. I froze, pressing myself against the cold stone wall. Moments later, a patrol of guards marched past, their torchlight flickering mere feet from where I stood.

Once they passed, Rashka cawed again, signaling it was safe to move. We continued this dance through the city—the raven warning, me hiding, then pressing on. It was slow going, but we were making progress.

Finally, we reached the castle where I had once lived. It felt surreal being back in the place I'd once called home, but instead of walking these halls with men bowing and stepping out of my way, I was navigating them like a thief, dipping in and out of darkness and hidden passageways avoiding detection. My heart hammered in my chest as I slipped out from a secret tunnel made to scurry the king away in an attack, and I stepped into the hall, navigating the familiar corridors until I reached Erik's quarters. Taking a deep breath, I eased the door open.

Erik lay sleeping, his face peaceful in the dim moonlight filtering through the window. For a moment, I hesitated. How would he feel seeing me again? It had only been a month since we'd parted, but so much had happened. So much had changed. It felt like a lifetime ago since I'd last seen him.

"Erik," I whispered, gently shaking his shoulder. "Wake up."

His eyes snapped open, hand instinctively reaching for the sword beside his bed. Then recognition dawned, and his expression morphed from alarm to disbelief.

"Asher?" he breathed, sitting up. "What in the name of—"

I clasped my hand over his mouth, silencing him. "Quiet," I hissed. "We can't risk anyone hearing."

Erik nodded, and I removed my hand. For a long moment, we just stared at each other. Then, without warning, Erik jumped to his feet and pulled me into a fierce embrace.

"You idiot," he muttered, his voice thick with emotion. "Do you have any idea what you've done?"

I returned the hug, relief washing over me. "I'm sorry, Erik. I truly am."

He pulled back, his eyes searching my face. "I'm proud of you," he said softly. "And furious. Gods, Asher, I almost lost my head because of you. Luckily, they let me keep it, but I've been demoted. The shame you brought on our family name..."

My heart sank. "You're not Head of the Kingsguard?"

Erik shook his head. "No. Sir Edmund holds that honor now."

I practically spat at the mention of Edmund's name. The man was a snake, cruel and ambitious. This complicated things significantly. It had been my hope that as Head of the Kingsguard he could use his powerful position to rally more men to fight beside us. But now the man in that position was one whose cruelty to women was renowned. He was exactly the kind of man Reyna and her army wanted to slaughter, and that meant he'd be pushing his Kingsguard to fight us with everything they had.

"Fuck," I grumbled beneath my breath.

Erik looked at me, unaware of the conflict now surging through my mind. "I'm sorry," I said again. "I never meant for you to suffer for my actions. But Erik, I couldn't do it. I couldn't kill her."

"The Rebel Rose they call her now," Erik said, his voice low. "So, you followed your heart after all. I knew you wouldn't be able to do it." A small smile pulled up on his lips. "Well, what happened?"

I launched into an explanation of everything that had happened since I'd left Ironheart. Erik listened, his expression growing more incredulous with each passing moment.

He pointed at Rhaska, who perched on the back of his dining chair. "So that's..."

"A kindrion. A bird linked to an Animara named Thalassa. The leader of the free women of Moonshadow Woods."

He gave the bird an awkward wave. "Uh, hi?"

Rhaska cawed back.

"Gods, this is unbelievable," he said shaking his head. "You're really serious? Ogres, magic, Cloudborn... it's all real?"

"It's all real."

He blew out a breath. "Fuck. This is madness."

"It is madness, but no more than this system we live in," I went on, "It's broken, Erik. The way we treat women, the way we enslave them—it's wrong. We have to change it."

Erik ran a hand through his hair, conflict clear on his face. "I know this, Asher. I was there when we freed our sister from it. And though I agree, do you really think this rebellion is the answer? Asher, it's madness. You're talking about overthrowing the entire kingdom!"

"It's not just me," I argued. "The Rebel Rose has an army. Cloudborn warriors, magical creatures—things we thought were myths. And if anyone stands against her, she'll slaughter them all."

Fear flickered in Erik's eyes. "You can't be serious."

"I am. Which is why I need your help. We need to stop the men from fighting when they come. Can you do that?"

Erik paced the room, agitation clear in every movement. "How? I'm not Head of the Kingsguard. My influence is limited."

"But you're respected," I pressed. "The men trust you. When we breech the walls, if you can convince them to stand down, to not engage when the Rebel Rose's army arrives, we can avoid a bloodbath. Reyna will not harm any man who stands aside."

For a long moment, Erik was silent, weighing my words. Finally, he nodded. "I'll do what I can. But Asher, I can't promise anything. For as many good men as I know want to see an end to this cruel system, there are as many who thrive in it. But I'll do my best. You have my word."

Relief flooded through me. "Thank you. There's one more thing—we need the gates opened when we arrive."

Erik's eyes widened. "Are you insane? That's impossible. It takes two men to open those gates, and how am I supposed to find someone to work with me and not just run and turn me in for treason?"

"I know it's a lot to ask," I said, desperation creeping into my voice. "But it's crucial. Without those gates open, we're sitting ducks for the archers on the walls. Please, Erik. I'm counting on you to be there, to find someone you can trust to help you."

Erik ran a hand over his face, the weight of my request clearly weighing on him. "I'll... I'll try. Gods, Asher, do you have any idea what you're asking of me?"

"I do," I said softly. "And I wouldn't ask if there was any other way. But this is our chance to change things, to make Ironheart better for everyone."

"And for her." He said it as fact, and not as a question.

I met his knowing eyes and nodded. "And for her. I love her, Erik. I love her with every ounce of my soul. My very being."

A long silence stretched between us. Finally, Erik smiled. "I'm happy for you, brother. I think you're crazy, but I'm happy for you."

I smiled back, clasping his shoulder. "I knew I could count on you."

"I'll do my best. But Asher, if this goes wrong..."

"It won't," I said, with more confidence than I felt. "I know you can do this. I believe in you, brother."

He let out an exaggerated breath, "You're going to get us all killed. Yourself and that woman included."

"We can do this. I know it. Just promise me you'll find a way to open that gate when you see us coming."

With a heavy sigh, he nodded. "I'll find a way."

My heart swelled with my love for the man who had been at my side my whole life, and I knew I could count on our bond holding steadfast through whatever came our way. "I knew you would, brother."

We embraced once more, and then it was time for me to go. I needed to get back out of the city while it slept and use the cover of darkness as my ally. We quickly discussed the final plans for how he would know to open the gates, then with Rhaska checking for guards outside and giving me the go ahead, I slipped out of Erik's room.

As I slunk through the hidden corridors leaving the castle, a nagging doubt gnawed at me. What if Erik decided to tell the king? He could regain the family honor, secure his position, and become richer than his wildest dreams if he turned me in. But as quickly as the thought invaded my mind, I pushed it away. He was my brother. My blood. And I trusted him with not only my life, but with Reyna's and every person who'd committed themselves to our cause.

Rashka led me back through the winding streets toward the secret passage I'd used to enter the city. We were almost there when the raven let out an urgent caw. I pressed myself against the wall, but the soft glow of the streetlight illuminated my position. I glanced left and right, trying to find a better hiding spot, but it was too late. Four guards emerged around the corner, their torchlight sweeping across me as I froze, hoping like hell they didn't recognize me.

But my heart sank as I recognized their leader—Sir Mark, a man I'd never gotten along with. He'd envied me since we were children, and I'd beat him at every game we'd ever played, then I'd become the youngest Head of the Kingsguard ever, stepping right over him. He'd always hated me just as much as I hated him.

His face split into a cruel grin. "Well, well," he drawled. "Look what we have here. The traitor returns."

Rhaska screamed again, and I reached for my sword, but before I could draw it, something struck me from behind. Stars exploded in my vision as I fell to my knees. Rough hands grabbed me, wrenching my arms behind my back.

"King Lothaire will reward us handsomely for your head, *traitor,*" Sir Mark sneered, grabbing my hair and yanking my head back.

They began to drag me through the deserted streets toward the castle. Panic clawed at my throat. This couldn't be how it ended. Not when we were so close.

Reyna.

Her face flashed through my mind, and I wondered if I'd ever see it again. If they got me to the castle, Lothaire would have me beheaded before I even left the throne room. As much as he loved a public show, my betrayal would cut too deep. He wouldn't wait for the executioner—he'd lop my head off the moment he laid eyes on me.

I started to struggle, knowing I could take them in a fair fight, but I stopped when I felt the blades pressing against my neck. With one flick of their wrists, they could split my throat open and end my fight right here in the streets. As we continued back toward the castle, plan after plan for my escape flickered through my mind, but just as quickly, I dismissed them as impossible.

Just when I started to succumb to the realization I was marching to my unavoidable death, a familiar caw pierced the night. Rashka swooped down, talons raking across Sir Mark's face. He yelled, swatting at the bird who darted out of the way.

Then, to my amazement, more animals appeared. Cats slunk out of the shadows, hissing and spitting. One launched itself onto a guard's face, its sharp claws and teeth raking at his skin and leaving blood in its wake before it jumped to safety. Rats swarmed around the guards' feet scurrying up their legs and causing them to scream as they tried to swat them off. Even a flock of chickens emerged from a nearby coop, pecking and flapping at the men.

In the chaos, the guards let go of me to fight off their animal attackers, and a wide grin stretched across my face.

Thalassa.

She was watching through Rashka's eyes and now calling on the city's animals to come to my aid.

"What the fuck?" Sir Mark shouted as a chicken flapped against his face.

He swatted it out of the air, and it flew away to safety. He turned, his eyes scanning the animals surrounding him, then they landed on mine. I knew I couldn't leave any of these men alive to report that they'd seen me, so I wasted no time. I drew my sword, launching across the small divide between us, his eyes flashing wide just before my blade slipped through his throat. As I stood there, face to face with him while he choked on his blood, I smiled.

"You've never beaten me at anything, Sir Mark. I don't know why you thought tonight would be any different."

I yanked out my sword, and he dropped to his knees, gurgling and choking as a red pool of blood grew around him.

I made quick work of the other three distracted guards, their bodies joining his in lifeless heaps on the cobblestones. I knew we'd likely drawn attention to ourselves with all the noise, and more guards would arrive soon, so I didn't linger.

"Thank you for your help. I appreciate it. Truly," I said to the animals, though it felt strange to do so and I had no idea if they could understand me.

The rats started to feast on the flesh of the fallen men, and I smiled. "Enjoy."

Wasting no more time, I followed Rashka, sprinting through the streets until we reached the secret passage, and I slipped inside, heart pounding. Only when I emerged outside the city walls did I allow myself to breathe. I'd made it. Against all odds, I'd succeeded in my mission.

As I made my way back to our camp, exhaustion and relief warred within me. I'd spoken to Erik, planted the seeds of our plan. But would it be enough? The image of those gates loomed large in my mind. Everything hinged on them opening when we arrived.

If they didn't... I shuddered at the thought of Reyna and our army trapped outside, easy targets for the archers on the walls. The potential for catastrophic bloodshed was all too real.

But I had to have faith. Faith in Erik, faith in our cause, faith in the bond between brothers that had weathered so much already.

As the first light of dawn began to paint the sky, I finally caught sight of our camp. Reyna stood at its edge, scanning the horizon. When she saw me, her face lit up with relief. She ran toward me, and I caught her in my arms, holding her tight.

"You made it," she breathed, her voice muffled against my chest.

I stroked her hair, savoring the warmth of her body against mine. "I did."

"I was worried, Asher. So worried. I was with Thalassa when you were captured. She saw it through Rashka's eyes. I thought the worst was going to happen."

"Thanks to her, I'm alive and back here with you. She saved me having all those animals come to my aid."

"It took her so much energy to communicate with that many animals at a distance that I thought it was going to kill her. She collapsed when it was over, and she's still recovering."

"Then I need to go and thank her. I wouldn't be here without her."

Reyna leaned up and kissed me, her lips soft but desperate. I held them against mine, just enjoying the feeling of her lips on mine thinking how close I was to almost never tasting them again.

Reyna pulled back, her green eyes searching my face. "Well, how did it go? Thalassa reported that things sounded good? Do you agree?"

I managed a tired smile. "I trust Erik is going to do everything in his power to help us. I'm not saying he may not fail. I've given him a difficult job, but he won't betray us. We have a chance, Reyna. A real chance."

She sighed, leaning up on her toes and kissing me once again. I took her hand, and as we walked back toward Thalassa's tent so I could thank her, I began to recount my adventure in the city. With each word, I felt the weight of our impending assault settle more firmly on my shoulders. We had set things in motion now, for better or worse.

Tomorrow, we would march on Ironheart. And the fate of the entire kingdom would hang in the balance.

CHAPTER TWENTY-NINE
Reyna

The air crackled with tension as we marched toward Ironheart. The rhythmic thud of ogre footsteps, the soft padding of bear and wolf paws, and the steady clop of horse hooves formed the cadence of our approach. Like nature's own war drums pulsing with the heartbeat of our unified force. The very atmosphere seemed alive with energy, as if the world itself held its breath, waiting for the storm of battle to break upon Ironheart's walls.

As we approached the spot I had designated for our initial encounter, I saw them—the Iron Swordmaidens, my former sisters-in-arms, standing in full force. A small smile tugged at my lips. It was working. They had come out in full strength, just as I had hoped.

But as we drew closer, doubt began to gnaw at me. What if I was wrong? What if the bond I shared with these women, forged through years of shared struggle and sacrifice, wasn't enough? In mere minutes, I could be facing an attack from the very sisters I had trained alongside, fought beside, bled with.

I glanced back at our army—a motley crew of Cloudborn warriors, Moonshadow tribe, and magical creatures. They were brave, but against the battle-hardened Iron Swordmaidens? The potential for devastating losses on both sides made my stomach churn.

Everything hinged on this moment. On my bond with Jaila. On the hope that the women I had led for so long would see the truth in our cause.

I urged Ember forward, breaking away from our lines. As I rode, I spotted a familiar figure advancing from the other side. Jaila, my old friend and second-in-command. My chest tightened with a mix of longing and apprehension.

We met in the space between our armies, the tension palpable. For a moment, we just stared at each other, drinking in the sight of a friend we thought we might never see again. Jaila's face was a mask of conflicting emotions—relief, anger, hope, fear.

"Reyna?" Jaila breathed, her voice barely above a whisper. "By the gods, is it really you?"

I nodded, fighting back tears. "It's me, Jaila. I've come back. I'm sorry," I murmured. "I'm so sorry I left you all behind."

"I thought you were dead," she choked out. "We all did." Jaila's composure cracked, and I saw her preparing to dismount, no doubt to hug me the way I wanted to hug her.

I shook my head. "Don't. We have to look like enemies," I said, staying atop Ember.

She furrowed her brow, settling back onto her horse, confusion and conflict filling her eyes. "Reyna, what are you doing? Do you have any idea the danger you're putting us in by coming here like this? Are you... are you seriously attacking us? Your sisters?"

I took a deep breath, steeling myself for what came next. "Gods, no. Of course not. I'm here to free you," I said, my voice steady despite the nerves fluttering in my stomach. "All of you. To give you a chance at the life we've always dreamed of."

Jaila's eyes widened in disbelief. "Free us? Reyna, have you lost your mind? Do you know what they'll do to us if we even consider such a thing?"

"I do," I said softly. "But Jaila, look behind me. Look at the army I've brought. We have a real chance here. A chance to end the rule of cruel men once and for all."

Jaila's gaze swept over our forces, a flicker of hope sparking in her eyes. But fear quickly doused it. "And if we fail?" she asked, her voice barely audible.

I gave her a look, letting the weight of my next sentence settle between us. "Then we fail fighting for our freedom," I replied. "Isn't that better than living another day under their rule?"

I could see the conflict raging within her, the weight of responsibility for the women under her command warring with the desire for freedom. I pressed on, pouring every ounce of passion and conviction I had into my words.

"Jaila, think of all we've endured. The battles we've been forced to fight, the sisters we've lost. We have a chance now—a real chance—to change everything. To build a world where our daughters won't have to live in fear, where they can choose their own paths."

Hope glistened in Jaila's eyes. "Do you really think we can do this?"

"We have allies," I said, gesturing to the diverse army behind me. "Powerful allies. And we have the element of surprise. But more than that, we have the strength of our conviction. We're not just fighting for ourselves, Jaila. We're fighting for every woman who's ever been silenced, every girl who's ever been told she's worth less because of her gender. Together, I know we can take this kingdom and end the reign of men. Today."

I could see the moment Jaila made her decision. Her shoulders straightened, and a fierce light entered her eyes. "Okay. We're in. What's the plan?" she asked, a smile tugging at her lips.

Relief and excitement surged through me as we quickly hashed out the details. When we'd finalized our plan, we exchanged the same look we'd always shared right before a battle. A look that said I have your back no matter what.

As I watched Jaila ride back to the Iron Swordmaidens, my heart swelled with hope and determination. The fight ahead would be fraught with danger, but with my sisters by my side once more,

I felt invincible. The real battle was about to begin, and we were ready.

Knowing now I would have the full force of the Iron Swordmaidens at my side when we attacked Ironheart, I rode back to my army and addressed them.

"We have the support of the Iron Swordmaidens," I said loudly. The simple statement brought a rumble of cheers from my forces, and I couldn't help but grin widely as Ember danced beneath me, feeling my excitement.

"Soon we will march on Ironheart, and Gods willing, we will tear down this system from the inside and ensure no woman in Ironheart will ever suffer the abuses of men again!"

The roar of my army shook the very ground around me.

I turned to the brave non-warriors from Moonshadow Woods who had come with us to bolster our appearance. "You've done your part," I told them, my heart swelling with gratitude. "You've made our army look larger, more intimidating, to draw out my old army. And it worked. But you're not trained for battle. The Cloudborn, the battlemaidens, and the Iron Swordmaidens can handle it from here. You don't need to risk your lives further."

To my surprise, a chorus of protests rose up. "We want to finish this," one woman called out. "We've come this far. Let us see it through!"

"You'll have fewer losses with a larger force," another pointed out.

I looked out at their determined faces, women who had known peace in Moonshadow Woods but were willing to risk everything for the freedom of others. Emotion welled up in my throat, nearly choking me.

"Thank you," I managed, my voice thick. "Your courage honors us all."

As I rejoined our lines, I caught Asher's eye. He gave me a nod, his face a mixture of pride and concern. I wanted to reach out to him, to draw strength from his unwavering support, but there was no time. The moment of truth had arrived.

Jaila gave the signal we had agreed upon, making it look like she was leading a charge. My heart pounding, I raised my sword high. "For freedom!" I shouted, my voice carrying across the field.

The air itself seemed to tremble as my army surged forward with a thunderous roar that shook the very earth. Across the field, the Iron Swordmaidens charged as well, their battle cries a fierce counterpoint to our own. For a heart-stopping moment, the world held its breath as two unstoppable forces hurtled toward each other, the promise of devastating carnage hanging heavy in the air. Then, to the shock of the Kingsguard watching from afar, our armies crashed together not in combat, but in unity. Like two mighty rivers converging into a single, unstoppable torrent, we merged forces, our battle cries now lifting into one. Our forces united, we pivoted westward, our combined might now focused on a single, shared purpose.

The power of our united army was overwhelming. Cloudborn warriors with their gleaming Aurorium weapons, fierce battlemaidens from various kingdoms, the brave women of Moonshadow Woods, magical creatures that defied belief, and my own Iron Swordmaidens—all fighting as one for a common cause.

As we thundered toward the gates, exhilaration filled every inch of my battle-readied body. We had done it. Against all odds, we had united. Victory was now within our grasp. But a small voice in the back of my mind whispered doubts. What if the gates didn't open? What if Erik betrayed us and we were rushing headlong into a trap?

I pushed the thoughts aside, focusing on the task at hand. I had to believe in our plan, in Asher's brother, in the righteousness of our cause. There was no room for doubt now.

Asher galloped along beside me, his face set in fierce determination. Our eyes met, and in that moment, I saw all the fear, hope, and love that I felt reflected in his gaze.

The gates of Ironheart loomed before us, growing larger with each passing second. My heart hammered in my chest, every fiber of my being focused on those massive iron barriers. Would they open? Or would they remain closed, leaving us trapped and vulnerable outside the walls?

The fate of our rebellion, of countless lives, hung on what happened in the next few moments. As we bore down on the gates, I sent up a silent prayer to whatever gods might be listening.

Let this be the day we change everything.

As we charged forward, time seemed to slow. I could hear the thundering of hooves, the battle cries of our warriors, the harsh pants of my own breath. But above it all, one thought echoed in my mind:

Open. Please, open.

CHAPTER THIRTY
Asher

The thundering of hooves and the battle cries of our united army filled the air as we charged towards the gates of Ironheart. Riding beside Reyna, I was struck by the fierce determination etched on her face. She was truly the Rebel Rose in this moment, a leader born to change the world.

Around us, the power of our forces was overwhelming. Jaila, the new Iron Rose, rode with us, her face hardened, eyes fixed on the gate ahead. Gaia and Thalassa flanked our sides, while Thorun and other Cloudborn warriors led the charge. The sight of ogres, wolves, and bears running alongside us was surreal, a scene straight out of legend.

As we drew closer to the gates, a hail of arrows suddenly darkened the sky. My heart clenched as I saw some of our forces fall, their cries of pain lost in the chaos of battle. But then, a sight that took my breath away — bursts of light as Cloudborn warriors activated their shields, deflecting arrows striking their armor with flashes of Aurorium energy. The arrows bounced off them, and they roared with anger as they charged on, their muscular horses thundering toward our enemies ahead.

Just when I thought the arrow assault might slow our charge, the sky filled with birds, coming in from all directions into a dark cloud that merged as one. They dove at the archers on the walls, their thick mass swallowing them up as they darted around, shrieking, pecking and clawing, creating a chaotic distraction. Thalassa's work, no doubt. Her power over animals was proving invaluable. The stream of arrows ceased as the archers screamed and shouted, some falling from the high walls as they tried to fight off their avian attackers.

Despite our momentum, fear gnawed at my insides as we neared the gates. What if they didn't open? What if Erik hadn't—couldn't come through? We'd be trapped, easy targets for the forces within. The potential for a massacre loomed large in my mind.

But then, like an answer to an unspoken prayer, the gates began to creak open. My heart soared as I caught sight of Erik, standing there with a triumphant smile.

I knew you'd come through for me, brother.

I couldn't stop the smile from spreading across my face as I locked eyes with him. He'd been there for me all my life, and he'd come through for me again now. He'd done it.

We were in.

With a roar, we charged through, our army squeezing into lines as we exploded through the gate and into Ironheart. The first wave of Kingsguard met us just inside the gates, but they were no match for our combined forces.

The wolves hit the Kingsguard first, their speed devastating as they swept from one solider to the next, their powerful jaws ripping through flesh as they tore man after man apart. One Cloakfang appeared out of thin air beside me, rising high on its hind legs and swiping down half a dozen Kingsguard with its powerful, poisonous claws.

It was hard for me not to worry if we were killing innocent men in this attack, but I had to push those thoughts aside and fight to survive, to make sure Reyna and our allies survived, until hopefully, once we were in, we could convince the others to stand down.

Cloudborn and Moonshadow warriors fought side by side, their skills evident as they battled back the Kingsguard. The ogres arrived next, and I saw the shocked flashes of white from the eyes of the remaining soldiers as they took in the sight of the massive, lumbering creatures. With their wooden clubs swinging into the enemy, they finished up the last of the forces that had been sent to stop us.

I scanned the soldiers' faces, searching for Sir Edmund, but found no trace of him. A cold feeling settled in my stomach—his absence from the front lines meant he was likely guarding his beloved King personally. My jaw clenched in disappointment, but I consoled myself with the knowledge that our confrontation was inevitable.

But then my gaze found Erik, and my heart soared seeing my brother again, alive and looking uninjured from the battle. The man who had come through for me against all odds. The one man I knew would have my back no matter how impossible a task I'd asked of him.

I leaped from my horse and embraced him.

"You did it," I said, my voice thick with emotion.

Erik's grip tightened. "We did it, brother."

"I knew you would pull through for me. I never doubted you."

He pulled back to look at me then arched an eyebrow. "Really? Not once? Because I doubted we could pull this off right up until the gates actually opened."

I laughed, clasping a hand on his shoulder. "Okay, maybe a twinge of doubt."

He grinned, shrugging. "Thanks to the help of Sir Laine, we managed to pull it off."

I looked for Laine to thank him, a friend of ours since childhood, but he was nowhere to be found.

Erik must have sensed my intent, then softly shook his head, and I knew instantly his meaning.

"No," I breathed, my heart constricting with the loss. A loss *I* had caused when I'd asked Erik to enlist the help of someone we trusted.

"He knew the risks," Erik said quickly. "And he died with a sword in his hand fighting for a cause he believed in for the first time in his life. You know what happened to his little sister."

I swallowed hard, giving a sharp nod as I remembered how he'd grieved her loss. She'd been sent to the brothel at eighteen and died only weeks later from the abuse she'd incurred. Erik had chosen his ally well. If anyone would want to fight to see women freed from their chains, it would have been Laine. But still, guilt and sorrow swelled inside me that he'd lost his life before he'd been able to see how we could change things.

"I wouldn't be here without you," I said, my voice thick with emotion. "None of this would have happened if you hadn't opened those gates."

"We're changing everything," he whispered. "Together. As we always said we would when we were boys."

"Though I doubt this is what we imagined," I said with a short laugh as we separated, gesturing to the chaos around us.

"Better," Erik replied, his eyes gleaming with purpose. "We're not just playing at being heroes anymore. We're actually doing something that matters."

A swell of emotion rushed up inside me, and I yanked him back against me in a powerful hug. He returned it with equal fervor, and I whispered, "Thank you for being the best brother."

"Well, I have to be better at you at *something*. I guess, yeah. I'm the best brother. I'll take it."

I laughed and released him, but our reunion was cut short as we spotted a second wave of Kingsguard approaching, far more numerous than the first. Their armor glinted in the sunlight, swords drawn and faces set with grim determination as they charged toward us.

I caught Reyna's eye across the courtyard. Without a word, she nodded, understanding passing between us. We'd fought together so many times now, learned each other's rhythms, strengths, and weaknesses. We were more than lovers; we were partners in battle, our movements a deadly dance choreographed through blood and fire.

"Together?" I called to her, drawing my sword.

She grinned, the wildness in her eyes sending a thrill through me. "Always," she replied, unsheathing her twin blades.

As the Kingsguard rushed toward us, Reyna and I met their charge head-on. Back-to-back, we moved as one entity, each anticipating the other's moves before they happened. When I ducked, she spun above me, her blades slicing through the exposed necks of our enemies. When she dropped to sweep the legs of a guard, I was already there to deliver the killing blow before he hit the ground.

"On your left!" Reyna shouted, and I swung my blade without hesitation, catching the guard who had tried to flank me. His eyes widened in shock as my sword found the gap between his armor plates.

"Behind you!" I warned, and Reyna dropped to her knees just as I swung over her head, my blade connecting with the throat of a Kingsguard who'd thought her vulnerable.

There was something beautiful in our brutality, something pure in how perfectly we complemented each other. Every move I made, she enhanced. Every opening I created, she exploited. Together, we carved a path through the Kingsguard like a storm through autumn leaves.

A particularly large guard managed to knock me off balance with a powerful blow. Before I could recover, he raised his sword for what would have been a killing stroke—but Reyna was there, her blade sliding between his ribs from behind. Our eyes met over his falling body, a moment of connection in the chaos.

"Thought you could use a hand," she said with a fierce smile.

"I had him right where I wanted him," I shot back, returning her smile.

"Of course you did."

Our moment was interrupted as three more guards rushed us. We turned to meet them, moving in perfect sync. I blocked a high strike while Reyna slid underneath my guard, taking out the knees of one attacker. As he fell, I finished him with a downward stroke while Reyna was already engaging the next two.

One guard managed to slice her arm, drawing blood. Before I could even react, she'd spun like a dervish, her blades flashing in an intricate pattern that left both men gurgling on the ground, clutching their throats.

We fought on, the battle a blur of steel and blood and desperate cries. But through it all, I was acutely aware of Reyna beside me—her breathing, her movements, her presence. I'd never fought alongside someone who felt so perfectly in tune with me, as though we shared one mind, one purpose, one heart.

As we finished up the second round of Kingsguard, I glanced around, my heart swelling to see Gaia, Thalassa, Thorun, and our other leaders still standing. The courtyard was littered with the bodies of Kingsguard, but still more were marching in from the inner ward.

"We need to get through to them," I said to Reyna, breathing hard. "Get them to lay down their arms. There's no need for all this death. I'm tired of killing men who could be our allies."

She gave me a sharp nod, then together, we quickly climbed to a high point where we could be seen and heard. As the next wave of Kingsguard drew closer, I raised my voice, praying that as their former Head of Kingsguard, my words would reach them.

"Brothers in arms!" I called out, my voice carrying across the courtyard. "I implore you to stop and listen!"

To my surprise, they halted, their eyes fixed on us. I pressed on, my heart pounding.

"For too long, we've been part of a system that treats women as property, as less than human. We've stood by while they've have been abused, enslaved, and slaughtered. But today, we have a chance to change everything."

I felt Reyna's presence beside me, her strength bolstering mine as I continued.

"Think of the women in your lives. Your mother. Your sister. Your wife. Your daughter. Don't they deserve freedom? Respect? The chance to choose their own paths?"

I saw confusion and conflict on many faces below.

Good. They were listening.

"We've been told that this is the natural order of things," I continued. "That men must rule and women must serve. But look around you! Look at the army that stands with us today. Women warriors of unmatched skill and courage. Magical beings we thought were mere legend. They've united for one purpose — to break the chains that bind half of humanity."

Reyna stepped forward, her voice joining mine, clear and powerful. "Imagine a world where your daughters can become whatever they dream. Where your sisters aren't forced into their husbands' beds or sent to die in senseless wars. Where your mothers are respected for their wisdom, not silenced for their gender."

I could see the impact of our words. Some men were nodding, others whispering amongst themselves.

"We stand at a crossroads," I declared. "We can cling to the old ways and be swept aside by the tide of change, or we can be part of building a better future. A future where men and women stand as equals, where we judge each other by the content of our character, not the accident of our birth."

"The choice is yours," Reyna finished, her voice ringing with authority. "But know this — change is coming, with or without you. Will you be remembered as those who stood in its way, or those who helped usher in a new era of justice and equality? If you set down your weapons, you won't be harmed, but if you rise up against us, if you rise up to support slavery and injustice, then we will have no choice but to cut you down. So, who's with us? Who will stand up to centuries of abuse and tyranny?"

A heavy silence fell over the courtyard. Men's eyes scanned our army, their faces showing a mix of fear and awe as they took in the sight of us. Women. Men. Ogres. Bears. Wolves. We were as terrifying as we were inspiring. We'd all joined together in this cause, and now I had to hope these men—who'd never known a world where choice existed—would join us too.

For a moment, it seemed as if the whole world held its breath, waiting to see what would happen next.

Then one of the Kingsguard stepped forward, removing his helmet and tossing it to the ground. Others followed, weapons clattering as they surrendered. Not all laid down their arms—some looked uncertain, torn between duty and conscience, while others remained firmly opposed. But the tide was turning.

Those who stood against us charged forward with a roar, while those who joined our cause turned to face their former comrades.

In a matter of seconds, the Kingsguard was fighting itself. Men who moments ago had stood shoulder to shoulder now crossed swords, their faces a mix of determination and anguish.

Reyna's voice rose above the din. "For freedom!" she cried, leading our forces into the fray.

I leaped down from our perch, Reyna at my side, and we joined the battle. It was chaos—friend and foe often indistinguishable in the melee. But slowly, surely, we were gaining the upper hand.

As I fought, I caught glimpses of our allies in action. Thorun, his Aurorium weapons flashing as he cut through opponents with ease. Gaia, fighting with a fury born of years of oppression. Thalassa, her eyes glowing as she directed a pack of city dogs to harass enemy fighters.

And always, always, I was aware of Reyna. We moved in and out of each other's orbits, sometimes fighting side by side, sometimes separated by the press of bodies, but always finding our way back to each other, as though drawn by some invisible force.

A large guard managed to knock Reyna's sword from her hand. Without missing a beat, I tossed her my dagger, which she caught and buried in her attacker's throat in one fluid motion. She flashed me a quick, fierce grin before retrieving her blade and rejoining the fight.

Moments later, I found myself surrounded by three Kingsguard. I parried desperately, knowing I couldn't hold them all off. Suddenly, Reyna was there, leaping over a fallen body and landing beside me, her blades a whirlwind of death as she cut down two of my attackers in the blink of an eye. Together, we dispatched the third with brutal efficiency.

"I had them," I panted, sweat and blood mingling on my face.

"I know," she replied, her eyes gleaming with battle-light. "But I couldn't let you have all the fun."

As the fighting began to wane, I caught sight of Erik surrounded by three Kingsguard who had cornered him against a wall. His face was bloodied, his sword arm clearly injured, but he fought on with grim determination.

"Erik!" I shouted, abandoning my own battle to reach my brother. One of the guards turned at my cry, but I was already moving, my blade catching him beneath the chin before he could raise his weapon.

The second guard swung at me, forcing me to parry and counter. Our blades clashed in a flurry of strikes, but he was no match for my fury. As he fell, I turned to see Erik drive his sword through the third guard with his off-hand—a move I'd taught him years ago.

"Still remember that trick," Erik panted, a grin breaking through the blood on his face.

"Didn't think you were paying attention when I showed you," I replied, clasping his uninjured arm.

"Always paid attention to you, big brother." His eyes met mine, serious now. "Even when I didn't agree with you, I was watching, learning."

The moment was interrupted as a group of loyalist Kingsguard broke through our lines nearby.

"Just like old times?" Erik asked, raising his sword despite his injury.

"Just like old times," I agreed, moving into position at his side. Back to back, we met the attackers, falling into the familiar rhythm we'd perfected in countless training sessions growing up.

Where I was precision and technique, Erik was instinct and unpredictability. Where I would parry, he would dodge. Where I would thrust, he would slash. Different styles, but perfectly complementary.

"Your left!" I called, and without hesitation, Erik pivoted, catching a blade that would have taken his arm.

"Duck!" he shouted a moment later, and I dropped just as his blade whistled over my head to catch an attacker I hadn't seen.

We moved together like dancers who had rehearsed the same steps a thousand times, each anticipating the other's movements, covering each other's vulnerabilities. Despite his injury, Erik fought with the same courage and skill that had made me proud to call him brother all these years.

As the last of our attackers fell, I caught sight of Reyna across the courtyard, battling alongside Jaila, the two women a blur of deadly motion. For a moment, our eyes met over the chaos, and a surge of love and pride filled me. She nodded once, a gesture of understanding and approval as she saw me fighting alongside my brother, before turning back to her own battle.

When the fighting finally ceased, Reyna appeared at my side, her face streaked with dirt and blood but her eyes shining with triumph. "Well done," she said softly, her hand finding mine.

I squeezed her hand, drawing strength from her touch. "It's not over yet," I reminded her.

She nodded, her expression hardening. "We need to get to Lothaire and find Cassia."

As if on cue, our forces began to regroup. The Cloudborn, the battlemaidens, the Iron Swordmaidens, and our newfound allies among the Kingsguard—all looked to Reyna, awaiting her command.

She raised her voice, every inch the leader she was born to be. "To the castle! Today, we end Lothaire's reign and free every woman in Ironheart!"

A cheer went up, echoing off the stone walls of the city. As we prepared to march through the streets towards the castle, I caught Erik's eye. He nodded, a silent understanding passing between us. Whatever came next, we would face it together.

The castle loomed in the distance, Lothaire's last bastion. As we set off, I couldn't help but marvel at how far we'd come. From a split-second decision to spare her life that day on the mountain to leading a rebellion that could change the face of the kingdom.

But I knew the hardest part still lay ahead. Lothaire wouldn't give up his power without a fight. And somewhere in that castle was Cassia, Reyna's sister, the spark that had ignited this revolution.

The final battle awaited us. And with it, the dawn of a new era for Ironheart.

CHAPTER THIRTY-ONE
Reyna

The streets of Ironheart echoed with the clash of steel and battle cries as we moved through the city taking out the remaining Kingsguard who refused to join our cause. My heart raced with a mixture of exhilaration and disbelief. We were doing it. My plan, a plan that emerged from a single desperate thought, had transformed into a powerful army now on the brink of success.

But what truly astounded me was the sight of men—Kingsguard and civilians alike—picking up swords to fight at our side. Asher had been right. His brother had opened the gates, and now, men I had once considered the enemy were fighting alongside us for freedom.

As we rounded a corner, I saw a group of townsfolk, both men and women, emerge from their homes, makeshift weapons in hand. They joined our ranks without hesitation, their faces set with determination. The sight brought tears to my eyes.

"Asher," I called out, my voice thick with emotion. He turned, his eyes finding mine. "You were right. About everything."

He gave me a small smile, understanding the weight of my admission. For years, I'd lived in the Warhold with no connection to the outside world, and I believed all men were evil, that they were the source of our oppression. But now, seeing so many risk everything to fight for change, I realized how wrong I'd been. They too had been slaves to the system, perhaps in ways I hadn't fully comprehended before.

A garrison of Kingsguard loyal to the king marched around the corner, and we turned our wrath onto them. Jaila appeared beside me, her grin wide as we fell into our familiar rhythm, our swords singing in harmony as they tore through flesh and bone. I grinned back at her, our looks needing no words as we relished every second of our reunion.

Our growing group continued quelling every uprising we encountered, and then as we passed the Warhold, a familiar figure caught my eye.

Sir Roland.

The cruel overseer who had taken such joy in mistreating the women under his charge froze when he saw us, turning on his heel to flee. My eyes narrowed, rage bubbling up inside me.

He was not one of the innocent men.

He was exactly the kind of monster I had believed all men to be.

The kind of monster I now hunted like a wolf closing in on its prey.

Before I could move, an arrow whizzed past me, striking Roland in the knee as he attempted to flee. I turned to see Gaia, her bow still raised, a fierce light in her eyes.

We approached Roland as he writhed on the ground, pathetic pleas for mercy spilling from his lips. "Please," he begged, "I'll fight with you. I'll do anything!"

Gaia stepped forward, her face a mask of cold fury. She knelt beside him, her voice a low growl. "Do you remember the nights you snuck into our quarters? The women you forced yourself on?"

Roland's eyes widened with fear as recognition dawned. Gaia continued, her voice breaking slightly. "You forced yourself on me. You forced yourself on Lorna, my love. I've been waiting a long time for this moment."

I kneeled down beside her, my eyes sparkling with merciless glee. "Hello, Sir Roland. It's good to see you again. The last time I saw you, I believe you threatened to..." I pressed a finger to my chin. "What was it you wanted to do to me again?"

"Please. Please. I'm sorry. I... I was wrong. Have mercy. You wouldn't hurt an unarmed man, would you?"

Gaia looked to me, and with how much rage and anger I saw burning in her eyes, though I wanted to be the one to end his miserable life, I gave her the honor with a quick nod.

In a flash, her blade was out. With a swift, merciless stroke, she sliced between Roland's legs. His agonizing howl echoed through the street.

She stared at him, a menacing smirk matching the hatred in her eyes as blood pooled beneath him while he wailed.

I turned to Roland, who was whimpering pitifully. "I know what you are, what you've done." I leaned in closer, a sinister smile curling up my lips. "I remember what you promised to do to me."

Fear erupted in his eyes as he lifted his hands, begging for his life.

I stared at him, tipping my head back and forth, relishing the pain and anguish in his eyes... the same pain and anguish I knew he'd caused many of my swordsisters when he'd sneak into their beds at night.

"As much as I want to kill you, I'm not going to." I said, and relief flooded his eyes. That relief evaporated instantly when I finished with, "This isn't my vengeance to take."

I stepped back, giving Gaia a final nod.

Roland's eyes flashed wide as she grinned.

"No, please!" he begged, but she didn't hesitate.

Her blade flashed once more across his throat, and Roland's cries were silenced forever as he choked on his own blood. A cheer went up from the swordsisters who had gathered around us, years of pent-up anger and fear released in that moment of justice.

As we moved on, leaving Roland's body behind, a weight lifted from my shoulders. It wasn't just about vengeance. It was about accountability, about making sure that those who had abused their power would never have the chance to do so again in the new world we were going to build.

We pressed on toward the castle, our forces growing with each street we passed. The sight of Cloudborn warriors fighting alongside former Kingsguard, of battlemaidens and townspeople standing shoulder to shoulder, filled me with a hope I had never dared to feel before.

As we neared the castle gates, a group of Kingsguard moved to block our path. I raised my weapon, ready for another fight, but to my surprise, one of them stepped forward, his sword pointed not at us, but at his fellow guards.

"Stand down," he commanded. "It's over. Lothaire's reign ends today."

The other guards hesitated, then slowly lowered their weapons. The one who had spoken turned to me, his eyes filled with a mixture of fear and determination.

"Rebel Rose," he said, his voice carrying across the suddenly quiet courtyard. "Lothaire knows you're coming. They said he's in the throne room, and..." he hesitated, his eyes flicking to Asher before returning to me. "He has your sister."

The world seemed to tilt beneath my feet. Cassia. After all this time, all this fighting, she was so close. And yet, the thought of her in Lothaire's grasp made my blood run cold.

"Nothing can protect him from me," I snarled, my grip tightening on my weapon.

Asher appeared at my side, his hand on my arm. "Reyna," he said softly, "we need to be careful. Lothaire isn't stupid. We need to be sure we aren't walking into a trap."

I took a deep breath, forcing myself to think past the rage and fear. He was right, of course. We needed a plan.

As we gathered our forces, preparing to enter the castle, I looked around at the faces of those who had fought beside me.

"Listen to me," I called out, my voice carrying across the courtyard. "Lothaire is cornered, and he's desperate. He's holding my sister hostage, thinking it will save him. But he's wrong. Today, we end his reign. Today, we free every woman in Ironheart. But we must be careful. We cannot risk innocent lives in our quest for justice."

I saw nods of agreement, determination written on every face.

"Thorun," I continued, "the Aegisari shielding abilities will be crucial. Stay in front of the group so you can deflect as much as you can if we face any attacks." His eyes narrowed in understanding, his chest heaving with his deep breaths. "Thalassa, can you use your connection with animals to scout ahead, maybe provide a distraction? But leave the wolves, ogres and bears out here to defend this group if they need it."

Thalassa nodded, her eyes already beginning to glow as she reached out to the creatures around us and in the castle.

"Asher, Erik," I turned to the brothers, "you know the layout of the castle better than anyone. We'll need your guidance to navigate quickly and efficiently."

They nodded, already beginning to discuss the best route to the throne room.

"Jaila and Gaia, you're with me. The rest of you," I addressed the remaining fighters, "stay out here and ready for anything. Lothaire will have his most loyal guards with him, but there could be other forces we don't know about. Guard the entrance and exit to make sure we don't get trapped between forces."

"Yaira," I said, turning to one of the Cloudborn warriors I'd seen fight with great skill, a tall woman with intricate, dark braids woven through her hair. She stepped forward, her green eyes locking with mine as she awaited my command. "You're in charge of this group until we return. Keep them safe."

She gave me one sharp nod then turned to the masses now under her command, including the two ogres looking like dangerous sentinels standing guard over our army.

As the rest of our group began to move toward the castle entrance, Asher pulled me aside. "Reyna," he said softly, his eyes filled with concern, "are you okay?"

I took a shaky breath. "I have to be," I replied. "Cassia needs me. All of Ironheart needs me. I can't falter now."

He squeezed my hand. "You won't. And you're not alone. We're all with you."

I nodded, drawing strength from his words and the warmth of his touch. "Thank you," I whispered. "For everything. For showing me that there's good in people, even when I couldn't see it. For believing in this cause, in me."

"Always," he said simply, and in that moment, I knew that whatever happened next, whatever challenges we faced in the throne room and beyond, I could face them with Asher by my side.

We turned back to our gathered forces. They stood ready, a united front all committed to a single cause. Freedom. Justice. A new dawn for Ironheart.

"For Cassia," I said, my voice steady. "For every woman who has suffered under Lothaire's rule. For a future where all are free. Let's end this."

With a collective roar of determination, my smaller group surged forward into the castle. As we moved through the grand halls, my mind raced with memories of Cassia. Her laugh, her unwavering support, the fierce determination to become a powerful swordsister. I had failed to protect her once. I would not fail again.

After cutting down the remaining Kingsguard loyal to Lothaire we encountered on our way, we finally arrived at the massive doors of the throne room, the last barrier between us and Lothaire. I took a deep breath, steadying myself for what was to come. Victory or heartbreak lay on the other side of the doors. One wrong move and I could lose Cassia forever.

"Are you ready?" Asher asked softly, his hand on my shoulder.

I nodded, my jaw set with determination. "Let's finish this."

With a shared look of resolve, we pushed open the doors, ready to face whatever awaited us within.

CHAPTER THIRTY-TWO
Reyna

As we burst into the throne room, my heart faltered. The grand chamber stretched before us, cold and imposing, with Lothaire seated on his ornate throne. But Cassia—my sister, my reason for fighting—was nowhere to be seen.

Lothaire sat with a smug smile playing on his lips. Eight of his largest, most powerful Kingsguard flanked him, weapons drawn and ready. In front of them stood a wall of at least thirty more guards, creating an impenetrable barrier between us and the king. Lothaire's eyes, cold and calculating, watched our entrance with a calm that sent chills down my spine.

"Ah. Finally," he said, his voice carrying across the cavernous room as if he'd been patiently waiting for this exact moment. "The prodigal rose returns," he sneered, his gaze fixed on me before shifting to Asher. "And look who she's dragged along. Tell me, boy, how does it feel to be so thoroughly whipped by a woman that you'd abandon your duty?"

Asher stepped forward, his voice steady. "My duty is to protect the innocent, not to prop up a tyrant. Your reign is over, Lothaire."

"Your duty is to protect your king!" He bellowed back. "I am your king, and you dare to betray me?"

Asher remained silent, the two men staring each other down.

"And for what?" His eyes locked onto mine, narrowing into slits. "For her? For a fucking cunt?" He laughed, a cold, cruel thing. "And you let her convince you to turn on king and kingdom, for what? To free her *sister*?" His eyes gleamed with malice.

My blood ran cold. "Where is she?" I demanded, my voice sharp as a blade. "What have you done with Cassia?"

The throne room, once a symbol of Lothaire's absolute power, now crackled with tension. The air itself seemed to thicken, heavy with the weight of the impending storm brewing between us.

Lothaire's laughter, cruel and mocking, echoed through the cavernous room. "She's quite safe... for now." His eyes narrowed. "My most loyal guards are with her at this very moment, awaiting my orders."

Rage, hot and potent, surged through me. I fought to keep my voice steady as I addressed the tyrant who had lorded over me since birth.

My eyes narrowed as I took in his relaxed posture on the throne. "You should have run while you had the chance. Give me my sister and maybe I'll make your death merciful."

Lothaire laughed, the sound echoing off the stone walls. "Is that what you thought was going to happen with this little display of yours? That I'd cower and flee? Get on my knees and beg? Bow to... a *woman*?" He shook his head, a smirk playing on his lips. "No. Here's how this is going to go."

He leaned forward, fingers steepled. "You're going to take your pathetic group of women and whatever the hell else you dragged in with you, leave my city, and leave Ironheart. When you're gone, I'll send your sister along after you. My Iron Swordmaidens stay. They're mine. But do this, and your beloved sister lives. If you defy me, if you kill me, she dies."

My blood boiled at his words.

My swordmaidens. They're mine.

As if they were possessions, objects to be owned rather than women with minds and hearts and wills of their own. I caught Jaila and Gaia's postures stiffen beside me, their hands tightening on their weapons. The rage in their eyes matched what burned through me—the same fury I'd felt every day as his Iron Swordmaiden leader before I made my flee to freedom.

Jaila took a half-step forward, her voice low and dangerous. "We are no one's property, Lothaire. Not anymore."

Gaia's eyes flashed with hatred born of countless humiliations. "We would rather die fighting then let one more woman live another day as your slave."

Lothaire dismissed them with a contemptuous wave, as if their words were nothing but the buzzing of insects. "Silence. I wasn't addressing you." His eyes remained fixed on me. "So, Rebel Rose. What will it be? Your sister, or your precious revolution? Because I can guarantee you, you can't have both."

"Where is she!" I demanded, my hand twitching with need to take my sword and slice it through his jugular.

His eyes narrowed, a predatory gleam in them. He glanced toward the high windows where the afternoon sun cast long shadows across the throne room floor. "The guards holding her have orders. If they don't hear the code word from me by sunset, they'll slit her throat without hesitation. You can kill me, Rebel Rose, but you'll never know the word. You'll never reach her in time."

I stared at him, trying to read the calculation behind his eyes. And in them, I saw his own certainty. His confidence, his certainty, that he could take Cassia from me if I didn't obey.

And it made my boiling blood run cold.

"Or, take my deal. Leave my kingdom. I'll even show mercy to the women of Ironheart who betrayed me," he continued, his voice silky. "No mass executions, no torture for their insolence. Though the gods know they deserve hanging for their treachery. I am, after all, a merciful king."

The weight of his words pressed down on me, each one a hammer blow to my resolve.

But if you don't retreat now, if you attempt to harm me or any of my loyal guards," Lothaire continued, his voice dropping to a menacing whisper. "Your sister dies. And these women you want to 'free' will beg for the old ways. What I'll do to them will ensure no woman ever dares to stand against me again."

His confidence infuriated me, but more so because I recognized the trap he'd laid. He'd stayed because he believed my love for Cassia would force me to retreat. In his mind, the rebellion was nothing but a sister's desperate attempt to save her sibling—a personal vendetta, not a revolution. He couldn't conceive that it had grown beyond that, that *I* had grown beyond that.

Time seemed to slow to a crawl as the weight of Lothaire's ultimatum settled over me. My sister, my beloved Cassia, had been the catalyst for this rebellion. Her capture had set me on this path, and I'd sworn to save her or die trying.

But then I thought of our forces—women and men who had risked everything for this cause. The Cloudborn warriors who had broken centuries of isolation to join us. The Moonshadow tribe who had emerged from their safety after generations of hiding. The Iron Swordmaidens who had thrown off their chains. The men who had chosen to stand against tyranny, to fight for a world where all could be free.

Could I betray them all for the sake of one life, no matter how precious?

The faces of countless women flashed before my eyes—women I had met on our journey, women I had fought beside, women I had never met but who were counting on us. I saw their hope, their fear, their desperate longing for freedom.

And then I saw the future—a future where Lothaire continued his reign of terror. Where women remained enslaved, where daughters were torn from their mothers, where the cycle of tyranny continued unbroken. A future where our rebellion became nothing more than a cautionary tale, a failed attempt at change that only led to harsher repression.

I couldn't let that happen. Not when we were so close.

The weight of leadership, of responsibility, pressed down on me like a mountain. In that raw, painful moment, I knew this was the true test of a leader—the willingness to sacrifice everything, even one's own heart, for the greater good.

My eyes found Asher's across the room. In his gaze, I saw understanding bloom—he knew what choice I was about to make, what I was about to sacrifice. Sympathy filled his eyes, softening their blue depths, but behind it was something else—pride. Pride in my strength, in my willingness to make the hardest choice a leader could face. His slight nod conveyed what words couldn't—that he loved me not despite this terrible choice, but because of the courage it took to make it. That he understood the agony coursing through my veins, and he would stand with me through whatever came next.

I met Lothaire's gaze, unflinching. "I know my sister," I said, my voice clear and steady despite the storm raging within me. "She would rather die a thousand deaths than see me abandon this fight. She would curse my name if I traded the freedom of all women for her life alone."

Surprise flickered across Lothaire's face, quickly masked by contempt. "You would sacrifice your own blood? Your own flesh?"

"I would sacrifice everything to ensure you can never control another woman again. Because unlike you, I fight for something greater than myself. This isn't about me. It isn't even about Cassia. It's about every woman who has ever lived under your boot, and every woman who will come after us."

Lothaire's face contorted with rage. "So be it," he snarled. "Her death will be on your hands."

"If she dies," I said, my voice deadly quiet, "I will make you pay for it a thousandfold."

Lothaire stood abruptly, his cloak swirling around him. "Enough of this." He gestured to his guards. "Kill them all. And send the signal to execute the sister."

The Kingsguard advanced, their weapons raised. But I was beyond fear now, beyond doubt. A cold clarity had settled over me, a singular purpose burning in my veins.

"For freedom!" I cried, raising my blade. Our forces surged forward, meeting the Kingsguard head-on.

As the clash of battle erupted around us, I kept my eyes fixed on Lothaire. He was backing away toward a previously concealed door behind the throne, his face a mask of fury and fear.

"I'm coming for you, Lothaire!" I shouted over the din of battle.

"You'll never succeed," he called back, his voice dripping with contempt. "I'll survive, and when I return to reclaim what's mine, every woman and girl in Ironheart will feel my wrath."

The arrogance, the cruelty in his voice ignited a roar of rage within me. Without thinking, I charged forward, determined to end him before he could escape, before he could carry out his threat against Cassia.

But as I reached the halfway point of the throne room, Lothaire pulled a torch from its sconce and threw it at his feet. In an instant, a wall of flame erupted between us, racing across the floor in all directions. The heat slammed into me like a physical blow, forcing me back as it cut off every path leading to him.

Horror dawned as I realized what he'd done. The floor had been soaked with oil, a trap laid in anticipation of our arrival. The flames spread rapidly, licking up the tapestries that lined the walls, engulfing the wooden furniture. Thick, black smoke began to fill the chamber.

"Enjoy my parting gift," Lothaire laughed over the roar of the flames. "While the flesh is being seared from your bones, I want you to remember your sister will be dying too. And you could have avoided it all." His eyes gleamed with malice through the wall of fire. "Your little rebellion ends now, and you accomplished *nothing!* When the ashes cool, I'll hunt down every woman who dared stand with you and make examples of them all!"

"I will find you, and I will kill you. There is nowhere in this world you can hide from me!" I shouted, the power of my words tearing apart my throat.

He spun and disappeared through the door, a Kingsguard pulling it shut behind them and sealing us all inside. Rage burned through me like the fires consuming the chamber. I had made the impossible choice—sacrificing my sister for the greater cause—and now he was escaping to kill her anyway. The unfairness of it clawed at my insides, threatening to consume me more thoroughly than any flame.

"It's a trap!" I shouted to our forces. "We need to get out!"

The battle took on a desperate quality as both sides fought not only each other but the rapidly spreading fire. The Kingsguard nearest the flames broke formation, some fleeing, others continuing to fight with renewed ferocity, their escape cut off.

"Reyna!" Asher appeared at my side, his face streaked with soot and blood. "We need to go!"

"Lothaire's escaping!" I shouted over the roar of the flames. "And Cassia—if he gets away, he's going to send word to kill her! We have to stop him, Asher!"

"We'll find another way!" Asher gripped my arm, his eyes intense with determination and fear. "But we can't help anyone if we die here! We have to go, now!"

A massive wooden beam, its ancient timber engulfed in raging flames, crashed down from the ceiling with a deafening crack. In a blur of motion, Asher shoved me hard, sending me stumbling backward just as the burning timber crashed where I'd been standing. The impact shook the floor beneath us as sparks and embers erupted in a violent cloud.

"Asher!" I screamed, heart stopping as flames temporarily obscured him from view. When he rolled into sight on the other side of the burning beam, relief flooded through me like a physical pain.

"Go, Reyna!" he shouted, his face illuminated in hellish oranges and reds. "This place is coming apart!"

All around us, the ancient mortar between the stones cracked from the intense heat, the sound like bones breaking. Chunks of ornate ceiling decorations rained down, smashing into deadly shards on the stone floor. The air had become a furnace, each breath searing my lungs.

Suddenly, Asher's expression transformed to pure horror, his eyes fixed on something beyond me.

"ERIK!" he bellowed, the name tearing from his throat with such force I felt it more than heard it through the inferno's roar.

I spun to see his brother across the chamber, locked in combat with two Kingsguard, completely unaware of the archer taking aim at his exposed back. Asher lunged forward instinctively, but the flaming beam trapped him, flames leaping higher as if mocking his desperation.

"NO!" he screamed again, his voice breaking as he watched helplessly, separated from his brother by an impassable wall of fire.

Through the wavering heat haze, I watched the archer's fingers begin to release the bowstring, his face a mask of cold determination. Time seemed to slow.

Erik. The man who had risked everything by opening the gates. Asher's brother. His family. The man he loved and would sacrifice his life for. The man who had made all of this possible.

For us.

For... me.

Without conscious thought, my body moved. A wave of power sent me moving faster than I'd ever imagined, and I hurled myself between Erik and the incoming arrow, a cry tearing from my throat. As I moved, I felt something stir deep within me, a power I had sensed but never fully grasped until now.

The arrow flew towards us, its deadly point aimed straight at my heart. But instead of the pain I expected on impact, I felt a surge of energy unlike anything I'd ever experienced. A blinding flash of light erupted from my body, expanding outward in a dome of pure, shimmering energy. Like a separate life force that had awakened and blended with mine, the power of my bloodline exploded from within.

The arrow bounced off the energy shield around me, and the nearby Kingsguard were thrown back by the force of the blast, crumpling against the walls.

As the light faded, I stood there, panting, my entire body tingling with residual power. For the first time, I truly felt the significance of my Aegisari blood. This was who I was meant to be—a protector, a shield for those who couldn't defend themselves.

Erik stared at me, his eyes wide with awe and gratitude. "You... you saved me," he breathed.

I nodded, my breath coming in short gasps. The shield that had eluded me for so long had finally manifested when I needed it most. Not to save myself, but to protect another.

Another section of ceiling beams crashed down, sending a wave of heat and smoke rolling over us. We were running out of time.

Asher fought his way to my side, his eyes widening as he took in what had just happened. "Reyna. Your shield—"

"Later," I cut him off, coughing as smoke filled my lungs. "Lothaire is getting away. I need to stop him, Asher! We have to find Cassia and save her!"

I scanned the room desperately, looking for any escape route. My mind and body felt physically torn apart as I tried to formulate a plan. Lothaire was escaping. Cassia would die if he got word to her guards. And we were trapped in a burning room.

"The side passage!" Asher pointed to a corridor where the flames hadn't yet spread. "We can get through there!"

"But Lothaire went that way!" I pointed to the hidden door behind the throne, now sealed shut and surrounded by fire. "He's going to escape! We have to stop him!"

"You can't reach him through that door," Asher said, gripping my shoulders. "It's sealed from the inside now. He's heading to the roof!"

My eyes landed on a large window to the side of the throne, completely engulfed in flames.

"There!" I pointed. "The window! I can go out and climb to the roof. Catch him before he escapes."

"That's suicide!" Asher protested. "It's burning, and if you fall, you'll die!"

I looked between the window and Asher, torn between my desperate need to save my sister and the knowledge that Lothaire could not be allowed to slip away, to regroup, to return with vengeance.

"Asher," I said, my voice steadying despite the chaos around us. "Where would they be keeping Cassia?"

His eyes widened with understanding. "There's a secret dungeon they use for interrogations. I know the way."

In that moment, something shifted inside me—a realization that had been slowly building throughout our journey. All my life, I'd carried every burden alone. I'd believed that trusting others meant weakness, that depending on anyone else would lead to failure and pain.

But looking at Asher now—this man who had risked everything for our cause, who had stood beside me through impossible odds—I understood the truth. I wasn't alone anymore. I didn't have to carry every weight by myself.

"You know where she is. I don't. So, I'm going after Lothaire," I said, gripping his hands tightly in mine. "And you're going to save Cassia."

"What? Reyna, you can't be serious—"

"I trust you," I interrupted, the words feeling both foreign and absolutely right on my tongue. "I trust you with my sister's life, Asher. If anyone can save her, it's you."

The realization was liberating—like setting down a weight I'd carried so long I'd forgotten it was there. All around us were people who had joined our cause, who fought beside us, who believed in the same future we did. I didn't have to be everything, do everything. I could trust them. I could trust him.

"I can get to the window through the flames. My armor will heal me from the worst of the burns," I continued. "I'll find a way up to the roof. I'll stop Lothaire. You find Cassia."

Asher stared at me, recognition dawning in his eyes. Not just of the plan, but of what it meant for me to entrust him with this—with the person I loved most in the world. He pulled me against him, enclosing me in his arms.

"I'll get her out," he promised, his voice fierce against my ear. "I swear it on my life." He pulled back, his eyes burning with determination. "And I trust you to find a way to survive. To kill Lothaire. End this. Today."

We stood frozen for a moment, the flames burning like an inferno around us as our eyes locked, a thousand words passing between us in that single heartbeat.

Love. Fear. Determination. Trust.

"Save her," I whispered, my voice breaking. "Please."

"I will," he promised. "I love you, Reyna."

"I love you too."

His hands framed my face as his lips found mine in a swift, fierce kiss that tasted of smoke and desperation. When we broke apart, he gave me one last look filled with love and determination.

"Go," he said. "End this."

I nodded, my heart somehow both heavy and lighter than it had ever been. "I'll see you when it's over."

And I prayed to gods I'd thought had forsaken me long ago that I would. The thought that this could be our last moment together—our final words, our final touch—clawed at my chest with icy fingers. I memorized his face, the blue of his eyes, the set of his jaw, storing away every detail like treasure. Danger would await him at every turn. But I had to trust him not just with Cassia's life, but with his own. To fight. To survive. To come back to me. And to do it all without me there at his side where I belonged.

He turned to Erik, Jaila, Gaia, Thalassa, Thorun, and others who had fought their way to our side. "Come with me! We're going to save Reyna's sister!"

As they raced toward the side passage that had not yet been consumed by flames, I faced the window—my only hope of reaching Lothaire in time.

The fire was closing in, the heat blistering against my skin. I took a deep breath, wincing as the hot air seared my lungs, then ran toward the window straight into the wall of flames, leaping through it in a shower of glass.

The impact was brutal, shards slicing my skin as I crashed through. My hands shot out, grasping desperately for the window ledge. My fingers caught the stone, my body swinging out violently and slamming into the castle wall with force that drove the breath from my smoke-filled lungs.

For a heart-stopping moment, I hung there, the ground dizzyingly far below, my fingers screaming with the strain of supporting my weight. Pain lanced through me—cuts from the glass, burns from the fire, the impact of my body against unyielding stone.

But I held on.

Hanging there from the window ledge, glass pieces embedded in my palms as smoke billowed out above me, I looked up toward the roof. Somewhere up there was Lothaire, the man who had ruled through cruelty and fear, who had torn Cassia from me, who now threatened everything and everyone I loved.

My wounds began to heal, the Aurorium in my armor sending waves of recovery through my battered body. Determination hardened within me, cold and deadly as forged steel.

"I'm coming for you, Lothaire," I whispered, beginning my climb upward. "Your reign ends today."

CHAPTER THIRTY-THREE
Asher

The smoke from the throne room still burned in my lungs as we raced through the castle corridors. The secret passageways I'd traversed countless times as Head of the Kingsguard now served a different purpose—not to protect a tyrant king, but to save an innocent woman. To save Reyna's sister.

"This way," I called to the others, my voice hoarse. "The dungeon is beneath the east wing."

"Actually, it's faster if we go this way," Erik pointed out, and I didn't argue, instead letting him lead the way.

Thorun, Jaila, Gaia, and Thalassa followed us close behind, our footsteps echoing off the stone walls. The castle was in chaos, servants and guards fleeing in all directions, some fighting, others simply trying to escape the chaos.

Thorun fell into step beside me, his massive frame dwarfing mine, the intricate patterns on his Aurorium armor catching the torchlight. His dark eyes studied me with barely concealed suspicion.

"You're certain you know where they're keeping her?" he rumbled, his deep voice carrying the accent of the Cloudborn.

"I'm certain," I replied, meeting his gaze. "It's where Lothaire keeps prisoners he doesn't want anyone to know about. The interrogation dungeon."

Thorun's jaw tightened. "And you would know, wouldn't you? How many women have you dragged there yourself, Kingsguard?"

The accusation stung, not because it was unfair, but because there was a kernel of truth to it. I had been part of this system—not its worst enforcer, but complicit nonetheless.

"Hey, he's trying to help," Erik interjected. "We all are. There's no point in dragging up the past right now."

Thorun just grunted, giving Erik the same suspicious stare I'd gotten from him ever since we'd met.

"I didn't take any women down there," I said firmly. "But I've been there. I know the way, and I know how it's guarded." I tried not to let my temper flare at his continued suspicions of me. Even after watching me fight for her, be ready to die for her, it still seemed like it wasn't enough to prove myself worthy of an Aegisari. Of *her.*

"He's okay, Thorun," Gaia stood up for me. "Asher is our ally even if he was once a Kingsguard. We're not going to keep holding it against him."

"Hmmm," was all he grunted, his massive hand resting on the hilt of his blade.

We reached a narrow staircase hidden behind a tapestry depicting one of Lothaire's hunting expeditions.

"Down here," I whispered, drawing my sword. "The guards won't be expecting us from this direction. Stay quiet."

The stone steps spiraled downward, the air growing colder and damper with each turn. The sounds of the chaos above faded, replaced by an oppressive silence broken only by the occasional distant drip of water.

At the bottom of the stairs, a narrow corridor stretched before us, lined with torches that cast long, dancing shadows. I held up a hand, signaling the others to stop.

"Four guards at the door," I breathed, peering around the corner. "Heavily armed. We need to take them by surprise."

"Leave it to me," Thalassa whispered, her eyes beginning to glow with an ethereal light. She closed them, her face a mask of concentration.

A moment later, a chorus of squeaks echoed through the corridor, and a wave of rats poured from the darkness, swarming over the guards' feet. The men shouted in surprise and disgust, momentarily distracted.

"Now!" I hissed, and we charged.

The guards were skilled, recovering quickly from their shock, but they were outnumbered and caught off guard. Jaila and Gaia took down one with brutal efficiency while Erik dispatched another. The third guard managed to parry my initial attack, but a swift kick to his knee followed by a slash to his throat ended his resistance.

The fourth guard, the largest of the group, roared as he swung a massive battle axe at my head. I ducked, feeling the air disturbed by the weapon's passing, but before I could counter, Thorun stepped between us, catching the axe's handle with his bare hand. With a twist of his wrist, he wrenched the weapon from the guard's grasp and drove his own blade through the man's chest in one fluid motion.

Our eyes met over the falling body, and I saw a flicker of something like respect in Thorun's gaze.

"You fight well... for a Kingsguard," he conceded, wiping his blade clean.

"And you fight well for someone who lives in the clouds," I replied with a hint of a smile.

He snorted, but I caught the barest twitch of his lips. It wasn't friendship, not yet, but it was a start.

We approached the heavy iron door at the end of the corridor. It was locked, as expected, but the key hung at the belt of one of the fallen guards.

"Be ready," I warned as I pushed the key into the lock. "There will be more guards inside, and possibly Sir Edmund. He's dangerous—one of the best swordsmen in Ironheart."

The lock turned with a heavy click, and I pushed the door open, wincing at the groan of hinges that could have used oil. The chamber beyond was large and dimly lit, the air thick with the smell of damp stone and fear.

My blood ran cold at what I saw. Cassia—her golden hair unmistakable even in the low light—hung suspended from chains attached to the ceiling, her arms stretched painfully above her head, her toes barely touching the ground. Blood stained her dress where she had clearly been beaten. Despite her condition, her head was held high, her eyes blazing with a defiance that reminded me so much of Reyna it made my chest ache.

And standing before her, a cruel smile on his face, was Sir Edmund.

He turned at our entrance, surprise quickly giving way to a sneer as he recognized me. "Asher. I was wondering when you'd make an appearance. Come to save your whore's sister?"

Five more guards flanked him, drawing their weapons as he spoke. Behind them, I could make out three more prisoners chained to the walls—women I didn't recognize, likely sent here for some infraction like disobeying a man's orders.

"Stand down, Edmund," I said, my voice steady despite the rage building inside me. "It's over. Lothaire has fled. The city has fallen."

Edmund laughed, a harsh, grating sound. "It's never over. Men like us, we always rise again. You've forgotten who you are, Asher. Forgotten your place in the natural order."

"I've remembered who I truly am," I countered. "A protector, not an oppressor. Now step away from her."

"Or what?" he taunted, drawing his sword. "You'll kill me? You don't have the stones for it, boy. You never did. Always too soft, too questioning. That's why I should have been Lothaire's true right hand, not you."

I didn't waste breath on further words. With a roar that held all my fury, I lunged forward. The others followed, and the dungeon erupted into chaos.

Edmund was as good as I'd remembered—his blade a blur as he parried my first attacks. The other guards engaged my companions, the clash of steel echoing off the stone walls as the battle began.

Out of the corner of my eye, I saw Thorun locked in combat with two guards, his massive form a whirlwind of controlled violence, his armor sending out blasts as he deflected blows. Jaila and Gaia fought back-to-back, their styles complementing each other perfectly. Erik defended Thalassa as she used her powers to call rats and spiders from the darkness, sending them to harass and distract our enemies.

Edmund and I circled each other, trading vicious blows. He was stronger than me, but I was quicker, using my agility to avoid his more powerful strikes.

"You're a disgrace," he spat, blood streaming from a cut above his eye where I'd managed to slip past his guard. "Fighting for these cunts, these lesser creatures. Your father would be ashamed."

"My father died believing in a lie," I shot back, deflecting a thrust aimed at my heart. "I fight for the truth."

Our blades locked, bringing us face to face. Edmund's breath was hot on my skin, his eyes filled with contempt. "The truth? The truth is that you're weak. That you let a woman lead you by your cock into treason."

With a roar of fury, I broke the lock and slashed at his face, my blade opening a red line across his cheek. He stumbled back, cursing.

Behind him, I saw movement—Cassia, using her suspended position to her advantage as a guard ventured too close. With a burst of strength that belied her injured state, she swung her body up, wrapping her legs around the unsuspecting guard's neck. The man clawed desperately at her thighs as she tightened her grip, cutting off his airflow with ruthless precision.

His face purpled as he struggled, but Cassia held on, her face a mask of cold determination. With a sickening crack, she twisted her body sharply, snapping the guard's neck. As his lifeless body slumped to the floor, Cassia hung there, her strength nearly spent from the effort.

Jaila, having dispatched her own opponent, raced to Cassia's side with keys she'd taken from a fallen guard. "Hold on," she said, reaching up to unlock the manacles that held Cassia suspended.

As Jaila freed Cassia from her chains, she collapsed into Jaila's arms. Despite the chaos of battle around them, they embraced tightly, years of shared struggle and sisterhood passing between them wordlessly. But their reunion was about to be cut short. While I parried another blow from Edmund, I saw a guard approaching from behind, his sword raised and poised to strike.

"Cassia! Jaila!" I shouted as I ducked another swing from Edmund.

Both women turned as one, Jaila swinging her blade up to stop the blow while Cassia, despite her weakened state, snatched up a fallen dagger and drove it into the guard's side. They moved with the practiced coordination of warriors who had trained together for years, covering each other's weaknesses, amplifying each other's strengths.

My momentary distraction cost me. Edmund seized the opportunity, his blade slicing into my arm. Pain lanced through me, but I gritted my teeth and held my ground.

"Eyes on me, traitor," Edmund snarled, pressing his advantage with a flurry of strikes that drove me backward.

I parried desperately, knowing one slip would mean my death. While he fought solely for himself, focused only on his survival and victory, my attention kept splitting between our duel and the others fighting around us. Every cry of pain, every moment of danger for my companions pulled at my awareness.

As I struggled to hold my own against Edmund, I noticed Thorun locked in combat with three guards at once. Despite his skill and strength, they gradually overwhelmed him, forcing him to divide his attention between multiple opponents.

"Thorun! On your left!" I shouted, seeing an opening in the guard's defense.

Without questioning me, Thorun pivoted, his blade finding the gap in the guard's armor that I'd spotted. The man fell with a cry, giving Thorun the breathing room he needed to dispatch the other two in quick succession.

Our eyes met across the chamber, and he gave me a quick nod of acknowledgment, perhaps even gratitude. No words were needed; we understood each other in that moment. We were warriors, fighting for the same cause despite our different paths.

Cassia, now fully free, had armed herself with two short swords from fallen guards. She fought with a ferocity that matched her sister's, her golden hair whirling around her as she cut down a guard who had been about to attack Erik from behind.

"Behind you!" I called to her.

She spun instantly, her blades catching the guard's sword in a scissoring motion that wrenched it from his grip. With a fluid follow-through, she drove one blade into his throat, her expression cold as ice.

"Thanks!" she called back, before turning to fend off another guard.

Edmund used my divided attention once again to press his attack, his blade slipping past my guard to open a shallow cut across my ribs. I hissed in pain but countered with a low slash that caught his thigh, drawing blood.

"You're slipping, Edmund," I taunted, capitalizing on his momentary pain to land another blow, this one across his shoulder. While Edmund was good with a blade, it was his temper that always cost him his precision. His inability to control his emotions was one of the reasons he'd been passed over as Kingsguard with me taking the coveted role instead. Knowing this about him, I continued taunting.

"You're not as good as I thought. No wonder they made me Kingsguard instead of you even though you've served twice as long. It took me leaving the position for you to finally get it. How does it feel knowing you never would have been Kingsguard if I'd stayed? And a pity position for you no less, only because Erik was being punished for my mistakes. You know they would have chosen him over you otherwise."

His face contorted with rage. "I'll show you who's Head of the Kingsguard!" He lunged forward recklessly, abandoning technique for pure aggression.

It was exactly what I'd been waiting for. I side-stepped his charge, allowing his momentum to carry him past me, then pivoted and drove my blade deep into his back.

Edmund gasped, his sword clattering to the stone floor as he fell to his knees. I stood over him, watching as blood spread across his fine uniform, staining the proud insignia of the Kingsguard.

"You... you've doomed us all," he rasped, blood bubbling at his lips. "When the... other kingdoms learn what you've done... they'll destroy you. They'll come for your whore and make her suffer in ways you can't even begin to imagine."

I leaned closer, my voice low. "No one will touch Reyna. Not you. Not them. Not anyone. I'll kill everyone and everything that tries to take her from me. And I'll start with you."

I pressed my blade into his neck, holding his gaze as it slipped through his flesh, blood pouring from the wound and spilling to the floor beneath him. With a final, rattling breath, Sir Edmund collapsed face-first onto the cold stone floor.

I stood there for a moment, watching Edmund's life drain away. I couldn't help but wonder what kind of man he might have become in a different world—one not built on the subjugation of women, one that didn't define manhood through domination and cruelty. But that world didn't exist yet, and Edmund had chosen his side. He'd embraced the system that gave men like us power, refused to question it as I had. He'd fought to preserve that broken order, and now he'd died for it, as so many other men today had. But I felt no guilt as I watched the last of the light leave his eyes. Edmund, like so many others, would never try to change. They'd never embrace the new way, and our changing world would be better without him. One less oppressor standing in the way of freedom.

Around us, the fighting had ceased. The remaining guards lay dead or had surrendered, and there was Cassia, standing amidst the carnage like an avenging angel, her blades still dripping with blood, her eyes scanning the chamber for any remaining threats. To think of the fate that had awaited such a powerful, capable woman only solidified my belief that I was on the right side of this fight.

"Cassia!" Jaila called, stepping over the corpses at her feet as she rushed forward.

Their eyes met in a moment of profound recognition as Cassia opened her arms and caught Jaila in them. Ignoring the carnage around them, they embraced tightly, the two women reunited in a hug so powerful I could almost feel it myself.

"I knew you'd come," Cassia whispered, her voice hoarse and shaky. "The moment I was taken, I knew eventually you would all find a way to free me. Reyna. Where is she?"

She let go of Jaila, her eyes scanning the strange faces of people she'd never met before.

"She's okay," Jaila said quickly. "She's gone after Lothaire."

"Thank the gods," Cassia breathed. "I was scared for a moment when I didn't see her here."

"Your sister isn't that easy to kill." I grinned. "And I can attest to that from personal experience."

She turned as I approached, weapons rising instinctively as her eyes narrowed.

"You're Sir Asher," she said, not a question but a statement. "The head of the Kingsguard."

"Former," I corrected, sheathing my sword to show I meant no threat. "Now I fight with your sister. For freedom."

Cassia studied me, her gaze so similar to Reyna's it was almost like looking at a reflection, though her hair was golden where Reyna's was dark as midnight and her eyes blue to Reyna's green.

"She sent me to find you while she went after Lothaire."

Confusion twisted her features. "Why would she ask you to save me? You're one of them."

"I was," I admitted. "Until I met Reyna. Until I saw the truth of the world we'd built, the suffering we'd caused. Now I'm trying to make it right."

"He loves her," Erik said, stepping forward. "And she loves him. Together, they've led this rebellion to save you, united people who have been divided for generations. They're changing the world, Cassia. And it all started for you."

Jaila stepped forward, placing a steadying hand on Cassia's shoulder. "He's with us now, Cass. I've seen it with my own eyes." Her voice softened. "Reyna loves him. And he loves her. They fight side by side as equals."

Cassia's eyes widened slightly, looking between Jaila and me. "Reyna? Our Reyna? And him?" She gestured at me with her blade.

"Strange days," Jaila said with a small smile. "But I've watched them today. He's proven himself worthy of her trust."

Cassia looked between us, her expression guarded. "So, the mighty Sir Asher, terror of the Kingsguard, fell in love with... my sister?" She laughed, a sound both bitter and amazed. "And somehow convinced her to love him back? That must have been quite a feat."

"I'll never understand it either, but I'll be grateful for it every day of my life," I said softly. "Love isn't something you can deny or argue into or out of existence. It simply... happens, even when it seems impossible. Even when it changes everything you thought you knew about the world."

She regarded me silently for a long moment, her eyes seeing through me in a way that reminded me painfully of Reyna. Then, slowly, she lowered her weapons.

"My sister has always been an excellent judge of character," she said finally. "If she trusts you with her heart, with this rebellion... with my life..." She took a deep breath. "Then I suppose I can trust you too. For now."

It wasn't unconditional acceptance, but it was a start. And in that moment, it was enough.

"Thank you," I said simply.

Gaia quickly introduced herself and our other companions, Cassia looking perplexed about the brief details she was given as to who Gaia, Thalassa, and Thorun were.

"When there is time later, we'll tell you everything," Gaia said. "And better yet, we'll let Reyna tell you the whole tale. She's been on quite an adventure trying to get you back."

"Wow. I missed a lot while I was being forced to learn proper dining etiquette fit for a king's wife." Cassia smiled, then winced, her hand going to a wound in her side that I hadn't noticed before.

"You're hurt," I said, moving to help her, but she waved me off.

"I've had worse," she replied, straightening with visible effort. "Where is Reyna now?"

"She was heading to the roof to confront Lothaire," I answered, my worry for Reyna flooding back.

Determination hardened Cassia's features. "Then that's where we need to be. I've waited years to see that bastard die. I want to be there when my sister ends him."

"You're wounded," Gaia protested, stepping forward. "You need rest, treatment—"

"What I need," Cassia cut her off, her voice like steel, "is to see my sister. And I hope I'm not too late to watch that bastard Lothaire die."

I looked at her—bloody, battered, but unbowed—and saw the same indomitable spirit that had drawn me to Reyna. These sisters, forged in suffering, tempered by resistance, had become something magnificent and terrible. Warriors in the truest sense.

"Go. We'll take care of the prisoners," Thalassa said. "You two get to Reyna."

With one last look, a strange tip of her head, Cassia shrugged. "Well, I guess it's you and me, Kingsguard. Let's go."

"Asher works just fine," I corrected with a smile.

"Asher it is then." She smiled back.

Together, we left behind our battered but determined group and headed off to find Reyna.

As we climbed the stairs out of the dungeon, I sent a silent prayer to whatever gods might be listening. *Keep her safe until we can reach her. Let her survive this final battle. I love her. I need her.*

Somewhere above us, on the rooftop of the castle, Reyna's final confrontation with Lothaire was likely already unfolding. And with it, the fate of everything we had fought for.

CHAPTER THIRTY-FOUR
Reyna

The climb was brutal. My blood-stained hands slipped on cold stone as I forced my aching muscles upward. The wind howled around me, tearing at my armor, threatening to rip me from the wall and send me plummeting to the courtyard far below. My fingers burned, scraping against the rough surface as I desperately searched for each new handhold.

Suddenly a sharp pain exploded through my bicep. I hissed in anger seeing the arrow embedded in my arm. I looked up to see two Kingsguard peering over the wall at me, one with an arrow nocked and aimed right at my head.

The arrow whistled past my ear, so close I felt the air displace around it. Then another, this one bouncing off my armor. I pressed myself closer to the wall, trying to make myself a smaller target as I continued my ascent.

The burns from the fire in the throne room still stung, though the Aurorium in my armor was already working to heal them. Between the cuts from the shattered window, the burns, and now an arrow in my arm, I was a mess of pain, and I remembered Thorun telling me my healing would slow the more wounds and damage I took. But pain was an old friend, and I refused to let it slow me down.

The archers continued their assault, arrows raining down like deadly hail. One grazed my cheek, hot blood trickling down my face and into my mouth, the taste of copper fueling my rage. Another struck my thigh, but the arrowhead couldn't penetrate the Aurorium plates of my armor.

I reached a narrow ledge just below the parapet, giving me a moment to catch my breath. With a grunt, I yanked the arrow from my bicep, biting back a cry as fresh blood flowed from the wound. It started to close, but slowly now, my powers already hard at work healing my burns and other injuries. The pain was intense but clarifying, sharpening my focus to a deadly point.

Eight more feet to the top.

Eight more feet between me and Lothaire.

Between me and justice for Cassia, for all women who had suffered under his reign.

I gathered my strength, muscles coiling like a cat preparing to pounce. Then I moved, faster than my injured body should have allowed. Hand over hand, foot finding purchase where there seemed to be none, I scrambled up the wall in a burst of speed that caught the archers off guard.

As I reached the parapet, an archer loosed another arrow, but I was ready. I twisted mid-climb, my body moving on instinct, and caught the shaft in mid-air. In one fluid motion, I pulled myself up and over the edge, driving the captured arrow through the archer's eye before he could reach for another.

The second archer dropped his bow and drew his sword, charging at me with a cry of rage. I rolled to my feet, drawing my twin blades in a fluid motion. Steel met Aurorium with a ring that carried over the howling wind. He was good—one of Lothaire's elite guard, trained from childhood in the art of killing.

But I was better.

I parried his aggressive strikes, reading his style, learning his patterns. He fought like most Kingsguard—technically proficient but predictable, taught to follow forms rather than adapt. When he tried a high slash at my neck, I dropped to one knee, my blade finding the gap beneath his breastplate. He gasped, blood bubbling from his lips, then crumpled to the stone.

As I rose, I saw six more Kingsguard spread out in a semi-circle, their armor gleaming in the fading rays of the sun. Behind them stood Lothaire, his face twisted with malice and fear.

"Kill her!" he shrieked, spittle flying from his lips. "I want her head!"

The Kingsguard advanced as one, moving with the precision of men who had trained together for years. These weren't ordinary soldiers; they were the king's personal guard, the best fighters in Ironheart.

Well, the best fighters besides *me.*

I settled into a fighting stance, my blades held loose and ready. "Come then," I said, my voice carrying across the rooftop. "Let's see what the king's best can do against one woman with a cause."

The first guard charged, faster than I expected, his longsword whistling toward my head. I parried, the impact jarring my arm, and countered with a thrust that he barely avoided. As we disengaged, two more attacked from my flanks, forcing me to dive and roll to avoid being caught between them.

I came up in a crouch, slashing at the nearest guard's legs. My blade found flesh, and he stumbled with a cry of pain. I pressed the advantage, driving my second blade up under his chin before he could recover.

But the moment of victory cost me. Something hard struck my back, sending me sprawling across the rooftop. The fourth guard wielded a spiked mace that had caught me between the armor plates. Pain exploded across my back, momentarily stealing my breath.

I rolled desperately as the mace came down again, the spikes striking sparks from the stone where my head had been a heartbeat before. The guard lifted the weapon for another strike, but I lashed out with my foot, catching his knee. There was a satisfying crack, and he howled, his leg buckling beneath him.

Before he could fall, I was on my feet, one blade driving through the gap beneath his helmet. The mace fell from lifeless fingers as he collapsed.

Two down, four to go, but they were learning. They approached more cautiously now, spreading out to surround me. I backed toward the edge of the roof, forcing them to constrict their circle, limiting their ability to flank me.

The tallest guard held a spear, keeping me at bay while the others looked for an opening. I feinted at him, drawing a predictable thrust that I slipped past, getting inside his reach. My blade opened his throat, but even as he fell, one of his companions landed a glancing blow on my shoulder.

I staggered, pain flaring down my arm. The guard pressed his advantage, raining heavy blows that I could only parry, not counter. Each impact sent fresh waves of agony through my injured shoulder. My back throbbed from the mace hit, and the arrow wound in my bicep had reopened, blood soaking my sleeve. I was gaining new wounds faster than the Aurorium could heal me.

For a moment, doubt crept in. There were still three guards, all skilled, and I was injured. Lothaire watched from the far side of the roof, a smile playing on his lips as he saw me falter.

I've come too far to fail now.

The thought of Cassia, of Asher, of all we had fought for, ignited something deep within me. But this time, it wasn't just determination—it was something older, stronger, something that had lain dormant in my blood for generations.

I felt it then—a warmth spreading from my core, coursing through my veins like liquid fire. The Aurorium in my armor began to glow, resonating with the power awakening inside me. This was my heritage, my birthright as an Aegisari. The power my mother had passed to me before she died in this cruel system. The legacy I had only just begun to understand.

I remembered her face that day they'd stolen her life. That look in her eye that she'd never break, not even in death. And in that remembrance, that memory of her final moments looking at me, I felt a surge of power flow through me.

My Aegisari blood.

Her blood.

"Mother," I whispered, the word both a prayer and an invocation.

The pain didn't just recede—it transformed, becoming fuel for the energy surging through me. The wounds on my body began to close at an accelerated rate, the Aurorium armor amplifying my natural healing abilities. I straightened, a new calm settling over me as I embraced what I truly was—a daughter of the Aegisari, a protector, a shield against darkness.

The next guard who came at me found not a wounded prey but a predator awakened to her true nature. I moved differently now—faster, stronger, my reflexes heightened by the Aegisari power flowing through me. The Aurorium in my armor pulsed with a faint glow, responding to the ancient power in my blood.

To the guard, it must have seemed as if I was almost a blur. I moved with impossible speed, no longer reactive but proactive, dictating the flow of the fight. When he swung his broadsword in a powerful arc, I didn't parry—I stepped inside the swing, too close for the blade to be effective. My dagger slid between his ribs before he could adjust, my strength enhanced by the power surging through me.

The fifth guard hesitated, seeing the change in me. Fear flickered in his eyes as he recognized something beyond human manifesting before him. That hesitation was fatal. I threw my dagger with deadly accuracy, the blade spinning end over end to bury itself in his throat. He clawed at it, eyes wide with shock, then toppled backward.

Only one left now—a massive man with a greatsword and a shield emblazoned with Lothaire's crest. Even he approached more cautiously than before, shield raised, sword held low for an upward strike. I could sense his fear beneath the practiced exterior—a fear not just of me, but of what I represented, what I had become.

"You fight well," he rumbled, circling me. "But you can't win this."

I retrieved my dagger from the fallen guard, wiping it clean on his cloak. "I've been told what I can and can't do my entire life," I replied, rolling my injured shoulder. "I'm done listening to men's words."

He attacked then, shield leading, trying to bash me off balance. I sidestepped, but he was quicker than his size suggested, his greatsword changing direction mid-swing to force me back. We exchanged blows, neither gaining the advantage, his reach and power balanced by my speed and precision.

I feinted again, drawing him into a powerful swing that I ducked under. As the momentum of his massive sword carried him slightly off-balance, I struck, not at him but at his shield, my blade sliding along its edge to slice through the leather straps binding it to his arm.

The shield fell away, and for a critical moment, he was exposed. My second blade found the gap in his armor at the armpit, sliding deep. His greatsword clattered to the stone as he fell to his knees, then face-forward onto the roof.

Six elite Kingsguard lay dead around me, their blood staining the stone. I stood in the center of the carnage, chest heaving, body aching, but undefeated.

Across the roof, Lothaire's smug smile had vanished, replaced by naked fear. He drew his own sword—a beautiful, ornate thing that had likely never seen real battle—and backed away toward the edge of the roof.

"Stay back!" he commanded, his voice cracking with panic. "I am your king!"

I advanced slowly, relentlessly, like the tide coming in. "You are no king of mine," I said, my voice low and deadly. "You never were."

"Guards!" he shouted, looking desperately toward the door. "More guards!"

But no one came. The door remained closed. We were alone on the roof, just the tyrant and the woman he had tried to squash beneath his boot.

"They're all dead," I told him, continuing my advance. "Or they've joined us. Your reign is over, Lothaire. It ends today."

He swung his sword wildly, the blade slicing through empty air as I easily sidestepped. "I'll kill you," he snarled, all pretense of regality gone. "I'll kill you and display your head on a pike. I'll find your precious sister and make her suffer for years before I grant her death."

I laughed, the sound shocking even me with its coldness. "You had your chance with both of us. Now your time is up."

He charged, his technique as poor as I'd expected. I deflected his blade with contemptuous ease, spinning past him to slash across his back. He howled, stumbling forward before turning to face me again, blood soaking through his fine clothes.

"Not so easy when your opponent can fight back, is it?" I taunted, circling him as a wolf circles wounded prey.

Lothaire's eyes darted from side to side, seeking escape. Finding none, he attacked again, more desperately this time. Our blades met, and I allowed him to press me back, letting him think he had the advantage.

"You see?" he gloated, mistaking my tactical retreat for weakness. "You're no match for me. I was born to rule. You were born to serve."

I parried another clumsy strike. "Is that what you told yourself when you ordered women slaughtered? When you tore daughters from their mothers? When you treated half of humanity as breeding stock?"

"It is the natural order of things," he spat, lunging again. "Men rule, women obey. It has always been thus. It will always be thus."

I deflected his blade and countered with a precise cut that opened his cheek, matching the scar I'd given myself as a girl to avoid his cruel fate for me.

"There," I said with cold satisfaction. "Now we match."

Rage contorted his features as blood streamed down his face. "You bitch!" he snarled, his attacks growing wilder, more frenzied.

I dodged and weaved, letting him exhaust himself, letting his fury consume his limited technique. When he overextended on a thrust, I stepped inside his guard, my blade finding his sword arm. He screamed as tendons severed, his weapon clattering to the stone.

Lothaire fell to his knees, clutching his useless arm. His eyes, once filled with contempt and cruelty, now showed only fear.

"Please," he begged, his voice breaking. "Mercy. I'll give you anything. Gold, lands, power—"

"I don't want your gifts," I cut him off, standing over him with my blade at his throat. "I want justice. For my sister. For every woman who suffered under your rule."

His eyes hardened suddenly, a last flicker of defiance. "If you kill me, you're no better than I am. You speak of justice, but this is vengeance, plain and simple."

I considered his words, my blade steady at his throat. "Perhaps it is both," I admitted. "But unlike you, I'm not killing for power or pleasure or to maintain an unjust system. I'm ending a reign of terror. I'm freeing countless women from bondage."

I leaned closer, my voice dropping to a whisper. "And yes, I'm avenging my sister, whom you tore from me. I'm avenging my mother that you sentenced to death for the simple crime of protecting her daughter from a brutal man. I'm avenging every woman broken by your laws, your soldiers, your cruelty."

"You'll fail," he hissed, blood from the wound on his face flowing onto his lips. "Another king will rise. Another kingdom will conquer you. The old ways will return, stronger than before."

I straightened, looking down at him—this man who had been the bogeyman of my childhood, the tyrant of my youth, the target of my rebellion. In the end, he seemed so small, so pathetic.

"Perhaps," I acknowledged. "But we will fight. We will always fight. And one day, we will win not just a battle, but the war. That is what you never understood about us, Lothaire. You can break our bodies, but never our spirits."

With a final surge of rage, he lunged at me, a hidden dagger appearing in his hand. The blade came at me with unexpected speed—even in his desperation, Lothaire was still dangerous.

In that moment of true peril, the power within me surged again. I didn't consciously summon it, but it responded to my need. A blinding flash of light erupted from my body, the shield of pure energy expanding outward. Lothaire's dagger struck the shimmering barrier and shattered, fragments of steel raining down harmlessly.

He stumbled back, his eyes wide with disbelief and terror as he stared at the pulsing shield of energy surrounding me. The golden light cast harsh shadows across his face, illuminating the fear that had replaced his arrogance.

"What... what are you?" he whispered, all pretense of strength gone from his voice.

The shield pulsed with my heartbeat as I stepped forward, the energy rippling around me like living armor. I met his gaze, letting him see the power of generations of women he had tried to destroy burning in my eyes.

"I am the end of your terror," I said, my voice resonating with the power of my bloodline. "I am the vengeance of every woman you've broken. I am the dawn after your long night of cruelty."

Before he could recover, I drove my blade through his chest in one fluid motion. His eyes widened further, the broken hilt falling from his fingers.

I leaned close as his life ebbed away. "This is for Cassia," I whispered. "And for my mother. And for every woman who ever suffered under your hand."

With a final twist of my blade, I stepped back. Lothaire swayed on his knees, blood pouring from the wound. Then, with a contemptuous kick, I sent him toppling over the edge of the roof.

His scream echoed all the way down before being cut short by the sickening thud of his body hitting the courtyard below.

For a moment, silence reigned. Then, from below, a cheer erupted—our forces, seeing the fall of the tyrant king.

I stood above them, the weight of this moment both freeing me from the shackles that had bound me my entire life and settling a new weight upon my shoulders. Below me gathered thousands who had joined my cause, my dream, and who would now look to me in this new world we would be forging together.

"Lothaire is dead!" I shouted to them, my voice thick with emotion. "And so is his world. It is ours now! You are free!"

The cheers and roars below me nearly shook the foundations of the castle I stood atop, just like we had shaken the very foundations of the system that had enslaved us all for so long.

Exhaustion crashed over me as I staggered back from the edge. I sank to my knees, my blades falling from numb fingers. It was done. After all the fighting, all the pain, all the sacrifice, it was finally done.

The door to the roof burst open, and I tensed, reaching for my weapons before recognizing the figure silhouetted against the light.

"Asher," I breathed, relief washing through me.

He rushed to my side, grasping my face in his hands and crushing my lips with a kiss that poured all of his love, his worry, and his relief into me. I sighed into his mouth, my own relief that he'd returned to me causing my heart to swell to bursting.

He softened his kiss, then leaned back, his face pale with worry as he took in my blood-soaked form. "Reyna! You're hurt—"

But I wasn't looking at him anymore. Behind him, standing in the doorway, golden hair catching the last rays of the setting sun, was a figure I had dreamed of seeing again for so long.

"Cassia," I whispered, hardly daring to believe it.

My sister. My heart.

"Reyna," she said, her voice breaking on my name.

And then we were moving, both of us, heedless of our wounds. We collided in the center of the blood-soaked roof, arms wrapping around each other so tightly it hurt. But it was a good pain, the kind that proves you're alive, that the person you love most in the world is alive and in your arms.

"You came for me," she sobbed into my shoulder, her entire body shaking. "You actually came for me."

"Always," I promised, pulling back just enough to see her face, to memorize every new line, every change. "I would have torn down the world to find you."

"Apparently, you did just that," she said with a watery laugh, gesturing at the carnage around us, the smoke rising from the burning castle, the sounds of celebration from below.

I laughed too, a sound of pure joy that I hadn't known I was still capable of making. "I had help," I admitted, looking over at Asher, who stood watching us with a gentle smile.

"So I've heard," Cassia said, following my gaze. "Your Kingsguard is quite the fighter. He saved me."

"Former Kingsguard," Asher corrected gently, stepping closer.

I reached out, drawing him into our embrace. "We saved each other," I said, holding both of the people I loved most in the world.

As we held each other on that blood-soaked rooftop, the sun began to set over Ironheart, painting the sky in hues of gold and crimson. Below us, the city erupted in celebration as word of Lothaire's death spread through the streets.

It was more than just the end of a day. It was the end of an era, and the dawn of a new age. An age of freedom, of possibility, of hope.

And I would face it with the two people I loved the most by my side.

CHAPTER THIRTY-FIVE
Asher

Standing atop the castle with Reyna, watching the sun set over Ironheart, I felt a sense of awe wash over me. We had done it. Against all odds, we had succeeded. Lothaire was dead, and a new era of freedom was dawning.

I glanced at Reyna, reunited at last with her beloved sister. The joy on their faces was palpable, a reminder of why we had fought so hard. Squeezing Reyna's hand gently, I said, "You two should catch up. I'll go check on the others."

She nodded gratefully, and I made my way back through the castle, littered with the bodies of the men who refused to join our cause as well as some of the bodies from those who sacrificed themselves for freedom. Though my heart weighed heavy for the losses, it didn't dampen the hope that swelled inside my chest.

We had done it. We had ended Lothaire's reign and freed countless women from beneath the stifling boot of oppression.

As I walked through the courtyard, I was met with a sea of familiar and new faces. Former Kingsguard who had chosen to stand with us clasped my arm, their eyes shining with a newfound purpose. Cloudborn warriors and women from Moonshadow Woods greeted me as an ally, a far cry from the suspicion they had once regarded me with.

Then, through the crowd, I saw him. Erik. My brother. For a moment, we stood frozen, staring at each other across the courtyard, then Erik's smile broke across his face, and we rushed toward each other.

We collided in a fierce embrace, and I hugged tight the man I'd known would have my back no matter what. The man who'd risked everything for the bonds of brotherhood.

"Ouch," I said when his squeeze tightened and put pressure on the deep wound Edmund had given me.

He stepped back. "Are you okay? I saw you take the blow. It looked bad."

"It's deep but it didn't hit anything I need. It will heal."

"Good, because I didn't get a chance to do this yet."

He playfully slapped me across the back of the head, something we did to each other often when the other did something foolish. "Do you know how close you were to getting yourself killed? Getting me killed? Getting half of Ironheart killed? If this had gone badly, the streets would look a whole lot different right now with women being whipped, traitors being beheaded, and just a whole lot of retaliation."

I rubbed where he'd hit. "But it didn't go badly. We did it. We freed the women of Ironheart. And we did in largely in part because of you. You opened the gate and let us in. Thank you," I said, my voice thick with emotion. "I knew I could trust you."

I embraced Erik again and his grip tightened. "Of course," he said, his voice equally strained. "We're brothers. I'll always have your back, Asher."

As we pulled apart, I saw the pride in his eyes. "What you've done here," he gestured to the celebrating crowd around us, "it's incredible. You've changed everything."

"We did it together," I corrected him. "All of us. I couldn't have done any of this without you, Erik."

A shadow passed over his face. "I just wish..." he trailed off, but I knew what he was thinking.

"Adira," I said softly, thinking of our sister. "I wish she could see this too. Be here, free, with us."

Erik nodded. "Do you think she's alright? Wherever she is?"

"I have to believe she is," I said. "We gave her a chance at freedom. I have to believe she's out there somewhere, living the life she deserves."

We stood in companionable silence for a moment, both lost in thoughts of our sister.

Finally, Erik sighed. "Well, wherever she is, I hope she's as happy as the women in Ironheart tonight."

"Me too." I smiled. "We did a good thing here, Erik. It was a big risk, but looking at all these women out there smiling and free, it was worth it."

He nodded in agreement, then we stepped aside to make way for a Cloudborn riding by on his horse. He tipped his head and greeted us, and as I looked at the grey horse, suddenly, a realization hit me.

"Wait!" I exclaimed. Without another word, I took off running toward the castle stables, my heart pounding with hope.

"Where are you going?" Erik called.

"I'll be right back!" I shouted, too excited to stop and explain.

With hope nearly exploding from within, I burst through the stable doors, my eyes scanning the stalls frantically. And then there, in the far stall, I saw him. Tempest, my loyal mount, the friend I had been forced to leave behind.

"Tempest," I breathed, a lump swelling inside my throat as I approached him. When I reached his stall, he nickered softly, pressing his muzzle against my outstretched hand. "Hey, old friend."

I opened the stall and stepped inside, then wrapped my arms around his neck, burying my face in his mane. His familiar scent enveloped me, bringing with it a flood of memories. "I've missed you," I whispered. "I'm so sorry I had to leave you behind. I hope you can forgive me."

As I stood there, reunited with my faithful companion, I felt a sense of completion. Reyna and Cassia were safe. The women of Ironheart were free. And now, I had both Erik and Tempest back. It felt like all the pieces of my life were finally falling into place.

"This is your horse?" a deep voice interrupted my thoughts. I turned to see Thorun standing in the stable doorway, his eyes appraising Tempest. "The one you gave up for Reyna?"

I nodded, one hand still resting on Tempest's neck. "Yes. This is Tempest. Thank you so much for letting me borrow Stormrunner. I appreciate it, but I'm so glad to have my boy back." I patted Tempest's muscular neck.

Thorun stepped closer, his expression softening. "He's a fine animal," he said. Then, to my surprise, he added, "I owe you an apology, Asher. I didn't trust you at first. I couldn't believe a man from Ironheart, and a Kingsguard no less, could truly stand with us. I was wrong."

His words caught me off guard. "Thank you, Thorun," I responded, truly surprised and touched by his admission. "That means a lot coming from you."

Thorun nodded, his eyes meeting mine and holding them with a powerful stare. "You've proven yourself a true ally. And more than that, you've proven yourself worthy of Reyna. She is Cloudborn, one of our clan. But you've earned your place at her side."

With that, he clasped my forearm in a warrior's grip, a gesture of respect and acceptance that meant more to me than I could express.

"Thank you, Thorun. It means the world to me that you think so."

His answer was a deep grunt, and as he turned to leave, I felt a weight lift from my shoulders. I had earned not just Reyna's love, but the respect of her people.

As Thorun's footsteps faded, I heard another set approaching. I turned to see Reyna standing in the doorway, her eyes shining with love and pride.

In an instant, I was before her, gathering her into my arms. I held her tight, reveling in the feel of her body against mine, the steady beat of her heart a reminder that we had survived. And not only survived, we had triumphed.

"We did it," I whispered, scarcely able to believe it myself.

Reyna pulled back slightly, her green eyes meeting mine. "We did," she agreed. "You were right, Asher. About so much. About the good in people, about the possibility of change. I couldn't have done this without you."

I cupped her face in my hands, my thumb gently tracing the scar on her cheek. "You're the bravest, most incredible person I've ever known, Reyna. You changed everything. You changed me. I love you, Reyna. Now and always."

My lips met hers with all the passion and love that had been building since the moment we met. It was a kiss of triumph, of relief, of a love that had been forged in the fires of rebellion and a love that had survived through it all.

When we finally parted, both breathless, I rested my forehead against hers. "What happens now?"

Reyna smiled, her eyes alight with hope and determination. "Now," she said, "we build something new. Together."

As we stood there in the stable, the sounds of celebration drifting in from the city beyond, I felt a sense of peace I had never known before. The road ahead would not be easy—dismantling centuries of oppression would be a daunting task. But with Reyna by my side, with the strength of our diverse allies, and with the fire of justice burning in our hearts, I knew we were equal to the task.

The sun had fully set now, but Ironheart was ablaze with the light of a new dawn. A dawn of freedom, of possibility, of hope.

And we would face it, hand in hand, ready to write the next chapter in our story.

CHAPTER THIRTY-SIX
Reyna

The great hall of Ironheart castle, once a symbol of oppression, now echoed with laughter and joy. Everywhere I looked, I saw scenes that warmed my heart: mothers, once forced into breeding, reunited with their children; sisters, separated by arbitrary class distinctions, embracing; former enemies sharing drinks and swapping stories.

Standing on a balcony overlooking the festivities, a sense of awe washed over me. Asher stood to my right, his hand warm in mine, while Cassia was on my left, her presence a constant reminder of why we had fought so hard.

"It's amazing," I breathed, still scarcely able to believe that tiny flicker of an idea I'd had during my flee to freedom had turned into a revolution that freed thousands of others. "We really did it."

Asher squeezed my hand, his blue eyes shining with pride. "We helped, but you made all of this possible."

As I surveyed the scene below, I couldn't stop the twinge of sadness from creeping into my heart. "I just wish all the kingdoms could be like this," I said softly. "It breaks my heart to think of the women still suffering in the other six realms."

Asher sighed, a hint of exasperation in his voice. "Reyna, can we just enjoy our victory for a moment before you start beating yourself up over what's happening out there? Just one night of enjoying the fact that thousands of women are free right here in front of us? Because of you?"

I couldn't help but laugh, the sound still strange to me how naturally it had started to come. Laughter wasn't commonplace in the Warhold. But now... now I could let the lighter emotions flow through me because I was... free. And so were they. "Okay, okay. You're right. Let's celebrate."

He took my hand, dragging me out to dance with the men and women all enjoying a freedom none of them had ever imagined they'd experience in their lifetime. We drank and danced, laughed and hugged, and then as the night wore on, I found a quiet moment with Cassia. We stood in a corner of the hall, our heads close together as we talked.

"I was so scared," Cassia admitted, her voice barely above a whisper. "When they took me away, I thought I'd never see you again."

I pulled her into a hug, careful not to squeeze her wounds. "I'm so sorry, Cassia. I should have protected you better."

She pulled back, her blue eyes blazing with determination. "No, Reyna. There was nothing you could have done differently that day. You did everything you could, and even though the odds were..." She paused and chuckled. "Impossible, really, you did protect me in the end. And not just that, you protected all of us. I'm so proud to be your sister, and I don't ever want to be apart again."

Tears pricked my eyes. "I promise, no one will ever separate us again. Whatever comes next, we face it together."

Our moment was interrupted by a chorus of voices calling my name. "Where is the Rebel Rose? Speech! Speech!" someone in the crowd chanted, then the others joined in the chorus.

"Oh, gods," I breathed, a flush of embarrassment creeping up my chest and cheeks.

"Go on, *Rebel Rose*," Cassia teased, giving me a shove. "You owe everyone a speech."

With a nervous laugh, I made my way to the center of the hall. I looked out over the sea of faces—women and men, young and old, warriors and townsfolk, all enjoying the evening together, and many free for the first time. I felt a surge of emotion so strong it nearly took my breath away.

"My friends," I began, my voice carrying across the suddenly quiet hall. "What we have accomplished here is nothing short of miraculous. We have broken chains that have bound us for generations. We have proven that when we stand together, there is nothing we cannot overcome."

As I spoke, I saw heads nodding, eyes shining with pride and hope. And suddenly, unplanned and unexpected words began to pour from my lips, surprising even me with their passion and conviction.

"But our work is not done," I continued, my voice growing stronger. "Even as we celebrate our freedom, there are still six kingdoms where women are enslaved right now at this very moment. Can we truly call ourselves free while our sisters near and far still suffer under the boot of oppression?"

A murmur ran through the crowd. I saw uncertainty on some faces, fear on others. But I also saw determination, a fire kindling in eyes that had only recently dared to hope.

"I say why stop here at Ironhold? Why should we be the only free women in the land?" The words I hadn't planned on saying rang out, clear and strong. "I say we march across the Southlands together and free them all! Together we can accomplish anything! Together we put an end to the needless suffering of women everywhere! Who will stand with me, to bring the light of freedom to every corner of our world?"

For a heartbeat, silence reigned. Then, like a wave crashing against the shore, a cheer erupted. It started small, but quickly grew, until the very walls seemed to shake with the force of it.

"Free the Southlands!" The cry went up, echoing through the hall.

"I'm with you!" Jaila shouted, raising her hand. "And I believe I can speak for the rest of the Iron Swordmaidens that *we* are with you!"

My sisters-in-arms roared their response, and I could feel it vibrating inside of my chest.

"And I!" Gaia shouted, and Thalassa stepped to her side giving me a sharp nod.

Thorun puffed up, his proud gaze meeting mine. "We are with you, Reyna of the Cloudborn Clan!"

A tidal wave of emotion crashed over me—exhilaration and trepidation intertwined, threatening to overwhelm me. In this one breathtaking moment, I felt the power of the people wash over me, and I knew with bone-deep certainty that we stood on the precipice of change, not just for ourselves, but for countless souls across the Southlands. The weight of responsibility settled on my shoulders, heavy like iron armor pressing down on me. A flicker of doubt whispered that I might be leading these newly freed people to their doom, but it was quickly consumed by the burning flame of hope that had ignited within us all.

Our victory today was not an end, but a beginning—a spark igniting a wildfire that would sweep across the Southlands and incinerate anyone who stood in our way. From Ironhold to the farthest reaches of Shadestone, we would shatter centuries of oppression, our cause echoing like a battle cry across the land: today Ironhold, tomorrow all six kingdoms. The dawn of a new era was breaking, and we were the harbingers of that long-awaited light.

The cheers rose again as one by one people stepped forward, pledging themselves to my cause. As the crowd's enthusiasm and my gratitude for them washed over me, I caught sight of Asher leaving against a pillar. The worry in his eyes was clear, but there was also pride, and something deeper—a love so profound it made my heart ache.

After the last of the free people pledged themselves to my cause, I finally made my way back to him.

The crowd had mostly dispersed, their cheers still echoing faintly down the stone corridors as the celebration went on.

He watched me approach. The expression on his face cut deeper than any blade. I stopped in front of him, a deep breath lifting my shoulders as I waited to speak, knowing without words what he was going to say.

"I thought the plan," he said slowly, voice tight, "was to save Cassia. That was the mission. Rescue your sister. Then disappear into the woods. Live. Be free. Happy."

I swallowed. "That *was* the plan."

He let out a short breath—half laugh, half frustration. "Then the plan became about Ironhold. Free the women here. Give them a chance. Gods, we did that. You did that." He smiled briefly then shook his head, jaw clenching. "Now the goal is *every* kingdom in the Southlands? Reyna, you keep moving the line."

My heart twisted. "I know."

His eyes met mine, sharp and searching. "When does it stop? When is it enough? When we've lost half this army? When I'm dragging your lifeless body from the battlefield? Or you dragging mine? Or my brother? Or your sister? Thorun? Gaia? Thalassa? Huh? When does this end?"

I didn't answer right away. I couldn't. Because he wasn't wrong.

So he pressed harder. "Let's take them—these women, these fighters—and vanish. Find somewhere safe. Moonshadow Woods. Mistveil Mountain. Somewhere no king can touch us. Let us all be free. Safe. We *did* something. That should be enough."

It should have been...but it wasn't.

"You don't understand," I said, quietly at first. "If we walk away now, how long before another king rides in and takes Ironhold back? How long before everything we've done gets undone?"

I stepped toward him, placing a hand on his chest, hovering over that heart I knew without question beat for me the way mine beat for him. "I can't disappear. Not when I know there are women still locked in cages. Still bleeding in the sand. Still begging to be saved."

His gaze dropped for a moment. When he looked back up, there was something weary in his voice.

"There's a whole world out there, Reyna. You've never seen it." He stepped closer, his voice lowering. "You've never marched outside Ironhold. You have no idea what awaits us. I have. I've traveled with the king. I've seen this world. The dangers. Stormspire's unscalable cliffs. The desert separating us from the kingdom of Goldcoast that burns during the day and freezes at night—and that's just the *terrain*, not to mention the creatures that live beneath the sand. The assassins hidden in the woods in Verdant. The politics you've never had to handle. There are things out there you've never fought. Creatures that make cloakfangs look tame. Kings with armies we've never faced. Spies. Poison. Death. It all awaits us out there, Reyna."

He paused, eyes softening. "It's a beautiful dream. Gods, I love this dream. March across the kingdoms and free them all. But it's just that Reyna. A dream. And I'm scared if you go down this path, it'll kill you."

I looked up at him, heat burning in my throat. "Then let it."

His eyes flared at my blunt admission.

"I would rather die trying to change the world than hide from it. I didn't plan for this, Asher, but it's mine now. And I can't walk away. Not while there's still someone out there praying for freedom the way we used to. You can't ask me not to fight."

"And you can't ask me just to stay silent and blindly follow you! What about what *I* want? Huh? What about the life *I* dream of? Me. You. My brother. Your sister. Our friends. All safe and free. Laughing and dancing every night. Me fucking you senseless beside the stream. Holding you in my arms until morning just to awaken to the beautiful world we built. Together. The world right there within our grasp right now."

I choked back the tears as I imagined the beautiful image of the life I knew awaited us. All I had to do was say yes. But I glanced at the women, now free, singing and laughing and dancing around the hall, and then I imagined the ones still crying for help as they endured the unimaginable, and I knew I could never be happy, never feel free, until I'd saved them all.

I reached out and slid my fingers across his cheeks. "You're right, Asher. It isn't fair for me to do this. It isn't fair for me to ask you to give up your dream for mine. But I'm asking anyway. Because to love me means to understand that I'll never be happy in this world we would build until I know I've done everything in my power to free as many as I can. I wouldn't be... me. And you love me, right?"

His eyes remained locked with mine, searching, as he stared at me. Hurt and anger and fear collided in those icy orbs before, finally, they softened.

With a sigh, he reached up, brushing a thumb across my cheek like he was memorizing it. Like he was saying goodbye to something.

"Of course I'll fight with you," he said. "I'll follow you across deserts and kingdoms and fight godsdamned monsters. But don't ask me to smile while I watch you walk into fire."

I leaned into his hand, letting his warmth steady me.

"I'm not asking you to smile," I whispered. "Just to stay."

"Then I'm here. Always. Even if it breaks me." He pulled me close. "You're going to get yourself killed, you know," he murmured, his voice tight with concern. "And I can't live without you now."

I cupped his face in my hands, willing him to understand. "Asher, if you love me, then you'll understand that this is who I am. I'm a protector. I'm Aegisari. It's in my very blood. I can't stop until every woman in the Southlands is free."

His silence stretched. His eyes searched mine, as if saying goodbye to the version of me that could stay safe, be the woman who could stop right here, right now, and follow him into the dream world awaiting us. The peace awaiting us.

Then, slowly, he nodded. "I understand," he said softly. "And of course, I'll be by your side. Always. But if we're doing this... I need to start making some of the calls."

He paused, voice low but steady. "You're the best warrior I've ever seen. But marching across six more kingdoms with an army isn't just about fighting. It's terrain. Politics. Supplies. Strategy. That's where I'm strong. That's what I know. If we're going to do this, I need to be more than your sword. I need to be your partner."

I nodded, the truth of his words sinking in. "Yes. Of course. You're right. I've never even left Ironhold. You know much more about the kingdoms and politics and everything awaiting us out there. I trust you. We're partners, Asher. Always."

"Always, Reyna. Always."

With his soft smile and his vow to fight beside me no matter where this battle took us, the relief that flooded through me was almost dizzying. I pulled him close, our lips meeting in a kiss that held the weight of battles won and challenges yet to come—a silent vow to face them all, side by side.

As the kiss deepened, the heat of battle transmuted into a different kind of fire. The adrenaline of victory, the joy of freedom, the anticipation of the coming chaos—all of it merged into a burning need for connection with the man who had become my partner in both battle and heart, a vital part of my very being.

We broke apart, our breaths heavy as our eyes locked, and I saw the same desire reflected in his azure eyes. Without a word, we slipped away from the celebration, finding a quiet corner of the castle that was ours alone.

The moment the door closed behind us, Asher's lips were on mine again, hungry and insistent. I matched his fervor, my hands roaming over the planes of his chest, marveling at the strength there.

"Whatever happens, Reyna. I'm with you. I love you, and I'm with you, always."

His words and his promise were like tossing kindling on the fire already raging inside of me. I pulled his lips to mine, relishing the exquisite pain of his fervor. Our hands moved together, our armor and clothing ripping away one piece at a time until we were naked.

"Mine," he growled, pushing me against the stone wall.

I gasped when my back hit it, but didn't release my grip on his hair, instead pulling him back down to my lips.

He reached down and cupped my ass, and with one quick pull, he yanked me up against him. I wrapped my legs around his waist, biting his lip when I felt his cock press against me.

"Fuck me, Asher," I whispered, angling my hips, begging him to enter me.

A playful fire ignited in his eyes, but instead of easing my ache with a thrust, he teased my entrance, his hard cock sliding up and down my wet heat.

"Please, Asher," I begged, my breath ragged and needy.

With a guttural growl, he thrust himself inside of me. I gasped, a whimper escaping my lips as I wrapped my body around him, clinging to him as if my life depended on it. The hard rocks dug into my back, but I felt no pain, only the exquisite fullness inside of me as I slid up and down on his cock.

"Gods, you feel good on my cock," his low voice rumbled into my ear, and he grabbed my hair, pulling my head back, his lips finding their way back to my neck.

I cried out, my pace quickening as I rubbed myself against him, the pleasure mounting inside of me while his lips and teeth worked their way up my neck until he kissed me again, catching my moans in his mouth.

With a shudder, I gripped him tightly, and we came together, our bodies connecting in a dance as old as time. As I panted in his arms, my body limp and held up only by his strength, I felt a sense of rightness, of completion. Every touch, every kiss, every shared breath was a reaffirmation of the bond between us.

Like iron repeatedly melted and reforged, our relationship had transformed—adversaries to allies, allies to lovers, lovers to something deeper. Each trial had tempered us into something stronger. Something I wanted to believe was unbreakable.

Later, as we lay tangled together, our skin cooling in the night air, I traced idle patterns on Asher's chest.

"Are you really okay with this?" I asked softly. "With marching on the other kingdoms?"

He was quiet for a long moment, his hand moving gently through my hair.

"I'd be lying if I said I wasn't scared," he said finally. "Do I wish we could stop now—live here together, safe and free? Gods, yes." He paused. "But I know you. And I love you. And I won't stand in your way."

I propped myself up on one elbow, looking down at him. The moonlight cast his features in silver—his jaw, his lips, his eyes. They looked calm. But I knew better now. I'd seen the flicker of fear he tried to hide.

"I couldn't do any of this without you," I said. "You know that, right?"

Asher smiled, reaching up to cup my cheek. "We're partners in this, Reyna. In everything. Whatever comes next... we'll face it together."

He kissed me softly.

"I meant it when I said I'm yours. Always."

I rested my head against his chest, letting the sound of his heartbeat anchor me.

"I am yours and you are mine." I kissed him softly, then settled back into his embrace.

But I couldn't stop the thought that whispered through the quiet between us:

He said he was with me. But what happens if my cause demands a sacrifice he isn't willing to make? A sacrifice like... me?

As I lay in his arms, I tried to quiet my mind from all the unknowns we'd be facing. The days ahead would bring new battles, new struggles. But for now, in the still of the night, wrapped in the arms of the man I loved, I allowed myself to simply be. To revel in our victory, in our love, in the promise of a future brighter than any I had dared to dream.

Soon, we would begin our march to free the Southlands. But tonight, in this moment, we had already won the greatest victory of all—the freedom to love, to hope, to dream of a better world. And that, I knew, was worth fighting for.

CHAPTER THIRTY-SEVEN
Reyna

Two weeks had passed since we'd freed Ironheart, and now we gathered inside its walls, an army two thousand strong preparing to sweep across the Southlands freeing every kingdom we descended upon. Though we could have used more time to rest and recover, we couldn't risk the other kingdoms gathering to attack us. We had to strike first. Be relentless. Take the fight to them before they had time to prepare for the wave of rebellion soon to wash over them.

The city itself seemed to pulse with energy, a living, breathing entity of its own as excitement and fear bubbled inside the waiting warriors. The clang of armor, the whinnying of horses, and the low murmur of voices blended into a symphony of anticipation. Banners bearing the symbol of our rebellion—a rose wrapped around a sword—fluttered in the morning breeze, a vibrant splash of color against the grey stone walls.

Amidst the organized chaos, I found myself facing a group of Cloudborn warriors. It would never cease to shock me to see my own green eyes staring back at me when I'd look at them.

"Thank you," I said, my voice thick with emotion. The words felt inadequate to express the depth of my gratitude. "For everything. We couldn't have done this without you."

Yaira, a tall woman with intricate braids, stepped forward. She clasped my forearm, her grip strong and reassuring.

"It was our honor, Rebel Rose," she said, giving me a gentle nod. "I wish we could all stay and fight with you, but we leave one-hundred-fifty of our finest warriors with you. The rest of us must return to defend Mistveil Mountain from any potential attacks from the north."

I nodded, understanding the weight of their sacrifice. They had left their home vulnerable to aid our cause. "When this is over," I promised, "I'll come visit. I want to learn more about our people, our history."

Thorun, who had been standing nearby, his massive frame a comforting presence, stepped forward. "You'll come home, you mean," he said, his gruff voice softened by a hint of affection that made my heart clench.

Home. The word echoed in my mind. For so long, home had been a concept beyond my reach—a luxury not afforded to a weapon of the king. The Warhold only housed us, but it was never a home. But now, looking at these people—my people—I felt the call of the Mistveil Mountains, and I vowed to make it back there again someday when this battle was over and the Southlands free.

Thorun's hand came to rest on my shoulder, warm and reassuring. "You'll always have a place with us, Reyna," he said, his eyes, usually hard as flint, now soft with an almost fraternal affection. "Remember that."

I covered his hand with mine, squeezing gently. "Thank you, Thorun. For everything."

"You can thank me when we take back the Southlands. You're not getting rid of me yet."

I smiled, so grateful to have him by my side to lead his people as we embarked on this dangerous but important mission. He nodded, a rare smile crossing his face before he moved to bid farewell to his departing warriors. I watched him go, marveling at how this gruff, initially suspicious man I'd faced down on the mountain had become someone I trusted implicitly.

As the Cloudborn warriors heading home filed out, Cassia pressed up near me. Her golden hair, so different from my dark locks, shimmered in the morning sun.

"It's still hard to believe, isn't it?" she said, watching them go. Her voice was filled with wonder. "That you're one of them. Cloudborn? Aegisari?"

I turned to my sister, seeing the awe in her eyes as she watched them, their Aurorium armor catching the sun and reflecting off their muscular frames.

"It's a part of me I'm still discovering," I admitted, reaching out to tuck a stray strand of hair behind her ear. "But I'm glad I get to do it with you by my side."

Cassia leaned into my touch, her eyes glistening with unshed tears. "Even though they're your family now, I hope you never forget I'm your family too."

I turned to face her, gazing at her firmly. "Never. You're my sister, and I could never replace you."

She smiled softly. "Good. It's always been you and me, and it's strange to think of sharing you after I just got you back. I was so afraid I'd lost you," she whispered. "When they took me... I thought I'd never see you again."

I pulled her into a fierce embrace, burying my face in her hair. "Nothing will ever separate us again, Cassia," I promised fiercely. "I may have a new family in the Cloudborn Clan, but you're always going to be my sister too. We're in this together, always."

We held each other for a long moment, a quiet moment between sisters amidst the preparations for war feeling precious and rare. When we finally pulled apart, Cassia's smile was watery but determined. "Together," she echoed.

Our moment was interrupted by the approach of the cloakfang ursids and the ogres, their massive forms dwarfing everything around them. The ground trembled with each step they took. Beside them walked Thalassa, tall and proud as her eyes took on a colorful glow as she communicated with her creatures.

"They wish to bid you goodbye," she said, her voice tinged with regret. "I'm afraid they must return to Moonshadow Woods. They want to protect what remains of our tribe. We can't leave our home undefended."

I nodded, trying to hide my disappointment. These magical creatures had been a formidable part of our force, their very presence a reminder of the impossible things we'd achieved. But I understood and respected their desire to remain with what was left of their tribe, protecting the woods and women they had kept so safe from the cruelty of the outside world.

But Thalassa wasn't finished. A smile played at her lips as she continued, "The swiftclaw wolves, however, are quite excited about running across the Southlands. They've agreed to join your cause. They will be a powerful asset to us."

As if on cue, the pack of the swiftclaw wolves appeared, their speed as they arrived startling, and their eyes gleaming with an intelligence that still took my breath away. I felt a surge of gratitude, remembering how these creatures had fought bravely beside us, and were willing to do it again.

"Thank you," I said to Thalassa and the creatures, my voice thick with emotion. "Thank you for joining our cause and helping us free Ironheart. We couldn't have done it without you. Keep the woods safe while we're gone," I said to the ogres and cloakfangs, then I turned to the wolves, "and we appreciate you continuing this journey with us."

Thalassa's eyes glowed as she conveyed my message, and then with a nod, the ogres turned and started away, the bears lumbering behind. Thalassa gave me a smile, then she and her wolves and her raven moved off together to join the rest of the fighters from Moonshadow Woods.

Jaila and Gaia approached next, their faces alight with a mixture of excitement and determination. Jaila, my old friend and the woman I'd trusted so completely that I'd let my entire plan hinge on her loyalty, clasped my arm.

"We're ready," she reported, her voice thrumming with anticipation. "The swordsisters can't wait to free our sisters in the other kingdoms."

Gaia nodded in agreement, her eyes burning with vengeance I understood too well. "If we can turn more battlemaidens to our cause as we go, our force will grow to be unstoppable."

"Let's hope you're right," I said, the enormity of our task settling over me once more. "We'll need every advantage we can get."

"It won't be easy," Jaila said, her eyes growing serious. "Each kingdom will present its own challenges, its own dangers."

Gaia nodded. "And as the attacking army, we will be at the mercy of their walls. The odds are... not in our favor."

"When have they ever been?" Jaila chuckled, a hint of her old mischief in her voice. "We've already done the impossible once. Why not six more times?"

Gaia crooked a wicked smile. "The kings of the Southlands have no idea what is coming for them."

I reached out, taking their hands in mine. "Whatever comes," I said softly, "we face it together."

I squeezed their hands, drawing strength from their touch, from the presence of these women who had become more than allies—they were family.

"You're right," I said. "The path ahead is dangerous. But look at what we've already accomplished. We have something our enemies can never match: the power of hope, of freedom, of love."

They both nodded, their eyes igniting with passion and hope, and then with a brief hug, we parted ways as they returned to the Iron Swordmaidens to prepare for our journey.

As the final preparations were made, I found myself standing beside Ember, my loyal mare pawing at the ground in anticipation. I stroked her neck, drawing comfort from her solid presence.

Asher approached, leading Tempest. The sight of him, handsome, tall and strong in his new armor—a mixture of his Kingsguard style but with our new emblem on it instead— made my heart skip a beat.

"Are you ready for this?" he asked softly as he drew near, his free hand coming to rest on my waist.

I leaned into his touch, loving how vulnerable I could be in his presence. "As ready as I'll ever be," I replied, searching his face. "Are you?"

A wry smile tugged at his lips. "To follow you into certain danger, possibly to our deaths?" His hand tightened on my waist, pulling me closer. "Always, Reyna. Where you go, I go. Whatever comes, we face it together."

Despite the gravity of the moment, I couldn't help but laugh. This man, who had given up everything to stand by my side, who had shown me that goodness could exist even in the darkest places—he was my rock, my compass in the storm of revolution.

I raised a hand to his cheek, my thumb tracing the line of his jaw. "I love you," I said softly, the words still new and precious between us. "Whatever happens out there, know that."

Asher's eyes softened, and he leaned down to press his forehead against mine. "And I love you, Reyna. More than I ever thought possible."

We shared a kiss, soft and sweet, a promise that our love would endure no matter what lay ahead for us. Then, with a final look acknowledging the weight of the challenges ahead, we mounted our horses.

Before us stretched the road through Ironhold where we would free every woman as we crossed the vast kingdom, and beyond

that, the other kingdoms of the Southlands. Behind us stood our army—a motley crew of Cloudborn warriors, swordsisters, swiftclaw wolves, and freedom fighters from every walk of life. The morning sun glinted off armor and weapons, a sea of determination ready to reshape the world.

Asher drew Tempest up beside me, his hand reaching out to clasp mine. "Quite a sight, isn't it?" he said, his voice filled with awe.

I nodded, unable to speak past the lump in my throat. This was more than an army. This was the beginning of a new world.

Taking a deep breath, I urged Ember forward, positioning myself to address the gathered forces.

"My friends," I called out, my voice carrying across the assembled crowd. "Just weeks ago, we achieved what many thought impossible. We freed Ironheart from tyranny and oppression. We proved that when we stand united, there is nothing we cannot overcome."

A cheer went up from the crowd, the sound echoing off the castle walls behind us.

"But our work is not finished," I continued, my voice growing stronger with each word. "Even now, women across the Southlands suffer under tyranny of men. They lay in bed at night as we did, hoping and praying that someday, somehow, they will know freedom. And I say we answer their call!"

Another cheer, louder this time.

"I want to be clear," I said, my tone softening slightly. "You are all free. No one is obligated to join this fight. If any of you wish to stay behind, to enjoy the freedom you've so bravely won, know that you do so with our gratitude and blessing."

I paused, letting my words sink in. Then, my voice rising once more, I declared, "But for those who choose to march with us, know this: together, we will take back the entire Southlands from the tyrannical grip of men who would see us as property rather than people. Together, we will light the flame of freedom in every corner of our world!"

The response was deafening. Swords were raised, battle cries echoed across the morning air. The passion and power of these people, united in purpose, was almost overwhelming.

But even through the thunderous cheers, a soft whisper infiltrated my mind—one I couldn't ignore.

Ruthio.

I hadn't seen his face since Ironheart, but I could feel his presence like a storm building on the horizon. He was out there, somewhere in the shadows of the Southlands. And as soon as he heard of our rebellion he would be waiting. Watching. Preparing.

The kings we were about to face as we swept across the kingdoms were dangerous. Every battle ahead would be hard-won. We would lose people. We would suffer. But when we finally reached Shadestone at the far reach of the Southlands... gods, we'd better be ready. Because that fight against his Shadestone Sentinels... *that* would be unlike anything we'd faced before.

And not just the strength of his army or the strength of his Nocturnium. We were strong. We had Aurorium. We could fight them. But from what Asher had told me, Ruthio was cunning. Patient. Powerful. The kind of threat that didn't just crush his enemies—he *consumed* them. If Asher was wary of him, I knew I needed to heed that instinct.

I'd seen it in his eyes every time Ruthio's name came up during strategy meetings as we prepared for this march. A flicker of hesitation—small, but unmistakable. Like he was already calculating how to protect me from whatever Ruthio was planning. Like some part of him feared we couldn't win. Feared he'd lose me to this fight.

He'd voiced it once—warned me I might be marching myself and this army to its death. I told him not to doubt us. And he promised to believe.

He hadn't spoken it since, but I could still see it in his eyes—that flicker of doubt he couldn't quite hide. And now it was creeping into me, slow and quiet, like a rot beneath the surface.

Could we really do this? Could we survive what was coming?

Or was I leading these brave souls straight into the fire that would consume us all?

I looked out at them. The women who had bled for this cause. The men who had risked everything to stand beside us. My sister. Asher. All of them.

And I knew the answer.

I would not stop fighting until every woman in the Southlands was free. Or I would die trying.

I would face every king.

Every man who dared to stand in our way.

I would break the chains.

I would tear down their walls.

I would free every woman still trapped beneath the boot of oppression.

And when the day came to face Ruthio, I would not flinch.

We would fight.

And we would win.

We had to.

They were all counting on me.

I spun Ember around and then with a shared nod, Asher and I spurred our horses forward. The gates of Ironheart swung open with the groan of ancient hinges, and we rode out, our army streaming behind us like a river of hope and determination.

As we left the city behind, I felt a sense of destiny settle over me. The road ahead would be long and fraught with danger. We would face armies, confront kings, and challenge centuries of entrenched beliefs. But in that moment, with Asher and our allies by my side and the strength of our united forces at my back, I had never felt more alive, more certain of our path.

We had done the impossible once. We had freed Ironheart, had united people who had once been enemies. Now, we would do it again, and again, until every woman in the Southlands could taste the sweetness of our newfound freedom.

As we rode into the unknown, I felt a surge of hope so strong it nearly took my breath away. This was more than a rebellion now. This was a revolution. And we would see it through to the end, no matter the cost.

The Rebel Rose and her army were on the march. And the Southlands would never be the same again.

***

Craving more rebellion, romance, and revenge?
The Rebel Rose trilogy has just begun, and it's only the start of a massive Fateforged Chronicles world filled with characters you're sure to love! Reyna's fight for freedom—and her dangerous desire for Asher—continues in Book 2 (coming soon).

Join the rebellion at ktmartinauthor.com and get:
- Release alerts for the Rebel Rose trilogy and other books coming in this world
- Exclusive updates and bonus content
- **Don't miss REAPER'S RUIN coming soon** - my dark, steamy fae romantasy where Death himself falls for the soul he's meant to claim

www.ktmartinauthor.com
Where Fates are Forged and Love is Legendary